NON SANZ DROICT.

William Shakespeare

The Life and Death of King John

Edited by William H. Matchett

The Famous History of the Life of King Henry VIII

Edited by S. Schoenbaum

With New and Updated
Critical Essays
and a Revised Bibliography

THE SIGNET CLASSIC SHAKESPEARE
General Editor: Sylvan Barnet

$\mathcal{C}$

A SIGNET CLASSIC

SIGNET CLASSIC
Published by New American Library, a division of
Penguin Group (USA) Inc., 375 Hudson Street,
New York, New York 10014, U.S.A.
Penguin Books Ltd, 80 Strand,
London WC2R 0RL, England
Penguin Books Australia Ltd, 250 Camberwell Road,
Camberwell, Victoria 3124, Australia
Penguin Books Canada Ltd, 10 Alcorn Avenue,
Toronto, Ontario, Canada M4V 3B2
Penguin Books (N.Z.) Ltd, Cnr Rosedale and Airborne Roads,
Albany, Auckland 1310, New Zealand

Penguin Books Ltd, Registered Offices:
80 Strand, London WC2R 0RL, England

Published by Signet Classic, an imprint of New American Library,
a division of Penguin Group (USA) Inc.

First Signet Classic Printing (Second Revised Edition), February 2004
10   9   8   7   6   5   4   3   2

Contents

Shakespeare: An Overview

Biographical Sketch

Between the record of his baptism in Stratford on 26 April 1564 and the record of his burial in Stratford on 25 April 1616, some forty official documents name Shakespeare, and many others name his parents, his children, and his grandchildren. Further, there are at least fifty literary references to him in the works of his contemporaries. More facts are known about William Shakespeare than about any other playwright of the period except Ben Jonson. The facts should, however, be distinguished from the legends. The latter, inevitably more engaging and better known, tell us that the Stratford boy killed a calf in high style, poached deer and rabbits, and was forced to flee to London, where he held horses outside a playhouse. These traditions are only traditions; they may be true, but no evidence supports them, and it is well to stick to the facts.

Mary Arden, the dramatist's mother, was the daughter of a substantial landowner; about 1557 she married John Shakespeare, a tanner, glove-maker, and trader in wool, grain, and other farm commodities. In 1557 John Shakespeare was a member of the council (the governing body of Stratford), in 1558 a constable of the borough, in 1561 one of the two town chamberlains, in 1565 an alderman (entitling him to the appellation of "Mr."), in 1568 high bailiff—the town's highest political office, equivalent to mayor. After 1577, for an unknown reason he drops out of local politics. What *is* known is that he had to mortgage his wife's property, and that he was involved in serious litigation.

The birthday of William Shakespeare, the third child and the eldest son of this locally prominent man, is unrecorded, but the Stratford parish register records that the infant was baptized on 26 April 1564. (It is quite possible that he was born on 23 April, but this date has probably been assigned by tradition because it is the date on which, fifty-two years later, he died, and perhaps because it is the feast day of St. George, patron saint of England.) The attendance records of the Stratford grammar school of the period are not extant, but it is reasonable to assume that the son of a prominent local official attended the free school—it had been established for the purpose of educating males precisely of his class—and received substantial training in Latin. The masters of the school from Shakespeare's seventh to fifteenth years held Oxford degrees; the Elizabethan curriculum excluded mathematics and the natural sciences but taught a good deal of Latin rhetoric, logic, and literature, including plays by Plautus, Terence, and Seneca.

On 27 November 1582 a marriage license was issued for the marriage of Shakespeare and Anne Hathaway, eight years his senior. The couple had a daughter, Susanna, in May 1583. Perhaps the marriage was necessary, but perhaps the couple had earlier engaged, in the presence of witnesses, in a formal "troth plight" which would render their children legitimate even if no further ceremony were performed. In February 1585, Anne Hathaway bore Shakespeare twins, Hamnet and Judith.

That Shakespeare was born is excellent; that he married and had children is pleasant; but that we know nothing about his departure from Stratford to London or about the beginning of his theatrical career is lamentable and must be admitted. We would gladly sacrifice details about his children's baptism for details about his earliest days in the theater. Perhaps the poaching episode is true (but it is first reported almost a century after Shakespeare's death), or perhaps he left Stratford to be a schoolmaster, as another tradition holds; perhaps he was moved (like Petruchio in *The Taming of the Shrew*) by

> Such wind as scatters young men through the world,
> To seek their fortunes farther than at home
> Where small experience grows.   (1.2.49–51)

In 1592, thanks to the cantankerousness of Robert Greene, we have our first reference, a snarling one, to Shakespeare as an actor and playwright. Greene, a graduate of St. John's College, Cambridge, had become a playwright and a pamphleteer in London, and in one of his pamphlets he warns three university-educated playwrights against an actor who has presumed to turn playwright:

> There is an upstart crow, beautified with our feathers, that with his *tiger's heart wrapped in a player's hide* supposes he is as well able to bombast out a blank verse as the best of you, and being an absolute Johannes-factotum [i.e., jack-of-all-trades] is in his own conceit the only Shake-scene in a country.

The reference to the player, as well as the allusion to Aesop's crow (who strutted in borrowed plumage, as an actor struts in fine words not his own), makes it clear that by this date Shakespeare had both acted and written. That Shakespeare is meant is indicated not only by *Shake-scene* but also by the parody of a line from one of Shakespeare's plays, *3 Henry VI*: "O, tiger's heart wrapped in a woman's hide" (1.4.137). If in 1592 Shakespeare was prominent enough to be attacked by an envious dramatist, he probably had served an apprenticeship in the theater for at least a few years.

In any case, although there are no extant references to Shakespeare between the record of the baptism of his twins in 1585 and Greene's hostile comment about "Shake-scene" in 1592, it is evident that during some of these "dark years" or "lost years" Shakespeare had acted and written. There are a number of subsequent references to him as an actor. Documents indicate that in 1598 he is a "principal comedian," in 1603 a "principal tragedian," in 1608 he is one of the "men players." (We do not have, however, any solid information about which roles he may have played; later traditions say he played Adam in *As You Like It* and the ghost in *Hamlet*, but nothing supports the assertions. Probably his role as dramatist came to supersede his role as actor.) The profession of actor was not for a gentleman, and it occasionally drew the scorn of university men like Greene who resented writing speeches for persons less educated than themselves, but it was respectable enough; players, if prosperous, were in effect members of the bourgeoisie, and there is nothing to suggest that Stratford considered William Shakespeare less than a solid citizen. When, in 1596, the Shakespeares were granted a coat of arms—i.e., the right to be considered gentlemen—the grant was made to Shakespeare's father, but probably William Shakespeare had arranged the matter on his own behalf. In subsequent transactions he is occasionally styled a gentleman.

Although in 1593 and 1594 Shakespeare published two narrative poems dedicated to the Earl of Southampton, *Venus and Adonis* and *The Rape of Lucrece*, and may well have written most or all of his sonnets in the middle nineties, Shakespeare's literary activity seems to have been almost entirely devoted to the theater. (It may be significant that the two narrative poems were written in years when the plague closed the theaters for several months.) In 1594 he was a charter member of a theatrical company called the Chamberlain's Men, which in 1603 became the royal company, the King's Men, making Shakespeare the king's playwright. Until he retired to Stratford (about 1611, apparently), he was with this remarkably stable company. From 1599 the company acted primarily at the Globe theater, in which Shakespeare held a one-tenth interest. Other Elizabethan dramatists are known to have acted, but no other is known also to have been entitled to a share of the profits.

Shakespeare's first eight published plays did not have his name on them, but this is not remarkable; the most popular play of the period, Thomas Kyd's *The Spanish Tragedy*, went through many editions without naming Kyd, and Kyd's authorship is known only because a book on the profession of acting happens to quote (and attribute to Kyd) some lines on the interest of Roman emperors in the drama. What is remarkable is that after 1598 Shakespeare's name commonly appears on printed plays—some of which are not his. Presumably his name was a drawing card, and publishers used it to attract potential buyers. Another indication of his popularity comes from Francis Meres, author of *Palladis Tamia: Wit's Treasury* (1598). In this anthology of snippets accompanied by an essay on literature, many playwrights are mentioned, but Shakespeare's name occurs more often than any other, and Shakespeare is the only play-wright whose plays are listed.

From his acting, his play writing, and his share in a playhouse, Shakespeare seems to have made considerable money. He put it to work, making substantial investments in Stratford real estate. As early as 1597 he bought New Place, the second-largest house in Stratford. His family moved in soon afterward, and the house remained in the family until a granddaughter died in 1670. When Shakespeare made his will in 1616, less than a month before he died, he sought to leave his property intact to his descendants. Of small bequests to relatives and to friends (including three actors, Richard Burbage, John Heminges, and Henry Condell), that to his wife of the second-best bed has provoked the most comment. It has sometimes been taken as a sign of an unhappy marriage (other supposed signs are the apparently hasty marriage, his wife's seniority of eight years, and his residence in London without his family). Perhaps the second-best bed was the bed the couple had slept in, the best bed being reserved for visitors. In any case, had Shakespeare not excepted it, the bed would have gone (with the rest of his household possessions) to his daughter and her husband.

On 25 April 1616 Shakespeare was buried within the chancel of the church at Stratford. An unattractive monument to his memory, placed on a wall near the grave, says that he died on 23 April. Over the grave itself are the lines, perhaps by Shakespeare, that (more than his literary fame) have kept his bones undisturbed in the crowded burial ground where old bones were often dislodged to make way for new:

> Good friend, for Jesus' sake forbear
> To dig the dust enclosed here.
> Blessed be the man that spares these stones
> And cursed be he that moves my bones.

A Note on the Anti-Stratfordians, Especially Baconians and Oxfordians

Not until 1769—more than a hundred and fifty years after Shakespeare's death—is there any record of anyone expressing doubt about Shakespeare's authorship of the plays and poems. In 1769, however, Herbert Lawrence nominated Francis Bacon (1561–1626) in *The Life and Adventures of Common Sense*. Since then, at least two dozen other nominees have been offered, including Christopher Marlowe, Sir Walter Raleigh, Queen Elizabeth I, and Edward de Vere, 17th earl of Oxford. The impulse behind all anti-Stratfordian movements is the scarcely concealed snobbish opinion that "the man from Stratford" simply could not have written the plays because he was a country fellow without a university education and without access to high society. Anyone, the argument goes, who used so many legal terms, medical terms, nautical terms, and so forth, and who showed some familiarity with classical writing, must have attended a university, and anyone who knew so much about courtly elegance and courtly deceit must himself have moved among courtiers. The plays do indeed reveal an author whose interests were exceptionally broad, but specialists in any given field—law, medicine, arms and armor, and so on—soon find that the plays do not reveal deep knowledge in specialized matters; indeed, the playwright often gets technical details wrong.

The claim on behalf of Bacon, forgotten almost as soon as it was put forth in 1769, was independently reasserted by Joseph C. Hart in 1848. In 1856 it was reaffirmed by W. H. Smith in a book, and also by Delia Bacon in an article; in 1857 Delia Bacon published a book, arguing that Francis Bacon had directed a group of intellectuals who wrote the plays.

Francis Bacon's claim has largely faded, perhaps because it was advanced with such evident craziness by Ignatius Donnelly, who in *The Great Cryptogram* (1888) claimed to break a code in the plays that proved Bacon had written not only the plays attributed to Shakespeare but also other Renaissance works, for instance the plays of Christopher Marlowe and the essays of Montaigne.

Consider the last two lines of the Epilogue in *The Tempest*:

> As you from crimes would pardoned be,
> Let your indulgence set me free.

What was Shakespeare—sorry, Francis Bacon, Baron Verulam—*really* saying in these two lines? According to Baconians, the lines are an anagram reading, "Tempest of Francis Bacon, Lord Verulam; do ye ne'er divulge me, ye words." Ingenious, and it is a pity that in the quotation the letter *a* appears only twice in the cryptogram, whereas in the deciphered message it appears three times. Oh, no problem; just alter "Verulam" to "Verul'm" and it works out very nicely.

Most people understand that with sufficient ingenuity one can torture any text and find in it what one wishes. For instance: Did Shakespeare have a hand in the King James Version of the Bible? It was nearing completion in 1610, when Shakespeare was forty-six years old. If you look at the 46th Psalm and count forward for forty-six words, you will find the word *shake*. Now if you go to the end of the psalm and count backward forty-six words, you will find the word *spear*. Clear evidence, according to some, that Shakespeare slyly left his mark in the book.

Bacon's candidacy has largely been replaced in the twentieth century by the candidacy of Edward de Vere (1550–1604), 17th earl of Oxford. The basic ideas behind the Oxford theory, advanced at greatest length by Dorothy and Charlton Ogburn in *This Star of England* (1952, rev. 1955), a book of 1297 pages, and by Charlton Ogburn in *The Mysterious William Shakespeare* (1984), a book of 892 pages, are these: (1) The man from Stratford could not possibly have had the mental equipment and the experience to have written the plays—only a courtier could have written them; (2) Oxford had the requisite background (social position, education, years at Queen Elizabeth's court); (3) Oxford did not wish his authorship to be known for two basic reasons: writing for the public theater was a vulgar pursuit, and the plays show so much courtly and royal disreputable behavior that they would have compromised Oxford's position at court. Oxfordians offer countless details to support the claim. For example, Hamlet's phrase "that ever I was born to set it right" (1.5.89) barely conceals "E. Ver, I was born to set it right," an unambiguous announcement of de Vere's authorship, according to *This Star of England* (p. 654). A second example: Consider Ben

Jonson's poem entitled "To the Memory of My Beloved Master William Shakespeare," prefixed to the first collected edition of Shakespeare's plays in 1623. According to Oxfordians, when Jonson in this poem speaks of the author of the plays as the "swan of Avon," he is alluding not to William Shakespeare, who was born and died in Stratford-on-Avon and who throughout his adult life owned property there; rather, he is alluding to Oxford, who, the Ogburns say, used "William Shakespeare" as his pen name, and whose manor at Bilton was on the Avon River. Oxfordians do not offer any evidence that Oxford took a pen name, and they do not care that Oxford had sold the manor in 1581, forty-two years before Jonson wrote his poem. Surely a reference to the Shakespeare who was born in Stratford, who had returned to Stratford, and who had died there only seven years before Jonson wrote the poem is more plausible. And exactly why Jonson, who elsewhere also spoke of Shakespeare as a playwright, and why Heminges and Condell, who had acted with Shakespeare for about twenty years, should speak of Shakespeare as the author in their dedication in the 1623 volume of collected plays is never adequately explained by Oxfordians. Either Jonson, Heminges and Condell, and numerous others were in on the conspiracy, or they were all duped—equally unlikely alternatives. Another difficulty in the Oxford theory is that Oxford died in 1604, and some of the plays are clearly indebted to works and events later than 1604. Among the Oxfordian responses are: At his death Oxford left some plays, and in later years these were touched up by hacks, who added the material that points to later dates. *The Tempest*, almost universally regarded as one of Shakespeare's greatest plays and pretty clearly dated to 1611, does indeed date from a period after the death of Oxford, but it is a crude piece of work that should not be included in the canon of works by Oxford.

The anti-Stratfordians, in addition to assuming that the author must have been a man of rank and a university man, usually assume two conspiracies: (1) a conspiracy in Elizabethan and Jacobean times, in which a surprisingly large number of persons connected with the theater knew that the actor Shakespeare did not write the plays attributed to him but for some reason or other pretended that he did; (2) a conspiracy of today's Stratfordians, the professors who teach Shakespeare in the colleges and universities, who are said to have a vested interest in preserving Shakespeare as the author of the plays they teach. In fact, (1) it is inconceivable that the secret of Shakespeare's nonauthorship could have been preserved by all of the people who supposedly were in on the conspiracy, and (2) academic fame awaits any scholar today who can disprove Shakespeare's authorship.

The Stratfordian case is convincing not only because hundreds or even thousands of anti-Stratford arguments—of the sort that say "ever I was born" has the secret double meaning "E. Ver, I was born"—add up to nothing at all but also because irrefutable evidence connects the man from Stratford with the London theater and with the authorship of particular plays. The anti-Stratfordians do not seem to understand that it is not enough to dismiss the Stratford case by saying that a fellow from the provinces simply couldn't have written the plays. Nor do they understand that it is not enough to dismiss all of the evidence connecting Shakespeare with the plays by asserting that it is perjured.

The Shakespeare Canon

We return to William Shakespeare. Thirty-seven plays as well as some nondramatic poems are generally held to constitute the Shakespeare canon, the body of authentic works. The exact dates of composition of most of the works are highly uncertain, but evidence of a starting point and/or of a final limiting point often provides a framework for informed guessing. For example, *Richard II* cannot be earlier than 1595, the publication date of some material to which it is indebted; *The Merchant of Venice* cannot be later than 1598, the year Francis Meres mentioned it. Sometimes arguments for a date hang on an alleged topical allusion, such as the lines about the unseasonable weather in *A Midsummer Night's Dream*, 2.1.81–117, but such an allusion, if indeed it is an allusion to an event in the real world, can be variously interpreted, and in any case there is always the possibility that a topical allusion was inserted years later, to bring the play up to date. (The issue of alterations in a text between the time that Shakespeare drafted it and the time that it was printed—alterations due to censorship or playhouse practice or Shakespeare's own second thoughts—will be discussed in "The Play Text as a Collaboration" later in this overview.) Dates are often attributed on the basis of style, and although conjectures about style usually rest on other conjectures (such as Shakespeare's development as a playwright, or the appropriateness of lines to character), sooner or later one must rely on one's literary sense. There is no documentary proof, for example, that *Othello* is not as early as *Romeo and Juliet*, but one feels that *Othello* is a later, more mature work, and because the first record of its performance is 1604, one is glad enough to set its composition at that date and not push it back into Shakespeare's early years. (*Romeo and Juliet* was first published in 1597, but evidence suggests that it was written a little earlier.) The following chronology, then, is indebted not only to facts but also to informed guesswork and sensitivity. The dates, necessarily imprecise for some works, indicate something like a scholarly consensus concerning the time of original composition. Some plays show evidence of later revision.

Plays. The first collected edition of Shakespeare, published in 1623, included thirty-six plays. These are all accepted as Shakespeare's, though for one of them, *Henry VIII*, he is thought to have had a collaborator. A thirty-seventh play, *Pericles*, published in 1609 and attributed to Shakespeare on the title page, is also widely accepted as being partly by Shakespeare even though it is not included in the 1623 volume. Still another play not in the 1623 volume, *The Two Noble Kinsmen*, was first published in 1634, with a title page attributing it to John Fletcher and Shakespeare. Probably most students of the subject now believe that Shakespeare did indeed have a hand in it. Of the remaining plays attributed at one time or another to Shakespeare, only one, *Edward III*, anonymously published in 1596, is now regarded by some scholars as a serious candidate. The prevailing opinion, however, is that this rather simple-minded play is not Shakespeare's; at most he may have revised some passages, chiefly scenes with the Countess of

Salisbury. We include *The Two Noble Kinsmen* but do not include *Edward III* in the following list.

1588–94	*The Comedy of Errors*
1588–94	*Love's Labor's Lost*
1589–91	*2 Henry VI*
1590–91	*3 Henry VI*
1589–92	*1 Henry VI*
1592–93	*Richard III*
1589–94	*Titus Andronicus*
1593–94	*The Taming of the Shrew*
1592–94	*The Two Gentlemen of Verona*
1594–96	*Romeo and Juliet*
1595	*Richard II*
1595–96	*A Midsummer Night's Dream*
1596–97	*King John*
1594–96	*The Merchant of Venice*
1596–97	*1 Henry IV*
1597	*The Merry Wives of Windsor*
1597–98	*2 Henry IV*
1598–99	*Much Ado About Nothing*
1598–99	*Henry V*
1599	*Julius Caesar*
1599–1600	*As You Like It*
1599–1600	*Twelfth Night*
1600–1601	*Hamlet*
1601–1602	*Troilus and Cressida*
1602–1604	*All's Well That Ends Well*
1603–1604	*Othello*
1604	*Measure for Measure*
1605–1606	*King Lear*
1605–1606	*Macbeth*
1606–1607	*Antony and Cleopatra*
1605–1608	*Timon of Athens*
1607–1608	*Coriolanus*
1607–1608	*Pericles*
1609–10	*Cymbeline*
1610–11	*The Winter's Tale*
1611	*The Tempest*

| 1612–13 | *Henry VIII* |
| 1613 | *The Two Noble Kinsmen* |

Poems. In 1989 Donald W. Foster published a book in which he argued that "A Funeral Elegy for Master William Peter," published in 1612, ascribed only to the initials W.S., *may* be by Shakespeare. Foster later published an article in a scholarly journal, *PMLA* 111 (1996), in which he asserted the claim more positively. The evidence begins with the initials, and includes the fact that the publisher and the printer of the elegy had published Shakespeare's *Sonnets* in 1609. But such facts add up to rather little, especially because no one has found any connection between Shakespeare and William Peter (an Oxford graduate about whom little is known, who was murdered at the age of twenty-nine). The argument is based chiefly on statistical examinations of word patterns, which are said to correlate with Shakespeare's known work. Despite such correlations, however, many readers feel that the poem does not sound like Shakespeare. True, Shakespeare has a great range of styles, but his work is consistently imaginative and interesting. Many readers find neither of these qualities in "A Funeral Elegy."

1592–93	*Venus and Adonis*
1593–94	*The Rape of Lucrece*
1593–1600	*Sonnets*
1600–1601	*The Phoenix and the Turtle*

Shakespeare's English

1. Spelling and Pronunciation. From the philologist's point of view, Shakespeare's English is modern English. It requires footnotes, but the inexperienced reader can comprehend substantial passages with very little help, whereas for the same reader Chaucer's Middle English is a foreign language. By the beginning of the fifteenth century the chief grammatical changes in English had taken place, and the final unaccented *-e* of Middle English had been lost (though it survives even today in spelling, as in *name*); during the fifteenth century the dialect of London, the commercial and political center, gradually displaced the provincial dialects, at least in writing; by the end of the century, printing had helped to regularize and stabilize the language, especially spelling. Elizabethan spelling may seem erratic to us (there were dozens of spellings of *Shakespeare*, and a simple word like *been* was also spelled *beene* and *bin*), but it had much in common with our spelling. Elizabethan spelling was conservative in that for the most part it reflected an older pronunciation (Middle English) rather than the sound of the language as it was then spoken, just as our spelling continues to reflect medieval pronunciation—most obviously in the now silent but formerly pronounced letters in a word such as *knight*. Elizabethan pronunciation, though not identical with ours, was much closer to ours than to that of the Middle Ages. Incidentally, though no one can be certain about what Elizabethan English sounded like, specialists tend to believe it was rather like the speech of a modern stage Irishman (*time* apparently was pronounced *toime*, *old* pronounced *awld*, *day* pronounced *die*, and *join* pronounced *jine*) and not at all like the Oxford speech that most of us think it was.

An awareness of the difference between our pronunciation and Shakespeare's is crucial in three areas—in accent, or number of syllables (many metrically regular lines may look irregular to us); in rhymes (which may not look like rhymes); and in puns (which may not look like puns). Examples will be useful. Some words that were at least on occasion stressed differently from today are *aspèct*, *còmplete*, *fòrlorn*, *revènue*, and *sepùlcher*. Words that sometimes had an additional syllable are *emp[e]ress*, *Hen[e]ry*, *mon[e]th*, and *villain* (three syllables, *vil-lay-in*). An additional syllable is often found in possessives, like *moon*'s (pronounced *moones*), and in words ending in *-tion* or *-sion*. Words that had one less syllable than they now have are *needle* (pronounced *neel*) and *violet* (pronounced *vilet*). Among rhymes now lost are *one* with *loan*, *love* with *prove*, *beast* with *jest*, *eat* with *great*. (In reading, trust your sense of metrics and your ear, more than your eye.) An example of a pun that has become obliterated by a change in pronunciation is Falstaff's reply to Prince Hal's "Come, tell us your

reason" in *1 Henry IV*: "Give you a reason on compulsion?
If reasons were as plentiful as blackberries, I would give no
man a reason upon compulsion, I" (2.4.237–40). The *ea* in
reason was pronounced rather like a long *a*, like the *ai* in
raisin, hence the comparison with blackberries.

Puns are not merely attempts to be funny; like metaphors
they often involve bringing into a meaningful relationship
areas of experience normally seen as remote. In *2 Henry IV*,
when Feeble is conscripted, he stoically says, "I care not. A
man can die but once. We owe God a death" (3.2.242–43),
punning on *debt*, which was the way *death* was pronounced.
Here an enormously significant fact of life is put into simple
commercial imagery, suggesting its commonplace quality.
Shakespeare used the same pun earlier in *1 Henry IV*, when
Prince Hal says to Falstaff, "Why, thou owest God a death,"
and Falstaff replies, " 'Tis not due yet: I would be loath
to pay him before his day. What need I be so forward with
him that calls not on me?" (5.1.126–29).

Sometimes the puns reveal a delightful playfulness;
sometimes they reveal aggressiveness, as when, replying to
Claudius's "But now, my cousin Hamlet, and my son,"
Hamlet says, "A little more than kin, and less than kind!"
(1.2.64–65). These are Hamlet's first words in the play, and
we already hear him warring verbally against Claudius.
Hamlet's "less than kind" probably means (1) Hamlet is not
of Claudius's family or nature, *kind* having the sense it still
has in our word *mankind*; (2) Hamlet is not kindly (affec-
tionately) disposed toward Claudius; (3) Claudius is not
naturally (but rather unnaturally, in a legal sense incestu-
ously) Hamlet's father. The puns evidently were not put in
as sops to the groundlings; they are an important way of
communicating a complex meaning.

2. *Vocabulary.* A conspicuous difficulty in reading Shakespeare is rooted in the fact that some of his words are no
longer in common use—for example, words concerned with
armor, astrology, clothing, coinage, hawking, horsemanship, law, medicine, sailing, and war. Shakespeare had a
large vocabulary—something near thirty thousand words—
but it was not so much a vocabulary of big words as a
vocabulary drawn from a wide range of life, and it is partly

his ability to call upon a great body of concrete language that gives his plays the sense of being in close contact with life. When the right word did not already exist, he made it up. Among words thought to be his coinages are *accommodation, all-knowing, amazement, bare-faced, countless, dexterously, dislocate, dwindle, fancy-free, frugal, indistinguishable, lackluster, laughable, overawe, premeditated, sea change, star-crossed.* Among those that have not survived are the verb *convive,* meaning to feast together, and *smilet,* a little smile.

Less overtly troublesome than the technical words but more treacherous are the words that seem readily intelligible to us but whose Elizabethan meanings differ from their modern ones. When Horatio describes the Ghost as an "erring spirit," he is saying not that the ghost has sinned or made an error but that it is wandering. Here is a short list of some of the most common words in Shakespeare's plays that often (but not always) have a meaning other than their most usual modern meaning:

'a	he
abuse	deceive
accident	occurrence
advertise	inform
an, and	if
annoy	harm
appeal	accuse
artificial	skillful
brave	fine, splendid
censure	opinion
cheer	(1) face (2) frame of mind
chorus	a single person who comments on the events
closet	small private room
competitor	partner
conceit	idea, imagination
cousin	kinsman
cunning	skillful
disaster	evil astrological influence
doom	judgment
entertain	receive into service

envy	malice
event	outcome
excrement	outgrowth (of hair)
fact	evil deed
fancy	(1) love (2) imagination
fell	cruel
fellow	(1) companion (2) low person (often an insulting term if addressed to someone of approximately equal rank)
fond	foolish
free	(1) innocent (2) generous
glass	mirror
hap, haply	chance, by chance
head	army
humor	(1) mood (2) bodily fluid thought to control one's psychology
imp	child
intelligence	news
kind	natural, acting according to nature
let	hinder
lewd	base
mere(ly)	utter(ly)
modern	commonplace
natural	a fool, an idiot
naughty	(1) wicked (2) worthless
next	nearest
nice	(1) trivial (2) fussy
noise	music
policy	(1) prudence (2) stratagem
presently	immediately
prevent	anticipate
proper	handsome
prove	test
quick	alive
sad	serious
saw	proverb
secure	without care, incautious
silly	innocent

sensible	capable of being perceived by the senses
shrewd	sharp
so	provided that
starve	die
still	always
success	that which follows
tall	brave
tell	count
tonight	last night
wanton	playful, careless
watch	keep awake
will	lust
wink	close both eyes
wit	mind, intelligence

All glosses, of course, are mere approximations; sometimes one of Shakespeare's words may hover between an older meaning and a modern one, and as we have seen, his words often have multiple meanings.

3. Grammar. A few matters of grammar may be surveyed, though it should be noted at the outset that Shakespeare sometimes made up his own grammar. As E.A. Abbott says in *A Shakespearian Grammar,* "Almost any part of speech can be used as any other part of speech": a noun as a verb ("he childed as I fathered"); a verb as a noun ("She hath made compare"); or an adverb as an adjective ("a seldom pleasure"). There are hundreds, perhaps thousands, of such instances in the plays, many of which at first glance would not seem at all irregular and would trouble only a pedant. Here are a few broad matters.

Nouns: The Elizabethans thought the *-s* genitive ending for nouns (as in *man's*) derived from *his*; thus the line " 'gainst the count his galleys I did some service," for "the count's galleys."

Adjectives: By Shakespeare's time adjectives had lost the endings that once indicated gender, number, and case. About the only difference between Shakespeare's adjectives and ours is the use of the now redundant *more* or *most* with the comparative ("some more fitter place") or superlative

("This was the most unkindest cut of all"). Like double comparatives and double superlatives, double negatives were acceptable; Mercutio "will not budge for no man's pleasure."

Pronouns: The greatest change was in pronouns. In Middle English *thou, thy,* and *thee* were used among familiars and in speaking to children and inferiors; *ye, your,* and *you* were used in speaking to superiors (servants to masters, nobles to the king) or to equals with whom the speaker was not familiar. Increasingly the "polite" forms were used in all direct address, regardless of rank, and the accusative *you* displaced the nominative *ye.* Shakespeare sometimes uses *ye* instead of *you,* but even in Shakespeare's day *ye* was archaic, and it occurs mostly in rhetorical appeals.

Thou, thy, and *thee* were not completely displaced, however, and Shakespeare occasionally makes significant use of them, sometimes to connote familiarity or intimacy and sometimes to connote contempt. In *Twelfth Night* Sir Toby advises Sir Andrew to insult Cesario by addressing him as *thou:* "If thou thou'st him some thrice, it shall not be amiss" (3.2.46–47). In *Othello* when Brabantio is addressing an unidentified voice in the dark he says, "What are you?" (1.1.91), but when the voice identifies itself as the foolish suitor Roderigo, Brabantio uses the contemptuous form, saying, "I have charged thee not to haunt about my doors" (93). He uses this form for a while, but later in the scene, when he comes to regard Roderigo as an ally, he shifts back to the polite *you,* beginning in line 163, "What said she to you?" and on to the end of the scene. For reasons not yet satisfactorily explained, Elizabethans used *thou* in addresses to God—"O God, thy arm was here," the king says in *Henry V* (4.8.108)—and to supernatural characters such as ghosts and witches. A subtle variation occurs in *Hamlet.* When Hamlet first talks with the Ghost in 1.5, he uses *thou,* but when he sees the Ghost in his mother's room, in 3.4, he uses *you,* presumably because he is now convinced that the Ghost is not a counterfeit but is his father.

Perhaps the most unusual use of pronouns, from our point of view, is the neuter singular. In place of our *its, his* was often used, as in "How far that little candle throws *his* beams." But the use of a masculine pronoun for a neuter noun came to seem unnatural, and so *it* was used for the possessive as well as the nominative: "The hedge-sparrow fed the cuckoo so long / That it had it head bit off by it young." In the late sixteenth century the possessive form *its* developed, apparently by analogy with the *-s* ending used to indicate a genitive noun, as in *book*'s, but *its* was not yet common usage in Shakespeare's day. He seems to have used *its* only ten times, mostly in his later plays. Other usages, such as "you have seen Cassio and she together" or the substitution of *who* for *whom,* cause little problem even when noticed.

Verbs, Adverbs, and Prepositions: Verbs cause almost no difficulty: The third person singular present form commonly ends in *-s,* as in modern English (e.g., "He blesses"), but sometimes in *-eth* (Portia explains to Shylock that mercy "blesseth him that gives and him that takes"). Broadly speaking, the *-eth* ending was old-fashioned or dignified or "literary" rather than colloquial, except for the words *doth, hath,* and *saith.* The *-eth* ending (regularly used in the King James Bible, 1611) is very rare in Shakespeare's dramatic prose, though not surprisingly it occurs twice in the rather formal prose summary of the narrative poem *Lucrece.* Sometimes a plural subject, especially if it has collective force, takes a verb ending in *-s,* as in "My old bones aches." Some of our strong or irregular preterites (such as *broke*) have a different form in Shakespeare (*brake*); some verbs that now have a weak or regular preterite (such as *helped*) in Shakespeare have a strong or irregular preterite (*holp*). Some adverbs that today end in *-ly* were not inflected: "grievous sick," "wondrous strange." Finally, prepositions often are not the ones we expect: "We are such stuff as dreams are made on," "I have a king here to my flatterer."

Again, none of the differences (except meanings that have substantially changed or been lost) will cause much difficulty. But it must be confessed that for some elliptical passages there is no widespread agreement on meaning. Wise editors resist saying more than they know, and when they are uncertain they add a question mark to their gloss.

Shakespeare's Theater

In Shakespeare's infancy, Elizabethan actors performed wherever they could—in great halls, at court, in the courtyards of inns. These venues implied not only different audiences but also different playing conditions. The innyards must have made rather unsatisfactory theaters: on some days they were unavailable because carters bringing goods to London used them as depots; when available, they had to be rented from the innkeeper. In 1567, presumably to avoid such difficulties, and also to avoid regulation by the Common Council of London, which was not well disposed toward theatricals, one John Brayne, brother-in-law of the carpenter turned actor James Burbage, built the Red Lion in an eastern suburb of London. We know nothing about its shape or its capacity; we can say only that it may have been the first building in Europe constructed for the purpose of giving plays since the end of antiquity, a thousand years earlier. Even after the building of the Red Lion theatrical activity continued in London in makeshift circumstances, in marketplaces and inns, and always uneasily. In 1574 the Common Council required that plays and playing places in London be licensed because

> sundry great disorders and inconveniences have been found to ensue to this city by the inordinate haunting of great multitudes of people, specially youth, to plays, interludes, and shows, namely occasion of frays and quarrels, evil practices of incontinency in great inns having chambers and secret places adjoining to their open stages and galleries.

The Common Council ordered that innkeepers who wished licenses to hold performance put up a bond and make contributions to the poor.

The requirement that plays and innyard theaters be licensed, along with the other drawbacks of playing at inns and presumably along with the success of the Red Lion, led James Burbage to rent a plot of land northeast of the city walls, on property outside the jurisdiction of the city. Here he built England's second playhouse, called simply the Theatre. About all that is known of its construction is that it was wood. It soon had imitators, the most famous being the Globe (1599), essentially an amphitheater built across the Thames (again outside the city's jurisdiction), constructed with timbers of the Theatre, which had been dismantled when Burbage's lease ran out.

Admission to the theater was one penny, which allowed spectators to stand at the sides and front of the stage that jutted into the yard. An additional penny bought a seat in a covered part of the theater, and a third penny bought a more comfortable seat and a better location. It is notoriously difficult to translate prices into today's money, since some things that are inexpensive today would have been expensive in the past and vice versa—a pipeful of tobacco (imported, of course) cost a lot of money, about three pennies, and an orange (also imported) cost two or three times what a chicken cost—but perhaps we can get some idea of the low cost of the penny admission when we realize that a penny could also buy a pot of ale. An unskilled laborer made about five or sixpence a day, an artisan about twelve pence a day, and the hired actors (as opposed to the sharers in the company, such as Shakespeare) made about ten pence a performance. A printed play cost five or sixpence. Of course a visit to the theater (like a visit to a baseball game today) usually cost more than the admission since the spectator probably would also buy food and drink. Still, the low entrance fee meant that the theater was available to all except the very poorest people, rather as movies and most athletic events are today. Evidence indicates that the audience ranged from apprentices who somehow managed to scrape together the minimum entrance fee and to escape from their masters for a few hours, to prosperous members of the middle class and aristocrats who paid the additional fee for admission to the galleries. The exact proportion of men to women cannot be determined, but women of all classes certainly were present. Theaters were open every afternoon but Sundays for much of the year, except in times of plague, when they were closed because of fear of infection. By the way, no evidence suggests the presence of toilet facilities. Presumably the patrons relieved themselves by making a quick trip to the fields surrounding the playhouses.

There are four important sources of information about the

structure of Elizabethan public playhouses—drawings, a contract, recent excavations, and stage directions in the plays. Of drawings, only the so-called de Witt drawing (c. 1596) of the Swan—really his friend Aernout van Buchell's copy of Johannes de Witt's drawing—is of much significance. The drawing, the only extant representation of the interior of an Elizabethan theater, shows an amphitheater of three tiers, with a stage jutting from a wall into the yard or

Johannes de Witt, a Continental visitor to London, made a drawing of the Swan theater in about the year 1596. The original drawing is lost; this is Aernout van Buchell's copy of it.

center of the building. The tiers are roofed, and part of the stage is covered by a roof that projects from the rear and is supported at its front on two posts, but the groundlings, who paid a penny to stand in front of the stage or at its sides, were exposed to the sky. (Performances in such a playhouse were held only in the daytime; artificial illumination was not used.) At the rear of the stage are two massive doors; above the stage is a gallery.

The second major source of information, the contract for the Fortune (built in 1600), specifies that although the Globe (built in 1599) is to be the model, the Fortune is to be square, eighty feet outside and fifty-five inside. The stage is to be forty-three feet broad, and is to extend into the middle of the yard, i.e., it is twenty-seven and a half feet deep.

The third source of information, the 1989 excavations of the Rose (built in 1587), indicate that the Rose was fourteen-sided, about seventy-two feet in diameter with an inner yard almost fifty feet in diameter. The stage at the Rose was about sixteen feet deep, thirty-seven feet wide at the rear, and twenty-seven feet wide downstage. The relatively small dimensions and the tapering stage, in contrast to the rectangular stage in the Swan drawing, surprised theater historians and have made them more cautious in generalizing about the Elizabethan theater. Excavations at the Globe have not yielded much information, though some historians believe that the fragmentary evidence suggests a larger theater, perhaps one hundred feet in diameter.

From the fourth chief source, stage directions in the plays, one learns that entrance to the stage was by the doors at the rear (*"Enter one citizen at one door, and another at the other"*). A curtain hanging across the doorway—or a curtain hanging between the two doorways—could provide a place where a character could conceal himself, as Polonius does, when he wishes to overhear the conversation between Hamlet and Gertrude. Similarly, withdrawing a curtain from the doorway could "discover" (reveal) a character or two. Such discovery scenes are very rare in Elizabethan drama, but a good example occurs in *The Tempest* (5.1.171), where a stage direction tells us, *"Here Prospero discovers Ferdinand and Miranda playing at chess."* There was also some sort of playing space "aloft" or "above" to represent, for instance, the top of a city's walls or a room above the street. Doubtless each theater had its own peculiarities, but perhaps we can talk about a "typical" Elizabethan theater if we realize that no theater need exactly fit the description, just as no mother is the average mother with 2.7 children.

This hypothetical theater is wooden, round, or polygonal (in *Henry V* Shakespeare calls it a "wooden *O*"), capable of holding some eight hundred spectators who stood in the yard around the projecting elevated stage—these spectators were the "groundlings"—and some fifteen hundred additional spectators who sat in the three roofed galleries. The stage, protected by a "shadow" or "heavens" or roof, is entered from two doors; behind the doors is the "tiring house" (attiring house, i.e., dressing room), and above the stage is some sort of gallery that may sometimes hold spectators but can be used (for example) as the bedroom from which Romeo—according to a stage direction in one text—"goeth down." Some evidence suggests that a throne can be lowered onto the platform stage, perhaps from the "shadow"; certainly characters can descend from the stage through a trap or traps into the cellar or "hell." Sometimes this space beneath the stage accommodates a sound-effects man or musician (in *Antony and Cleopatra* "*music of the hautboys* [oboes] *is under the stage*") or an actor (in *Hamlet* the "*Ghost cries under the stage*"). Most characters simply walk on and off through the doors, but because there is no curtain in front of the platform, corpses will have to be carried off (Hamlet obligingly clears the stage of Polonius's corpse, when he says, "I'll lug the guts into the neighbor room"). Other characters may have fallen at the rear, where a curtain on a doorway could be drawn to conceal them.

Such may have been the "public theater," so called because its inexpensive admission made it available to a wide range of the populace. Another kind of theater has been called the "private theater" because its much greater admission charge (sixpence versus the penny for general admission at the public theater) limited its audience to the wealthy or the prodigal. The private theater was basically a large room, entirely roofed and therefore artificially illuminated, with a stage at one end. The theaters thus were distinct in two ways: One was essentially an amphitheater that catered to the general public; the other was a hall that catered to the wealthy. In 1576 a hall theater was established in Blackfriars, a Dominican priory in London that had been suppressed in 1538 and confiscated by the Crown and thus was not under the city's jurisdiction. All the actors in this Blackfriars theater were boys about eight to thirteen years old (in the public theaters similar boys played female parts; a boy Lady Macbeth played to a man Macbeth). Near the end of this section on Shakespeare's theater we will talk at some length about possible implications in this convention of using boys to play female roles, but for the moment we should say that it doubtless accounts for the relative lack of female roles in Elizabethan drama. Thus, in *A Midsummer Night's Dream*, out of twenty-one named roles, only four are female; in *Hamlet*, out of twenty-four, only two (Gertrude and Ophelia) are female. Many of Shakespeare's characters have fathers but no mothers—for instance, King Lear's daughters. We need not bring in Freud to explain the disparity; a dramatic company had only a few boys in it.

To return to the private theaters, in some of which all of the performers were children—the "eyrie of . . . little eyases" (nest of unfledged hawks—2.2.347–48) which Rosencrantz mentions when he and Guildenstern talk with Hamlet. The theater in Blackfriars had a precarious existence, and ceased operations in 1584. In 1596 James Burbage, who had already made theatrical history by building the Theatre, began to construct a second Blackfriars theater. He died in 1597, and for several years this second Blackfriars theater was used by a troupe of boys, but in 1608 two of Burbage's sons and five other actors (including Shakespeare) became joint operators of the theater, using it in the winter when the open-air Globe was unsuitable. Perhaps such a smaller theater, roofed, artificially illuminated, and with a tradition of a wealthy audience, exerted an influence in Shakespeare's late plays.

Performances in the private theaters may well have had intermissions during which music was played, but in the public theaters the action was probably uninterrupted, flowing from scene to scene almost without a break. Actors would enter, speak, exit, and others would immediately enter and establish (if necessary) the new locale by a few properties and by words and gestures. To indicate that the scene took place at night, a player or two would carry a torch. Here are some samples of Shakespeare establishing the scene:

This is Illyria, lady.   (*Twelfth Night*, 1.2.2)

Well, this is the Forest of Arden.   (*As You Like It*, 2.4.14)

This castle has a pleasant seat; the air
Nimbly and sweetly recommends itself
Unto our gentle senses.   (*Macbeth*, 1.6.1–3)

The west yet glimmers with some streaks of day.
                                        (*Macbeth*, 3.3.5)

Sometimes a speech will go far beyond evoking the minimal setting of place and time, and will, so to speak, evoke the social world in which the characters move. For instance, early in the first scene of *The Merchant of Venice* Salerio suggests an explanation for Antonio's melancholy. (In the following passage, *pageants* are decorated wagons, floats, and *cursy* is the verb "to curtsy," or "to bow.")

Your mind is tossing on the ocean,
There where your argosies with portly sail—
Like signiors and rich burghers on the flood,
Or as it were the pageants of the sea—
Do overpeer the petty traffickers
That cursy to them, do them reverence,
As they fly by them with their woven wings.   (1.1.8–14)

Late in the nineteenth century, when Henry Irving produced the play with elaborate illusionistic sets, the first scene showed a ship moored in the harbor, with fruit vendors and dock laborers, in an effort to evoke the bustling and exotic life of Venice. But Shakespeare's words give us this exotic, rich world of commerce in his highly descriptive language when Salerio speaks of "argosies with portly sail" that fly with "woven wings"; equally important, through Salerio Shakespeare conveys a sense of the orderly, hierarchical society in which the lesser ships, "the petty traffickers," curtsy and thereby "do . . . reverence" to their superiors, the merchant prince's ships, which are "Like signiors and rich burghers."

On the other hand, it is a mistake to think that except for verbal pictures the Elizabethan stage was bare. Although Shakespeare's Chorus in *Henry V* calls the stage an "unworthy scaffold" (Prologue 1.10) and urges the spectators to "eke out our performance with your mind" (Prologue 3.35), there was considerable spectacle. The last act of *Macbeth*, for instance, has five stage directions calling for *"drum and colors,"* and another sort of appeal to the eye is indicated by the stage direction *"Enter Macduff, with Macbeth's head."* Some scenery and properties may have been substantial; doubtless a throne was used, but the pillars supporting the roof would have served for the trees on which Orlando pins his poems in *As You Like It*.

Having talked about the public theater—"this wooden *O*"—at some length, we should mention again that Shakespeare's plays were performed also in other locales. Alvin Kernan, in *Shakespeare, the King's Playwright: Theater in the Stuart Court 1603–1613* (1995), points out that "several of [Shakespeare's] plays contain brief theatrical performances, set always in a court or some noble house. When Shakespeare portrayed a theater, he did not, except for the choruses in *Henry V*, imagine a public theater" (p. 195). (Examples include episodes in *The Taming of the Shrew*, *A Midsummer Night's Dream*, *Hamlet*, and *The Tempest*.)

A Note on the Use of Boy Actors in Female Roles

Until fairly recently, scholars were content to mention that the convention existed; they sometimes also mentioned that it continued the medieval practice of using males in female roles, and that other theaters, notably in ancient Greece and in China and Japan, also used males in female roles. (In classical Noh drama in Japan, males still play the female roles.) Prudery may have been at the root of the academic failure to talk much about the use of boy actors, or maybe there really is not much more to say than that it was a convention of a male-centered culture (Stephen Greenblatt's view, in *Shakespearean Negotiations* [1988]). Further, the very nature of a convention is that it is not thought about: Hamlet is a Dane and Julius Caesar is a Roman, but in Shakespeare's plays they speak English, and we in the audience never give this odd fact a thought. Similarly, a character may speak in the presence of others and we understand, again without thinking about it, that he or she is not heard by the figures on the stage (the aside); a character alone on the stage may speak (the soliloquy), and we do not take the character to be unhinged; in a realistic (box) set, the fourth wall, which allows us to see what is going on, is miraculously missing. The no-nonsense view, then, is that the boy actor was an accepted convention, accepted unthinkingly—just as today we know that Kenneth Branagh is not Hamlet, Al Pacino is not Richard III, and Denzel Washington is not the Prince of Aragon. In this view, the audience takes the performer for the role, and that is that; such is the argument we now make for race-free casting, in which African-Americans and Asians can play roles of persons who lived in medieval Denmark and ancient Rome. But gender perhaps is different, at least today. It is a matter of abundant academic study: The Elizabethan theater is now sometimes called a transvestite theater, and we hear much about cross-dressing.

Shakespeare himself in a very few passages calls attention to the use of boys in female roles. At the end of *As You Like It* the boy who played Rosalind addresses the audience, and says, "O men, . . . if I were a woman, I would kiss as many of you as had beards that pleased me." But this is in the Epilogue; the plot is over, and the actor is stepping out of the play and into the audience's everyday world. A second reference to the practice of boys playing female roles occurs in *Antony and Cleopatra*, when Cleopatra imagines that she and Antony will be the subject of crude plays, her role being performed by a boy:

> The quick comedians
> Extemporally will stage us, and present
> Our Alexandrian revels: Antony
> Shall be brought drunken forth, and I shall see
> Some squeaking Cleopatra boy my greatness.   (5.2.216–20)

In a few other passages, Shakespeare is more indirect. For instance, in *Twelfth Night* Viola, played of course by a boy, disguises herself as a young man and seeks service in the house of a lord. She enlists the help of a Captain, and (by way of explaining away her voice and her beardlessness) says,

> I'll serve this duke
> Thou shalt present me as an eunuch to him.   (1.2.55–56)

In *Hamlet*, when the players arrive in 2.2, Hamlet jokes with the boy who plays a female role. The boy has grown since Hamlet last saw him: "By'r Lady, your ladyship is nearer to heaven than when I saw you last by the altitude of a chopine" (a lady's thick-soled shoe). He goes on: "Pray God your voice . . . be not cracked" (434–38).

Exactly how sexual, how erotic, this material was and is, is now much disputed. Again, the use of boys may have been unnoticed, or rather not thought about—an unexamined convention—by most or all spectators most of the time, perhaps *all* of the time, except when Shakespeare calls the convention to the attention of the audience, as in the passages just quoted. Still, an occasional bit seems to invite erotic thoughts. The clearest example is the name that Rosalind takes in *As You Like It*, Ganymede—the beautiful youth whom Zeus abducted. Did boys dressed to play female roles carry homoerotic appeal for straight men (Lisa Jardine's view, in *Still Harping on Daughters* [1983]), or for gay men, or for some or all women in the audience? Further, when the boy actor played a woman who (for the purposes of the plot) disguised herself as a male, as Rosalind, Viola, and Portia do—so we get a boy playing a woman playing a man—what sort of appeal was generated, and for what sort of spectator?

Some scholars have argued that the convention empowered women by letting female characters display a freedom unavailable in Renaissance patriarchal society; the convention, it is said, undermined rigid gender distinctions. In this view, the convention (along with plots in which female characters for a while disguised themselves as young men) allowed Shakespeare to say what some modern gender

critics say: Gender is a constructed role rather than a bio-
logical given, something we make, rather than a fixed binary
opposition of male and female (see Juliet Dusinberre, in
Shakespeare and the Nature of Women [1975]). On the other
hand, some scholars have maintained that the male disguise
assumed by some female characters serves only to reaffirm
traditional social distinctions since female characters who
don male garb (notably Portia in *The Merchant of Venice*
and Rosalind in *As You Like It*) return to their female garb
and at least implicitly (these critics say) reaffirm the status
quo. (For this last view, see Clara Claiborne Park, in an
essay in *The Woman's Part*, ed. Carolyn Ruth Swift Lenz et
al. [1980].) Perhaps no one answer is right for all plays; in
As You Like It cross-dressing empowers Rosalind, but in
Twelfth Night cross-dressing comically traps Viola.

Shakespeare's Dramatic Language: Costumes, Gestures and Silences; Prose and Poetry

Because Shakespeare was a dramatist, not merely a poet,
he worked not only with language but also with costume,
sound effects, gestures, and even silences. We have already
discussed some kinds of spectacle in the preceding section,
and now we will begin with other aspects of visual language;
a theater, after all, is literally a "place for seeing." Consider
the opening stage direction in *The Tempest*, the first play in
the first published collection of Shakespeare's plays: *"A
tempestuous noise of thunder and Lightning heard: Enter a
Ship-master, and a Boteswain."*

Costumes: What did that shipmaster and that boatswain
wear? Doubtless they wore something that identified them
as men of the sea. Not much is known about the costumes
that Elizabethan actors wore, but at least three points are
clear: (1) many of the costumes were splendid versions of
contemporary Elizabethan dress; (2) some attempts were
made to approximate the dress of certain occupations and of
antique or exotic characters such as Romans, Turks, and
Jews; (3) some costumes indicated that the wearer was

supernatural. Evidence for elaborate Elizabethan clothing can be found in the plays themselves and in contemporary comments about the "sumptuous" players who wore the discarded clothing of noblemen, as well as in account books that itemize such things as "a scarlet cloak with two broad gold laces, with gold buttons down the sides."

The attempts at approximation of the dress of certain occupations and nationalities also can be documented from the plays themselves, and it derives additional confirmation from a drawing of the first scene of Shakespeare's *Titus Andronicus*—the only extant Elizabethan picture of an identifiable episode in a play. (See pp. xxxviii–xxxix.) The drawing, probably done in 1594 or 1595, shows Queen Tamora pleading for mercy. She wears a somewhat medieval-looking robe and a crown; Titus wears a toga and a wreath, but two soldiers behind him wear costumes fairly close to Elizabethan dress. We do not know, however, if the drawing represents an actual stage production in the public theater, or perhaps a private production, or maybe only a reader's visualization of an episode. Further, there is some conflicting evidence: In *Julius Caesar* a reference is made to Caesar's doublet (a close-fitting jacket), which, if taken literally, suggests that even the protagonist did not wear Roman clothing; and certainly the lesser characters, who are said to wear hats, did not wear Roman garb.

It should be mentioned, too, that even ordinary clothing can be symbolic: Hamlet's "inky cloak," for example, sets him apart from the brightly dressed members of Claudius's court and symbolizes his mourning; the fresh clothes that are put on King Lear partly symbolize his return to sanity. Consider, too, the removal of disguises near the end of some plays. For instance, Rosalind in *As You Like It* and Portia and Nerissa in *The Merchant of Venice* remove their male attire, thus again becoming fully themselves.

Gestures and Silences: Gestures are an important part of a dramatist's language. King Lear kneels before his daughter Cordelia for a benediction (4.7.57–59), an act of humility that contrasts with his earlier speeches banishing her and that contrasts also with a comparable gesture, his ironic

kneeling before Regan (2.4.153–55). Northumberland's failure to kneel before King Richard II (3.3.71–72) speaks volumes. As for silences, consider a moment in *Coriolanus*: Before the protagonist yields to his mother's entreaties (5.3.182), there is this stage direction: *"Holds her by the hand, silent."* Another example of "speech in dumbness" occurs in *Macbeth*, when Macduff learns that his wife and children have been murdered. He is silent at first, as Malcolm's speech indicates: "What, man! Ne'er pull your hat upon your brows. Give sorrow words" (4.3.208–9). (For a discussion of such moments, see Philip C. McGuire's *Speechless Dialect: Shakespeare's Open Silences* [1985].)

Of course when we think of Shakespeare's work, we think primarily of his language, both the poetry and the prose.

Prose: Although two of his plays (*Richard II* and *King John*) have no prose at all, about half the others have at least one quarter of the dialogue in prose, and some have notably more: *1 Henry IV* and *2 Henry IV*, about half; *As You Like It*

and *Twelfth Night*, a little more than half; *Much Ado About Nothing*, more than three quarters; and *The Merry Wives of Windsor*, a little more than five sixths. We should remember that despite Molière's joke about M. Jourdain, who was amazed to learn that he spoke prose, most of us do not speak prose. Rather, we normally utter repetitive, shapeless, and often ungrammatical torrents; prose is something very different—a sort of literary imitation of speech at its most coherent.

Today we may think of prose as "natural" for drama; or even if we think that poetry is appropriate for high tragedy we may still think that prose is the right medium for comedy. Greek, Roman, and early English comedies, however, were written in verse. In fact, prose was not generally considered a literary medium in England until the late fifteenth century; Chaucer tells even his bawdy stories in verse. By the end of the 1580s, however, prose had established itself on the English comic stage. In tragedy, Marlowe made some use of prose, not simply in the speeches of clownish servants but even in the speech of a tragic hero, Doctor Faustus. Still, before Shakespeare, prose normally was used in the theater only for special circumstances: (1) letters and proclamations, to set them off from the poetic dialogue; (2) mad characters, to indicate that normal thinking has become disordered; and (3) low comedy, or speeches uttered by clowns even when they are not being comic. Shakespeare made use of these conventions, but he also went far beyond them. Sometimes he begins a scene in prose and then shifts into verse as the emotion is heightened; or conversely, he may shift from verse to prose when a speaker is lowering the emotional level, as when Brutus speaks in the Forum.

Shakespeare's prose usually is not prosaic. Hamlet's prose includes not only small talk with Rosencrantz and Guildenstern but also princely reflections on "What a piece of work is a man" (2.2.312). In conversation with Ophelia, he shifts from light talk in verse to a passionate prose denunciation of women (3.1.103), though the shift to prose here is perhaps also intended to suggest the possibility of madness. (Consult Brian Vickers, *The Artistry of Shakespeare's Prose* [1968].)

Poetry: Drama in rhyme in England goes back to the Middle Ages, but by Shakespeare's day rhyme no longer dominated poetic drama; a finer medium, blank verse (strictly speaking, unrhymed lines of ten syllables, with the stress on every second syllable) had been adopted. But before looking at unrhymed poetry, a few things should be said about the chief uses of rhyme in Shakespeare's plays. (1) A couplet (a pair of rhyming lines) is sometimes used to convey emotional heightening at the end of a blank verse speech; (2) characters sometimes speak a couplet as they leave the stage, suggesting closure; (3) except in the latest plays, scenes fairly often conclude with a couplet, and sometimes, as in *Richard II*, 2.1.145–46, the entrance of a new character within a scene is preceded by a couplet, which wraps up the earlier portion of that scene; (4) speeches of two characters occasionally are linked by rhyme, most notably in *Romeo and Juliet*, 1.5.95–108, where the lovers speak a sonnet between them; elsewhere a taunting reply occasionally rhymes with the previous speaker's last line; (5) speeches with sententious or gnomic remarks are sometimes in rhyme, as in the duke's speech in *Othello* (1.3.199–206); (6) speeches of sardonic mockery are sometimes in rhyme—for example, Iago's speech on women in *Othello* (2.1.146–58)—and they sometimes conclude with an emphatic couplet, as in Bolingbroke's speech on comforting words in *Richard II* (1.3.301–2); (7) some characters are associated with rhyme, such as the fairies in *A Midsummer Night's Dream*; (8) in the early plays, especially *The Comedy of Errors* and *The Taming of the Shrew*, comic scenes that in later plays would be in prose are in jingling rhymes; (9) prologues, choruses, plays-within-the-play, inscriptions, vows, epilogues, and so on are often in rhyme, and the songs in the plays are rhymed.

Neither prose nor rhyme immediately comes to mind when we first think of Shakespeare's medium: It is blank verse, unrhymed iambic pentameter. (In a mechanically exact line there are five iambic feet. An iambic foot consists of two syllables, the second accented, as in *away*; five feet make a pentameter line. Thus, a strict line of iambic pentameter contains ten syllables, the even syllables being stressed more heavily than the odd syllables. Fortunately, Shakespeare usually varies the line somewhat.) The first speech in *A Midsummer Night's Dream*, spoken by Duke Theseus to his betrothed, is an example of blank verse:

> Now, fair Hippolyta, our nuptial hour
> Draws on apace. Four happy days bring in
> Another moon; but, O, methinks, how slow
> This old moon wanes! She lingers my desires,
> Like to a stepdame, or a dowager,
> Long withering out a young man's revenue. (1.1.1–6)

As this passage shows, Shakespeare's blank verse is not mechanically unvarying. Though the predominant foot is the iamb (as in *apace* or *desires*), there are numerous variations. In the first line the stress can be placed on "fair," as the regular metrical pattern suggests, but it is likely that "Now" gets almost as much emphasis; probably in the second line "Draws" is more heavily emphasized than "on," giving us a trochee (a stressed syllable followed by an unstressed one); and in the fourth line each word in the phrase "This old moon wanes" is probably stressed fairly heavily, conveying by two spondees (two feet, each of two stresses) the oppressive tedium that Theseus feels.

In Shakespeare's early plays much of the blank verse is end-stopped (that is, it has a heavy pause at the end of each line), but he later developed the ability to write iambic pentameter verse paragraphs (rather than lines) that give the illusion of speech. His chief techniques are (1) enjambing, i.e., running the thought beyond the single line, as in the first three lines of the speech just quoted; (2) occasionally replacing an iamb with another foot; (3) varying the position of the chief pause (the caesura) within a line; (4) adding an occasional unstressed syllable at the end of a line, traditionally called a feminine ending; and (5) beginning or ending a speech with a half line.

Shakespeare's mature blank verse has much of the rhythmic flexibility of his prose; both the language, though richly figurative and sometimes dense, and the syntax seem natural. It is also often highly appropriate to a particular character. Consider, for instance, this speech from *Hamlet*, in which Claudius, King of Denmark ("the Dane"), speaks to Laertes:

> And now, Laertes, what's the news with you?
> You told us of some suit. What is't, Laertes?
> You cannot speak of reason to the Dane
> And lose your voice. What wouldst thou beg, Laertes,
> That shall not be my offer, not thy asking?   (1.2.42–46)

Notice the short sentences and the repetition of the name "Laertes," to whom the speech is addressed. Notice, too, the shift from the royal "us" in the second line to the more intimate "my" in the last line, and from "you" in the first three lines to the more intimate "thou" and "thy" in the last two lines. Claudius knows how to ingratiate himself with Laertes.

For a second example of the flexibility of Shakespeare's blank verse, consider a passage from *Macbeth*. Distressed by the doctor's inability to cure Lady Macbeth and by the imminent battle, Macbeth addresses some of his remarks to the doctor and others to the servant who is arming him. The entire speech, with its pauses, interruptions, and irresolution (in "Pull't off, I say," Macbeth orders the servant to remove the armor that the servant has been putting on him), catches Macbeth's disintegration. (In the first line, *physic* means "medicine," and in the fourth and fifth lines, *cast the water* means "analyze the urine.")

> Throw physic to the dogs, I'll none of it.
> Come, put mine armor on. Give me my staff.
> Seyton, send out.—Doctor, the thanes fly from me.—
> Come, sir, dispatch. If thou couldst, doctor, cast
> The water of my land, find her disease
> And purge it to a sound and pristine health,
> I would applaud thee to the very echo,
> That should applaud again.—Pull't off, I say.—
> What rhubarb, senna, or what purgative drug,
> Would scour these English hence? Hear'st thou of them?
>
> (5.3.47–56)

Blank verse, then, can be much more than unrhymed iambic pentameter, and even within a single play Shakespeare's blank verse often consists of several styles, depending on the speaker and on the speaker's emotion at the moment.

The Play Text as a Collaboration

Shakespeare's fellow dramatist Ben Jonson reported that the actors said of Shakespeare, "In his writing, whatsoever he penned, he never blotted out line," i.e., never crossed out material and revised his work while composing. None of Shakespeare's plays survives in manuscript (with the possible exception of a scene in *Sir Thomas More*), so we cannot fully evaluate the comment, but in a few instances the published work clearly shows that he revised his manuscript. Consider the following passage (shown here in facsimile) from the best early text of *Romeo and Juliet*, the Second Quarto (1599):

Ro. Would I were ſleepe and peace ſo ſwcet to reſt
The grey eyde morne ſmiles on the frowning night,
Checkring the Eaſterne Clouds with ſtreaks of light,
And darkneſſe fleckted like a drunkard reeles,
From forth daies pathway,made by *Tytans* wheeles.
Hence will I to my ghoſtly Friers cloſe cell,
His helpe to craue,and my deare hap to tell.

                                        Exit.

Enter Frier alone with a basket.   (night,
Fri. The grey-eyed morne ſmiles on the frowning
Checking the Eaſterne clowdes with ſtreaks of light:
And fleckeld darkneſſe like a drunkard reeles,
From forth daies path,and *Titans* burning wheeles:
Now ere the ſun aduance his burning eie,

Romeo rather elaborately tells us that the sun at dawn is
dispelling the night (morning is smiling, the eastern clouds
are checked with light, and the sun's chariot—Titan's
wheels—advances), and he will seek out his spiritual father,
the Friar. He exits and, oddly, the Friar enters and says pretty
much the same thing about the sun. Both speakers say that
"the gray-eyed morn smiles on the frowning night," but there
are small differences, perhaps having more to do with the
business of printing the book than with the author's
composition: For Romeo's "checkring," "fleckted," and
"pathway," we get the Friar's "checking," "fleckeld," and
"path." (Notice, by the way, the inconsistency in Elizabethan
spelling: Romeo's "clouds" become the Friar's "clowdes.")

   Both versions must have been in the printer's copy, and it
seems safe to assume that both were in Shakespeare's manuscript. He must have written one version—let's say he first
wrote Romeo's closing lines for this scene—and then he
decided, no, it's better to give this lyrical passage to the
Friar, as the opening of a new scene, but he neglected to
delete the first version. Editors must make a choice, and they
may feel that the reasonable thing to do is to print the text as
Shakespeare intended it. But how can we know what he
intended? Almost all modern editors delete the lines from

Romeo's speech, and retain the Friar's lines. They don't do this because they know Shakespeare's intention, however. They give the lines to the Friar because the first published version (1597) of *Romeo and Juliet* gives only the Friar's version, and this text (though in many ways inferior to the 1599 text) is thought to derive from the memory of some actors, that is, it is thought to represent a performance, not just a script. Maybe during the course of rehearsals Shakespeare—an actor as well as an author—unilaterally decided that the Friar should speak the lines; if so (remember that we don't know this to be a fact) his final intention was to give the speech to the Friar. Maybe, however, the actors talked it over and settled on the Friar, with or without Shakespeare's approval. On the other hand, despite the 1597 version, one might argue (if only weakly) on behalf of giving the lines to Romeo rather than to the Friar, thus: (1) Romeo's comment on the coming of the daylight emphasizes his separation from Juliet, and (2) the figurative language seems more appropriate to Romeo than to the Friar. Having said this, in the Signet edition we have decided in this instance to draw on the evidence provided by earlier text and to give the lines to the Friar, on the grounds that since Q1 reflects a production, in the theater (at least on one occasion) the lines were spoken by the Friar.

A playwright sold a script to a theatrical company. The script thus belonged to the company, not the author, and author and company alike must have regarded this script not as a literary work but as the basis for a play that the actors would create on the stage. We speak of Shakespeare as the author of the plays, but readers should bear in mind that the texts they read, even when derived from a single text, such as the First Folio (1623), are inevitably the collaborative work not simply of Shakespeare with his company—doubtless during rehearsals the actors would suggest alterations—but also with other forces of the age. One force was governmental censorship. In 1606 parliament passed "an Act to restrain abuses of players," prohibiting the utterance of oaths and the name of God. So where the earliest text of *Othello* gives us "By heaven" (3.3.106), the first Folio gives "Alas," presumably reflecting the compliance of stage practice with the law. Similarly, the 1623 version of *King Lear* omits the oath "Fut" (probably from "By God's foot") at 1.2.142, again presumably reflecting the line as it was spoken on the stage. Editors who seek to give the reader the play that Shakespeare initially conceived—the "authentic" play conceived by the solitary Shakespeare—probably will restore the missing oaths and references to God. Other editors, who see the play as a collaborative work, a construction made not only by Shakespeare but also by actors and compositors and even government censors, may claim that what counts is the play as it was actually performed. Such editors regard the censored text as legitimate, since it is the play that was (presumably) finally put on. A performed text, they argue, has more historical reality than a text produced by an editor who has sought to get at what Shakespeare initially wrote. In this view, the text of a play is rather like the script of a film; the script is not the film, and the play text is not the performed play. Even if we want to talk about the play that Shakespeare "intended," we will find ourselves talking about a script that he handed over to a company with the intention that it be implemented by actors. The "intended" play is the one that the actors—we might almost say "society"—would help to construct.

Further, it is now widely held that a play is also the work of readers and spectators, who do not simply receive meaning, but who create it when they respond to the play. This idea is fully in accord with contemporary poststructuralist critical thinking, notably Roland Barthes's "The Death of the Author," in *Image-Music-Text* (1977) and Michel Foucault's "What Is an Author?", in *The Foucault Reader* (1984). The gist of the idea is that an author is not an isolated genius; rather, authors are subject to the politics and other social structures of their age. A dramatist especially is a worker in a collaborative project, working most obviously with actors—parts may be written for particular actors—but working also with the audience. Consider the words of Samuel Johnson, written to be spoken by the actor David Garrick at the opening of a theater in 1747:

> The stage but echoes back the public voice;
> The drama's laws, the drama's patrons give,
> For we that live to please, must please to live.

The audience—the public taste as understood by the playwright—helps to determine what the play is. Moreover, even members of the public who are not part of the playwright's immediate audience may exert an influence through censorship. We have already glanced at governmental censorship, but there are also other kinds. Take one of Shakespeare's most beloved characters, Falstaff, who appears in three of Shakespeare's plays, the two parts of *Henry IV* and *The Merry Wives of Windsor*. He appears with this name in the earliest printed version of the first of these plays, *1 Henry IV*, but we know that Shakespeare originally called him (after an historical figure) Sir John Oldcastle. Oldcastle appears in Shakespeare's source (partly reprinted in the Signet edition of *1 Henry IV*), and a trace of the name survives in Shakespeare's play, 1.2.43–44, where Prince Hal punningly addresses Falstaff as "my old lad of the castle." But for some reason—perhaps because the family of the historical Oldcastle complained—Shakespeare had to change the name. In short, the play as we have it was (at least in this detail) subject to some sort of censorship. If we think that a text should present what we take to be the author's intention, we probably will want to replace *Falstaff* with *Oldcastle*. But if we recognize that a play is a collaboration, we may welcome the change, even if it was forced on Shakespeare. Somehow *Falstaff*, with its hint of *false-staff*, i.e., inadequate prop, seems just right for this fat knight who, to our delight, entertains the young prince with untruths. We can go as far as saying that, at least so far as a play is concerned, an insistence on the author's original intention (even if we could know it) can sometimes impoverish the text.

The tiny example of Falstaff's name illustrates the point that the text we read is inevitably only a version—something in effect produced by the collaboration of the playwright with his actors, audiences, compositors, and editors—of a fluid text that Shakespeare once wrote, just as the *Hamlet* that we see on the screen starring Kenneth Branagh is not the *Hamlet* that Shakespeare saw in an open-air playhouse starring Richard Burbage. *Hamlet* itself, as we shall note in a moment, also exists in several versions. It is not surprising that there is now much talk about the *instability* of Shakespeare's texts.

Because he was not only a playwright but was also an actor and a shareholder in a theatrical company, Shakespeare probably was much involved with the translation of the play from a manuscript to a stage production. He may or may not have done some rewriting during rehearsals, and he may or may not have been happy with cuts that were made. Some plays, notably *Hamlet* and *King Lear*, are so long that it is most unlikely that the texts we read were acted in their entirety. Further, for both of these plays we have more than one early text that demands consideration. In *Hamlet*, the Second Quarto (1604) includes some two hundred lines not found in the Folio (1623). Among the passages missing from the Folio are two of Hamlet's reflective speeches, the "dram of evil" speech (1.4.13–38) and "How all occasions do inform against me" (4.4.32–66). Since the Folio has more numerous and often fuller stage directions, it certainly looks as though in the Folio we get a theatrical version of the play, a text whose cuts were probably made—this is only a hunch, of course—not because Shakespeare was changing his conception of Hamlet but because the playhouse demanded a modified play. (The problem is complicated, since the Folio not only cuts some of the Quarto but adds some material. Various explanations have been offered.)

Or take an example from *King Lear*. In the First and Second Quarto (1608, 1619), the final speech of the play is given to Albany, Lear's surviving son-in-law, but in the First Folio version (1623), the speech is given to Edgar. The Quarto version is in accord with tradition—usually the highest-ranking character in a tragedy speaks the final words. Why does the Folio give the speech to Edgar? One possible answer is this: The Folio version omits some of Albany's speeches in earlier scenes, so perhaps it was decided (by Shakespeare? by the players?) not to give the final lines to so pale a character. In fact, the discrepancies are so many between the two texts, that some scholars argue we do not simply have texts showing different theatrical productions. Rather, these scholars say, Shakespeare substantially revised the play, and we really have two versions of *King Lear* (and of *Othello* also, say some)—two different plays—not simply two texts, each of which is in some ways imperfect.

In this view, the 1608 version of *Lear* may derive from Shakespeare's manuscript, and the 1623 version may derive from his later revision. The Quartos have almost three hundred lines not in the Folio, and the Folio has about a hundred lines not in the Quartos. It used to be held that all the texts were imperfect in various ways and from various causes— some passages in the Quartos were thought to have been set from a manuscript that was not entirely legible, other passages were thought to have been set by a compositor who was new to setting plays, and still other passages were thought to have been provided by an actor who misremembered some of the lines. This traditional view held that an editor must draw on the Quartos and the Folio in order to get Shakespeare's "real" play. The new argument holds (although not without considerable strain) that we have two authentic plays, Shakespeare's early version (in the Quarto) and Shakespeare's—or his theatrical company's—revised version (in the Folio). Not only theatrical demands but also Shakespeare's own artistic sense, it is argued, called for extensive revisions. Even the titles vary: Q1 is called *True Chronicle Historie of the life and death of King Lear and his three Daughters*, whereas the Folio text is called *The Tragedie of King Lear*. To combine the two texts in order to produce what the editor thinks is the play that Shakespeare intended to write is, according to this view, to produce a text that is false to the history of the play. If the new view is correct, and we do have texts of two distinct versions of *Lear* rather than two imperfect versions of one play, it supports in a textual way the poststructuralist view that we cannot possibly have an unmediated vision of (in this case) a play by Shakespeare; we can only recognize a plurality of visions.

Editing Texts

Though eighteen of his plays were published during his lifetime, Shakespeare seems never to have supervised their publication. There is nothing unusual here; when a playwright sold a play to a theatrical company he surrendered his ownership to it. Normally a company would not publish the play, because to publish it meant to allow competitors to acquire the piece. Some plays did get published: Apparently hard-up actors sometimes pieced together a play for a publisher; sometimes a company in need of money sold a play; and sometimes a company allowed publication of a play that no longer drew audiences. That Shakespeare did not concern himself with publication is not remarkable; of his contemporaries, only Ben Jonson carefully supervised the publication of his own plays.

In 1623, seven years after Shakespeare's death, John Heminges and Henry Condell (two senior members of Shakespeare's company, who had worked with him for about twenty years) collected his plays—published and unpublished—into a large volume, of a kind called a folio. (A folio is a volume consisting of large sheets that have been folded once, each sheet thus making two leaves, or four pages. The size of the page of course depends on the size of the sheet—a folio can range in height from twelve to sixteen inches, and in width from eight to eleven; the pages in the 1623 edition of Shakespeare, commonly called the First Folio, are approximately thirteen inches tall and eight inches wide.) The eighteen plays published during Shakespeare's lifetime had been issued one play per volume in small formats called quartos. (Each sheet in a quarto has been folded twice, making four leaves, or eight pages, each page being about nine inches tall and seven inches wide, roughly the size of a large paperback.)

Heminges and Condell suggest in an address "To the great variety of readers" that the republished plays are presented in better form than in the quartos:

> Before you were abused with diverse stolen and surreptitious copies, maimed and deformed by the frauds and stealths of injurious impostors that exposed them; even those, are now offered to your view cured and perfect of their limbs, and all the rest absolute in their numbers, as he [i.e., Shakespeare] conceived them.

There is a good deal of truth to this statement, but some of the quarto versions are better than others; some are in fact preferable to the Folio text.

Whoever was assigned to prepare the texts for publication

in the first Folio seems to have taken the job seriously and yet not to have performed it with uniform care. The sources of the texts seem to have been, in general, good unpublished copies or the best published copies. The first play in the collection, *The Tempest*, is divided into acts and scenes, has unusually full stage directions and descriptions of spectacle, and concludes with a list of the characters, but the editor was not able (or willing) to present all of the succeeding texts so fully dressed. Later texts occasionally show signs of carelessness: in one scene of *Much Ado About Nothing* the names of actors, instead of characters, appear as speech prefixes, as they had in the Quarto, which the Folio reprints; proofreading throughout the Folio is spotty and apparently was done without reference to the printer's copy; the pagination of *Hamlet* jumps from 156 to 257. Further, the proofreading was done while the presses continued to print, so that each play in each volume contains a mix of corrected and uncorrected pages.

Modern editors of Shakespeare must first select their copy; no problem if the play exists only in the Folio, but a considerable problem if the relationship between a Quarto and the Folio—or an early Quarto and a later one—is unclear. In the case of *Romeo and Juliet*, the First Quarto (Q1), published in 1597, is vastly inferior to the Second (Q2), published in 1599. The basis of Q1 apparently is a version put together from memory by some actors. Not surprisingly, it garbles many passages and is much shorter than Q2. On the other hand, occasionally Q1 makes better sense than Q2. For instance, near the end of the play, when the parents have assembled and learned of the deaths of Romeo and Juliet, in Q2 the Prince says (5.3.208–9),

Come, *Montague;* for thou art early vp
To see thy sonne and heire, now earling downe.

The last three words of this speech surely do not make sense, and many editors turn to Q1, which instead of "now earling downe" has "more early downe." Some modern editors take only "early" from Q1, and print "now early down"; others take "more early," and print "more early down." Further, Q1 (though, again, quite clearly a garbled and abbreviated text) includes some stage directions that are not found in Q2, and today many editors who base their text on Q2 are glad to add these stage directions, because the directions help to give us a sense of what the play looked like on Shakespeare's stage. Thus, in 4.3.58, after Juliet drinks the potion, Q1 gives us this stage direction, not in Q2: *"She falls upon her bed within the curtains."*

In short, an editor's decisions do not end with the choice of a single copy text. First of all, editors must reckon with Elizabethan spelling. If they are not producing a facsimile, they probably modernize the spelling, but ought they to preserve the old forms of words that apparently were pronounced quite unlike their modern forms—*lanthorn, alablaster*? If they preserve these forms are they really preserving Shakespeare's forms or perhaps those of a compositor in the printing house? What is one to do when one finds *lanthorn* and *lantern* in adjacent lines? (The editors of this series in general, but not invariably, assume that words should be spelled in their modern form, unless, for instance, a rhyme is involved.) Elizabethan punctuation, too, presents problems. For example, in the First Folio, the only text for the play, Macbeth rejects his wife's idea that he can wash the blood from his hand (2.2.60–62):

> No: this my Hand will rather
> The multitudinous Seas incarnardine,
> Making the Greene one, Red.

Obviously an editor will remove the superfluous capitals, and will probably alter the spelling to "incarnadine," but what about the comma before "Red"? If we retain the comma, Macbeth is calling the sea "the green one." If we drop the comma, Macbeth is saying that his bloody hand will make the sea ("the Green") *uniformly* red.

An editor will sometimes have to change more than spelling and punctuation. Macbeth says to his wife (1.7.46–47):

> I dare do all that may become a man,
> Who dares no more, is none.

For two centuries editors have agreed that the second line is unsatisfactory, and have emended "no" to "do": "Who dares do more is none." But when in the same play (4.2.21–22) Ross says that fearful persons

> Floate vpon a wilde and violent Sea
> Each way, and moue,

need we emend the passage? On the assumption that the compositor misread the manuscript, some editors emend "each way, and move" to "and move each way"; others emend "move" to "none" (i.e., "Each way and none"). Other editors, however, let the passage stand as in the original. The editors of the Signet Classic Shakespeare have restrained themselves from making abundant emendations. In their minds they hear Samuel Johnson on the dangers of emendation: "I have adopted the Roman sentiment, that it is more honorable to save a citizen than to kill an enemy." Some departures (in addition to spelling, punctuation, and lineation) from the copy text have of course been made, but the original readings are listed in a note following the play, so that readers can evaluate the changes for themselves.

Following tradition, the editors of the Signet Classic Shakespeare have prefaced each play with a list of characters, and throughout the play have regularized the names of the speakers. Thus, in our text of *Romeo and Juliet*, all speeches by Juliet's mother are prefixed "Lady Capulet," although the 1599 Quarto of the play, which provides our copy text, uses at various points seven speech tags for this one character: *Capu. Wi.* (i.e., Capulet's wife), *Ca. Wi., Wi., Wife, Old La.* (i.e., Old Lady), *La.,* and *Mo.* (i.e., Mother). Similarly, in *All's Well That Ends Well*, the character whom we regularly call "Countess" is in the Folio (the copy text) variously identified as *Mother, Countess, Old Countess, Lady,* and *Old Lady.* Admittedly there is some loss in regularizing, since the various prefixes may give us a hint of the way Shakespeare (or a scribe who copied Shakespeare's manuscript) was thinking of the character in a particular scene—for instance, as a mother, or as an old lady. But too much can be made of these differing prefixes, since the social relationships implied are *not* always relevant to the given scene.

We have also added line numbers and in many cases act and scene divisions as well as indications of locale at the beginning of scenes. The Folio divided most of the plays into acts and some into scenes. Early eighteenth-century editors increased the divisions. These divisions, which provide a convenient way of referring to passages in the plays, have been retained, but when not in the text chosen as the basis for the Signet Classic text they are enclosed within square brackets, [ ], to indicate that they are editorial additions. Similarly, though no play of Shakespeare's was equipped with indications of the locale at the heads of scene divisions, locales have here been added in square brackets for the convenience of readers, who lack the information that costumes, properties, gestures, and scenery afford to spectators. Spectators can tell at a glance they are in the throne room, but without an editorial indication the reader may be puzzled for a while. It should be mentioned, incidentally, that there are a few authentic stage directions—perhaps Shakespeare's, perhaps a prompter's—that suggest locales, such as *"Enter Brutus in his orchard,"* and *"They go up into the Senate house."* It is hoped that the bracketed additions in the Signet text will provide readers with the sort of help provided by these two authentic directions, but it is equally hoped that the reader will remember that the stage was not loaded with scenery.

Shakespeare on the Stage

Each volume in the Signet Classic Shakespeare includes a brief stage (and sometimes film) history of the play. When we read about earlier productions, we are likely to find them eccentric, obviously wrongheaded—for instance, Nahum Tate's version of *King Lear*, with a happy ending, which held the stage for about a century and a half, from the late seventeenth century until the end of the first quarter of the nineteenth. We see engravings of David Garrick, the greatest actor of the eighteenth century, in eighteenth-century garb as King Lear, and we smile, thinking how absurd the production must have been. If we are more thoughtful, we say, with the English novelist L. P. Hartley, "The past is a foreign country: they do things differently there." But if the eighteenth-century staging is a foreign country, what of the plays of the late sixteenth and seventeenth centuries? A foreign language, a foreign theater, a foreign audience.

Probably all viewers of Shakespeare's plays, beginning with Shakespeare himself, at times have been unhappy with the plays on the stage. Consider three comments about production that we find in the plays themselves, which suggest Shakespeare's concerns. The Chorus in *Henry V* complains that the heroic story cannot possibly be adequately staged:

> But pardon, gentles all,
> The flat unraisèd spirits that hath dared
> On this unworthy scaffold to bring forth
> So great an object. Can this cockpit hold
> The vasty fields of France? Or may we cram
> Within this wooden *O* the very casques
> That did affright the air at Agincourt?
> . . . .
> Piece out our imperfections with your thoughts.
>
> (Prologue 1.8–14,23)

Second, here are a few sentences (which may or may not represent Shakespeare's own views) from Hamlet's longish lecture to the players:

> Speak the speech, I pray you, as I pronounced it to you, trippingly on the tongue. But if you mouth it, as many of our players do, I had as lief the town crier spoke my lines. . . . O, it offends me to the soul to hear a robustious periwig-pated fellow tear a passion to tatters, to very rags, to split the ears of the groundlings. . . . And let those that play your clowns speak no more than is set down for them, for there be of them that will themselves laugh, to set on some quantity of barren spectators to laugh too, though in the meantime some necessary question of the play be then to be considered. That's villainous and shows a most pitiful ambition in the fool that uses it. (3.2.1–47)

Finally, we can quote again from the passage cited earlier in this introduction, concerning the boy actors who played the female roles. Cleopatra imagines with horror a theatrical version of her activities with Antony:

> The quick comedians
> Extemporally will stage us, and present
> Our Alexandrian revels: Antony
> Shall be brought drunken forth, and I shall see
> Some squeaking Cleopatra boy my greatness
> I' th' posture of a whore.
>
> (5.2.216–21)

It is impossible to know how much weight to put on such passages—perhaps Shakespeare was just being modest about his theater's abilities—but it is easy enough to think that he was unhappy with some aspects of Elizabethan production. Probably no production can fully satisfy a playwright, and for that matter, few productions can fully satisfy *us;* we regret this or that cut, this or that way of costuming the play, this or that bit of business.

One's first thought may be this: Why don't they just do "authentic" Shakespeare, "straight" Shakespeare, the play as Shakespeare wrote it? But as we read the plays—words written to be performed—it sometimes becomes clear that we do not know *how* to perform them. For instance, in *Antony and Cleopatra* Antony, the Roman general who has succumbed to Cleopatra and to Egyptian ways, says, "The nobleness of life / Is to do thus" (1.1.36–37). But what is "thus"? Does Antony at this point embrace Cleopatra? Does he embrace and kiss her? (There are, by the way, very few scenes of kissing on Shakespeare's stage, possibly because boys played the female roles.) Or does he make a sweeping gesture, indicating the Egyptian way of life?

This is not an isolated example; the plays are filled with lines that call for gestures, but we are not sure what the gestures should be. *Interpretation* is inevitable. Consider a passage in *Hamlet*. In 3.1, Polonius persuades his daughter, Ophelia, to talk to Hamlet while Polonius and Claudius eavesdrop. The two men conceal themselves, and Hamlet encounters Ophelia. At 3.1.131 Hamlet suddenly says to her, "Where's your father?" Why does Hamlet, apparently out of nowhere—they have not been talking about Polonius—ask this question? Is this an example of the "antic disposition" (fantastic behavior) that Hamlet earlier (1.5.172) had told Horatio and others—including us—he would display? That is, is the question about the whereabouts of her father a seemingly irrational one, like his earlier question (3.1.103) to Ophelia, "Ha, ha! Are you honest?" Or, on the other hand, has Hamlet (as in many productions) suddenly glimpsed Polonius's foot protruding from beneath a drapery at the rear? That is, does Hamlet ask the question because he has suddenly seen something suspicious and now is testing Ophelia? (By the way, in productions that do give Hamlet a physical cue, it is almost always Polonius rather than Claudius who provides the clue. This itself is an act of interpretation on the part of the director.) Or (a third possibility) does Hamlet get a clue from Ophelia, who inadvertently betrays the spies by nervously glancing at their place of hiding? This is the interpretation used in the BBC television version, where Ophelia glances in fear toward the hiding place just after Hamlet says "Why wouldst thou be a breeder of sinners?" (121–22). Hamlet, realizing that he is being observed, glances here and there *before* he asks "Where's your father?" The question thus is a climax to what he has been doing while speaking the preceding lines. Or (a fourth interpretation) does Hamlet suddenly, without the aid of any clue whatsoever, intuitively (insightfully, mysteriously, wonderfully) sense that someone is spying? Directors must decide, of course—and so must readers.

Recall, too, the preceding discussion of the texts of the plays, which argued that the texts—though they seem to be before us in permanent black on white—are unstable. The Signet text of *Hamlet*, which draws on the Second Quarto (1604) and the First Folio (1623) is considerably longer than any version staged in Shakespeare's time. Our version, even if spoken very briskly and played without any intermission, would take close to four hours, far beyond "the two hours' traffic of our stage" mentioned in the Prologue to *Romeo and Juliet*. (There are a few contemporary references to the duration of a play, but none mentions more than three hours.) Of Shakespeare's plays, only *The Comedy of Errors*, *Macbeth*, and *The Tempest* can be done in less than three hours without cutting. And even if we take a play that exists only in a short text, *Macbeth*, we cannot claim that we are experiencing the very play that Shakespeare conceived, partly because some of the Witches' songs almost surely are non-Shakespearean additions, and partly because we are not willing to watch the play performed without an intermission and with boys in the female roles.

Further, as the earlier discussion of costumes mentioned, the plays apparently were given chiefly in contemporary, that is, in Elizabethan dress. If today we give them in the costumes that Shakespeare probably saw, the plays seem not contemporary but curiously dated. Yet if we use our own dress, we find lines of dialogue that are at odds with what we see; we may feel that the language, so clearly not our own, is inappropriate coming out of people in today's dress. A common solution, incidentally, has been to set the plays in the nineteenth century, on the grounds that this attractively distances the plays (gives them a degree of foreignness, allowing for interesting costumes) and yet doesn't put them into a museum world of Elizabethan England.

Inevitably our productions are adaptations, *our* adaptations, and inevitably they will look dated, not in a century but in twenty years, or perhaps even in a decade. Still, we cannot escape from our own conceptions. As the director Peter Brook has said, in *The Empty Space* (1968):

> It is not only the hair-styles, costumes and make-ups that look dated. All the different elements of staging—the shorthands of behavior that stand for emotions; gestures, gesticulations and tones of voice—are all fluctuating on an invisible stock exchange all the time. . . . A living theatre that thinks it can stand aloof from anything as trivial as fashion will wilt. (p. 16)

As Brook indicates, it is through today's hairstyles, costumes, makeup, gestures, gesticulations, tones of voice—this includes our *conception* of earlier hairstyles, costumes, and so forth if we stage the play in a period other than our own—that we inevitably stage the plays.

It is a truism that every age invents its own Shakespeare, just as, for instance, every age has invented its own classical world. Our view of ancient Greece, a slave-holding society in which even free Athenian women were severely circum-scribed, does not much resemble the Victorians' view of ancient Greece as a glorious democracy, just as, perhaps, our view of Victorianism itself does not much resemble theirs. We cannot claim that the Shakespeare on our stage is the true Shakespeare, but in our stage productions we find a Shakespeare that speaks to us, a Shakespeare that our ances-tors doubtless did not know but one that seems to us to be the true Shakespeare—at least for a while.

Our age is remarkable for the wide variety of kinds of staging that it uses for Shakespeare, but one development deserves special mention. This is the now common practice of race-blind or color-blind or nontraditional casting, which allows persons who are not white to play in Shakespeare. Previously blacks performing in Shakespeare were limited to a mere three roles, Othello, Aaron (in *Titus Andronicus*), and the Prince of Morocco (in *The Merchant of Venice*), and there were no roles at all for Asians. Indeed, African-Americans rarely could play even one of these three roles, since they were not welcome in white companies. Ira Aldridge (c.1806–1867), a black actor of undoubted talent, was forced to make his living by performing Shakespeare in England and in Europe, where he could play not only Othello but also—in whiteface—other tragic roles such as King Lear. Paul Robeson (1898–1976) made theatrical his-tory when he played Othello in London in 1930, and there was some talk about bringing the production to the United States, but there was more talk about whether American audiences would tolerate the sight of a black man—a real black man, not a white man in blackface—kissing and then killing a white woman. The idea was tried out in summer stock in 1942, the reviews were enthusiastic, and in the fol-lowing year Robeson opened on Broadway in a production that ran an astounding 296 performances. An occasional all-black company sometimes performed Shakespeare's plays, but otherwise blacks (and other minority members) were in effect shut out from performing Shakespeare. Only since about 1970 has it been common for nonwhites to play major roles along with whites. Thus, in a 1996–97 production of *Antony and Cleopatra*, a white Cleopatra, Vanessa Red-grave, played opposite a black Antony, David Harewood.

Multiracial casting is now especially common at the New York Shakespeare Festival, founded in 1954 by Joseph Papp, and in England, where even siblings such as Claudio and Isabella in *Measure for Measure* or Lear's three daughters may be of different races. Probably most viewers today soon stop worrying about the lack of realism, and move beyond the color of the performers' skin to the quality of the performance.

Nontraditional casting is not only a matter of color or race; it includes sex. In the past, occasionally a distinguished woman of the theater has taken on a male role—Sarah Bernhardt (1844–1923) as Hamlet is perhaps the most famous example—but such performances were widely regarded as eccentric. Although today there have been some performances involving cross-dressing (a drag *As You Like It* staged by the National Theatre in England in 1966 and in the United States in 1974 has achieved considerable fame in the annals of stage history), what is more interesting is the casting of women in roles that traditionally are male but that need not be. Thus, a 1993–94 English production of *Henry V* used a woman—*not* cross-dressed—in the role of the governor of Harfleur. According to Peter Holland, who reviewed the production in *Shakespeare Survey* 48 (1995), "having a female Governor of Harfleur feminized the city and provided a direct response to the horrendous threat of rape and murder that Henry had offered, his language and her body in direct connection and opposition" (p. 210). Ten years from now the device may not play so effectively, but today it speaks to us. Shakespeare, born in the Elizabethan Age, has been dead nearly four hundred years, yet he is, as Ben Jonson said, "not of an age but for all time." We must understand, however, that he is "for all time" precisely because each age finds in his abundance something for itself and something of itself.

And here we come back to two issues discussed earlier in this introduction—the instability of the text and, curiously, the Bacon/Oxford heresy concerning the authorship of the plays. *Of course* Shakespeare wrote the plays, and we should daily fall on our knees to thank him for them—and yet there is something to the idea that he is not their only author. Every editor, every director and actor, and every reader to some degree shapes them, too, for when we edit, direct, act, or read, we inevitably become Shakespeare's collaborator and re-create the plays. The plays, one might say, are so cunningly contrived that they guide our responses, tell us how we ought to feel, and make a mark on us, but (for better or for worse) we also make a mark on them.

—SYLVAN BARNET
Tufts University

The Life and Death of
KING JOHN

Introduction*
to *King John*

    The Life and Death of King John was probably not Shakespeare's title. The editors of the 1623 Folio harmonized the plays they grouped as "Histories" by giving them titles as nearly alike as possible. *Richard II,* for example, is also "The Life and Death of . . ." in the Folio, though, prior to 1623, it had appeared as "The Tragedy of . . . ." The Folio titles are designed to fit the plays into a general pattern.

    This point is worth attention only because so many readers assume, on the basis of the title, that John must be the hero of the play. He is not. He is no more the hero of the play bearing his name than Henry IV is the hero of either of the plays bearing his name or, for that matter, Julius Caesar of the play bearing his. Each of Shakespeare's plays is best considered an individual experiment in dramatic structure; too often they are distorted for the sake of fitting them into some generic theory, understood in terms designed to make them conform to a definition. In the plays based on English history, Shakespeare is less involved with the exploits of kings, or indeed with the actual history of the period, than he is with exploring situations that test moral or political theory against complex psychological reality. Only in *Richard III* does the king dominate the stage: *Richard II* balances its verbose king against the silent Bolingbroke as the wronger becomes the wronged, the wronged the wronger; and the primary balance of moral positions in *Henry IV [Part One]* is triple—Hal played off against Hotspur and Falstaff, each in his own way both attractive and reprehensible. *King John* is also built upon a triple balance. To attain it, Shakespeare has

---

*Portions of this introduction have been recast from passages of my article "Richard's Divided Heritage in *King John,*" *Essays in Criticism,* XII (1962), 231–53, by permission of the editors.

mingled freely reordered historical material with pure fiction; just as he invented Falstaff and took years from Hotspur for the sake of that dramatic structure, so he invented the Bastard and took years from Arthur for the sake of this. His is a drama of ideas and not just a chronicle history.

A second stumbling block to appreciating Shakespeare's accomplishment in *King John* has been the general assumption that his play is based on another, *The Troublesome Reign of John, King of England,* which can thus be used to "explain" Shakespeare's departures from history (the Bastard, the ignoring of Magna Charta, etc.). We are told that we may not blame these on—or credit them to—Shakespeare, who "merely took them over from his source." The note on sources on page 135 gives a brief account of my reasons for thinking that *King John* is not dependent on *The Troublesome Reign* but that the dependence is the other way around. (Indeed, "The Troublesome Reign of King John" is more likely to have been Shakespeare's original title, taken over by the imitation, than is the title given it by the editors of the Folio.) It is sufficient here to say that, even if I were wrong, even if Shakespeare *had* based his play on the other, we would still have to consider the result as a finished play deserving independent judgment. John is the rightful king at the beginning of *The Troublesome Reign;* the Bastard is but a shadow of Shakespeare's character.

The King John of history came to the throne legitimately, the heir named by his dying brother, Richard I. True, their nephew Arthur was the son of a brother older than John, and some supported his claim, but John's was in fact the better. Primogeniture was not the only legal route to a crown. John enters Shakespeare's play, however, as an acknowledged usurper. Unlike his mother, he offers no objection to Chatillion's reference to his "borrowed majesty" (1.1.4), and even Queen Elinor's objection is a political gesture, not an assertion of principle, as is clear as soon as Chatillion has left the stage. By thus transforming history, Shakespeare is able to play John's "possession" against Arthur's "right," the *de facto* king against the king *de jure,* and by that means to pose a political and moral question. By adding the Bastard to this balance, he further divides the claims to the throne and makes the questions more significant. Richard's illegitimate son, with neither possession of, nor right to, the crown, has yet inherited his father's personal qualities—"The very spirit of Plantagenet!" (167)—which would make him a better king than either John or Arthur. It is this division of qualifications that the playwright both invents and explores.

The memory of Richard *Coeur de Lion* haunts this play as the mythically heightened image of a good and heroic king. He triumphantly combined the royal right, possession, and character which the first act distinguishes as having been divided among his nephew, the child Arthur; his brother, the man John; and his son, the youthful Bastard. The division is an imbalance demanding resolution: which—right, possession, or character—is the essential ingredient for a king? As we are introduced to the abstract issues in the early lines of the play, we are prone to the easy assumption that the throne obviously *ought* to go to Arthur, to whom by right it belongs. This point, so clear in the first act before we have seen Arthur, becomes more ambiguous in the second; we meet Arthur in circumstances which overshadow his right. While his immaturity and weakness attract some personal sympathy, sympathy for his cause is dissipated as we observe the company he keeps. King Richard's rightful heir is first seen agreeing to "Embrace . . . love . . . welcome" and "forgive" (2.1.11–12) Austria, the man who killed King Richard. He is a pawn moved by an ambitious mother and surrounded by an unscrupulous, self-seeking, foreign league. Were he to gain his right and become king, the results would presumably be disastrous for England.

With the death of Arthur, the failure and eventual collapse of John, and, through the course of the play, the Bastard's increasing perception of the distinction between self-interest and true honor, it would appear that the Bastard is being groomed to take over as king, as the most deserving of that position. And, indeed, so he is. In order to lead our expectations more firmly in that direction, Shakespeare has let us think the Bastard will be the only one left, withholding the historical fact of the existence of another heir; only in the final scenes of his play does he first mention John's son, Prince Henry. Bringing him in defeats these expectations, but it does not subvert the issue; it shifts the emphasis from the original questions to a deeper consideration of the requirements of honor. The very qualities that constitute the Bastard's fitness for the throne lead to his repudiation of personal ambition and his kneeling to Prince Henry. True honor, a matter not of prestige and power but of duty, is decided on the basis of what is best for England. The Bastard, in kneeling, renounces his recently established claim to the throne and thus prevents further civil war. True honor makes the Bastard the best of subjects in a unified England, and this, in the logic of the play, is more important than the character of the king.

Insofar as the play has a hero, then, it is the Bastard, and, indeed, a large part of the first act is devoted to introducing him to us. He repeats the national situation on a domestic scale. He also is in possession of an estate to which another, his half brother Robert, is the rightful heir. Our sympathies, like John's, are of course with the "good blunt fellow" (1.1.71); under the influence of those sympathies, however, both "right" and "honor" begin to twist in our hands. Robert's assumed moral right to his inheritance is denied by John in the name of another right, the legal fiction of the Bastard's legitimacy. Everyone knows that Robert, for lack of sufficient proof, like Arthur, for lack of sufficient power, is being "legally" cheated.

But the Bastard, unlike John, is not permitted to enjoy his dishonorably held possessions. To save him for his later role in the play, he is presented with a choice between "honor" and possessions. He chooses "honor" (here merely "reputation"), and his ambitious choice immediately pays off, for John knights him. There is in his response an impetuous decisiveness, uncalculating, heedless of consequences, a little naïve. He is not one to ask, like John, "What follows if we disallow of this?" (16), but says at once, "I'll take my chance" (151).

Many have been bothered by the contradiction between the self-sufficient character of the Bastard and his pursuit here of an honor that is merely reputation. They try to explain it away, just as they tell us he "does not really mean what he says" in his "Commodity" speech at the end of 2.1. The contradiction exists. The Bastard's discovery and handling of it is a primary development in the play. But the reputation he chooses in Act 1 is one to which he has, in fact, a right; gambling on future "chance," he trades his spurious respectability for an honest reputation as a royal bastard. He makes the right choice for the wrong reason; he has yet to add insight to the character which is intrinsic—"I am I, howe'er I was begot" (175). It is safe to say that the first act leaves the audience more interested in what will happen to him than in the immediate challenge to John.

The second act, however, is concerned almost entirely with the dynastic struggle, and the Bastard, though he attempts once, unsuccessfully, to control the action, serves primarily as an observant commentator. His presence as an observer needs to be stressed since, in the shade of his lively comments, one might overlook its importance: his political education is beginning and he has much to learn. By the end of the act the once naïve young man has found the proper name for the political motivation he observes.

Tracing this view of the main structure of the play unfortunately involves slighting many of its subsidiary felicities, as well as some of its weaknesses. John, Elinor, and Pandulph would each repay closer attention than can be given them here, but earlier generations would be particularly incensed at such neglect of Constance, whose laments for her son in this act made her, for actresses and audiences alike, the most attractive character in the play. This is a view I cannot share, though she is indeed forceful in her claims for sympathy. I find it noteworthy that many actresses, in creating their conception of her suffering motherhood, found it necessary to omit some of her more violent speeches, especially in her screeching exchanges with Elinor. Constance *is* a suffering mother, there is no doubt, but she is also an ambitious one, a strident, domineering tigress. No one would think of applying to her Lear's praise of Cordelia's voice, "ever soft,/Gentle and low—an excellent thing in woman" (5.3.274–5). Friend and enemy alike fail in their continuous attempts to silence her. John is brutal—"Bedlam, have done" (2.1.183)—while Austria (134) and King Philip (195) are merely trying to reconcile her to the etiquette of political duplicity, but even Arthur joins the chorus—"Good my mother, peace!" (163)— to no avail. She is equally uncontrollable in her appearances in the next act and is ultimately reported to have died "in a frenzy" (4.2.122). She is wronged, indeed, but she is one of the reasons that Arthur would be such a disastrous king for England.

In direct contrast with Arthur, the Bastard shows an immediate antipathy to Austria, motivated of course by the lion-skin Richard's killer is wearing. (Shakespeare is already thinking in terms of total dramatic effect on a stage, not just in terms of lines.) Whatever the moral masquerades of the political schemers, the Bastard, as Richard's son, has a personal loyalty which he will not deny. If this personal warmth is in contrast with the calculated zeal of the other opponents, it is in even greater contrast with the dispassionately calculated neutrality of Hubert.

Given the opposed armies at his gates, Hubert's position has all the appearance of eminent sense: "we are the King of England's subjects . . . he that proves the King,/To him will we prove loyal" (2.1.267–71). But, however appealing the arguments on the virtues of neutrality, Hubert's position is unacceptable in *King John*. This is not the moral superiority of "A plague o' both your houses!" with which Mercutio, "the prince's near ally," rejects the parochial quarrel that has caused his death (*Romeo and Juliet,* 3.1.108–11); this is the willingness of common citizens to accept either of two contradictory national loyalties. It has the sound sense of self-preservation—and perhaps today that seems enough—but it is meant to have little else: as comes increasingly clear in Hubert's progressive responses, it is not a moral position at all, but a refusal to face the issue. (That the issue is not resolvable in the terms in which it has been set does not, apparently, excuse a man from involvement.)

Hubert's response sounds fine until probed: "he that proves the King,/To him will we prove loyal." What kind of loyalty is this? Like "honor" in the first act, it is not the real article, but a calculated substitute; what ought to be the warm and total response of a committed man is here the small change of a self-indulgent apathy. What "proves the King"— the issue itself—is precisely what Hubert avoids, and his restatements, the "worthiest" or "greatest" (281, 332), are equally hollow, assuming only that might makes right. Hubert abdicates the citizen's duty to act according to his best moral lights and, selfishly holding himself aloof, leaves the decision to naked force.

Though superior to Hubert here in his loyalty and his freedom from selfish calculation, the Bastard is not himself facing any moral issues. His response is warm and total, but it is not yet what one would call perceptive. He, no less than Hubert, leaves the decision to naked force; the difference is his willingness to involve himself on the side to which he is loyal. This involvement leads to his first venture in political strategy, his "wild" (395) suggestion that the kings join forces against Angiers before turning back to their own quarrel. His "Smacks it not something of the policy?" (396) shows his naïve pride in what he is pleased to consider his approach to political wisdom, but what is the rash response of naïve loyalty in the Bastard becomes insane ruthlessness when it is accepted and given royal sanction by John.

It is from Blanch, however, that the Bastard learns the most. Though her role in the play is brief, it is crucial. Hubert's suggestion that she be married to the Dauphin disgusts the Bastard, but both kings see in the suggestion a way of saving face while abandoning their sterile enmity. Lewis, too, plays the game with a will, and his ability to switch rapidly from enemy to lover, patently insincere, gilding his political opportunism with the language of a sonneteer, is in sharp contrast not only with the Bastard's disgusted and less flexible sincerity, but with the honesty of his bride-to-be. Blanch is as much a political pawn as Arthur but, without loss of dignity or feminine propriety, she is hardly less plain-spoken—when called upon to speak—than the Bastard: "Further I will not flatter you, my lord,/That all I see in you is worthy love . . ." (516–17). When John asks for her formal assent, she pronounces herself "bound in honor still to do/What you in wisdom still vouchsafe to say" (522–23). This is the only use of the word "honor" in the second act (it had been used—misused—eight times before) and its first appearance in the play as a high-minded sense of personal obligation, a trait of character rather than a mere claim for public approval. Blanch is controlled by her honor, whatever the personal consequences. The Bastard is silent, but his education has now truly begun, as comes clear when he is left alone at the end of the scene.

In his well-known soliloquy—"Mad world! Mad kings!

Mad composition!" (561)—with new insight he gives the name, missing so far in the play, to the primary motivating force behind what we have seen: "Commodity," the unprincipled self-interest which perverts "all indifferency, ... direction, purpose, course, intent" (579–80), and brings the noblest-sounding resolutions to the most ignominious results. Having named it, he formally adopts it, for the Bastard's final words are "Gain, be my lord, for I will worship thee!" (598). Many of the difficulties commentators have with this speech arise from their attempts to make of it a summation of the Bastard's character, a final position rather than a stage in his development. He is not static, and it is enough in the second act that he has begun to consider where he is. What was blind loyalty now sees madness on both sides. For the first time he is critical of John. Though he is wrong in his estimate of King Philip's original motive, accepting the public declaration for the fact, the important point is that he is beginning to judge for himself and no longer just following chance. The word "honorable" in the Bastard's mouth now, though we may demur from "honorable war" (585), is not what it was in the first act, but what he has learned from Blanch.

After this insight into the kings, there is surely a hesitation (between lines 586 and 587) when, in his honesty, the Bastard recognizes the application to himself: "And why rail I on this commodity?/But for because he hath not wooed me yet" (587–88). Must we demand conversion at the very incipience of self-knowledge? The Bastard, realizing that he has been living in the same spirit he has condemned in the kings, concludes most humanly by reversing his complaint and turning their conduct into a rationalization for his own. But he has found a name for such conduct; he has seen commodity and its opposite. Never again can he remain unconscious in following chance. It is enough for now. It is a place to end a scene but not a play.

The Bastard is not the only one who is educated during the course of this play. Hubert, the man who thought he could hold himself aloof from commitment, is caught between the claims of political allegiance and those of simple compassion. The warmth of John's fawning—"O my gentle Hubert,/We owe thee much!" (3.2.29–30)—has a multiple motivation. John is not merely flattering Hubert in order to bring him to murder Arthur, but indeed owes Hubert much, just as he says: he may owe him the very capture of Arthur, as the entry would seem to imply, and he presumably owes him Angiers, Hubert apparently having made his choice after France broke the league. John is promising a reward already due and hinting for just one further service. Whatever the circumstances that determined him, Hubert is no longer in a position to maintain his neutrality; he has made, or has been forced to make, his choice, and the loyalty once so coldly promised to the stronger must now be delivered. After a number of false starts, John finally manages the most pointed of commissions, as though his will were less tainted for showing naked so briefly:

> *King John.* Death.
> *Hubert.*   My lord.
> *King John.*   A grave.
> *Hubert.*   He shall not live.
> *King John.*   Enough.
>   (76)

John leaves the promised reward unspecified, but the more significant ambiguity lies in the sinister irony of his final statement to Arthur that Hubert will attend on him "With all true duty" (83). True to whom? to what? in what sense? The nature of "true duty"—whether Hubert's, John's, the Bastard's, Blanch's, King Philip's, Pandulph's, Lady Faulconbridge's, Robert Faulconbridge's, the English nobles' or Melun's—is precisely what is at issue in this play, whether we call it that, or "loyalty," or "honor."

However unexpected, and even illogical, the shift in intent from murder to blinding—or, more likely, to murder as an "accident" during blinding—the resultant stage business is an image of the moral situation, an image that is echoed and reechoed in the lines. It is Hubert's "duty" that is iron; human sympathy is the living eye that he must put out. Hubert, with his hot irons and concealed accomplices, is brute power; the child Arthur is powerless innocence, wronged right. In the difficulty of putting innocent goodness on the stage, Shakespeare makes of Arthur, as he does of

Blanch at the end of 3.1, a formal image of victimized virtue—
Arthur the image of suffering innocence, Blanch of suffering
integrity. Perhaps the ultimate horror in the viciousness of
"this iron age" (4.1.60) is the recognition by innocence that
its own appearance must be suspect: "Nay, you may think
my love was crafty love,/And call it cunning" (53–54).

The choice between theory and humanity forced upon
Hubert is rather like the choice facing the Duke of York in
the final act of *Richard II,* but that old man, pursuing an
abstraction (as he does with consistently high-minded inef-
ficacy throughout the play), becomes ridiculous in his prose-
cution of his son, while Hubert, choosing humane mercy
over political theory, grows towards probity. His decision to
spare Arthur, his choice of a higher duty over a lower, creates no moral millennium, however; only the most naïve
faith would expect such a result. He is immediately involved
in duplicity—he must lie to John—and in "Much danger"
(133).

Hubert and the Bastard discover each other, as it were,
over the body of Arthur. The Bastard is sent to England in
3.2, so that he is off the stage when John gives his charge to
Hubert, which, for the sake of later developments, Shakespeare could not permit him to witness. The Bastard and
Hubert are also kept apart from each other during 4.2,
sharing the stage only as the Bastard reports on his travels
"through the land" (143) and on the prophecy of Peter of
Pomfret. Thus the Bastard observes neither the effect of
Hubert's false announcement of Arthur's death nor John's
later struggle to shift the responsibility and Hubert's revelation of his disobedient innocence. Hubert, in turn, has little
chance to recognize the new maturity of the Bastard: he
hears the Bastard's annoyance with John—"But if you be
afeard to hear the worst,/Then let the worst unheard fall on
your head" (135–36)—but not the Bastard's invitation for
the denial which John does not make—"I met [the English
lords]/ . . . going to seek the grave/Of Arthur, whom they say
is killed tonight/On your suggestion" (162–66). The Bastard
is no less open, no less loyal, but he approaches decisions
more slowly, suspending judgment without concealing his
suspicion.

The scene in which these two, the Bastard and Hubert,

recognize each other's worth is superbly constructed. Arthur's body lies unfound while the English lords reveal that they have already been in treasonable correspondence with Pandulph; their claim to outraged principles has been but an act, a pretext for saving their skins during the expected French invasion. In contrast, though he shares their suspicions that John has killed Arthur, the Bastard puts his duty to England first. Discovery of Arthur's body should confirm all suspicions, and the audience waits in suspense for the Bastard's response while the lords indulge in self-justifying superlatives of horror. "Sir Richard, what think you?" Salisbury asks (4.3.41), but he and Pembroke both favor the Bastard with their own I-told-you-so's before—following surely a lengthy pause—he answers simply and directly: "It is a damnèd and a bloody work,/The graceless action of a heavy hand,/If that it be the work of any hand" (57–59). His conditional conclusion, which can only strike the eager lords as pusillanimous, is a sign of his increasing wisdom, undergirded for the audience by our knowledge that the death was in fact accidental.

Hubert's untimely message that Arthur lives can hardly be expected to convince anyone, and the Bastard is forced to defend him from the lords' wrath, though his "If" is still unresolved. Shown Arthur's body, Hubert weeps, which the hypocrites naturally take for hypocrisy but, held off by the Bastard, they cannot attack him, and they leave to join the Dauphin. Though willing to defend Hubert from attack while the facts are unclear, the Bastard has not abandoned his own strong suspicions. Hubert, in spite of his choice of a higher duty, is entangled in circumstantial evidence. The Bastard demands a direct answer ("Knew you of this fair work?" [116]), and indicates both his stand if the answer is *yes* ("There is not yet so ugly a fiend of hell/As thou shalt be, if thou didst kill this child" [123–24]) and his honest opinion ("I do suspect thee very grievously" [134]). This is the new, more thoughtful, less hotheaded but no less forthright man that the Bastard has grown to be, a far cry from the unthinking enthusiast he was in the first act. And he need only listen to the quality of Hubert's brief denial to accept it without further question. In a world of commodity, the two who have abandoned it look into each other's hearts and recognize what they have found.

Having accepted Hubert's innocence, however, the Bastard is left with his suspicions of John. The issues surrounding Arthur's death are more complex, more muddled and human than many have been willing to allow. The moral responsibility naturally depends on whether one emphasizes the accident or the justified fear of John which forced Arthur to take the chance. What John wanted was Arthur's death without the responsibility for it. The consequences of the alleged death have no sooner forced him to welcome the news that Arthur is still alive than fate gives him exactly what he had wanted. But it is too late, and the thing he wanted becomes its own opposite: though, as it turned out, he lacked the power, he is left with the responsibility—or at least the apparent responsibility, which does equal harm. The Bastard knows less of this than we, and his response is the appropriate one for any conscientious man: "I am amazed, methinks, and lose my way/Among the thorns and dangers of this world" (140–41). The moral life is rarely, for a perceptive man, a simple choice between well-marked paths, but life in a maze. The ambiguity of the Bastard's ensuing soliloquy reflects the ambiguity of the issues themselves, and his conclusion the necessity to act in spite of it. He recognizes both Arthur's right to the throne and the fact that the very question is no longer relevant; that "England," the rightful king, is dead, but that England, the country, remains to suffer, "and vast confusion waits,/As doth a raven on a sick-fall'n beast,/The imminent decay of wrested pomp" (152–54). This is what commodity has cost. Though he recognizes now that John's pomp was wrested, the Bastard sees no honorable choice for one who would serve England but continuing loyalty: "I'll to the King" (157).

Arriving with his bad news, he is again closely observing John and controlling his disgust only with difficulty. The conclusion of his report—"And wild amazement hurries up and down/The little number of your doubtful friends" (5.1.35–36)—is not only general but pointedly personal ("I am amazed"); though others may be "doubtful friends" because they are both fearful and untrusting, he is a trustworthy and fearless friend tormented by doubt. John's assumption that

Arthur yet lives sounds to the Bastard like the sheerest evasion and almost leads to a break. Given the Bastard's suspicions, "some damned hand" (41) is dangerously blunt, backing down not at all from the firm position already taken when Arthur's body was found. There is a crescendo of excitement when John, in horror and guilt, attempts again to place the blame on Hubert, and the Bastard, convinced of Hubert's innocence, responds with a direct insinuation of John's responsibility for murder:

> *King John.* That villain Hubert told me he did live.
> *Bastard.* So, on my soul, he did, for aught he knew.
>
> (42–43)

The final pronoun, clearing Hubert, accuses John. This exchange, in which tempers have risen on both sides, must be followed by a long, electric silence, while John cringes and the Bastard cools to consider what he is doing. England must again be uppermost in his thoughts, for he stops his attack in midstream and turns to rallying John's spirits for the battle with the invaders. This self-control, this ability to quell his passionate outrage in order to undertake what is required by a higher loyalty, demonstrates the maturity the Bastard has reached. His moral superiority to John is obvious; it is one of his glorious moments and prepares us to accept what follows.

Though the Bastard has, technically, misjudged the details of Arthur's death, he has not in fact misjudged John. He pleads now only that the man act with the outer semblance of a king in order to inspire his followers. But John has just abandoned his authority to Pandulph and, pleased merely to have retained his throne, considers it a "happy peace" (63). Such peace with an invading army horrifies the Bastard—"O inglorious league!" (65)—and leads to so overwhelming a remonstrance that John, having yielded to Pandulph, yields his authority again, this time to the Bastard: "Have thou the ordering of this present time" (77). John, though a vigorous usurper, and swift to defend Angiers in the first act, has not been able to maintain his grasp. Once he has given way to the temptation to order Arthur's death, his fortunes decline: his nobles abandon him; the

French invade England; his mother dies; he capitulates to
Pandulph. He has proven a king incapable of kingship and
now is finally replaced in action by the man most capable
of it.

The Bastard has in fact become the king. Though he
speaks to Pandulph and Lewis of "the scope/And warrant
limited unto my tongue" (5.2.122–23), we know that his
warrant has not in fact been limited. Such a pose is but a way
of keeping his own counsel, of postponing decision until he
learns how things stand; once he knows the situation, he
assumes full authority: "Now hear our English king,/For
thus his royalty doth speak in me" (128–29). The king of and
for whom he speaks—who "is prepared" (130), who "doth
smile" (134) at the invasion, "the gallant monarch" (148),
"warlike John" (176)—is of course not the man John but a
verbal image of the king England needs. The image is not a
fiction, however, for it is personified in the Bastard himself.
As though to ensure this distinction between the image and
the fact, the brief third scene shows us, in direct contrast to
"warlike John," the utter impotence of the man beneath the
public image. Ill with fever, he is ordered from the field by
the Bastard, lest he confuse and dishearten the soldiers. The
kingly role has been entirely transferred. Richard's son
has become "Richard" (5.3.12); "That misbegotten devil,
Faulconbridge,/In spite of spite, alone upholds the day"
(5.4.4–5).

It is against the quality of this man that Shakespeare
displays the formalizations of allegiance, the hollow rites
which political practice substitutes for such living loyalty:
Arthur's "embracing" of Austria, Lewis' marriage to Blanch
and the treaty it attests; the "king's oath" (2.2.10) which
Constance has from Philip; the casuistry of Pandulph's
"falsehood falsehood cures" (3.1.203); John's second coronation, enforcing new oaths of allegiance after excommunication has freed his followers from their former oaths;
excommunication itself, not here a spiritual issue but merely
the weapon of another power politician; the show of outrage
with which the nobles cover their desertion; John's yielding
his crown to, and accepting it back from, Pandulph, again with
no religious significance but simply as a political bargain—
"Now keep your holy word: go meet the French" (5.1.5).

The fourth scene of Act 5 twists the ironic complications of meaningless oaths and meaningful loyalty about as far as they can be wrung. The dying Melun, breaking an oath (his to the Dauphin) which broke an oath (the Dauphin's and his to the English nobles) which broke an oath (the nobles' to John), reveals to the nobles that the Dauphin intends to execute them as soon as his battle is won. Abandoning their "holy vow" (4.3.67), they hasten to return to John. Who is to disentangle true honor from such a web as this? But Melun, saving their lives, says that he does so for the love of "one Hubert" (5.4.40–41), and because he himself had an English grandfather. This personal loyalty stands out above the meaningless oaths as a return to sanity and honor. The men thus saved by his love for Hubert are, however, the very men who most misjudged and misused Hubert for their selfish ends. They are saved by love for the man they scorned, a cutting of the web which carries distinct overtones of Christian forgiveness.

The two who have lifted themselves above commodity come together in another key scene when Hubert brings the Bastard the news that John is dying. No time is wasted in the play on the mechanics of John's death—poisoning by a monk is supplied by history as Shakespeare knew it; his attention, however, is not on John but on the effect of the approaching death on the Bastard. As they meet in the night, Hubert's "Who art thou?" (5.6.9) is precisely the question that remains to be settled, and the Bastard's "Who thou wilt" in answer, coupled with the reminder of his Plantagenet blood, stresses the possibility toward which the play has apparently been aiming. We have seen Hubert grow from his attempt at a coldly rational avoidance of the problem of choice between loyalties to a realization that a man is forced to commit himself and can only try to do so honorably. We have seen the Bastard grow from a naïve enthusiast following chance to a man of mature insight and ability. What Hubert brings the Bastard now is, in effect, an invitation to take the throne, to assume the role he has in fact been filling and for which the character he inherited from his father has proven so eminently fitted. Arthur is dead; John is dying; he is the obvious successor. It is all understated, but the implications are clear: "I left him almost speechless, and broke out/To acquaint you with this evil, that you might/The better arm you to the sudden time" (24–26). Hubert foresees a struggle, and he wants the Bastard to have the throne—as do we. A struggle with whom? "The lords are all come back" (33). Clearly they must not gain control. But then the surprising new complication is introduced: "And brought Prince Henry in their company" (34). This is the first mention in the play that John has a son and heir; dramatically it is startling news.

Nor is the structure of the play affected by whether or not the audience "knows all the time" that John must, historically, be followed on the throne by his son Henry. The "structure of expectation" may be affected—Henry's arrival could, in fact, fulfill a historical expectation—but an audience expecting Henry should still see his arrival as cutting across the prior course of the action, upsetting a suggested balance. For, whether or not the audience is surprised by the conclusion, the fact remains that the play, in its original division of claimants to the throne and its eventual elimination of two of them, appears to be moving toward the coronation of the third claimant, and only alters that appearance at the last minute by introducing the hitherto unmentioned heir. Not only has Henry been unmentioned, but Shakespeare has not even acknowledged that John had a wife (two, in fact). Suppressing Isabell, as he suppressed Constance's third husband, allows him to develop the relationship between John and his mother without dramatic confusion; it also serves to keep Henry better hidden.

Prince Henry is apparently, like Arthur, a young successor surrounded by a self-seeking league. The Bastard is in the situation that faced John upon the death of Richard, and the question is, will he, like John, usurp the throne? However self-seeking such a move might appear, it could well be considered, given the Bastard's kingly character and Prince Henry's companions, the best hope for England. The Bastard's immediate response is a prayer, as much for England as for himself: "Withhold thine indignation, mighty God,/And tempt us not to bear above our power!" (37–38). It is not a decision, but it is surely an aspiration to withstand the temptations of commodity. He is, in fact, not even willing at the moment to entertain the possibility of usurpation. His immediate revelation that he has lost "half my power this night" (39) has been taken to mean that he is forced to his dynastic decision only by his inability to muster sufficient strength to seize the throne from the combined forces of the returning noblemen. It is rather the explanation to Hubert of his prayer that God withhold his indignation. His worry is, as always, for England, facing the invaders now with decimated forces. The invasion, not the succession, is his business at the moment. And the question is doubly untimely, for John is still "the King" (43).

But we know, as the Bastard does not, that Lewis has also suffered grievous losses. Structurally, it remains only for John to die and the Bastard to reach his decision. Shakespeare first shows us Prince Henry, however, though the lines give no clue as to how the author may have advised his fellow-actor to play the part. The Prince's few speeches leave him sounding a sensitive enough young man facing the death of his father, but it would be equally possible to play him as a weakling reminiscent of Arthur or as a young man of promising strength of character, reminiscent of the Bastard. And the effect he creates will naturally cast its light on the Bastard's decision. If he is Arthur all over again, surrounded by the returning nobles, the Bastard's kneeling to him will flood the end of the play with a dreadful irony; if he has a suggestion of the royal character as well as the royal right, the Bastard's homage, acknowledging his possession of the throne, will create a triumphant rejoining of the qualifications divided at the beginning of the play.

The director and the actor, I would suggest, are called upon to attempt a compromise: Henry must be kept young enough to underline the similarity between the Bastard's choice and that which originally faced John; at the same time, he must show vitality and promise, for a suggestion of his complete dominance by the former traitors would be out of key with the generally hopeful conclusion of the play. This ambiguity in the Prince's role is in part indicative of the fact that our attention no longer remains solely on the question of what qualifies a king, but has shifted over to that of how, given this situation, the Bastard ought to act.

John, who commenced the play as a successful usurper, dies miserably as he listens to the Bastard's news of England's losses. Even as John lies dying, his faithful follower pays him the compliment of not tempering the truth. And, though "God He knows how we shall answer" Lewis (5.7.60), John is no sooner dead than the Bastard turns to rallying the defense. But defense is not necessary, for the others know that Lewis has already sued for peace. There remains then but the single question, and it is quickly settled: the Bastard turns and kneels to Prince Henry. Whether the Prince combines the true kingly character with the possession and the right here acknowledged, the lines give us little chance of knowing. It is going to be up to the director. That, however, is no longer the main point. The very strength of character which made the Bastard the most worthy of Richard's heirs leads him to relinquish any divisive personal ambitions and to acknowledge a true duty to support the new king. This is the heir who alone remains of those who were established in the first act as having a share in Richard's heritage; this is the young man who once said, "Gain, be my lord, for I will worship thee!"; this is the efficient commander who, as John failed, has actually been wielding the royal power, filling the role of England's king. In spite of all these indications of a contrary denouement, he kneels to Prince Henry, acknowledging him King Henry. In a world of self-seekers, his conception of honor has grown until he is capable of this self-denying loyalty to England. It is, of course, one of the tragic ironies of politics that a man may be cut off from authority by the very act which best demonstrates his worthiness to wield it.

Though it has taken a paragraph to sketch the implications of the Bastard's kneeling—and more could be said—he is not to be seen as one who has thought it all through. He is as impulsive at the close as he was at the beginning, but his impulses are those of one whose original promise has come to maturity. His closing speech, with its ringing final couplet, has sometimes been dismissed as a platitudinous set piece, as "Armada rhetoric." But Armada rhetoric can be moving if one has just survived the threat of the Armada, and the Bastard's speech is platitudinous only when lifted out of its historical and textual context, only when we fail to see that the play has demonstrated most effectively the moral complexity of the problem of loyalty, while the Bastard has shown us (as, in his lesser role, has Hubert) the self-denying acceptance of a higher duty which true loyalty demands from the man of honor.

—WILLIAM H. MATCHETT
University of Washington

The Life and Death of
KING JOHN

The Life and Death of
KING JOHN

ACT 1

Scene 1. [*England. King John's court.*]

*Enter King John, Queen Elinor, Pembroke, Essex,
and Salisbury, with Chatillion of France.*

King John. Now say, Chatillion, what would France
    with us?

Chatillion. Thus, after greeting, speaks the King of
    France
  In my behavior° to the majesty,
  The borrowed° majesty, of England here.

Elinor. A strange beginning: "borrowed majesty"!   *5*

King John. Silence, good mother; hear the embassy.

Chatillion. Philip of France, in right and true behalf
  Of thy deceasèd brother Geoffrey's son,
  Arthur Plantagenet, lays most lawful claim
  To this fair island and the territories: *10*
  To Ireland, Poictiers, Anjou, Touraine, Maine,

1.1.3 **In my behavior** through me   4 **borrowed** usurped

Desiring thee to lay aside the sword
Which sways usurpingly these several titles,
And put the same into young Arthur's hand,
15   Thy nephew and right royal sovereign.

King John. What follows if we disallow of° this?

Chatillion. The proud control° of fierce and bloody war,
To enforce these rights so forcibly withheld.

King John. Here have we war for war and blood for blood,
20   Controlment° for controlment: so answer France.

Chatillion. Then take my king's defiance from my mouth,
The farthest limit of° my embassy.

King John. Bear mine to him, and so depart in peace.
Be thou as lightning in the eyes of France,
25   For, ere thou canst report,° I will be there:
The thunder of my cannon shall be heard.
So, hence! Be thou the trumpet° of our wrath
And sullen presage of your own decay.°
An honorable conduct° let him have:
30   Pembroke, look to 't. Farewell, Chatillion.
                    Exit Chatillion and Pembroke.

Elinor. What now, my son! Have I not ever said
How that ambitious Constance would not cease
Till she had kindled France and all the world
Upon the right and party of her son?
35   This might have been prevented and made whole
With very easy arguments of love,°
Which now the manage° of two kingdoms must
With fearful bloody issue arbitrate.

16 **disallow of** deny 17 **proud control** resolute compulsion 20 **Controlment** compulsion 22 **farthest limit of** most extreme measure permitted by 25 **report** (1) give an account (2) make a noise like a gun (cf. line 26 "thunder") 27 **trumpet** herald 28 **sullen presage ... decay** gloomy foreteller of your own destruction 29 **conduct** escort 36 **arguments of love** (1) expressions of love (2) friendly discussions (?) 37 **manage** government(s)

King John. Our strong possession and our right for us.

Elinor. Your strong possession much more than your
　　right,　　　　　　　　　　　　　　　　　　　40
　Or else it must go wrong with you and me;
　So much my conscience whispers in your ear,
　Which none but God, and you, and I, shall hear.

Enter a Sheriff.

Essex. My liege, here is the strangest controversy,
　Come from the country to be judged by you,　　45
　That e'er I heard. Shall I produce the men?

King John. Let them approach.
　Our abbeys and our priories shall pay
　This expeditious charge.°

*Enter Robert Faulconbridge, and Philip [his
　　bastard brother].*

　　　　　　　What men° are you?

Bastard. Your faithful subject, I, a gentleman,　　50
　Born in Northamptonshire, and eldest son,
　As I suppose, to Robert Faulconbridge,
　A soldier, by the honor-giving hand
　Of Cordelion° knighted in the field.

King John. What art thou?　　　　　　　　　55

Robert. The son and heir to that same Faulconbridge.

King John. Is that the elder, and art thou the heir?
　You came not of one mother then, it seems.

Bastard. Most certain of one mother, mighty king;
　That is well known; and, as I think, one father:　60
　But for the certain knowledge of that truth
　I put you o'er° to God and to my mother;
　Of that I doubt, as all men's children may.

---

49 **expeditious charge** (1) sudden expense (2) speedy attack　49
What men who (of what name)　54 **Cordelion** *Coeur de lion* (Lionhearted), i.e., King Richard I, John's older brother　62 **put you o'er**
refer you

Elinor. Out on thee, rude man! Thou dost shame thy
          mother,
65   And wound her honor with this diffidence.°

Bastard. I, madam? No, I have no reason for it;
          That is my brother's plea and none of mine;
          The which if he can prove, 'a° pops me out
          At least from fair five hundred pound a year.
70   Heaven guard my mother's honor and my land!

King John. A good blunt fellow. Why, being younger
          born,
          Doth he lay claim to thine inheritance?

Bastard. I know not why, except to get the land.
          But once he slandered me with bastardy.
75   But whe'r° I be as true begot or no,
          That still I lay upon my mother's head;°
          But that I am as well begot, my liege—
          Fair fall° the bones that took the pains for me—
          Compare our faces and be judge yourself.
80   If old Sir Robert did beget us both,
          And were our father, and this son like him,
          O old Sir Robert, father, on my knee
          I give heaven thanks I was not like to thee!

King John. Why, what a madcap hath heaven lent us
          here!

85 *Elinor.* He hath a trick° of Cordelion's face;
          The accent of his tongue affecteth° him:
          Do you not read some tokens of my son
          In the large composition° of this man?

King John. Mine eye hath well examinèd his parts,
90   And finds them perfect Richard. Sirrah, speak,
          What doth move you° to claim your brother's land?

---

65 **diffidence** mistrust 68 **'a** he 75 **whe'r** whether 76 **lay upon
my mother's head** leave up to my mother 78 **Fair fall** may good
befall 85 **trick** distinctive trait 86 **affecteth** tends toward, resembles 88 **large composition** (1) large size (2) general features
91 **you** Robert (John shows his partiality for the Bastard by the shift
of pronoun—cf. line 55—and by his use of the slightly contemptuous
"Sirrah")

Bastard. Because he hath a half-face° like my father!
  With half that face° would he have all my land—
  A half-faced groat° five hundred pound a year!

Robert. My gracious liege, when that my father lived,   *95*
  Your brother did employ my father much—

Bastard. Well sir, by this you cannot get my land:
  Your tale must be how he employed my mother.

Robert. And once dispatched° him in an embassy
  To Germany, there with the emperor   *100*
  To treat of high affairs touching that time.
  Th' advantage of his absence took the King,
  And in the mean time sojourned at my father's,
  Where how he did prevail I shame to speak—
  But truth is truth: large lengths of seas and shores   *105*
  Between my father and my mother lay,
  As I have heard my father speak himself,
  When this same lusty° gentleman was got.°
  Upon his deathbed he by will bequeathed
  His lands to me, and took it on his death°   *110*
  That this my mother's son was none of his;
  And if° he were, he came into the world
  Full fourteen weeks before the course of time.
  Then, good my liege, let me have what is mine,
  My father's land, as was my father's will.   *115*

King John. Sirrah, your brother is legitimate.
  Your father's wife did after wedlock bear him;
  And if she did play false, the fault was hers;
  Which fault lies on° the hazards of all husbands
  That marry wives. Tell me, how if my brother,   *120*
  Who, as you say, took pains to get this son,
  Had of your father claimed this son for his?
  In sooth, good friend, your father might have kept

92 **half-face** (1) profile (2) imperfect or emaciated face   93 **With half that face** (1) with a face like that (2) with such impudence   94 **half-faced groat** (1) small silver coin with a profile stamped on it (2) imperfect or clipped coin   99 **dispatched** (1) sent (2) disposed of   108 **lusty** merry   108 **got** conceived   110 **took it on his death** swore at the peril of his soul   112 **And if** if (a frequent Elizabethan usage)   119 **lies on** is among

    This calf, bred from his cow, from all the world.
125   In sooth he might; then, if he were my brother's,
    My brother might not claim him, nor your father,
    Being none of his, refuse him: this concludes.°
    My mother's son did get your father's heir;
    Your father's heir must have your father's land.

130 *Robert.* Shall then my father's will be of no force
    To dispossess that child which is not his?

Bastard. Of no more force to dispossess me, sir,
    Than was his will to get me, as I think.

Elinor. Whether hadst thou° rather be, a Faulcon-
      bridge,
135   And like thy brother,° to enjoy thy land,
    Or the reputed son of Cordelion,
    Lord of thy presence° and no land beside?

Bastard. Madam, and if my brother had my shape
    And I had his, Sir Robert's his,° like him,
140   And if my legs were two such riding-rods,°
    My arms such eel-skins stuffed, my face so thin
    That in mine ear I durst not stick a rose
    Lest men should say, "Look, where three-farthings°
      goes!"
    And, to° his shape, were heir to all this land,
145   Would I might never stir from off this place,
    I would give it every foot to have this face:
    I would not be Sir Nob° in any case.°

Elinor. I like thee well: wilt thou forsake thy fortune,

---

127 **concludes** is decisive   134 **Whether hadst thou** which would you   135 **like thy brother** resembling Robert (in physique and character)   137 **Lord of thy presence** master of your own physique and character   139 **Sir Robert's his** Sir Robert's (a double genitive)   140 **riding-rods** switches for horses   143 **three-farthings** (the smallest of a number of coins which were distinguished from coins of similar sizes by the presence of a rose behind the ear in Queen Elizabeth's portrait)   144 **to** in addition to   147 **Nob** nickname for Robert (?—perhaps with puns on "head" and "knob," continuing mockery of his brother's appearance)   147 **in any case** (1) under any circumstances (2) in any covering (clothing, body)

Bequeath° thy land to him, and follow me?
I am a soldier and now bound to France.   150

Bastard. Brother, take you my land, I'll take my
        chance.
    Your face hath got five hundred pound a year,
    Yet sell your face for five pence and 'tis dear.
    Madam, I'll follow you unto the death.

Elinor. Nay, I would have you go before me thither. 155

Bastard. Our country manners give our betters way.

King John. What is thy name?

Bastard. Philip, my liege, so is my name begun—
    Philip, good old Sir Robert's wife's eldest son.

King John. From henceforth bear his name whose
        form thou bearest: 160
    Kneel thou down Philip, but rise more great,
    Arise Sir Richard, and Plantagenet.°

Bastard. Brother by th' mother's side, give me your
        hand:
    My father gave me honor, yours gave land.
    Now blessèd be the hour,° by night or day,   165
    When I was got, Sir Robert was away!

Elinor. The very spirit of Plantagenet!
    I am thy grandam, Richard; call me so.

Bastard. Madam, by chance but not by truth;° what
        though?
    Something about,° a little from the right,   170
    In at the window, or else o'er the hatch:
    Who dares not stir by day must walk by night,
    And have is have, however men do catch.
    Near or far off, well won is still well shot,°
    And I am I, howe'er I was begot.   175

149 **Bequeath** legally transfer (immediately; his death is not implied)
162 **Plantagenet** (surname of the royal family)   165 **hour** (1) hour
(2) whore (then identically pronounced)   169 **truth** virtue   170
Something about a bit off course   171–74 **In at the window ... well
shot** (all proverbial expressions)

 King John. Go, Faulconbridge. Now hast thou thy
   desire:
  A landless knight makes° thee a landed squire.
  Come, madam, and come, Richard, we must speed
  For France, for France, for it is more than need.

180 *Bastard.* Brother, adieu: good fortune come to thee!
  For thou wast got i' th' way of honesty.
         Exeunt all but Bastard.
  A foot of honor better than I was,
  But many a many foot of land the worse.
  Well, now can I make any Joan° a lady.
  "Good den, Sir Richard!"—"God-a-mercy,° fel-
185   low"°—
  And if his name be George, I'll call him Peter,
  For new-made honor doth forget men's names:
  'Tis too respective and too sociable
  For your conversion.° Now your traveler,
190   He and his toothpick° at my worship's mess,°
  And when my knightly stomach is sufficed,
  Why then I suck my teeth° and catechize
  My pickèd° man of countries: "My dear sir"—
  Thus, leaning on mine elbow, I begin—
195   "I shall beseech you"—that is Question now;
  And then comes Answer like an Absey-book:°
  "O, sir," says Answer, "at your best command,
  At your employment, at your service, sir";
  "No, sir," says Question, "I, sweet sir, at yours";
200   And so, ere Answer knows what Question would,
  Saving in dialogue of compliment,
  And talking of the Alps and Apennines,

---

177 **A landless knight makes** (1) the Bastard makes (2) making the
Bastard landless makes 184 **Joan** common girl 185 **Good den,
God-a-mercy** (usual greetings, elisions of "God give you good
evening" and "God have mercy on you") 185 **fellow** (used for one
of lower rank) 188–89 **'Tis too respective ... conversion** it (remembering names) is too respectful and too amiable for my change
in rank ("your" is general and vague: any conversion) 190 **toothpick** (an un-English affectation) 190 **mess** dinner table 192 **suck
my teeth** (scorning a toothpick) 193 **pickèd** (1) affected (2) with his
teeth picked 196 **Absey-book** A B C book, a child's question-and-
answer primer

The Pyrenean and the river Po,
It draws toward supper in conclusion so.
But this is worshipful society,   *205*
And fits the mounting spirit like myself;
For he is but a bastard to the time°
That doth not smack of observation.°
And so am I, whether I smack or no:
And not alone in habit and device,°   *210*
Exterior form, outward accoutrement,
But from the inward motion° to deliver
Sweet, sweet, sweet poison° for the age's tooth,
Which, though I will not practice to deceive,
Yet, to avoid deceit,° I mean to learn;   *215*
For it shall strew the footsteps of my rising.°
But who comes in such haste in riding-robes?
What woman-post° is this? Hath she no husband
That will take pains to blow a horn before her?°

Enter Lady Faulconbridge and James Gurney.

O me! 'Tis my mother. How now, good lady!   *220*
What brings you here to court so hastily?

Lady Faulconbridge. Where is that slave, thy brother?
     Where is he,
That holds in chase° mine honor up and down?

Bastard. My brother Robert? Old Sir Robert's son?
Colbrand the giant,° that same mighty man?   *225*
Is it Sir Robert's son that you seek so?

---

207 but a bastard to the time not a true child of his time   **208 observation** (1) paying attention (2) obsequiousness   **210 habit and device** dress and emblem (the heraldic symbol on his shield will be crossed by a black band, the "bar sinister" denoting a bastard)   **212 motion** incitement, intention   **213 sweet poison** flattery   **215 deceit** deception (i.e., being deceived)   **216 it shall strew ... rising** flattery will be thrown before me as I rise just as flowers are thrown to welcome a great man   **218 woman-post** female messenger   **219 blow a horn before her** (1) clear the way for her (as a herald announced an important arrival, or as the speeding post blew his post horn) (2) announce her adultery (the cuckold was said to wear horns)   **223 holds in chase** pursues (as a huntsman)   **225 Colbrand the giant** (Guy of Warwick's final opponent in the popular old romances)

Lady Faulconbridge. Sir Robert's son? Aye, thou un-
    reverend boy,
    Sir Robert's son! Why scorn'st thou at Sir Robert?
    He is Sir Robert's son, and so art thou.

230 *Bastard.* James Gurney, wilt thou give us leave awhile?

Gurney. Good leave,° good Philip.

Bastard.   Philip, sparrow!° James,
    There's toys° abroad; anon I'll tell thee more.

                                  Exit James.
    Madam, I was not old Sir Robert's son.
    Sir Robert might have eat his part in me
235 Upon Good Friday and ne'er broke his fast:
    Sir Robert could do well—marry, to confess°—
    Could he get me! Sir Robert could not do it.
    We know his handiwork: therefore, good mother,
    To whom am I beholding for these limbs?
240 Sir Robert never holp° to make this leg.°

Lady Faulconbridge. Hast thou conspirèd with thy
    brother too,
    That for thine own gain shouldst defend mine
    honor?
    What means this scorn, thou most untoward°
    knave?

Bastard. Knight, knight, good mother, Basilisco-like.°
245 What! I am dubbed; I have it on my shoulder.
    But, mother, I am not Sir Robert's son;
    I have disclaimed Sir Robert and my land;
    Legitimation, name, and all is gone.
    Then, good my mother, let me know my father;
250 Some proper° man I hope: who was it, mother?

---

231 **Good leave** willingly   231 **Philip, sparrow!** (Philip, a common
name for a pet sparrow, is too paltry for the newly knighted Bastard)
232 **toys** trifling gifts, i.e., knighthoods, or rumors (?)   236 **marry, to
confess** indeed, to speak the truth   240 **holp** helped   240 **to make this
leg** (1) to form a leg like mine (2) to give me courtly manners like this
("to make a leg" is to bow; the Bastard must bow, perhaps ironically,
as he requests her answer)   243 **untoward** perverse, ill-mannered
244 **Basilisco** (a bragging knight in an earlier play, *Soliman and Per-
seda*)   250 **proper** handsome, respectable

Lady Faulconbridge. Hast thou denied thyself a Faul-
     conbridge?

Bastard. As faithfully as I deny the devil.

Lady Faulconbridge. King Richard Cordelion was thy
     father.
   By long and vehement suit I was seduced
   To make room for him in my husband's bed.   255
   Heaven lay not my transgression to my charge,
   That art° the issue of my dear offense,
   Which was so strongly urged past my defense.

Bastard. Now, by this light, were I to get° again,
   Madam, I would not wish a better father.   260
   Some sins do bear their privilege° on earth,
   And so doth yours: your fault was not your folly.
   Needs must you lay your heart at his dispose,
   Subjected tribute° to commanding love,
   Against whose fury and unmatchèd force   265
   The aweless lion could not wage the fight,
   Nor keep his princely heart from Richard's hand.°
   He that perforce robs lions of their hearts
   May easily win a woman's. Ay, my mother,
   With all my heart I thank thee for my father!°   270
   Who lives and dares but say thou didst not well
   When I was got, I'll send his soul to hell.
   Come, lady, I will show thee to my kin,
   And they shall say, when Richard me begot,
   If thou hadst said him nay, it had been sin.   275
   Who says it was, he lies; I say 'twas not!°   *Exeunt.*

---

257 **That art** thou that art   259 **get** be conceived   261 **bear their
privilege** carry their immunity (because of their good results?)   264
Subjected tribute tribute required of a vassal   266–67 **The aweless
lion . . . Richard's hand** (the legend was that Richard's epithet came
from his having eaten the heart he tore out by reaching, bare-handed,
down the throat of a living lion)   270 **for my father** (1) on behalf
of my father (2) for the father you have given me   276 **not** (1) not
(2) naught, i.e., nothing (3) naught, i.e., wickedness (sexual immoral-
ity; cf. *Richard III*, 1.1.97–100)

ACT 2

[Scene 1. *France.*]

*Enter before [the gate of] Angiers, King Philip of
France, Lewis the Dauphin, Constance, Arthur,
and their Attendants and, from the other side,
Austria and his Attendants.*

King Philip. Before Angiers well met, brave Austria.
    Arthur, that great forerunner of thy blood,°
    Richard, that robbed the lion of his heart
    And fought the holy wars in Palestine,
5   By this brave duke° came early to his grave;
    And for amends to his posterity,
    At our importance° hither is he come
    To spread his colors,° boy, in thy behalf,
    And to rebuke the usurpation
10   Of thy unnatural uncle, English John:
    Embrace him, love him, give him welcome hither.

Arthur. God shall forgive you Cordelion's death

2.1.2 **forerunner of thy blood** predecessor in your line (Arthur was
Richard's nephew)   5 **this brave duke** Austria (that Austria killed
Richard is not historical, but see note to 3.1.40)   7 **importance**
importunity   8 **spread his colors** unfurl his battle flags

The rather that you give his offspring life,
Shadowing° their right under your wings of war.
I give you welcome with a powerless hand,   15
But with a heart full of unstainèd love:
Welcome before the gates of Angiers, Duke.

Lewis. Ah, noble boy, who would not do thee right?

Austria. Upon thy cheek lay I this zealous kiss,
As seal to this indenture° of my love: 20
That to my home I will no more return
Till Angiers, and the right thou hast in France,
Together with that pale, that white-faced shore,°
Whose foot spurns back the ocean's roaring tides
And coops° from other lands her islanders,   25
Even till that England, hedged in with the main,
That water-wallèd bulwark, still° secure
And confident from foreign purposes,
Even till that utmost corner of the west
Salute thee for her king; till then, fair boy,   30
Will I not think of home, but follow arms.

Constance. O take his mother's thanks, a widow's
        thanks,
Till your strong hand shall help to give him strength
To make a more requital to° your love.

Austria. The peace of heaven is theirs that lift their
        swords   35
In such a just and charitable war.

King Philip. Well then, to work: our cannon shall be
        bent°
Against the brows of this resisting town.
Call for our chiefest men of discipline,°
To cull the plots of best advantages.°   40

---

14 **Shadowing** sheltering   20 **indenture** sealed agreement   23 **that pale, that white-faced shore** (reference to the chalk cliffs on England's southern coast; a "pale" is also a limited territory)   25 **coops** encloses for protection   27 **still** always   34 **a more requital to** a larger recompense for   37 **bent** aimed (as is a bow)   39 **discipline** military training   40 **To cull ... advantages** to choose the best location (for the cannons)

We'll lay before this town our royal bones,
Wade to the marketplace in Frenchmen's blood:
But we will make it subject to this boy.

Constance. Stay for an answer to your embassy,
45   Lest unadvised you stain your swords with blood.
My Lord Chatillion may from England bring
That right in peace which here we urge in war,
And then we shall repent each drop of blood
That hot rash haste so indirectly° shed.

Enter Chatillion.

50 *King Philip.* A wonder, lady! Lo, upon thy wish,
Our messenger Chatillion is arrived!
What England says, say briefly, gentle lord;
We coldly pause for thee; Chatillion, speak.

Chatillion. Then turn your forces from this paltry siege
55   And stir them up against a mightier task:
England, impatient of your just demands,
Hath put himself in arms; the adverse winds,
Whose leisure I have stayed, have given him time
To land his legions all as soon as I;
60   His marches are expedient° to this town,
His forces strong, his soldiers confident.
With him along is come the mother-queen,
An Ate,° stirring him to blood and strife;
With her her niece, the Lady Blanch of Spain;
65   With them a bastard of the king's deceased;°
And all th' unsettled humors° of the land,
Rash, inconsiderate, fiery voluntaries,°
With ladies' faces and fierce dragons' spleens,°
Have sold their fortunes at their native homes,
70   Bearing their birthrights proudly on their backs,°

---

49 **indirectly** wrongly   60 **expedient** speedy   63 **Ate** goddess of vengeance   65 **of the king's deceased** of the deceased king   66 **unsettled humors** unsteady rabble ("humors" were bodily fluids, the balance of which supposedly determined a man's disposition)   67 **voluntaries** volunteers   68 **spleens** (the spleen was considered the location of the emotions)   70 **Bearing ... backs** i.e., having invested their patrimonies in armor

To make a hazard of° new fortunes here.
In brief, a braver choice of dauntless spirits
Than now the English bottoms° have waft o'er
Did never float upon the swelling tide,
To do offense and scathe in Christendom.   75

                                        Drum beats.

The interruption of their churlish drums
Cuts off more circumstance:° they are at hand,
To parley or to fight; therefore prepare.

King Philip. How much unlooked for is this expedi-
    tion!°

Austria. By how much unexpected, by so much   80
    We must awake endeavor for defense,
    For courage mounteth with occasion:
    Let them be welcome then; we are prepared.

    *Enter King [John] of England, Bastard, Queen
    [Elinor], Blanch, Pembroke, and others.*

King John. Peace be to France, if France in peace
    permit
    Our just and lineal° entrance to our own;   85
    If not, bleed France, and peace ascend to heaven,
    Whiles we, God's wrathful agent, do correct°
    Their proud contempt that beats His peace to
        heaven.

King Philip. Peace be to England, if that war return
    From France to England, there to live in peace.   90
    England we love, and for that England's sake
    With burden of our armor here we sweat.
    This toil of ours should be a work of thine,
    But thou from loving England art so far
    That thou hast under wrought° his lawful king,   95
    Cut off the sequence of posterity,
    Outfacèd infant state,° and done a rape
    Upon the maiden virtue of the crown.
    Look here upon thy brother Geoffrey's face:

71 **make a hazard of** take a chance on winning 73 **bottoms** ships
77 **circumstance** detailed information 79 **expedition** speed 85
lineal inherited 87 **correct** chastise 95 **underwrought** undermined
97 **Outfacèd infant state** arrogantly defiled the child king

100 These eyes, these brows, were molded out of his;
    This little abstract° doth contain that large
    Which died in Geoffrey, and the hand of time
    Shall draw this brief into as huge a volume.
    That Geoffrey was thy elder brother born,
105 And this his son; England was Geoffrey's right
    And this° is Geoffrey's in the name of God.
    How comes it then that thou art called a king,
    When living blood doth in these temples beat,
    Which owe° the crown that thou o'ermasterest?

King John. From whom hast thou this great commis-
110 sion, France,
    To draw my answer from thy articles?°

King Philip. From that supernal judge that stirs good
        thoughts
    In any breast of strong authority
    To look into the blots and stains of right;
115 That judge hath made me guardian to this boy,
    Under whose warrant I impeach thy wrong
    And by whose help I mean to chastise it.

King John. Alack, thou dost usurp authority.

King Philip. Excuse it is to beat usurping down.

120 *Elinor.* Who is it thou dost call usurper, France?

Constance. Let me make answer: thy usurping son.

Elinor. Out, insolent! Thy bastard shall be king
    That thou mayst be a queen° and check the world!

Constance. My bed was ever to thy son as true
125 As thine was to thy husband, and this boy
    Liker in feature to his father Geoffrey
    Than thou and John in manners, being as like
    As rain to water, or devil to his dam.

---

101 **abstract** summary, abridgment (cf. "brief" and "volume" in line
103) 106 **this** (possibly the English crown, which John is wearing,
the city of Angiers, or Arthur himself) 109 **owe** own 111 **To
draw ... articles** to compel me to answer your accusations 123
queen (1) queen (2) quean = whore (3) queen in chess (cf. "check")

My boy a bastard! By my soul I think
His father never was so true begot: *130*
It cannot be and if thou wert his mother.

Elinor. There's a good mother, boy, that blots thy
    father.

Constance. There's a good grandam, boy, that would
    blot thee.

Austria. Peace!

Bastard.   Hear the crier.°

Austria.   What the devil art thou?

Bastard. One that will play the devil, sir, with you,   *135*
And 'a° may catch your hide° and you alone:
You are the hare of whom the proverb goes,
Whose valor plucks dead lions by the beard.
I'll smoke° your skin-coat, and I catch you right;
Sirrah, look to 't; i' faith, I will, i' faith.   *140*

Blanch. O well did he become that lion's robe,
That did disrobe the lion of that robe!

Bastard. It lies as sightly° on the back of him
As great Alcides' shoes upon an ass.°
But, ass, I'll take that burden from your back,   *145*
Or lay on that shall make your shoulders crack.

Austria. What cracker° is this same that deafs our ears
With this abundance of superfluous breath?
King Philip, determine what we shall do straight.

King Philip. Women and fools, break off your con- *150*
    ference.
King John, this is the very sum of all:

---

134 **crier** law-court official who called for silence   136 **And 'a** if he
136 **hide** Richard's lion-skin, which Austria is wearing   139 **smoke**
(1) disinfect (2) beat   143 **sightly** handsomely   144 **Alcides' shoes
upon an ass** (1) Hercules' shoes (proverbial) on an ass (2) Hercules
appears (Folio's "shooes" may also = shows) mounted on an ass
(3) Hercules' lion-skin (he wore the skin of the Nemean lion which
he had killed) appears on an ass   147 **cracker** (1) braggart (2) fire-
cracker

England and Ireland, Anjou, Touraine, Maine,
In right of Arthur do I claim of thee:
Wilt thou resign them and lay down thy arms?

155 *King John.* My life as soon! I do defy thee, France.
Arthur of Britain,° yield thee to my hand,
And out of my dear love I'll give thee more
Than e'er the coward hand of France can win;
Submit thee, boy.

Elinor.   Come to thy grandam, child.

160 *Constance.* Do, child, go to it grandam, child;
Give grandam kingdom, and it grandam will
Give it a plum, a cherry, and a fig;
There's a good grandam.°

Arthur.   Good my mother, peace!
I would that I were low laid in my grave.
165 I am not worth this coil° that's made for me.

Elinor. His mother shames him so, poor boy, he
weeps.

Constance. Now shame upon you, whe'r she does
or no!
His grandam's wrongs, and not his mother's shames,
Draws° those heaven-moving pearls from his poor
eyes,
170 Which heaven shall take in nature of° a fee:
Ay, with these crystal beads heaven shall be bribed°
To do him justice and revenge on you.

Elinor. Thou monstrous slanderer of heaven and
earth!

Constance. Thou monstrous injurer of heaven and
earth!
175 Call not me slanderer; thou and thine usurp

---

156 **Britain** Brittany   160–63 **Do, child ... grandam** (baby talk)
165 **coil** fuss   169 **Draws** draw (it is not unusual for a plural subject
to have a verb in -*s*)   170 **in nature of** in place of, as though it were
171 **with these ... bribed** i.e., these crystal beads—pearls, tears—
will bribe heaven both as precious gems and as prayer beads

The dominations,° royalties, and rights
Of this oppressèd boy: this is thy eldest son's son,°
Infortunate in nothing but in thee:
Thy sins are visited° in this poor child;
The canon of the law° is laid on him,   180
Being but the second generation
Removed from thy sin-conceiving womb.

King John. Bedlam,° have done.

Constance.   I have but this to say,
That he is not only plaguèd for her sin,
But God hath made her sin° and her the plague°   185
On this removèd issue,° plagued for her
And with her plague; her sin his injury,
Her injury the beadle° to her sin,
All punished in the person of this child,
And all for her; a plague upon her!   190

Elinor. Thou unadvisèd scold, I can produce
A will° that bars the title of thy son.

Constance. Aye, who doubts that? A will! A wicked
     will;
A woman's will;° a cankered grandam's will!

King Philip. Peace, lady! Pause, or be more temperate: 195
It ill beseems this presence° to cry aim
To° these ill-tunèd repetitions.
Some trumpet summon hither to the walls
These men of Angiers. Let us hear them speak
Whose title they admit, Arthur's or John's.   200
                         Trumpet sounds.

---

176 **dominations** dominions   177 **eldest son's son** oldest grand-
son (*not* oldest-son's son)   179 **visited** punished   180 **canon of
the law** i.e., Exodus 20:5   183 **Bedlam** lunatic   185 **her sin**
John (?)   185 **the plague** (the great plagues were commonly explained as punishment for a sinful nation—Elinor is both the
cause of Arthur's punishment and that punishment itself)   186
this removèd issue this remote descendant, i.e., Arthur   188
beadle parish official who whipped sinners   192 **A will** (Richard's will named John his heir; Shakespeare plays this down to
present John as a usurper)   194 **A woman's will** (Constance
suggests that Elinor wrote the will, and women's wills were not
legal)   196 **presence** royal assembly   196–97 **cry aim/To** encourage

Enter Hubert upon the walls.

Hubert. Who is it that hath warned° us to the walls?

King Philip. 'Tis France, for England.

King John.   England for itself.
You men of Angiers, and my loving subjects—

King Philip. You loving men of Angiers, Arthur's sub-
            jects,
205   Our trumpet called you to this gentle parle°—

King John. For our advantage; therefore hear us first:
        These flags of France, that are advancèd° here
        Before the eye and prospect of your town,
        Have hither marched to your endamagement.
210   The cannons have their bowels full of wrath,
        And ready mounted are they to spit forth
        Their iron indignation 'gainst your walls.
        All preparation for a bloody siege
        And merciless proceeding by these French
215   Confronts your city's eyes, your winking° gates,
        And but for our approach those sleeping stones,
        That as a waist° doth girdle you about,
        By the compulsion of their ordinance°
        By this time from their fixèd beds of lime
220   Had been dishabited,° and wide havoc made
        For bloody power to rush upon your peace.
        But on the sight of us your lawful king,
        Who painfully with much expedient march
        Have brought a countercheck before your gates,
225   To save unscratched your city's threatened cheeks,
        Behold, the French, amazed, vouchsafe a parle;
        And now, instead of bullets wrapped in fire,
        To make a shaking fever in your walls,
        They shoot but calm words folded up in smoke,
230   To make a faithless error° in your ears;
        Which trust accordingly, kind citizens,

201 **warned** summoned   205 **parle** parley   207 **advancèd** raised
215 **winking** able to open and shut (the gates are like eyelids)   217
waist belt or sash   218 **ordinance** cannons   220 **dishabited** disin-
habited, dislodged   230 **faithless error** treacherous lie

And let us in, your king, whose labored° spirits,
Forwearied° in this action of swift speed,
Craves harborage within your city walls.

King Philip. When I have said,° make answer to us
    both.   235
Lo, in this right hand, whose protection
Is most divinely vowed upon the right
Of him it holds, stands young Plantagenet,
Son to the elder brother of this man,
And king o'er him and all that he enjoys: 240
For this downtrodden equity° we tread
In warlike march these greens before your town,
Being no further enemy to you
Than the constraint of hospitable zeal°
In the relief of this oppressèd child   245
Religiously provokes. Be pleasèd then
To pay that duty which you truly owe
To him that owes° it, namely this young prince;
And then our arms, like to a muzzled bear,
Save in aspect, hath° all offense sealed up: 250
Our cannons' malice vainly shall be spent
Against th' invulnerable clouds of heaven,
And with a blessèd and unvexed retire,°
With unhacked swords and helmets all unbruised,
We will bear home that lusty blood again   255
Which here we came to spout against your town,
And leave your children, wives, and you in peace.
But if you fondly pass° our proffered offer,
'Tis not the roundure° of your old-faced walls°
Can hide you from our messengers of war,   260
Though all these English and their discipline
Were harbored in their rude circumference.
Then tell us, shall your city call us° lord,

232 **labored** overworked   233 **Forwearied** tired out   235 **said** finished speaking   241 **equity** right   244 **the constraint of hospitable
zeal** the obligations of generous resolution   248 **owes** owns   250
hath will have   253 **unvexed retire** orderly departure   258 **fondly
pass** foolishly disregard   259 **roundure** roundness   259 **old-faced
walls** walls so well built they had not required refacing   263 **us**
i.e., King Philip (England, with Arthur as king, would be subordinate
to France)

In that behalf which° we have challenged it?
265 Or shall we give the signal to our rage
And stalk in blood to our possession?

Hubert. In brief, we are the King of England's subjects:
For him, and in his right, we hold this town.

King John. Acknowledge then the King, and let me in.

Hubert. That can we not; but he that proves° the
270 King,
To him will we prove loyal: till that time
Have we rammed up° our gates against the world.

King John. Doth not the crown of England prove the
King?
And if not that, I bring you witnesses,
275 Twice fifteen thousand hearts of England's breed—

Bastard. Bastards, and else.°

King John. To verify our title with their lives.

King Philip. As many and as well-born bloods° as
those—

Bastard. Some bastards, too.

280 *King Philip.* Stand in his face to contradict his claim.

Hubert. Till you compound° whose right is worthiest,
We for the worthiest hold the right from both.

King John. Then God forgive the sin of all those souls
That to their everlasting residence,
285 Before the dew of evening fall, shall fleet,°
In dreadful trial of our kingdom's king!

King Philip. Amen, amen! Mount, chevaliers! To
arms!

---

264 **In that behalf which** on behalf of him for whom   270 **proves**
proves to be   272 **rammed up** barricaded   276 **else** others   278
bloods (1) men of courage (2) men of good family   281 **compound**
settle   285 **fleet** pass away, fly

Bastard. Saint George, that swinged° the dragon, and
    e'er since
    Sits on's horseback at mine hostess' door,°
    Teach us some fence!° [*To Austria*] Sirrah, were I
    at home   290
    At your den, sirrah, with your lioness,
    I would set an ox head to your lion's hide,
    And make a monster° of you.

Austria.   Peace! No more.

Bastard. O tremble, for you hear the lion roar.

King John. Up higher to the plain, where we'll set
    forth   295
    In best appointment all our regiments.

Bastard. Speed then, to take advantage of the field.

King Philip. It shall be so; and at the other hill
    Command the rest to stand. God, and our right!
                            Exeunt.

Here, after excursions,° enter the Herald of France
with Trumpets, to the gates.

French Herald. You men of Angiers, open wide your
    gates,   300
    And let young Arthur, Duke of Britain, in,
    Who by the hand of France this day hath made
    Much work for tears in many an English mother,
    Whose sons lie scattered on the bleeding ground:
    Many a widow's husband groveling lies,   305
    Coldly embracing the discolored earth,
    And victory with little loss doth play
    Upon the dancing banners of the French,
    Who are at hand, triumphantly displayed,°
    To enter conquerors and to proclaim   310
    Arthur of Britain England's king, and yours.

---

288 **swinged** beat 289 **Sits ... hostess' door** i.e., painted on an
inn sign 290 **fence** skill with the sword 293 **monster** (1) ox-headed
lion (2) cuckold 299s.d. **excursions** sallies, raids (in the theater,
stage-crossings and clashes to represent a battle) 309 **displayed**
spread out (for a parade, not for a battle)

Enter English Herald, with Trumpet.

   English Herald. Rejoice, you men of Angiers, ring
     your bells:
    King John, your king and England's, doth ap-
     proach,
    Commander of this hot malicious day.
315   Their armors, that marched hence so silver-bright,
    Hither return all gilt° with Frenchmen's blood;
    There stuck no plume in any English crest
    That is removèd by a staff° of France.
    Our colors do return in those same hands
320   That did display them when we first marched forth,
    And, like a jolly troop of huntsmen, come
    Our lusty English, all with purpled hands,
    Dyed in the dying slaughter° of their foes.
    Open your gates and give the victors way.

325 *Hubert.* Heralds, from off our tow'rs we might behold,
    From first to last, the onset and retire°
    Of both your armies, whose equality
    By our best eyes cannot be censurèd.°
    Blood hath bought blood, and blows have answered
     blows,
    Strength matched with strength, and power con-
330   fronted power.
    Both are alike, and both alike we like:
    One must prove greatest. While they weigh so even,
    We hold our town for neither, yet for both.

Enter the two Kings, with their powers,
at several° doors.

   King John. France, hast thou yet more blood to cast
    away?
335   Say, shall the current of our right roam on?
    Whose passage, vexed with thy impediment,

---

316 **gilt** gilded, i.e., reddened (gold was considered red, as in "his
golden blood," *Macbeth,* 2.3.114) 318 **staff** spear, lance 323
Dyed in the dying slaughter hunters customarily dipped their hands
in the deer's blood, cf. *Julius Caesar* (3.1.106ff.) 326 **retire** withdrawal 328 **censurèd** judged 333s.d. **several** separate

    Shall leave his native channel and o'erswell,
    With course disturbed, even thy confining shores,
    Unless thou let his silver water keep
    A peaceful progress to the ocean.   340

King Philip. England, thou hast not saved one drop of
      blood
    In this hot trial more than we of France;
    Rather, lost more. And by this hand I swear,
    That sways the earth this climate overlooks,
    Before we will lay down our just-borne arms,   345
    We'll put thee down, 'gainst whom these arms we
      bear,
    Or add a royal number° to the dead,
    Gracing the scroll that tells of this war's loss
    With slaughter coupled to the name of kings.°

Bastard. Ha, majesty! How high thy glory tow'rs°   350
    When the rich blood of kings is set on fire!
    O now doth death line his dead chaps° with steel;
    The swords of soldiers are his teeth, his fangs;
    And now he feasts, mousing° the flesh of men
    In undetermined differences° of kings: 355
    Why stand these royal fronts° amazèd thus?
    Cry "Havoc!"° kings; back to the stainèd field,
    You equal potents,° fiery kindled spirits!
    Then let confusion° of one part° confirm
    The other's peace; till then, blows, blood, and death!   360

King John. Whose party do the townsmen yet° admit?

King Philip. Speak, citizens, for England: who's your
    king?

Hubert. The King of England, when we know the
    King.

---

347 **royal number** king's name as one item in the list   349 **With
slaughter ... kings** with a king slaughtered as well as slaughtering
350 **tow'rs** soars (hawking jargon)   352 **chaps** jaws   354 **mousing**
tearing, biting   355 **undetermined differences** unsettled disputes
356 **fronts** foreheads   357 **"Havoc!"** (the call for general slaughter
with no taking of prisoners)   358 **potents** potentates, powers   359
confusion defeat   359 **part** party   361 **yet** now

King Philip. Know him in us, that here hold up his
     right.

365 *King John.* In us, that are our own great deputy,
          And bear possession of our person° here,
          Lord of our presence,° Angiers, and of you.

Hubert. A greater pow'r than we denies all this,
          And, till it be undoubted, we do lock
370   Our former scruple in our strong-barred gates,
          Kings of our fear,° until our fears, resolved,
          Be by some certain king purged and deposed.

Bastard. By heaven, these scroyles° of Angiers flout
          you, kings,
          And stand securely on their battlements
375   As in a theater, whence they gape and point
          At your industrious scenes and acts of death.
          Your royal presences be ruled by me:
          Do like the mutines° of Jerusalem,
          Be friends awhile and both conjointly bend
380   Your sharpest deeds of malice on this town.
          By east and west let France and England mount
          Their battering cannon chargèd to the mouths,
          Till their soul-fearing° clamors have brawled down°
          The flinty ribs of this contemptuous city.
385   I'd play incessantly upon° these jades,°
          Even till unfencèd° desolation
          Leave them as naked as the vulgar° air.
          That done, dissever your united strengths,
          And part your mingled colors once again;
390   Turn face to face and bloody point to point.

---

366 **bear possession of our person** owe no allegiance to anyone else
(unlike Arthur, who has apparently done homage to Philip—cf. line
263) 367 **presence** person 371 **Kings of our fear** kings as a result
of our fear (forced by our fears to be our own kings) 373 **scroyles**
scoundrels 378 **mutines** mutineers (factions fighting each other in
Jerusalem in A.D. 70 united to fight the Romans) 383 **soul-fearing**
causing the soul to fear 383 **brawled down** noisily laid waste
385 **play … upon** (1) play guns upon (2) make sport of 385 **jades**
wretches (a "jade" is a worn-out horse or a wanton woman) 386
unfencèd unfortified 387 **vulgar** common

Then, in a moment, fortune shall cull° forth
Out of one side her happy minion,°
To whom in favor she shall give the day,
And kiss him with a glorious victory.
How like you this wild counsel, mighty states?°   *395*
Smacks it not something of the policy?°

King John. Now, by the sky that hangs above our
     heads,
I like it well. France, shall we knit our pow'rs
And lay this Angiers even with the ground,
Then after fight who shall be king of it?   *400*

Bastard. And if thou hast the mettle of a king,
Being wronged as we are by this peevish town,
Turn thou the mouth of thy artillery,
As we will ours, against these saucy walls;
And when that we have dashed them to the ground,   *405*
Why then defy each other, and, pell-mell,°
Make work° upon ourselves, for heaven or hell.°

King Philip. Let it be so. Say, where will you assault?

King John. We from the west will send destruction
Into this city's bosom.   *410*

Austria. I from the north.

King Philip.   Our thunder° from the south
Shall rain their drift° of bullets on this town.

Bastard. [*Aside*] O prudent discipline! From north to
     south
Austria and France shoot in each other's mouth.
I'll stir them to it: come, away, away!   *415*

Hubert. Hear us, great kings: vouchsafe a while to
     stay
And I shall show you peace and fair-faced league,

---

391 **cull** (1) choose (2) fondle, hug   392 **minion** darling, favorite
395 **states** kings   396 **the policy** political skill, perhaps specifically
Machiavellian political cunning   406 **pell-mell** headlong, tumultu-
ously   407 **Make work** work havoc   407 **for heaven or hell** to the
death   411 **thunder** cannons   412 **drift** shower

Win you this city without stroke or wound,
Rescue those breathing lives to die in beds,
420 That here come sacrifices for the field.
Persever not, but hear me, mighty kings.

King John. Speak on with favor; we are bent° to hear.

Hubert. That daughter there of Spain, the Lady
      Blanch,
Is near to England:° look upon the years
425 Of Lewis the Dolphin° and that lovely maid.
If lusty love should go in quest of beauty,
Where should he find it fairer than in Blanch?
If zealous° love should go in search of virtue,
Where should he find it purer than in Blanch?
430 If love, ambitious, sought a match of birth,
Whose veins bound° richer blood than Lady
      Blanch?
Such as she is, in beauty, virtue, birth,
Is the young Dolphin every way complete;°
If not complete of,° say he is not she,
435 And she again wants° nothing, to name want,°
If want it be not° that she is not he.
He is the half part of a blessèd man,
Left to be finishèd by such as she,
And she a fair divided excellence,
440 Whose fullness of perfection lies in him.
O, two such silver currents when they join
Do glorify the banks that bound them in;
And two such shores, to two such streams made
      one,
Two such controlling bounds shall you be, kings,
445 To these two princes, if you marry them.°

422 **bent** determined   424 **near to England** closely related to King
John (she was the daughter of John's sister and of the King of
Castile)   425 **Dolphin** Dauphin   428 **zealous** sanctified   431 **bound**
hold   433 **complete** fully endowed   434 **of** therein   435 **wants** lacks
435 **to name want** to speak of defects   436 **If want it be not** if it is
not a deficiency (the verbal quibbling of these lines is more to the
Elizabethan taste than to ours, but it marks also the impersonal
formality of Hubert's proposal)   445 **if you marry them** i.e., to each
other

This union shall do more than battery can
To our fast-closèd gates: for at this match,°
With swifter spleen° than powder can enforce,
The mouth of passage shall we fling wide ope,
And give you entrance. But without this match,   450
The sea enragèd is not half so deaf,
Lions more confident, mountains and rocks
More free from motion, no, not death himself
In mortal fury half so peremptory,°
As we to keep this city.

Bastard.   Here's a stay°   455
That shakes the rotten carcass of old death
Out of his rags! Here's a large mouth, indeed,
That spits forth death and mountains, rocks and
    seas,
Talks as familiarly of roaring lions
As maids of thirteen do of puppy-dogs.   460
What cannoneer begot this lusty blood?
He speaks plain cannon fire, and smoke, and
    bounce;°
He gives the bastinado° with his tongue:
Our ears are cudgeled; not a word of his
But buffets better than a fist of France.   465
Zounds!° I was never so bethumped with words
Since I first called my brother's father dad.

Elinor. Son, list to this conjunction,° make this match;
Give with our niece a dowry large enough,
For by this knot thou shalt so surely tie   470
Thy now unsured assurance° to the crown
That yon green boy shall have no sun to ripe
The bloom that promiseth a mighty fruit.
I see a yielding in the looks of France:
Mark how they whisper. Urge them while their souls   475
Are capable of this ambition,°

447 **match** (1) marriage (2) wick for igniting powder 448 **spleen**
impetuosity 454 **peremptory** resolute 455 **stay** check, hindrance
462 **bounce** explosive noise 463 **bastinado** cudgeling 466 **Zounds!**
by God's wounds! 468 **list to this conjunction** listen to (accept) this
union 471 **unsured assurance** uncertain title 476 **capable of this
ambition** ready to accept this desire for alliance

Lest zeal,° now melted by the windy breath
Of soft petitions, pity, and remorse,
Cool and congeal again to what it was.

480 *Hubert.* Why answer not the double majesties
This friendly treaty° of our threatened town?

King Philip. Speak England first, that hath been forward first
To speak unto this city: what say you?

King John. If that the Dolphin there, thy princely son,
485 Can in this book of beauty read "I love,"
Her dowry shall weigh equal with a queen:
For Anjou and fair Touraine, Maine, Poictiers,
And all that we upon this side the sea°—
Except this city now by us besieged—
490 Find liable° to our crown and dignity,
Shall gild her bridal bed and make her rich
In titles, honors, and promotions,
As she in beauty, education, blood,
Holds hand with° any princess of the world.

King Philip. What sayst thou, boy? Look in the lady's
495 face.

Lewis. I do, my lord, and in her eye I find
A wonder, or a wondrous miracle,
The shadow° of myself formed in her eye,
Which, being but the shadow of your son,
500 Becomes a sun, and makes your son a shadow:
I do protest I never loved myself
Till now infixèd I beheld myself,
Drawn in the flattering table° of her eye.
                              Whispers with Blanch.

Bastard. Drawn° in the flattering table of her eye!

477 **zeal** i.e., King Philip's eagerness to support Arthur   481 **treaty**
proposal   488 **sea** i.e., the English Channel   490 **liable** subject
494 **Holds hand with** is the equal of   498 **shadow** image   503
Drawn in the flattering table portrayed on the flattering surface (the
whole of the Dauphin's speech—eye, sun, son, shadow—is conventional; he simply says what is expected of him)   504 **Drawn** (1)
portrayed (2) disemboweled

　　Hanged in the frowning wrinkle of her brow!　　　505
　　And quartered° in her heart! He doth espy
　　Himself love's traitor; this is pity now,
　　That, hanged and drawn and quartered, there
　　　　should be
　　In such a love so vile a lout as he.

Blanch. [*To Lewis*] My uncle's will in this respect is
　　　　mine:　　　　　　　　　　　　　　　　　510
　　If he see aught in you that makes him like,
　　That anything he sees which moves his liking,
　　I can with ease translate it to my will;°
　　Or, if you will, to speak more properly,
　　I will enforce it eas'ly to my love.　　　　　515
　　Further I will not flatter you, my lord,
　　That all I see in you is worthy love,
　　Than this: that nothing do I see in you,
　　Though churlish thoughts themselves should be
　　　　your judge,
　　That I can find should merit any hate.　　　　520

King John. What say these young ones? What say you,
　　　　my niece?

Blanch. That she is bound in honor still° to do
　　What you in wisdom still vouchsafe to say.

King John. Speak then, Prince Dolphin: can you love
　　　　this lady?

Lewis. Nay, ask me if I can refrain from love,　　　525
　　For I do love her most unfeignèdly.

King John. Then do I give Volquessen, Touraine,
　　　　Maine,
　　Poictiers, and Anjou, these five provinces,
　　With her to thee; and this addition more,
　　Full thirty thousand marks of English coin.　　　530

---

506 **quartered** (1) lodged (2) cut or torn in four parts (traitors were
hanged, drawn and quartered)　513 **translate it to my will** i.e., I can
bend my will to my uncle's desires (Blanch is much less conventional,
and much more honest, than Lewis)　522 **still** always

Philip of France, if thou be pleased withal,
Command thy son and daughter to join hands.

King Philip. It likes us° well. Young princes, close
    your hands.

Austria. And your lips too, for I am well assured
535   That I did so when I was first assured.°

King Philip. Now, citizens of Angiers, ope your gates;
    Let in that amity which you have made,
    For at Saint Mary's chapel presently
    The rites of marriage shall be solemnized.
540   Is not the Lady Constance in this troop?
    I know she is not, for this match made up
    Her presence would have interrupted much.
    Where is she and her son? Tell me, who knows.

Lewis. She is sad and passionate° at your Highness'
    tent.

King Philip. And, by my faith, this league that we
545   have made
    Will give her sadness very little cure.
    Brother of England, how may we content
    This widow lady? In her right we came,
    Which we, God knows, have turned another way,
    To our own vantage.

550 *King John.*   We will heal up all,
    For we'll create young Arthur Duke of Britain
    And Earl of Richmond, and this rich fair town
    We make him lord of. Call the Lady Constance.
    Some speedy messenger bid her repair
555   To our solemnity.° I trust we shall,
    If not fill up the measure of her will,
    Yet in some measure satisfy her so
    That we shall stop her exclamation.°

533 **It likes us** we like it   535 **assured** engaged to be married   544
passionate enraged   555 **solemnity** ceremony (the wedding and the
granting of titles to Arthur)   558 **stop her exclamation** silence her
complaining

Go we, as well as haste will suffer us,
To this unlooked for, unpreparèd pomp.°   560
                    Exeunt [all but the Bastard].

Bastard. Mad world! Mad kings! Mad composition!°
  John, to stop Arthur's title in the whole,
  Hath willingly departed with° a part,
  And France, whose armor conscience buckled on,
  Whom zeal and charity brought to the field   565
  As God's own soldier, rounded in the ear
  With° that same purpose-changer, that sly devil,
  That broker° that still breaks the pate of faith,
  That daily break-vow, he that wins of all,
  Of kings, of beggars, old men, young men, maids,   570
  Who,° having no external thing to lose
  But the word "maid," cheats the poor maid of that,
  That smooth-faced° gentleman, tickling° commod-
    ity,°
  Commodity, the bias° of the world,
  The world, who of itself is peisèd° well,   575
  Made to run even upon even ground,
  Till this advantage, this vile drawing° bias,
  This sway° of motion,° this commodity,
  Makes it take head° from all indifferency,°
  From all direction, purpose, course, intent.   580
  And this same bias, this commodity,
  This bawd, this broker, this all-changing word,
  Clapped on the outward eye° of fickle France,

---

560 **pomp** ceremony   561 **composition** compromise   563 **departed
with** given away   566–67 **rounded in the ear/With** whispered to by
568 **broker** pander   571 **Who** (elliptical; begins by referring to
"maids," ends, as the subject of "cheats," by referring to° "commodity," the subject of this whole series of appositions)   573
smooth-faced ingratiating, deceitful   573 **tickling** (1) teasing—the
maids (2) flattering—anyone   573 **commodity** self-interest   574
bias oblique course (in bowling, the bowl went on an oblique course
because of the weight built into one side; "bias" was the word for
either the course or the weight itself)   575 **peisèd** weighted   577
vile drawing (two adjectives, but also "vile-drawing," drawing to evil)
578 **sway** (that which sways) diverter, corrupter   578 **motion** (1)
movement (2) intention   579 **take head** run   579 **indifferency** im-
partiality, disinterestedness   583 **outward eye** (1) physical vision,
as opposed to moral vision or conscience (2) in bowling, the bowl
had an "eye" which received the weight, the bias

       Hath drawn him from his own determined aid,
585   From a resolved° and honorable war,
       To a most base and vile-concluded peace.
       And why rail I on this commodity?
       But for because° he hath not wooed me yet:
       Not that I have the power to clutch my hand,°
590   When his fair angels° would salute my palm,
       But for my hand, as unattempted° yet,
       Like a poor beggar, raileth on the rich.
       Well, whiles I am a beggar, I will rail
       And say there is no sin but to be rich;
595   And being rich, my virtue then shall be
       To say there is no vice but beggary.
       Since kings break faith upon° commodity,
       Gain, be my lord, for I will worship thee!   *Exit.*

               Scene 2. [*King Philip's tent.*]

          Enter Constance, Arthur, and Salisbury.

  Constance. Gone to be married! Gone to swear a
          peace!
       False blood to false blood joined! Gone to be
          friends!
       Shall Lewis have Blanch, and Blanch those prov-
          inces?
       It is not so; thou hast misspoke, misheard;
5   Be well advised, tell o'er thy tale again.
       It cannot be; thou dost but say 'tis so.
       I trust I may not trust thee, for thy word

585 **resolved** the decision to undertake it having been made   588 **But
for because** only because   589 **clutch my hand** i.e., refuse the bribe
590 **angels** (1) commodity's agents, the fallen angels (2) gold coins
called "angels" because they carried a picture of the archangel
Michael killing a dragon   591 **unattempted** untested, untempted
597 **upon** as a result of

Is but the vain breath of a common man;
Believe me, I do not believe thee, man:
I have a king's oath to the contrary.   10
Thou shalt be punished for thus frighting me,
For I am sick and capable of fears,
Oppressed with wrongs, and therefore full of fears,
A widow, husbandless,° subject to fears,
A woman naturally born to fears;   15
And though thou now confess thou didst but jest,
With my vexed spirits I cannot take a truce,°
But they will quake and tremble all this day.
What dost thou mean by shaking of thy head?
Why dost thou look so sadly on my son?   20
What means that hand upon that breast of thine?
Why holds thine eye that lamentable rheum,°
Like a proud river peering o'er° his bounds?
Be these sad signs confirmers of thy words?
Then speak again, not all thy former tale,   25
But this one word, whether thy tale be true.

Salisbury. As true as I believe you think them false
  That give you cause to prove my saying true.

Constance. O if thou teach me to believe this sorrow,
  Teach thou this sorrow how to make me die!   30
  And let belief and life encounter so
  As doth the fury of two desperate men
  Which in the very meeting fall and die.
  Lewis marry Blanch! O boy, then where art thou?
  France friend with England, what becomes of me?   35
  Fellow, be gone! I cannot brook thy sight.
  This news hath made thee a most ugly man.

Salisbury. What other harm have I, good lady, done,
  But spoke the harm that is by others done?

2.2.14 **A widow, husbandless** (not necessarily a tautology: the historical Constance, though Geoffrey's widow, was at this time married
to her third husband; his presence would, however, be a dramatic
confusion, and Shakespeare simplifies to increase her isolation)
17 **take a truce** make peace   22 **that lamentable rheum** those sorrowful tears   23 **peering o'er** overflowing

40 *Constance.* Which harm within itself so heinous is
      As it makes harmful all that speak of it.

    Arthur. I do beseech you, madam, be content.°

    Constance. If thou, that bid'st me be content, wert
          grim,
      Ugly and sland'rous° to thy mother's womb,
45   Full of unpleasing blots° and sightless° stains,
      Lame, foolish, crooked, swart, prodigious,°
      Patched with foul moles and eye-offending marks,
      I would not care, I then would be content,
      For then I should not love thee: no, nor thou
50   Become thy great birth, nor deserve a crown.
      But thou art fair, and at thy birth, dear boy,
      Nature and fortune joined to make thee great.
      Of nature's gifts thou mayst with lilies boast
      And with the half-blown° rose. But fortune, O,
55   She is corrupted, changed, and won from thee;
      Sh' adulterates hourly° with thine uncle John,
      And with her golden hand° hath plucked on°
          France
      To tread down fair respect of sovereignty,
      And made his majesty the bawd to theirs.
60   France is a bawd to fortune and King John,
      That strumpet fortune, that usurping John!
      Tell me, thou fellow, is not France forsworn?
      Envenom° him with words, or get thee gone
      And leave those woes alone which I alone
      Am bound to underbear.°

65 *Salisbury.*   Pardon me, madam,
      I may not go without you to the kings.

    Constance. Thou mayst; thou shalt: I will not go with
          thee.

    42 **content** calm, satisfied 44 **sland'rous** a disgrace, giving cause for
    slander 45 **blots** spots, disfigurements 45 **sightless** unsightly 46
    prodigious deformed, hence a prodigy or bad omen 54 **half-blown**
    half-opened 56 **hourly** (1) every hour (2) like a whore (cf. 1.1.165)
    57 **golden hand** hand which dispenses gold 57 **plucked on** drawn
    along 63 **Envenom** (1) poison (2) curse 65 **underbear** endure,
    suffer

I will instruct my sorrows to be proud,°
For grief is proud° and makes his owner stoop.°
To me and to the state° of my great grief   70
Let kings assemble, for my grief's so great
That no supporter but the huge firm earth
Can hold it up: here I and sorrows sit;
Here is my throne; bid kings come bow to it.
                    [*Seats herself on the ground.*
                    Exeunt Salisbury and Arthur.]°

68, 69 **proud** (1) proud (2) prou'd = proved = tested   69 **stoop**
bow down (Constance is made to bow down under her grief,
but she will also make the kings bow down to it)   70 **state**
(1) condition (2) high rank (3) government (4) throne   74s.d.
Exeunt Salisbury and Arthur (it is not clear whether Salisbury
should lead Arthur off or they should go in opposite directions;
it is only clear that they are not present during the next scene
and that Arthur next appears, in 3.2, as John's prisoner)

ACT 3

Scene 1. [*King Philip's tent.*]

Enter King John, [King Philip of] France, [Lewis, the]
Dauphin, Blanch, Elinor, Philip [the Bastard], Austria
[and Attendants, to] Constance, [seated on
the ground].°

King Philip. 'Tis true, fair daughter, and this blessèd
    day
    Ever in France shall be kept festival:°
    To solemnize this day the glorious sun
    Stays in his course and plays the alchemist,
5   Turning with splendor of his precious eye
    The meager cloddy earth to glittering gold.
    The yearly course that brings this day about
    Shall never see it but a holy day.

Constance. [*Rising*] A wicked day, and not a holy day!
10   What hath this day deserved? what hath it done
    That it in golden letters should be set
    Among the high tides° in the calendar?

3.1.s.d. **seated on the ground** (the action is of course continuous
from the end of the second act) 2 **festival** as a holiday 12 **high
tides** principal anniversaries

Nay, rather turn this day out of the week,
This day of shame, oppression, perjury.
Or, if it must stand still,° let wives with child   15
Pray that their burdens may not fall this day,
Lest that their hopes prodigiously be crossed:°
But° on this day let seamen fear no wrack;°
No bargains° break that are not this day made;
This day all things begun come to ill end,   20
Yea, faith itself to hollow falsehood change!

King Philip. By heaven, lady, you shall have no cause
To curse the fair proceedings of this day:
Have I not pawned to you my majesty?°

Constance. You have beguiled me with a counterfeit°   25
Resembling majesty, which, being touched and
    tried,°
Proves valueless: you are forsworn, forsworn!
You came in arms to spill mine enemies' blood,
But now, in arms,° you strengthen it with yours.
The grappling vigor and rough frown of war   30
Is cold in amity and painted peace,°
And our oppression° hath made up this league.
Arm, arm, you heavens, against these perjured
    kings!
A widow cries; be husband to me, heavens!
Let not the hours of this ungodly day   35
Wear out° the day in peace; but, ere sunset,
Set armèd discord 'twixt these perjured kings!
Hear me! O, hear me!

Austria.   Lady Constance, peace!

Constance. War! War! No peace! Peace is to me a
    war.

15 **stand still** always remain   17 **prodigiously be crossed** be denied
by the birth of a deformed child   18 **But** except   18 **wrack** disaster
(here, of course, shipwreck)   19 **bargains** agreements   24 **pawned
to you my majesty** pledged you my word as a king   25 **counterfeit**
false coin   26 **touched and tried** its gold tested on a touchstone
28–29 **in arms ... in arms** armed ... embracing   31 **Is cold ...
peace** lies dead in your friendship and false peace   32 **our oppression** your oppression of us   36 **Wear out** last through

40   O, Lymoges!° O, Austria! Thou dost shame
      That bloody spoil:° thou slave, thou wretch, thou
            coward!
      Thou little valiant, great in villainy!
      Thou ever strong upon the stronger side!
      Thou fortune's champion, that dost never fight
45   But when her humorous° ladyship is by
      To teach thee safety! Thou art perjured too,
      And sooth'st up° greatness. What a fool art thou,
      A ramping° fool, to brag and stamp and swear
      Upon my party!° Thou cold-blooded slave,
50   Hast thou not spoke like thunder on my side?
      Been sworn my soldier, bidding me depend
      Upon thy stars, thy fortune, and thy strength,
      And dost thou now fall over° to my foes?
      Thou wear a lion's hide! Doff it for shame,
55   And hang a calfskin° on those recreant° limbs.

Austria. O that a man should speak those words to
      me!

Bastard. And hang a calfskin on those recreant limbs.

Austria. Thou dar'st not say so, villain, for thy life!

Bastard. And hang a calfskin on those recreant limbs.

60 *King John.* We like not this; thou dost forget thyself.

                    Enter Pandulph.

King Philip. Here comes the holy legate of the Pope.

Pandulph. Hail, you anointed deputies of heaven!
      To thee, King John, my holy errand is.
      I Pandulph, of fair Milan cardinal,

---

40 **Lymoges** (Limoges and Austria were, historically, two men, but
are here combined; Richard *Coeur de Lion* was actually killed, not
by Austria, but while besieging Limoges) 41 **bloody spoil** i.e., the
lion-skin 45 **humorous** full of humors, capricious 47 **sooth'st up**
flatterest 48 **ramping** (1) raging (2) threatening—chiefly said of
lions (3) standing on the hind legs, like a heraldic lion 49 **Upon
my party** as one of my supporters 53 **fall over** go over 55 **calfskin**
(1) indicating a calf, or meek, cowardly fellow, in sharpest contrast
with a lion (2) traditional coat (?) for a household fool or idiot kept
for amusement 55 **recreant** cowardly

And from Pope Innocent the legate here,   65
Do in his name religiously demand
Why thou against the church, our holy mother,
So willfully dost spurn;° and force perforce°
Keep Stephen Langton, chosen Archbishop
Of Canterbury, from that holy see: 70
This, in our foresaid holy father's name,
Pope Innocent, I do demand of thee.

King John. What earthy name to interrogatories°
Can task the free breath of a sacred king?°
Thou canst not, Cardinal, devise a name   75
So slight, unworthy and ridiculous,
To charge me to an answer,° as the Pope.
Tell him this tale, and from the mouth of England
Add thus much more, that no Italian priest
Shall tithe or toll° in our dominions;   80
But as we, under God, are supreme head,
So under Him that great supremacy
Where we do reign, we will alone uphold
Without th' assistance of a mortal hand:
So tell the Pope, all reverence set apart   85
To him and his usurped authority.

King Philip. Brother of England, you blaspheme in
this.

King John. Though you and all the kings of Christen-
dom
Are led so grossly° by this meddling priest,°
Dreading the curse that money may buy out,°   90
And by the merit of vile gold, dross, dust,
Purchase corrupted pardon of a man,
Who in that sale sells pardon from himself:°
Though you and all the rest, so grossly led,

68 **spurn** kick contemptuously   68 **force perforce** by violent means
73 **interrogatories** questions asked formally in a law court   73–74
What earthy name ... king what mortal can force a king to answer
charges   77 **charge me to an answer** command an answer from me
80 **tithe or toll** collect church revenues   89 **grossly** (1) stupidly (2)
materially—as opposed to spiritually   89 **this meddling priest** i.e.,
the Pope   90 **buy out** remove   93 **sells pardon from himself** (1) i.e.,
not from God (2) loses his own pardon through the transaction

95   This juggling witchcraft with revenue cherish,°
    Yet I alone, alone do me oppose
    Against the Pope, and count his friends my foes.

Pandulph. Then, by the lawful power that I have,
    Thou shalt stand curst and excommunicate:
100   And blessèd shall he be that doth revolt
    From his allegiance to an heretic;
    And meritorious shall that hand be called,
    Canonized and worshiped as a saint,
    That takes away by any secret course
    Thy hateful life.

105 *Constance.*   O lawful let it be
    That I have room with Rome° to curse awhile!
    Good Father Cardinal, cry thou "Amen"
    To my keen curses, for without my wrong
    There is no tongue hath power to curse him right.

110 *Pandulph.* There's law and warrant, lady, for my curse.

Constance. And for mine too: when law can do no right,
    Let it be lawful that law bar no wrong!
    Law cannot give my child his kingdom here,
    For he that holds his kingdom holds the law;
115   Therefore, since law itself is perfect wrong,
    How can the law forbid my tongue to curse?

Pandulph. Philip of France, on peril of a curse,
    Let go the hand of that arch-heretic,
    And raise the power of France upon his head,°
120   Unless he do submit himself to Rome.

Elinor. Look'st thou pale, France? Do not let go thy hand.

Constance. Look to that, Devil, lest that France repent,
    And by disjoining hands, hell lose a soul.

---

95 **This juggling … cherish** cling to, and nourish financially, this deceptive wickedness   106 **room with Rome** (the words were presumably homonyms)   119 **upon his head** against him

Austria. King Philip, listen to the Cardinal.

Bastard. And hang a calfskin on his recreant limbs.   125

Austria. Well, ruffian, I must pocket up these wrongs,
  Because—

Bastard.   Your breeches best may carry them.

King John. Philip, what sayst thou to the Cardinal?

Constance. What should he say, but as the Cardinal?

Lewis. Bethink you, father, for the difference   130
  Is purchase of a heavy curse from Rome,
  Or the light loss of England for a friend:
  Forgo the easier.°

Blanch.   That's the curse of Rome.

Constance. O Lewis, stand fast! The devil tempts thee
    here
  In likeness of a new untrimmèd° bride.   135

Blanch. The Lady Constance speaks not from her
    faith,
  But from her need.°

Constance.   O, if thou grant my need,
  Which only lives but by the death of faith,
  That need must needs infer° this principle,
  That faith would live again by death of need.   140
  O then tread down my need, and faith mounts up;
  Keep my need up, and faith is trodden down!

King John. The King is moved, and answers not to
    this.

Constance. O be removed from him, and answer well!

Austria. Do so, King Philip; hang no more in doubt.   145

Bastard. Hang nothing but a calfskin, most sweet lout.

---

133 **the easier** the lighter, the less oppressive 135 **untrimmèd** still
possessing her maidenhead 136–37 **speaks not ... need** is not
interested in truth but in advancing her cause 139 **infer** imply

King Philip. I am perplexed, and know not what to say.

Pandulph. What canst thou say but will perplex thee more,
If thou stand excommunicate and cursed?

King Philip. Good reverend Father, make my person yours,°
150 And tell me how you would bestow yourself.
This royal hand and mine are newly knit,
And the conjunction of our inward souls
Married in league, coupled and linked together
155 With all religious strength of sacred vows;
The latest breath that gave the sound of words
Was deep-sworn faith, peace, amity, true love
Between our kingdoms and our royal selves;
And even before this truce, but new° before,
160 No longer than we well could wash our hands
To clap this royal bargain up of peace,°
Heaven knows, they were besmeared and over-stained
With slaughter's pencil,° where revenge did paint
The fearful difference° of incensèd kings:
165 And shall these hands, so lately purged of blood,
So newly joined in love, so strong in both,°
Unyoke this seizure and this kind regreet?°
Play fast and loose° with faith? so jest with heaven,
Make such unconstant children of ourselves
170 As now again to snatch our palm from palm,°
Unswear faith sworn, and on the marriage bed
Of smiling peace to march a bloody host,
And make a riot on the gentle brow
Of true sincerity? O holy sir,
175 My reverend Father, let it not be so!

---

150 **make my person yours** put yourself in my place   159 **new** just
161 **clap ... peace** shake hands on this agreement, this royal peace
treaty   163 **pencil** paintbrush   164 **difference** dissension   166 **so
strong in both** (1) hands so strong in both blood and love (2) love so
strong in both kings (?)   167 **Unyoke ... regreet** release their clasp
and friendly counterclasp   168 **Play fast and loose** cheat   170 **palm**
(1) hand (2) symbol of peace

  Out of your grace, devise, ordain, impose
  Some gentle order, and then we shall be blessed
  To do your pleasure and continue friends.

Pandulph. All form is formless, order orderless,
  Save what is opposite to England's love.   *180*
  Therefore to arms! Be champion of our church,
  Or let the church, our mother, breathe her curse,
  A mother's curse, on her revolting son.
  France, thou mayst hold a serpent by the tongue,
  A casèd° lion by the mortal° paw,   *185*
  A fasting tiger safer by the tooth,
  Than keep in peace that hand which thou dost hold.

King Philip. I may disjoin my hand, but not my faith.

Pandulph. So mak'st thou faith an enemy to faith,°
  And like a civil war set'st oath to oath,   *190*
  Thy tongue against thy tongue. O, let thy vow,
  First made to heaven, first be to heaven performed,
  That is, to be the champion of our church.
  What since thou swor'st° is sworn against thyself
  And may not be performèd by thyself,   *195*
  For that which thou hast sworn to do amiss
  Is not amiss when it is truly done;°
  And being not done, where doing tends to ill,
  The truth is then most done not doing it.
  The better act of purposes mistook   *200*
  Is to mistake again; though indirect,
  Yet indirection thereby grows direct,
  And falsehood falsehood cures, as fire cools fire
  Within the scorchèd veins of one new burned.
  It is religion that doth make vows kept,   *205*
  But thou hast sworn against religion

185 **casèd** caged (?) wearing its own hide, i.e., living (?)   185 **mortal**
deadly   189 **So mak'st ... to faith** thus you make your loyalty to
your oath to John an enemy to your loyalty to the true faith, the
church   194 **What since thou swor'st** what you have sworn at any
time after your original vow to the church   197 **truly done** done as
it ought to be done, rather than done in accordance with your unsound oath (this argument for swearing one thing and doing another
is the so-called "doctrine of equivocation" for which Elizabethan
Protestants particularly hated and feared the Jesuits)

(By what thou swear'st against the thing thou
    swear'st)°
And mak'st an oath the surety for thy truth
(Against an oath the truth);° thou art unsure
210 To swear°—swears only not to be forsworn,°
Else what a mockery should it be to swear!
But thou dost swear only to be forsworn,
And most forsworn, to keep° what thou dost swear;
Therefore thy later vows against thy first
215 Is in thyself rebellion to thyself:
And better conquest never canst thou make
Than arm° thy constant and thy nobler parts
Against these giddy loose suggestions;°
Upon which better part° our prayers come in,
220 If thou vouchsafe° them. But if not, then know
The peril of our curses light on thee
So heavy as thou shalt not shake them off,
But in despair die under their black weight.

Austria. Rebellion, flat rebellion!

Bastard.   Will 't not be?°
225 Will not a calfskin stop that mouth of thine?

Lewis. Father, to arms!

Blanch.   Upon thy wedding day?
Against the blood that thou hast married?
What, shall our feast be kept with slaughtered men?
Shall braying trumpets and loud churlish drums,
230 Clamors of hell, be measures° to our pomp?

---

207 **(By what ... swear'st)** by your oath to John against your religion
209 **(Against an oath the truth)** the truth itself (religion) stands
against the oath (to John) which you make the basis of your loyalty
209–10 **thou art unsure/To swear** you are untrustworthy in your
oaths 210 **swears ... forsworn** one swears in the first place to
ensure that one will not later swear the opposite (the complex
parenthetical style of Pandulph's argument creates a dramatic effect
of quibbling ingenuity as opposed to an effect of plainspoken truth)
213 **And most forsworn, to keep** and you would be most forsworn
if you were to keep 217 **arm** to arm 218 **giddy loose suggestions**
inconstant, unrestrained temptations 219 **Upon which better part**
in behalf of which preferable party or faction 220 **vouchsafe** permit
224 **Will 't not be** will this not cease 230 **measures** melodies

O husband, hear me! Ay, alack, how new
Is "husband" in my mouth! Even for that name,
Which till this time my tongue did ne'er pronounce,
Upon my knee I beg, go not to arms
Against mine uncle.

Constance.   O, upon my knee,   235
Made hard with kneeling, I do pray to thee,
Thou virtuous Dolphin, alter not the doom
Forethought by God!°

Blanch. Now shall I see thy love: what motive may
Be stronger with thee than the name of wife?   240

Constance. That which upholdeth him that thee upholds,
His honor: O thine honor, Lewis, thine honor!

Lewis. I muse your Majesty doth seem so cold,
When such profound respects° do pull you on!

Pandulph. I will denounce° a curse upon his head.   245

King Philip. Thou shalt not need. England, I will fall
from° thee.

Constance. O fair return of banished majesty!

Elinor. O foul revolt of French inconstancy!

King John. France, thou shalt rue this hour within
this hour.

Bastard. Old Time the clock-setter, that bald sexton°
Time,   250
Is it as he will?° Well then, France shall rue.

Blanch. The sun's o'ercast with blood: fair day, adieu!
Which is the side that I must go withal?
I am with both: each army hath a hand,
And in their rage, I having hold of both,   255
They whirl asunder and dismember me.

237–38 **alter not ... God** don't interfere with divine intervention
244 **respects** inducements 245 **denounce** pronounce 246 **fall from**
desert 250 **sexton** gravedigger and bell-ringer 251 **Is it as he will**
is that the way he wants it

Husband, I cannot pray that thou mayst win;
Uncle, I needs must pray that thou mayst lose;
Father,° I may not wish the fortune thine;
260 Grandam, I will not wish thy wishes thrive:
Whoever wins, on that side shall I lose;
Assurèd loss before the match be played.

Lewis. Lady, with me, with me thy fortune lies.

Blanch. There where my fortune lives, there my life
dies.

265 *King John.* Cousin,° go draw our puissance° together.
[*Exit Bastard.*]
France, I am burned up with inflaming wrath,
A rage whose heat hath this condition,°
That nothing can allay, nothing but blood,
The blood, and dearest-valued blood, of France.

King Philip. Thy rage shall burn thee up, and thou
270 shalt turn
To ashes, ere our blood shall quench that fire!
Look to thyself, thou art in jeopardy.

King John. No more than he that threats. To arms
let's hie! *Exeunt.*

---

259 **Father** father-in-law (King Philip) 265 **Cousin** kinsman (commonly, as here, nephew) 265 **puissance** army 267 **condition** characteristic

Scene 2. [*Battlefield near Angiers.*]

*Alarums,° excursions. Enter Bastard, with
Austria's head.°*

Bastard. Now, by my life, this day° grows wondrous
hot.
Some airy devil hovers in the sky
And pours down mischief.° Austria's head lie there,

Enter [King] John, Arthur, Hubert.

While Philip breathes.°

King John. Hubert, keep this boy. Philip, make up:°   5
My mother is assailèd in our tent,
And ta'en, I fear.

Bastard.   My lord, I rescued her;°
Her Highness is in safety, fear you not:
But on, my liege, for very little pains
Will bring this labor to an happy end.   *Exit [all].°*   10

*Alarums, excursions, retreat. [Re]enter [King]
John, Elinor, Arthur, Bastard, Hubert, Lords.*

King John. [*To Elinor*] So shall it be: your Grace shall
stay behind
So strongly guarded. [*To Arthur*] Cousin, look not
sad:

3.2.s.d. Alarums trumpets, battle cries   s.d. **with Austria's head**
(though there is no mention of the lion-skin, the Bastard should presumably wear it in this scene and perhaps from now on; his complaint of the heat may be in part a comic reference to this addition
to his costume)   1 **this day** (1) the day itself (2) the battle   2–3
Some airy ... mischief some invisible devil has made the day so hot,
or the battle so fierce   4 **breathes** catches his breath   5 **make up**
advance, press on   7 **I rescued her** (Shakespeare gives the Bastard
credit for a rescue historically effected by John)   10s.d. **Exit [all]**
(because the stage is cleared, many editors begin a new scene here)

Thy grandam loves thee, and thy uncle will
As dear be to thee as thy father was.

15 *Arthur.* O this will make my mother die with grief!

King John. [*To the Bastard*] Cousin, away for Eng-
land! Haste before,°
And, ere our coming, see thou shake the bags°
Of hoarding abbots; imprisoned angels°
Set at liberty: the fat ribs of peace
20 Must by the hungry now be fed upon!
Use our commission in his° utmost force.

Bastard. Bell, book, and candle° shall not drive me
back
When gold and silver becks° me to come on.
I leave your Highness. Grandam, I will pray
25 (If ever I remember to be holy)
For your fair safety; so I kiss your hand.

Elinor. Farewell, gentle cousin.

King John.   Coz,° farewell. [*Exit Bastard.*]

Elinor. Come hither, little kinsman. Hark, a word.
[*She takes Arthur aside.*]

King John. Come hither, Hubert. O my gentle Hubert,
30 We owe thee much!° Within this wall of flesh
There is a soul counts thee her creditor,
And with advantage° means to pay° thy love;
And, my good friend, thy voluntary oath
Lives in this bosom, dearly cherishèd.
35 Give me thy hand. I had a thing to say,
But I will fit it with some better tune.°

---

16 **before** ahead of us 17 **shake the bags** empty the moneybags
("Shak[e]bag" is a "desperate ruffi[a]n" in *Arden of Feversham,*
1592) 18 **angels** coins; cf. 2.1.590 21 **his** its 22 **Bell, book, and
candle** excommunication 23 **becks** beckons 27 **Coz** cousin, kinsman 30 **We owe thee much** (perhaps the entry after line 3 indicates
that Hubert is responsible for the capture of Arthur. At any rate,
Hubert is now clearly loyal to John, not to France) 32 **advantage**
interest 32 **pay** recompense, repay 36 **fit it ... tune** (1) set it to
more appropriate music (2) render it in a better style (i.e., reward
you with more than words)

By heaven, Hubert, I am almost ashamed
To say what good respect° I have of thee.

Hubert. I am much bounden° to your Majesty.

King John. Good friend, thou hast no cause to say
    so yet,   40
But thou shalt have; and creep time ne'er so slow,
Yet it shall come for me to do thee good.
I had a thing to say, but let it go.
The sun is in the heaven, and the proud day,
Attended with the pleasures of the world,   45
Is all too wanton and too full of gauds
To give me audience.° If the midnight bell
Did, with his iron tongue and brazen mouth,
Sound on into the drowsy race° of night;
If this same were a churchyard where we stand,   50
And thou possessèd with a thousand wrongs;
Or if that surly spirit, melancholy,
Had baked thy blood and made it heavy, thick,
Which else runs tickling up and down the veins,
Making that idiot, laughter, keep° men's eyes   55
And strain° their cheeks to idle merriment,
A passion hateful to my purposes;
Or if that thou couldst see me without eyes,
Hear me without thine ears, and make reply
Without a tongue, using conceit° alone,   60
Without eyes, ears, and harmful sound of words;
Then, in despite of brooded° watchful day,
I would into thy bosom pour my thoughts:
But, ah, I will not; yet I love thee well,
And, by my troth, I think thou lov'st me well.   65

Hubert. So well, that what you bid me undertake,

---

38 **good respect** high regard   39 **bounden** bound, indebted   46–47
too full … audience (1) the mind of the day is too full of trinkets
to listen to me (2) the day is too full of florid beauties for you to
pay proper attention to my harsh meaning   49 **race** course, progress
(many editors substitute "ear" for "race," but this destroys the
oxymoron "drowsy race")   55 **keep** employ for its own purposes
56 **strain** constrain, limit   60 **conceit** imagination, understanding
62 **brooded** brooding

Though that my death were adjunct to° my act,
By heaven, I would do it.

King John.   Do not I know thou wouldst?
Good Hubert, Hubert, Hubert, throw thine eye
70 On yon young boy; I'll tell thee what, my friend,
He is a very serpent in my way,
And wheresoe'er this foot of mine doth tread
He lies before me: dost thou understand me?
Thou art his keeper.

Hubert.   And I'll keep him so
75 That he shall not offend your Majesty.

King John. Death.

Hubert.   My lord.

King John.   A grave.

Hubert.   He shall not live.

King John.   Enough.
I could be merry now. Hubert, I love thee.
Well, I'll not say what I intend for thee:
Remember. Madam, fare you well.
80 I'll send those powers o'er to your Majesty.

Elinor. My blessing go with thee!

King John.   For England, cousin, go.
Hubert shall be your man,° attend on you
With all true duty. On toward Calais,° ho!   Exeunt.

67 **adjunct to** an essential constituent of 82 **man** servant 83
Calais (pronounced to rhyme with "palace")

Scene 3. [*King Philip's tent.*]

*Enter [King Philip of] France, [Lewis, the] Dauphin,
Pandulph, Attendants.*

King Philip. So, by a roaring tempest on the flood,°
    A whole armado° of convicted° sail
    Is scattered and disjoined from fellowship.

Pandulph. Courage and comfort! All shall yet go well.

King Philip. What can go well, when we have run°
        so ill?   5
    Are we not beaten? Is not Angiers lost?
    Arthur ta'en prisoner? divers° dear friends slain?
    And bloody England into England gone,
    O'erbearing interruption, spite of° France?

Lewis. What he hath won, that hath he fortified.   10
    So hot a speed with such advice disposed,°
    Such temperate order in so fierce a cause,
    Doth want example:° who hath read or heard
    Of any kindred action like to this?

King Philip. Well could I bear that England had this
        praise,   15
    So° we could find some pattern° of our shame.

                    Enter Constance.

    Look, who comes here! a grave unto a soul,
    Holding th' eternal spirit, against her will,

3.3.1 **flood** sea 2 **armado** armada, fleet of armed ships 2 **con-
victed** doomed 5 **run** (1) proceeded (2) run away 7 **divers** various
9 **spite of** in spite of 11 **with such advice disposed** carried out with
such determination 13 **Doth want example** is without parallel
16 **So** if 16 **pattern** example, parallel

In the vile prison of afflicted breath.°
20   I prithee, lady, go away with me.

Constance. Lo, now! now see the issue of your peace!

King Philip. Patience, good lady! Comfort, gentle
        Constance!

Constance. No, I defy° all counsel, all redress,
        But that which ends all counsel, true redress:
25   Death, death, O, amiable, lovely death!
        Thou odoriferous stench! sound rottenness!
        Arise forth from the couch of lasting night,°
        Thou hate and terror to prosperity,
        And I will kiss thy detestable bones,
30   And put my eyeballs in thy vaulty° brows,
        And ring these fingers with thy household worms,
        And stop this gap of breath° with fulsome° dust,
        And be a carrion monster like thyself:
        Come, grin on me, and I will think thou smil'st
35   And buss° thee as thy wife! Misery's love,
        O, come to me!

King Philip.   O fair affliction,° peace!

Constance. No, no, I will not, having breath to cry!
        O that my tongue were in the thunder's mouth!
        Then with a passion would I shake the world,
40   And rouse from sleep that fell anatomy°
        Which cannot hear a lady's feeble voice,
        Which scorns a modern invocation.°

Pandulph. Lady, you utter madness, and not sorrow.

Constance. Thou art holy to belie me so!°
45   I am not mad: this hair I tear is mine;

19 **afflicted breath** tormented life   23 **defy** reject   27 **couch of
lasting night** lair of eternal night, i.e., Hell   30 **vaulty** (1) arched
(2) tomblike   32 **stop this gap of breath** stop up this mouth   32
fulsome loathsome   35 **buss** kiss   36 **affliction** (1) afflicted one (2)
one who now afflicts us   40 **fell anatomy** cruel skeleton, i.e., death
42 **modern invocation** common or ordinary entreaty   44 **Thou . . .
so** (as it stands, the line must be sarcastic; it is short a syllable, and
many editors follow the fourth edition of the Folio, 1685, in supplying "not" before "holy")

My name is Constance; I was Geoffrey's wife;
Young Arthur is my son, and he is lost!
I am not mad: I would to heaven I were,
For then 'tis like° I should forget myself!
O, if I could, what grief should I forget!   50
Preach some philosophy to make me mad,
And thou shalt be canonized, Cardinal.
For, being not mad but sensible of° grief,
My reasonable part produces reason
How° I may be delivered of° these woes,   55
And teaches me to kill or hang myself:
If I were mad, I should forget my son,
Or madly think a babe of clouts° were he.
I am not mad: too well, too well I feel
The different plague of each calamity.   60

King Philip. Bind up those tresses! O, what love I note
In the fair multitude of those her hairs!
Where but by chance a silver drop° hath fall'n,
Even to that drop ten thousand wiry friends°
Do glue° themselves in sociable grief,   65
Like true, inseparable, faithful loves,
Sticking together in calamity.

Constance. To England, if you will.°

King Philip.   Bind up your hairs.

Constance. Yes, that I will; and wherefore will I do it?
I tore them from their bonds and cried aloud,   70
"O that these hands could so redeem my son,
As they have given these hairs their liberty!"
But now I envy at° their liberty,
And will again commit them to their bonds,

49 **like** likely   53 **sensible of** capable of feeling   54–55 **reason/How**
the idea of a way in which   55 **be delivered of** (1) give birth to
(2) be delivered from   58 **babe of clouts** rag doll   63 **drop** tear   64
wiry friends hairs ("wiry" was a common, and not pejorative, epithet
for hair)   65 **glue** sympathetically attach   68 **To England, if you
will** (Constance here responds to King Philip's invitation at line 20;
the separation is often taken as evidence that her "mad scene" is an
interpolation, though the leap back to an earlier subject may simply
be another symptom of her agitation)   73 **envy at** am envious of

75   Because my poor child is a prisoner.
        And, Father Cardinal, I have heard you say
        That we shall see and know our friends in heaven:
        If that be true, I shall see my boy again,
        For since the birth of Cain, the first male child,
80   To him that did but yesterday suspire,
        There was not such a gracious° creature born.
        But now will canker-sorrow° eat my bud
        And chase the native beauty from his cheek,
        And he will look as hollow as a ghost,
85   As dim and meager as an ague's fit,
        And so he'll die; and rising so again,
        When I shall meet him in the court of heaven
        I shall not know him: therefore never, never
        Must I° behold my pretty Arthur more.

90   *Pandulph.* You hold too heinous a respect° of grief.

        Constance. He talks to me that never had a son.

        King Philip. You are as fond of° grief as of your child.

        Constance. Grief fills the room up of my absent child,
        Lies in his bed, walks up and down with me,
95   Puts on his pretty looks, repeats his words,
        Remembers° me of all his gracious parts,
        Stuffs out his vacant garments with his form;
        Then have I reason to be fond of grief!
        Fare you well: had you such a loss as I,
100   I could give better comfort than you do.
        I will not keep this form° upon my head,
        When there is such disorder in my wit!°
        O Lord! My boy, my Arthur, my fair son!
        My life, my joy, my food, my all the world!
105   My widow-comfort, and my sorrows' cure!   *Exit.*

        King Philip. I fear some outrage, and I'll follow
            her.   *Exit.*

81 **gracious** (1) attractive, pleasing (2) holy, expressing and meriting
divine grace 82 **canker-sorrow** sorrow as a cankerworm 89 **Must
I** can I 90 **heinous a respect** atrocious a conception 92 **fond of**
foolishly enamored with 96 **Remembers** reminds 101 **form** order
(she had bound up her hair at lines 69–75, and now unbinds it again)
102 **wit** mind

Lewis. There's nothing in this world can make me joy;
    Life is as tedious as a twice-told tale,
    Vexing the dull ear of a drowsy man,
    And bitter shame hath spoiled the sweet words'
      taste,°   *110*
    That it yields nought but shame and bitterness.

Pandulph. Before the curing of a strong disease,
    Even in the instant of repair° and health,
    The fit is strongest: evils that take leave,
    On their departure most of all show evil.   *115*
    What have you lost by losing of this day?°

Lewis. All days of glory, joy, and happiness.

Pandulph. If you had won it, certainly you had.
    No, no; when fortune means to men most good,
    She looks upon them with a threat'ning eye: *120*
    'Tis strange to think how much King John hath lost
    In this which he accounts so clearly won—
    Are not you grieved that Arthur is his prisoner?

Lewis. As heartily as he is glad he hath him.

Pandulph. Your mind is all as youthful as your blood. *125*
    Now hear me speak with a prophetic spirit,
    For even the breath of what I mean to speak
    Shall blow each dust,° each straw, each little rub,°
    Out of the path which shall directly lead
    Thy foot to England's throne. And therefore mark: *130*
    John hath seized Arthur, and it cannot be
    That, whiles warm life plays in that infant's veins,
    The misplaced° John should entertain an hour,
    One minute, nay, one quiet breath of rest.
    A scepter snatched with an unruly hand   *135*
    Must be as boisterously° maintained as gained,

---

110 **the sweet words' taste** (the words of the tale, sweet on first telling,
are bitter on second telling. Many editors follow Pope in emending
the Folio's "words'" to "world's")   113 **repair** recovery 116 **losing
of this day** losing today's battle 128 **dust** particle of dust 128 **rub**
obstacle (from bowling, a roughness in the path of the bowl) 133
misplaced out of his proper place, i.e., usurping 136 **boisterously**
violently

And he that stands upon a slipp'ry place
Makes nice of no vile hold to stay him up:°
That John may stand, then Arthur needs must fall;
140   So be it, for it cannot be but so.

Lewis. But what shall I gain by young Arthur's fall?

Pandulph. You, in the right of Lady Blanch your wife,
May then make all the claim that Arthur did.

Lewis. And lose it, life and all, as Arthur did.

Pandulph. How green you are and fresh in this old
145   world!
John lays you plots;° the times conspire with you,
For he that steeps his safety in true blood°
Shall find but bloody safety and untrue.
This act so evilly borne° shall cool the hearts
150   Of all his people, and freeze up their zeal,
That none so small advantage° shall step forth
To check his reign, but they will cherish it;
No natural exhalation° in the sky,
No scope of nature,° no distempered° day,
155   No common wind, no customèd event,
But they will pluck away his° natural cause
And call them meteors,° prodigies, and signs,
Abortives,° presages, and tongues of heaven,
Plainly denouncing vengeance upon John.

160 *Lewis.* May be he will not touch young Arthur's life,
But hold himself safe in his prisonment.

Pandulph. O sir, when he shall hear of your approach,
If that young Arthur be not gone already,

138 **Makes nice ... up** is not fastidious about his means of holding
himself up   146 **lays you plots** prepares the course for you to follow
147 **steeps his safety in true blood** saturates his own security in loyal,
or legitimate, blood (the specific aim of Pandulph's generalization is,
of course, John's inevitable need to murder the true king, Arthur)
149 **borne** (1) born (2) carried out   151 **none so small advantage** no
opportunity, however small   153 **exhalation** meteor   154 **scope of
nature** event at the limit of natural possibility   154 **distempered**
stormy   156 **his** its   157 **meteors** supernatural omens (opposed to
the "natural exhalation" of line 153)   158 **Abortives** misshaped cre-
ations (also considered omens)

Even at that news he dies; and then the hearts
Of all his people shall revolt from him   *165*
And kiss the lips of unacquainted change,°
And pick strong matter° of revolt and wrath
Out of the bloody fingers' ends of John.
Methinks I see this hurly° all on foot;°
And, O, what better matter breeds° for you   *170*
Than I have named! The bastard Faulconbridge
Is now in England ransacking the church,
Offending charity:° if but a dozen French
Were there in arms, they would be as a call°
To train° ten thousand English to their side,   *175*
Or as a little snow, tumbled about,
Anon° becomes a mountain. O noble Dolphin,
Go with me to the King: 'tis wonderful
What may be wrought out of their discontent,
Now that their souls are topful of offense.°   *180*
For England go; I will whet on° the King.

Lewis. Strong reasons makes° strange actions! Let us
    go:
If you say aye, the King will not say no.   *Exeunt.*

166 **kiss ... change** amorously welcome any alteration   167 **matter**
(1) reason, cause (2) corrupt matter, pus   169 **hurly** turmoil   169
on foot under way   170 **breeds** is being prepared   173 **charity** right
feeling among Christians   174 **call** decoy   175 **train** entice   177
Anon at once   180 **topful of offense** (1) filled to the brim with John's
offenses (2) thoroughly offended   181 **whet on** urge   182 **makes**
make (the verb form may imply "having strong reasons")

ACT 4

Scene 1. [*England. A room in a castle.*]

Enter Hubert and Executioners.

Hubert. Heat me these irons hot, and look thou stand
　　Within the arras.° When I strike my foot
　　Upon the bosom of the ground, rush forth
　　And bind the boy which you shall find with me
5　Fast to the chair. Be heedful. Hence, and watch.

Executioner. I hope your warrant will bear out° the
　　deed.

Hubert. Uncleanly° scruples! Fear not you! Look to 't.
　　　　　　　　　　　　　　[*Executioners hide.*]
　　Young lad, come forth; I have to say with° you.

Enter Arthur.

Arthur. Good morrow, Hubert.

Hubert.　　　　　　　　Good morrow, little prince.

4.1.2 **Within the arras** behind the curtain　6 **bear out** vindicate, give
authority for　7 **Uncleanly** improper　8 **to say with** something to
say to

Arthur. As little prince, having so great a title   10
   To be more prince, as may be.° You are sad.

Hubert. Indeed, I have been merrier.

Arthur.   Mercy on me!
   Methinks nobody should be sad but I:
   Yet I remember, when I was in France,
   Young gentlemen would be as sad as night,   15
   Only for wantonness.° By my Christendom,°
   So° I were out of prison, and kept sheep,
   I should be as merry as the day is long;
   And so I would be here, but that I doubt°
   My uncle practices° more harm to me.   20
   He is afraid of me, and I of him:
   Is it my fault that I was Geoffrey's son?
   No, indeed, is 't not; and I would to heaven
   I were your son, so you would love me, Hubert.

Hubert. [*Aside*] If I talk to him, with his innocent
      prate°   25
   He will awake my mercy, which lies dead:
   Therefore I will be sudden and dispatch.°

Arthur. Are you sick, Hubert? You look pale today.
   In sooth, I would you were a little sick,
   That I might sit all night and watch with you.   30
   I warrant I love you more than you do me.

Hubert. [*Aside*] His words do take possession of my
      bosom.
   [*To Arthur*] Read here, young Arthur.
                         [*Showing a paper.*]
                    [*Aside*] How now, foolish rheum!°
   Turning dispiteous torture° out of door!
   I must be brief, lest resolution drop   35

10–11 **As little ... may be** considering my title (King) to be even
greater, I am presently as little prince as may be   16 **wantonness**
whim   16 **By my Christendom** as I am a Christian (perhaps literally
"by my baptism")   17 **So** if only   19 **doubt** fear   20 **practices** schemes
25 **prate** prattle   27 **dispatch** finish the job quickly   33 **rheum** (1) tears
(2) room (in his bosom, Arthur's words threatening to displace the torture
there)   34 **dispiteous torture** merciless torture (1) threatened to Arthur
(2) now tormenting Hubert

Out at mine eyes in tender womanish tears.
[*To Arthur*] Can you not read it? Is it not fair writ?°

Arthur. Too fairly, Hubert, for so foul effect:°
Must you with hot irons burn out both mine eyes?

Hubert. Young boy, I must.

Arthur.   And will you?

40 *Hubert.*   And I will.

Arthur. Have you the heart? When your head did but
   ache,
I knit my handkercher about your brows
(The best I had, a princess wrought it me°—
And I did never ask it you° again)
45 And with my hand at midnight held your head,
And like the watchful minutes to the hour,°
Still and anon° cheered up the heavy time,
Saying, "What lack you?" and "Where lies your
   grief?"
Or "What good love° may I perform for you?"
50 Many a poor man's son would have lien° still,
And ne'er have spoke a loving word to you;
But you at your sick service had° a prince.
Nay, you may think my love was crafty° love,
And call it cunning. Do and if you will.
55 If heaven be pleased that you must use me ill,
Why then you must. Will you put out mine eyes?
These eyes that never did nor never shall
So much as frown on you?

Hubert.   I have sworn to do it,
And with hot irons must I burn them out.

60 *Arthur.* Ah, none but in this iron age would do it!
The iron of itself, though heat° red-hot,

37 **fair writ** written clearly   38 **effect** purpose   43 **wrought it me**
worked (embroidered) it for me   44 **ask it you** ask you for it   46
like the ... hour as frequently as there are observable minutes in an
hour (?)   47 **Still and anon** continually   49 **love** labor of love   50
lien (two syllables) lain   52 **you at your sick service had** you, sick,
had at your service   53 **crafty** feigned   61 **heat** heated

Approaching near these eyes, would drink my tears
And quench this fiery indignation
Even in the matter° of mine innocence!
Nay, after that, consume away in rust,　　　　　　65
But for° containing fire to harm mine eye!
Are you more stubborn-hard than hammered iron?
And if an angel should have come to me
And told me Hubert should put out mine eyes,
I would not have believed him—no tongue but
　　Hubert's.　　　　　　70

Hubert. [*Stamps*] Come forth.

　　　[*Executioners come forth with a cord, irons, etc.*]

　　　　　　　　Do as I bid you do.

Arthur. O save me, Hubert, save me! My eyes are out
Even with the fierce looks of these bloody men.

Hubert. Give me the iron, I say, and bind him here.

Arthur. Alas, what need you be so boist'rous rough?　　75
I will not struggle; I will stand stone still!
For God's sake, Hubert, let me not be bound!
Nay, hear me, Hubert! Drive these men away,
And I will sit as quiet as a lamb.
I will not stir, nor winch,° nor speak a word,　　　　80
Nor look upon the iron angerly:
Thrust but these men away, and I'll forgive you,
Whatever torment you do put me to.

Hubert. Go, stand within; let me alone with him.

Executioner. I am best pleased to be from° such a
　　deed.　　　　　　　[*Exeunt Executioners.*]　　85

Arthur. Alas, I then have chid away my friend!
He hath a stern look, but a gentle heart:
Let him come back, that his compassion may
Give life to yours.

Hubert.　　　　　　Come, boy, prepare yourself.

64 **matter** substance, i.e., tears　66 **But for** merely as a result of
80 **winch** wince　85 **from** away from

Arthur. Is there no remedy?

90 *Hubert.*   None, but to lose your eyes.

Arthur. O heaven, that there were but a mote in yours,
    A grain, a dust, a gnat, a wandering hair,
    Any annoyance in that precious sense:
    Then feeling what small things are boisterous° there,
95   Your vile intent must needs seem horrible.

Hubert. Is this your promise? Go to,° hold your
    tongue.

Arthur. Hubert, the utterance of a brace° of tongues
    Must needs want° pleading for a pair of eyes:
    Let me not hold my tongue! let me not,° Hubert!
100 Or, Hubert, if you will, cut out my tongue,
    So° I may keep mine eyes. O, spare mine eyes,
    Though to no use but still to look on you!
    Lo, by my troth, the instrument is cold
    And would not° harm me.

Hubert.   I can heat it, boy.

105 *Arthur.* No, in good sooth; the fire is dead with grief,
    Being create° for comfort, to be used°
    In undeserved extremes.° See else° yourself.
    There is no malice in this burning coal.
    The breath of heaven hath blown his spirit out
110 And strewed repentant ashes on his head.

Hubert. But with my breath I can revive it, boy.

Arthur. And if you do, you will but make it blush
    And glow with shame of your proceedings, Hubert:
    Nay, it perchance will sparkle in° your eyes,
115 And, like a dog that is compelled to fight,

94 **boisterous** painful 96 **Go to** (disapproving exclamation, equivalent, perhaps, to "come, come") 97 **brace** pair 98 **want** be
insufficient 99 **let me not** (1) repeating the previous plea (2) hinder
me not 101 **So** if thereby 104 **would not** (1) would not be able
to (2) does not wish to 106 **create** created 106 **to be used** at the
prospect of being used 107 **In undeserved extremes** for undeserved
cruelties (with pun on Latin *in extremis,* in the final agonies of dying)
107 **else** further 114 **sparkle in** throw sparks into

Snatch at his master that doth tarre him on.°
All things that you should use to do me wrong
Deny their office:° only you do lack
That mercy which fierce fire and iron extends,°
Creatures of note for mercy-lacking uses.°   120

Hubert. Well, see to live: I will not touch thine eye
For all the treasure that thine uncle owes;°
Yet am I sworn and I did purpose, boy,
With this same very iron to burn them out.

Arthur. O, now you look like Hubert! All this while   125
You were disguisèd.

Hubert.   Peace! No more. Adieu.
Your uncle must not know but° you are dead.
I'll fill these doggèd° spies with false reports;
And, pretty child, sleep doubtless and secure°
That Hubert, for the wealth of all the world,   130
Will not offend thee.

Arthur.   O heaven! I thank you, Hubert.

Hubert. Silence! No more! Go closely° in with me.
Much danger do I undergo for thee.   *Exeunt.*

---

116 **tarre him on** incite him   118 **Deny their office** contradict their
customary functions   119 **extends** extend, grant   120 **Creatures . . .
uses** creatures (i.e., fire and iron) famous for cruel uses   122 **owes**
owns   127 **but** anything but that   128 **doggèd** surly   129 **doubtless
and secure** certain and assured   132 **closely** secretly

Scene 2. [*King John's court.*]

Enter [King] John, Pembroke, Salisbury,
and other Lords.

King John. Here once again we sit, once again
   crowned,°
   And looked upon, I hope, with cheerful eyes.

Pembroke. This "once again," but that your Highness
      pleased,
   Was once superfluous:° you were crowned before,
5 And that high royalty was ne'er plucked off,
   The faiths of men ne'er stainèd with revolt;
   Fresh expectation° troubled not the land
   With any longed-for change or better state.°

Salisbury. Therefore, to be possessed with double
      pomp,°
10 To guard° a title that was rich before,
   To gild refinèd gold, to paint the lily,
   To throw a perfume on the violet,
   To smooth the ice, or add another hue
   Unto the rainbow, or with taper-light
15 To seek the beauteous eye of heaven to garnish,°
   Is wasteful and ridiculous excess.°

4.2.1 **once again crowned** (John has just had a second coronation,
enforcing new oaths of allegiance to counteract the excommunication which freed his followers from their original oaths. See
3.1.100–1) 4 **once superfluous** one time more than necessary
7 **Fresh expectation** (1) eager anticipation (2) anticipation of something new 8 **state** (1) government (2) condition 9 **pomp** ceremony, i.e., coronation 10 **guard** (1) ornament (2) defend 14–15
with taper-light ... garnish to seek to embellish the sun's beauty
with a candle 16 **excess** extravagance ("excess" also = usury—see
Merchant of Venice 1.3.59—and may here connote Salisbury's sense
that John is extorting too much money from his subjects)

Pembroke. But that your royal pleasure must be done,
    This act is as an ancient tale new told,
    And, in the last repeating, troublesome,
    Being urgèd at a time unseasonable.   20

Salisbury. In this the antique and well-noted° face
    Of plain old form° is much disfigurèd,
    And like a shifted wind unto a sail,
    It makes the course of thoughts to fetch about,°
    Startles and frights consideration,°   25
    Makes sound opinion sick and truth suspected,
    For putting on so new a fashioned robe.°

Pembroke. When workmen strive to do better than
    well,
    They do confound° their skill in covetousness,°
    And oftentimes excusing of a fault   30
    Doth make the fault the worse by th' excuse,
    As patches set upon a little breach°
    Discredit more in hiding of the fault
    Than did the fault before it was so patched.

Salisbury. To this effect, before you were new
    crowned,   35
    We breathed° our counsel: but it pleased your
    Highness
    To overbear it, and we are all well pleased,°
    Since all and every part of what we would°
    Doth make a stand at° what your Highness will.°

---

21 **well-noted** well-known 22 **old form** customary methods 24
fetch about (nautical) take a new tack 25 **frights consideration**
frightens contemplation (raising the whole question of his right to
the crown) 27 **so new a fashioned robe** (1) a robe so newly made,
as opposed to John's original coronation robe (2) a robe of such new
style, as opposed to "plain old form," line 22 29 **confound** disrupt,
destroy 29 **covetousness** (1) desire to do better (2) greed 32
breach tear in a garment, perhaps with a pun on the garment itself
36 **breathed** uttered quietly or hesitantly 37 **we are all well pleased**
(it is becoming increasingly clear that they are not in the least
pleased) 38 **would** would do, wish 39 **Doth make a stand at** stops
at (the limits of) 39 **will** wishes to do

40   *King John.* Some reasons of this double coronation
       I have possessed you with,° and think them strong;
       And more, more strong, when lesser is my fear,
       I shall indue° you with. Meantime but ask
       What you would have reformed that is not well,
45   And well shall you perceive how willingly
       I will both hear and grant you your requests.

       Pembroke. Then I, as one that am the tongue of these
       To sound the purposes° of all their hearts,
       Both for myself and them—but, chief of all,
50   Your safety, for the which, myself and them°
       Bend their best studies°—heartily request
       Th' enfranchisement of Arthur, whose restraint
       Doth move the murmuring lips of discontent
       To break into this dangerous argument:
55   If what in rest° you have, in right you hold,
       Why then° your fears, which, as they say, attend
       The steps of wrong, should move you to mew up
       Your tender kinsman, and to choke his days
       With barbarous ignorance, and deny his youth
60   The rich advantage of good exercise?°
       That the time's enemies° may not have this
       To grace occasions,° let it be our suit,
       That you have bid us ask his liberty,°
       Which for our goods° we do no further ask
65   Than whereupon our weal,° on you depending,
       Counts it your weal he have his liberty.

---

41 **possessed you with** given you   43 **indue** endow, supply   48 **sound the purposes** give sound to the intentions   50 **them** they (themselves?)   51 **Bend their best studies** exert their (our?) hardest efforts   55 **rest** peace   56 **Why then** why, then, is it that   60 **exercise** education in those qualities befitting a gentleman   61 **the time's enemies** those opposed to present arrangements   62 **grace occasions** embellish their excuses or opportunities (for rebellion)   63 **That you ... liberty** (as punctuated here—and in the Folio—Pembroke asks that it be given out that John encouraged them to ask for Arthur's liberty. Many editors, following Rowe, place a comma after "ask" to mean: "let his liberty be the suit you have offered to grant us")   64 **our goods** our own good   65 **whereupon our weal** in so far as our own well-being

Enter Hubert.

King John. Let it be so:° I do commit his youth
   To your direction. Hubert, what news with you?
                        [Takes him aside.]

Pembroke. This is the man should do the bloody deed:
   He showed his warrant to a friend of mine.   70
   The image of a wicked heinous fault
   Lives in his eye; that close aspect° of his
   Does show the mood of a much troubled breast,
   And I do fearfully believe 'tis done,
   What we so feared he had a charge to do.   75

Salisbury. The color of the King doth come and go
   Between his purpose and his conscience,
   Like heralds 'twixt two dreadful battles° set:
   His passion is so ripe, it needs must break.

Pembroke. And when it breaks, I fear will issue thence   80
   The foul corruption° of a sweet child's death.

King John. We cannot hold° mortality's strong hand.
   Good lords, although my will to give is living,
   The suit which you demand is gone and dead.
   He tells us Arthur is deceased tonight.   85

Salisbury. Indeed we feared his sickness was past cure.

Pembroke. Indeed we heard how near his death he
   was,
   Before the child himself felt he was sick:
   This must be answered either here or hence.°

King John. Why do you bend such solemn brows°
   on me?   90

---

67 **Let it be so** (John, seeing Hubert, grants their request on the supposition that Arthur is already dead. Many editors, following Dr.
Johnson, have destroyed this detail by moving the entry to the middle
of line 68)   72 **close aspect** severe appearance, guarded look   78
battles armies drawn up for battle   81 **corruption** pus   82 **hold**
restrain   89 **This must … hence** amends must be made for this
either in this world or the next   90 **bend … brows** scowl

Think you I bear the shears of destiny?°
Have I commandment on the pulse of life?

Salisbury. It is apparent foul play, and 'tis shame
That greatness should so grossly offer it:°
95 So thrive it in your game!° and so, farewell.

Pembroke. Stay yet, Lord Salisbury. I'll go with thee
And find th' inheritance of this poor child,
His little kingdom of a forcèd° grave.
That blood which owed° the breadth of all this isle,
100 Three foot of it doth hold: bad world the while!°
This must not be thus borne; this will break out
To all our sorrows, and ere long, I doubt.°

Exeunt [Lords].

King John. They burn in indignation. I repent.

Enter Messenger.

There is no sure foundation set on blood,
105 No certain life achieved by others' death.
A fearful eye thou hast. Where is that blood
That I have seen inhabit in those cheeks?
So foul a sky clears not without a storm;
Pour down thy weather: how goes all in France?

Messenger. From France to England; never such a
110 pow'r
For any foreign preparation°
Was levied in the body of a land.
The copy of your speed is learned by them:°
For when you should be told they do prepare,
115 The tidings comes that they are all arrived.

King John. O, where hath our intelligence° been
drunk?

91 **shears of destiny** with which Atropos, one of the three Fates, cuts
the thread of life 94 **so grossly offer it** present [such foul play] so
flagrantly 95 **So thrive it in your game** may your schemes come to
the same end 98 **forcèd** enforced, violently brought about 99
blood which owed life which owned 100 **the while** during the time
this can be true 102 **doubt** fear 111 **foreign preparation** force for
foreign invasion 113 **The copy … by them** they have learned to
copy your speed 116 **intelligence** spy service

Where hath it slept? Where is my mother's care,
That such an army could be drawn in France
And she not hear of it?

Messenger.   My liege, her ear
Is stopped with dust: the first of April died   *120*
Your noble mother; and, as I hear, my lord,
The Lady Constance in a frenzy died
Three days° before—but this from rumor's tongue
I idly° heard; if true or false I know not.

King John. Withhold thy speed, dreadful occasion!°   *125*
O, make a league with me, till I have pleased
My discontented peers. What! Mother dead!
How wildly then walks my estate in France!
Under whose conduct came those pow'rs of France
That thou for truth giv'st out are landed here?   *130*

Messenger. Under the Dolphin.

           Enter Bastard and Peter of Pomfret.

King John.   Thou hast made me giddy
With these ill tidings. [*To Bastard*] Now, what says
    the world
To your proceedings? Do not seek to stuff
My head with more ill news, for it is full.

Bastard. But if you be afeard to hear the worst,   *135*
Then let the worst unheard fall on your head.

King John. Bear with me, cousin, for I was amazed°
Under the tide; but now I breathe again
Aloft° the flood, and can give audience
To any tongue, speak it of what it will.   *140*

Bastard. How I have sped° among the clergymen,
The sums I have collected shall express.

---

123 **Three days** (Shakespeare compresses three years to three days)
124 **idly** carelessly, without paying attention   125 **occasion** course
of events   137 **amazed** in a maze, bewildered   139 **Aloft** on top of
141 **sped** fared

But as I travailed° hither through the land,
I find the people strangely fantasied,°
145 Possessed with rumors, full of idle dreams,
Not knowing what they fear, but full of fear.
And here's a prophet that I brought with me
From forth the streets of Pomfret,° whom I found
With many hundreds treading on his heels,
150 To whom he sung, in rude harsh-sounding rhymes,
That ere the next Ascension-day at noon,
Your Highness should deliver up your crown.

King John. Thou idle dreamer, wherefore didst thou
so?

Peter. Foreknowing that the truth will fall out so.

155 *King John.* Hubert, away with him: imprison him,
And on that day at noon, whereon he says
I shall yield up my crown, let him be hanged.
Deliver him to safety° and return,
For I must use thee.

                    [*Exit Hubert with Peter.*]
                    O my gentle° cousin,
160 Hear'st thou the news abroad, who are arrived?

Bastard. The French, my lord; men's mouths are full
of it—
Besides, I met Lord Bigot and Lord Salisbury,
With eyes as red as new-enkindled fire,
And others more, going to seek the grave
165 Of Arthur, whom they say is killed tonight
On your suggestion.

King John.   Gentle kinsman, go,
And thrust thyself into their companies.
I have a way to win their loves again;
Bring them before me.

Bastard.   I will seek them out.

143 **travailed** (1) labored (2) traveled (the words had not yet been separated) 144 **strangely fantasied** filled with strange fancies 148 **Pomfret** Pontefract, in the West Riding of Yorkshire 158 **safety** close custody 159 **gentle** noble, wellborn

King John. Nay, but make haste: the better foot
    before!°   *170*
   O, let me have no subject enemies,
   When adverse foreigners affright my towns
   With dreadful pomp of stout invasion.
   Be Mercury,° set feathers to thy heels,
   And fly, like thought, from them to me again.   *175*

Bastard. The spirit of the time shall teach me speed.

                                         Exit.

King John. Spoke like a sprightful° noble gentleman.
   Go after him, for he perhaps shall need
   Some messenger betwixt me and the peers,
   And be thou he.

Messenger.   With all my heart, my liege. [*Exit.*]   *180*

King John. My mother dead!

                 Enter Hubert.

Hubert. My lord, they say five moons were seen to-
    night:
   Four fixèd, and the fifth did whirl about
   The other four in wondrous motion.

King John. Five moons?

Hubert.   Old men and beldams° in the streets   *185*
   Do prophesy upon it° dangerously;
   Young Arthur's death is common in their mouths,
   And, when they talk of him, they shake their heads
   And whisper one another in the ear,
   And he that speaks doth gripe the hearer's wrist,   *190*
   Whilst he that hears makes fearful action,
   With wrinkled brows, with nods, with rolling eyes.
   I saw a smith stand with his hammer, thus,
   The whilst his iron did on the anvil cool,
   With open mouth swallowing a tailor's news,   *195*

---

170 **the better foot before** as fast as you can   174 **Mercury** messenger of the gods, who wore winged sandals   177 **sprightful** full of spirit   185 **beldams** grandmothers   186 **prophesy upon it** expound its meaning

Who, with his shears and measure in his hand,
Standing on slippers, which his nimble haste
Had falsely thrust upon contrary feet,
Told of a many thousand warlike French,
200   That were embattailèd° and ranked in Kent.
Another lean unwashed artificer
Cuts off his tale and talks of Arthur's death.

King John. Why seek'st thou to possess me with these
    fears?
Why urgest thou so oft young Arthur's death?
205   Thy hand hath murdered him: I had a mighty cause
To wish him dead, but thou hadst none to kill him.

Hubert. No had,° my lord? Why, did you not pro-
    voke° me?

King John. It is the curse of kings to be attended
By slaves that take their humors° for a warrant
210   To break within the bloody house of life,
And on the winking of authority
To understand a law,° to know the meaning
Of dangerous majesty, when perchance it frowns
More upon humor than advised respect.°

215 *Hubert.* Here is your hand and seal for what I did.

King John. O, when the last accompt° twixt heaven
    and earth
Is to be made, then shall this hand and seal
Witness against us to damnation!
How oft the sight of means to do ill deeds
220   Make deeds ill done!° Hadst not thou been by,
A fellow by the hand of nature marked,
Quoted° and signed° to do a deed of shame,

200 **embattailèd** marshaled for battle   207 **No had** had I not   207
provoke urge (order?)   209 **humors** moods, whims   211–12 **on the
winking ... a law** take as law the mere hints (or oversights) of one
in authority   214 **advised respect** deliberate consideration   216 **accompt** account   220 **deeds ill done** (1) evil deeds done (2) deeds
done badly   222 **Quoted** (1) marked, as with a line in the margin of
a book (2) noted, recorded   222 **signed** (1) marked with some dis-
tinguishing characteristic, such as, e.g., the sign of Cain (2) assigned,
appointed

This murder had not come into my mind;
But taking note of thy abhorred aspect,
Finding thee fit for bloody villainy,   225
Apt, liable° to be employed in danger,
I faintly broke with thee of° Arthur's death;
And thou, to be endearèd to a king,
Made it no conscience to destroy° a prince.

Hubert. My lord—   230

King John. Hadst thou but shook thy head or made a
    pause
When I spake darkly° what I purposèd,
Or turned an eye of doubt upon my face,
As° bid me tell my tale in express words,
Deep shame had struck me dumb, made me break
    off,   235
And those thy fears might have wrought fears in me.
But thou didst understand me by my signs
And didst in signs again parley with sin;°
Yea, without stop,° didst let thy heart consent,
And consequently thy rude hand to act   240
The deed, which both our tongues held vile to name.
Out of my sight, and never see me more!
My nobles leave me, and my state is braved,°
Even at my gates, with ranks of foreign pow'rs;
Nay, in the body of this fleshly land,°   245
This kingdom, this confine° of blood and breath,
Hostility and civil tumult reigns
Between my conscience and my cousin's death.

Hubert. Arm you against your other enemies:
I'll make a peace between your soul and you.   250
Young Arthur is alive! This hand of mine
Is yet a maiden and an innocent hand,
Not painted with the crimson spots of blood.

---

226 **liable** suitable 227 **broke with thee of** disclosed to thee my
desire for 229 **Made it no conscience to destroy** had no scruples
about destroying 232 **darkly** obscurely 234 **As** as to 238 **sin** (1)
sin (2) sign 239 **stop** hesitation 243 **braved** challenged 245 **the
body of this fleshly land** my own body (conceived as a microcosm)
246 **confine** limited territory

Within this bosom never entered yet
255 The dreadful motion° of a murderous thought,
And you have slandered nature in my form,°
Which, howsoever rude exteriorly,
Is yet the cover of a fairer mind
Than to be butcher of an innocent child.

King John. Doth Arthur live? O, haste thee to the
260 peers!
Throw this report on their incensèd rage,
And make them tame to their obedience.°
Forgive the comment that my passion made
Upon thy feature, for my rage was blind,
265 And foul imaginary eyes of blood°
Presented thee more hideous than thou art.
O, answer not, but to my closet° bring
The angry lords with all expedient haste.
I conjure° thee but slowly: run more fast. *Exeunt.*

Scene 3. [*Before a castle.*]

Enter Arthur, on the walls.

Arthur. The wall is high, and yet will I leap down.
Good ground, be pitiful and hurt me not!
There's few or none do know me; if they did,
This ship-boy's semblance hath disguised me quite.
5 I am afraid, and yet I'll venture it.
If I get down, and do not break my limbs,
I'll find a thousand shifts° to get away.
As good to die and go, as die and stay.

[*Leaps down.*]

255 **motion** impulse, inclination 256 **form** features 262 **tame to
their obedience** subject to their oaths 265 **imaginary eyes of blood**
(1) John's eyes, imagining bloodshed (2) Hubert's eyes, imagined
bloodthirsty (3) Arthur's eyes, imagined as empty sockets 267
closet private council-chamber 269 **conjure** entreat 4.3.7 **shifts**
tricks

O me! my uncle's spirit is in these stones!
Heaven take my soul, and England keep my bones!   10
                 Dies.

     Enter Pembroke, Salisbury, and Bigot.

Salisbury. Lords, I will meet him at Saint Edmunds-
    bury.°
  It is our safety, and we must embrace
  This gentle offer of the perilous time.

Pembroke. Who brought that letter from the Cardinal?

Salisbury. The Count Meloone, a noble lord of France,   15
  Whose private with° me of the Dolphin's love
  Is much more general° than these lines import.

Bigot. Tomorrow morning let us meet him then.

Salisbury. Or rather then set forward, for 'twill be
  Two long days' journey, lords, or ere° we meet.   20

       Enter Bastard.

Bastard. Once more today well met, distempered°
    lords!
  The King by me requests your presence straight.°

Salisbury. The King hath dispossessed himself of us;
  We will not line his thin bestainèd cloak
  With our pure honors, nor attend the foot   25
  That leaves the print of blood where'er it walks.
  Return and tell him so: we know the worst.

Bastard. Whate'er you think, good words, I think,
    were best.

Salisbury. Our griefs, and not our manners, reason°
    now.

Bastard. But there is little reason in your grief!   30
  Therefore 'twere reason you had manners now.

---

11 **Saint Edmundsbury** Bury St. Edmunds, in Suffolk 16 **private with** private message to 17 **general** comprehensive 20 **or ere** before 21 **distempered** peevish 22 **straight** immediately 29 **reason** control our conduct

Pembroke. Sir, sir, impatience hath his privilege.

Bastard. 'Tis true, to hurt his master, no man else.

Salisbury. This is the prison. [*Sees Arthur.*] What is
    he lies here?

Pembroke. O death, made proud with pure and
35   princely beauty!
    The earth had not a hole to hide this deed.

Salisbury. Murder, as hating what himself hath done,
    Doth lay it open to urge on revenge.

Bigot. Or when he doomed this beauty to a grave,
40   Found it too precious princely for a grave.°

Salisbury. Sir Richard, what think you? You have
    beheld:
    Or have you° read or heard, or could you think,
    Or do you almost think, although you see,
    That° you do see? Could thought, without this
    object,
45   Form such another? This is the very top,
    The height, the crest, or crest unto the crest,
    Of murder's arms:° this is the bloodiest shame,
    The wildest savagery, the vilest stroke,
    That ever wall-eyed° wrath or staring rage°
50   Presented to the tears of soft remorse.°

Pembroke. All murders past do stand excused in this:
    And this, so sole and so unmatchable,
    Shall give a holiness, a purity,
    To the yet unbegotten sin of times,°
55   And prove a deadly bloodshed but a jest,
    Exampled by° this heinous spectacle.

Bastard. It is a damnèd and a bloody work,

---

40 **too ... princely for a grave** (the bodies of royalty were not buried
but placed in monuments) 42 **Or have you** have you either 44
That that which 47 **arms** (1) heraldic insignia (2) power 49 **wall-
eyed** glaring 49 **rage** insanity 50 **remorse** pity 54 **times** future
times 56 **Exampled by** in comparison with

The graceless° action of a heavy° hand,
If that it be the work of any hand.

Salisbury. If that it be the work of any hand!   60
We had a kind of light° what would ensue:
It is the shameful work of Hubert's hand,
The practice° and the purpose of the King—
From whose obedience I forbid my soul,
Kneeling before this ruin of sweet life,   65
And breathing to his breathless excellence
The incense of a vow, a holy vow,
Never to taste the pleasures of the world,
Never to be infected with delight,°
Nor conversant with ease and idleness,   70
Till I have set a glory to this hand,
By giving it the worship of revenge.°

Pembroke. ⎫
Bigot.   ⎬ Our souls religiously confirm thy words.

Enter Hubert.

Hubert. Lords, I am hot with haste in seeking you:
Arthur doth live; the King hath sent for you.   75

Salisbury. O, he is bold and blushes not at death.
Avaunt, thou hateful villain, get thee gone!

Hubert. I am no villain.

Salisbury.   [*Drawing his sword*] Must I rob the law?

Bastard. Your sword is bright, sir; put it up again.

Salisbury. Not till I sheathe it in a murderer's skin.   80

Hubert. Stand back, Lord Salisbury, stand back, I say!

---

58 **graceless** lacking divine sanction, damned   58 **heavy** oppressive, evil   61 **light** intimation (perhaps with the sarcastic connotation of "divinely inspired," following upon the Bastard's "damnèd" and "graceless")   63 **practice** plot   69 **infected with delight** (given these circumstances, delight would be unhealthy)   71–72 **set a glory to ... revenge** put a halo around Arthur's hand (as opposed to Hubert's, in line 62) by showing my veneration through revenge (he will make Arthur a saint by worshiping him as one. Some editors would read "this hand" as Salisbury's own, but that causes difficulties with the religious imagery)

By heaven, I think my sword's as sharp as yours.
I would not have you, lord, forget yourself,
Nor tempt° the danger of my true defense,
85   Lest I, by marking of° your rage, forget
Your worth, your greatness, and nobility.

Bigot. Out, dunghill! dar'st thou brave° a nobleman?

Hubert. Not for my life: but yet I dare defend
My innocent life against an emperor.

Salisbury. Thou art a murderer.

90   *Hubert.*   Do not prove me so:°
Yet° I am none. Whose tongue soe'er speaks false,
Not truly speaks; who speaks not truly, lies.

Pembroke. Cut him to pieces!°

Bastard.   Keep the peace, I say.

Salisbury. Stand by,° or I shall gall° you, Faulconbridge.

95   *Bastard.* Thou wert better gall the devil, Salisbury.
If thou but frown on me, or stir thy foot,
Or teach thy hasty spleen° to do me shame,°
I'll strike thee dead. Put up thy sword betime,°
Or I'll so maul you and your toasting-iron
100   That you shall think the devil is come from hell.

Bigot. What wilt thou do, renownèd Faulconbridge?
Second a villain and a murderer?

Hubert. Lord Bigot, I am none.

Bigot.   Who killed this prince?

---

84 **tempt** test   85 **marking of** (1) observing (2) striking at   87 **brave**
challenge   90 **Do not prove me so** (by forcing me to kill you)
91 **Yet** up to now   93 **Cut him to pieces** (Hubert, as a mere citizen,
is not considered worthy of the dueling code. The lords' honor
demands that they kill him for calling them liars, but they will not
bother to kill him as a gentleman)   94 **by** aside   94 **gall** wound
97 **spleen** ill temper   97 **do me shame** treat me contemptuously (as
you have Hubert)   98 **betime** soon, before it is too late

Hubert. 'Tis not an hour since I left him well:
　I honored him, I loved him, and will weep　　　　　　105
　My date° of life out for his sweet life's loss.

Salisbury. Trust not those cunning waters of his eyes,
　For villainy is not without such rheum,
　And he, long traded° in it, makes it seem
　Like rivers of remorse and innocency.　　　　　　　110
　Away with me, all you whose souls abhor
　Th' uncleanly savors of a slaughterhouse,
　For I am stifled with this smell of sin.

Bigot. Away toward Bury, to the Dolphin there!

Pembroke. There tell the King he may inquire us out.　115
　　　　　　　　　　　　　　　　　Exeunt Lords.

Bastard. Here's a good world! Knew you of this fair
　　work?
　Beyond the infinite and boundless reach
　Of mercy, if thou didst this deed of death,
　Art thou damned, Hubert.

Hubert. Do but hear me, sir—

Bastard.　　　　　　　　Ha! I'll tell thee what:　120
　Thou'rt damned as black—nay, nothing is so
　　black—
　Thou art more deep damned than Prince Lucifer:
　There is not yet so ugly a fiend of hell
　As thou shalt be, if thou didst kill this child.

Hubert. Upon my soul—

Bastard.　　　　　　　If thou didst but consent　125
　To this most cruel act, do but despair,°
　And if thou want'st a cord, the smallest thread
　That ever spider twisted from her womb
　Will serve to strangle thee! A rush will be a beam
　To hang thee on. Or wouldst thou drown thyself,　130
　Put but a little water in a spoon

---

106 **date** period　109 **traded** practiced　126 **do but despair** do nothing other than commit suicide (you are damned already; it is your
only choice)

And it shall be as all the ocean,
Enough to stifle such a villain° up.
I do suspect thee very grievously.

135 *Hubert.* If I in act, consent, or sin of thought,
Be guilty of the stealing that sweet breath
Which was embounded in this beauteous clay,
Let hell want pains enough to torture me!
I left him well.

Bastard.   Go, bear him in thine arms.
140 I am amazed,° methinks, and lose my way
Among the thorns and dangers of this world.
How easy dost thou take all England° up!
From forth this morsel of dead royalty,
The life, the right and truth of all this realm
145 Is fled to heaven, and England now is left
To tug and scamble° and to part by th' teeth°
The unowed interest° of proud swelling state.
Now for the bare-picked bone of majesty
Doth doggèd° war bristle his angry crest
150 And snarleth in the gentle eyes of peace:
Now powers from home and discontents at home
Meet in one line,° and vast confusion waits,
As doth a raven on a sick-fall'n beast,
The imminent decay of wrested pomp.°
155 Now happy he whose cloak and center° can

133 **such a villain** (apparently, the greater the villain, the easier
suicide) 140 **amazed** in a maze, bewildered 142 **all England** (in
calling Arthur "England," the Bastard acknowledges his right to the
throne) 146 **scamble** scramble 146 **part by th' teeth** tear apart as
would a pack of dogs or wolves 147 **unowed interest** (1) unowned
title (2) the interest (duty, obedience) not owed to any king 149
doggèd cruel 151–52 **powers from home ... one line** (a confusing
image: it may mean either that English deserters fight face to face
with English defenders who are themselves discontented, or that
foreign invaders—powers from their homes—are allied in a
single army with English rebels. Both senses are apt, and the complexity is an appropriate preparation for the "vast confusion" which
impends) 154 **wrested pomp** (1) the royal magnificence John
usurped from Arthur (2) the position which his enemies threaten to
wrest from John 155 **center** cincture, belt

Hold out this tempest. Bear away that child,
And follow me with speed: I'll to the King.
A thousand businesses are brief in hand,°
And heaven itself doth frown upon the land.

Exit [*both*].

158 **brief in hand** immediately demanded ("brief," used here in some apparently unique adjectival sense, is perhaps related to the noun meaning "a royal mandate" or "a summary statement".

ACT 5

Scene 1. [*King John's court.*]

Enter King John and Pandulph [with] Attendants.

[*King John gives Pandulph his crown.*]

King John. Thus have I yielded up into your hand
    The circle of my glory.

Pandulph. [*Returning him the crown*] Take again
    From this my hand, as holding of° the Pope,
    Your sovereign greatness and authority.

King John. Now keep your holy word: go meet the
5   French,
    And from his Holiness use all your power
    To stop their marches 'fore we are enflamed.
    Our discontented counties° do revolt;
    Our people quarrel with obedience,
10   Swearing allegiance and the love of soul°
    To stranger blood, to foreign royalty.

5.1.3 **as holding of** as a leasehold from   8 **counties** shires; nobles (?)
10 **love of soul** soul's love, loyalty

This inundation of mistempered humor
Rests by you only to be qualified.°
Then pause not, for the present time's so sick
That present med'cine must be ministered,   15
Or overthrow incurable ensues.

Pandulph. It was my breath that blew this tempest up,
Upon° your stubborn usage of the Pope,
But since you are a gentle convertite,°
My tongue shall hush again this storm of war   20
And make fair weather in your blust'ring land.
On this Ascension-day, remember well,
Upon your oath of service to the Pope,
Go I to make the French lay down their arms. *Exit.*

King John. Is this Ascension-day? Did not the prophet 25
Say that before Ascension-day at noon
My crown I should give off?° Even so I have!
I did suppose it should be on constraint,
But, heaven be thanked, it is but voluntary.

                Enter Bastard.

Bastard. All Kent hath yielded—nothing there holds
  out   30
But Dover Castle—London hath received,
Like a kind host, the Dolphin and his powers.
Your nobles will not hear you, but are gone
To offer service to your enemy;
And wild amazement° hurries up and down   35
The little number of your doubtful° friends.°

King John. Would not my lords return to me again
After they heard young Arthur was alive?

12–13 **This inundation ... qualified** only you can moderate this flood-
ing of the body (of the state) with turbulent humor (in medieval
physiology, health and disposition were considered dependent upon
the balance maintained among four bodily fluids, called humors)
18 **Upon** as a result of   19 **convertite** convert   27 **give off** relinquish
35 **amazement** confusion, uncertainty   36 **doubtful** (1) fearful (2)
untrustworthy   35–36 **hurries ... friends** (either "hurries them up
and down" or "hurries among them")

Bastard. They found him dead and cast into the
        streets,
40   An empty casket, where the jewel of life
        By some damned hand was robbed and ta'en away.

King John. That villain Hubert told me he did live.

Bastard. So, on my soul, he did, for aught he knew.
        But wherefore do you droop? Why look you sad?
45   Be great in act, as you have been in thought;
        Let not the world see fear and sad distrust°
        Govern the motion of a kingly eye;
        Be stirring° as the time; be fire with fire.
        Threaten the threat'ner, and outface° the brow
50   Of bragging° horror: so shall inferior eyes,
        That borrow their behaviors from the great,
        Grow great by your example and put on
        The dauntless spirit of resolution.
        Away, and glister like the god of war
55   When he intendeth to become° the field:
        Show boldness and aspiring confidence!
        What, shall they seek the lion in his den,
        And fright him there? and make him tremble there?
        O, let it not be said! Forage,° and run
60   To meet displeasure farther from the doors,
        And grapple with him ere he come so nigh.

King John. The legate of the Pope hath been with me,
        And I have made a happy° peace with him,
        And he hath promised to dismiss the powers
        Led by the Dolphin.

65 *Bastard.*   O inglorious league!
        Shall we, upon the footing of our land,°
        Send fair-play orders° and make compromise,
        Insinuation,° parley, and base truce
        To arms invasive? Shall a beardless boy,

46 **sad distrust** sorrowful lack of self-confidence 48 **stirring** energetic 49 **outface** defy, stare down 50 **bragging** threatening 55
become grace 59 **Forage** sally forth 63 **happy** blessed, favorable
66 **upon the footing of our land** based upon our native land
67 **fair-play orders** challenges and injunctions following the rules
of chivalry 68 **Insinuation** ingratiating actions

A cockered° silken wanton,° brave° our fields   70
And flesh° his spirit in a warlike soil,
Mocking the air with colors idly° spread,
And find no check? Let us, my liege, to arms!
Perchance the Cardinal cannot make your peace;
Or if he do, let it at least be said   75
They saw we had a purpose of defense.

King John. Have thou the ordering of this present
    time.

Bastard. Away then, with good courage! Yet, I know,
    Our party may well meet a prouder° foe.   *Exeunt.*

Scene 2. [*Bury St. Edmunds. The Dauphin's camp.*]

    Enter, in arms, [Lewis, the] Dauphin, Salisbury,
      Melun, Pembroke, Bigot, [and] Soldiers.

Lewis. My Lord Meloone, let this be copied out,
    And keep it safe for our remembrance;
    Return the precedent° to those lords again,
    That, having our fair order° written down,
    Both they and we, perusing o'er these notes,   5
    May know wherefore we took the sacrament,
    And keep our faiths firm and inviolable.

Salisbury. Upon our sides it never shall be broken.
    And, noble Dolphin, albeit we swear
    A voluntary zeal and an unurged faith   10
    To your proceedings, yet believe me, Prince,
    I am not glad that such a sore of time

---

70 **cockered** pampered   70 **wanton** spoiled child   70 **brave** (1) defy
(2) display his splendid outfit in   71 **flesh** initiate   72 **idly** (1) carelessly (2) uselessly (if they meet no defense)   79 **prouder** (1) more
powerful (2) more splendid (a last scoff at the Dauphin)   5.2.3
precedent original (the "this" of line 1)   4 **fair order** reasonable
terms of agreement

Should seek a plaster° by contemned° revolt,
And heal the inveterate canker° of one wound
15   By making many. O, it grieves my soul
That I must draw this metal° from my side
To be a widow-maker! O, and there
Where honorable rescue° and defense
Cries out upon° the name of Salisbury!
20   But such is the infection of the time
That, for the health and physic° of our right,
We cannot deal° but with the very hand
Of stern injustice and confusèd wrong.
And is 't not pity, O my grievèd friends,
25   That we, the sons and children of this isle,
Were born to see so sad an hour as this
Wherein we step after a stranger, march
Upon her gentle bosom, and fill up
Her enemies' ranks—I must withdraw and weep
30   Upon the spot° of this enforcèd cause—
To grace° the gentry of a land remote,
And follow unacquainted colors° here?
What, here? O nation, that thou couldst remove!°
That Neptune's arms, who clippeth° thee about,
35   Would bear° thee from the knowledge of thyself,
And cripple° thee, unto a pagan shore
Where these two Christian armies might combine
The blood of malice in a vein° of league,
And not to spend it so unneighborly!°

40   *Lewis.* A noble temper dost thou show in this,

---

13 **plaster** medical dressing   13 **contemned** despised   14 **inveterate canker** persistent ulcer   16 **metal** (1) sword (2) mettle, courage   18 **Where honorable rescue** (England) where (the need for) honorable rescue (or, where noblemen needing rescue)   19 **Cries out upon** appeal to   21 **physic** medical treatment   22 **deal** contend   30 **Upon the spot** (1) on the location (2) because of the disgrace   31 **grace** (1) embellish (2) be gracious to, welcome, honor   32 **unacquainted colors** foreign flags   33 **remove** go somewhere else   34 **clippeth** embraces   35 **bear** (1) carry (2) bare, strip   36 **cripple** disable (playing upon the sound-echo of "clippeth")   38 **vein** (1) blood vessel (2) inclination   39 **unneighborly** (meiosis, or understatement for rhetorical effect—Salisbury has created the image of a brutal rape by Neptune which would be preferable to the present "unneighborly" prospect)

And great affections° wrestling in thy bosom
Doth make an earthquake of nobility.
O, what a noble combat hast thou fought
Between compulsion and a brave respect!°
Let me wipe off this honorable dew,   45
That silverly doth progress° on thy cheeks:
My heart hath melted at a lady's tears,
Being an ordinary inundation,
But this effusion of such manly drops,
This show'r, blown up by tempest of the soul,   50
Startles mine eyes, and makes me more amazed
Than had I seen the vaulty top of heaven
Figured quite o'er with° burning meteors.
Lift up thy brow, renownèd Salisbury,
And with a great heart heave away this storm.   55
Commend° these waters to those baby eyes
That never saw the giant-world° enraged,
Nor met with fortune, other than at feasts,
Full warm of blood,° of mirth, of gossiping.
Come, come; for thou shalt thrust thy hand as deep   60
Into the purse of rich prosperity
As Lewis himself: so, nobles, shall you all,
That knit your sinews to the strength of mine.

Enter Pandulph.

And even there, methinks, an angel° spake.
Look where the holy legate comes apace,   65
To give us warrant from the hand of God,

41 **affections** passions (perhaps "affection's" to make "wrestling"
the subject of "Doth") 44 **Between ... respect** between what you
were compelled to do and a courageous (or ostentatious?) consideration (or carefulness) 46 **progress** make a ceremonious journey   53
Figured ... o'er with with a complete pattern of   56 **Commend**
entrust, deliver to the keeping of   57 **giant-world** (1) the baby's
world of giants (2) the large world beyond the baby's perception
59 **Full warm of blood** fully warmed with human feeling   64 **angel**
various possibilities: (1) Lewis himself, punning on "angel" as a coin
(following "purse" and "nobles," a "noble" also being a coin) and
attesting his sincerity (2) Pandulph, who has just arrived with, Lewis
thinks, heavenly assistance (3) a trumpet, which has just announced
Pandulph's arrival

And on our actions set° the name of right
With holy breath.

Pandulph.   Hail, noble prince of France!
The next is this: King John hath reconciled
70 Himself to Rome; his spirit is come in,°
That so stood out against the holy church,
The great metropolis and see of Rome.
Therefore thy threat'ning colors now wind up,
And tame the savage spirit of wild war,
75 That, like a lion fostered up at hand,
It may lie gently at the foot of peace,
And be no further harmful than in show.

Lewis. Your Grace shall° pardon me, I will not back:°
I am too high-born to be propertied,°
80 To be a secondary at control,°
Or useful servingman and instrument
To any sovereign state throughout the world.
Your breath first kindled the dead coal of wars
Between this chastised kingdom and myself,
85 And brought in matter° that should feed this fire;
And now 'tis far too huge to be blown out
With that same weak wind which enkindled it!
You taught me how to know the face of right,
Acquainted me with interest° to this land,
90 Yea, thrust this enterprise into my heart;
And come ye now to tell me John hath made
His peace with Rome? What is that peace to me?
I, by the honor of my marriage bed,
After young Arthur, claim this land for mine,
95 And, now it is half-conquered, must I back
Because that John hath made his peace with Rome?
Am I Rome's slave? What penny hath Rome borne?
What men provided? what munition sent,
To underprop this action? Is 't not I

67 **set** place, as an official seal   70 **is come in** has submitted   78
shall must   78 **back** go back   79 **propertied** treated as a property,
made a means to some other end   80 **a secondary at control** a subordinate under the control of another   85 **matter** (1) fuel (2) arguments   89 **interest** title

That undergo this charge?° Who else but I,   *100*
And such as to my claim are liable,°
Sweat in this business and maintain this war?
Have I not heard these islanders shout out,
"Vive le roi!" as I have banked° their towns?
Have I not here the best cards for the game   *105*
To win this easy match played for a crown?
And shall I now give o'er the yielded set?°
No, no, on my soul, it never shall be said.

Pandulph. You look but on the outside of this work.

Lewis. Outside or inside, I will not return   *110*
Till my attempt so much be glorified
As to my ample hope was promisèd
Before I drew this gallant head of war,°
And culled° these fiery spirits from the world,
To outlook° conquest and to win renown   *115*
Even in the jaws of danger and of death.

                             [Trumpet sounds.]
What lusty trumpet thus doth summon us?

                 Enter Bastard.

Bastard. According to the fair-play° of the world,
Let me have audience; I am sent to speak:
My holy Lord of Milan, from the King   *120*
I come, to learn how you have dealt for him,
And, as you answer, I do know the scope
And warrant limited unto my tongue.°

Pandulph. The Dolphin is too willful-opposite,°
And will not temporize° with my entreaties: *125*
He flatly says he'll not lay down his arms.

---

100 **charge** burden, expense   101 **liable** subject   104 **banked** coasted past (?) built military embankments around (?) (with *Vive le roi!* this is also part of the card-playing metaphor)   107 **set** contest   113 **drew this gallant head of war** assembled this gallant army   114 **culled** selected   115 **outlook** stare down   118 **fair-play** accepted rules for battle   122–23 **as you answer ... tongue** depending upon your answer, I know what I am authorized to say   124 **willful-opposite** obstinately quarrelsome   125 **temporize** make terms

Bastard. By all the blood that ever fury breathed,
          The youth says well. Now hear our English king,
          For thus his royalty doth speak in me:
130   He is prepared, and reason to he should°—
          This apish and unmannerly approach,
          This harnessed masque and unadvisèd revel,°
          This unhaired° sauciness and boyish troops,
          The King doth smile at, and is well prepared
135   To whip this dwarfish war, this° pigmy arms,
          From out the circle of his territories.
          That hand which had the strength, even at your
                    door,
          To cudgel you and make you take the hatch,°
          To dive like buckets in concealèd wells,
140   To crouch in litter° of your stable planks,
          To lie like pawns,° locked up in chests and trunks,
          To hug with swine, to seek sweet safety out
          In vaults and prisons, and to thrill and shake
          Even at the crying of your nation's crow,°
145   Thinking this voice an armèd Englishman—
          Shall that victorious hand be feebled here
          That in your chambers gave you chastisement?
          No! Know the gallant monarch is in arms
          And, like an eagle, o'er his aerie tow'rs,°
150   To souse° annoyance° that comes near his nest.
          And you degenerate, you ingrate revolts,°
          You bloody Neroes,° ripping up the womb
          Of your dear mother England, blush for shame:
          For your own ladies and pale-visaged maids,

130 **reason to he should** there is reason also (too) that he should be
prepared (?) reason to be prepared he indeed has (?) he should also
debate, or give his reasons (?) 132 **harnessed ... revel** masque
performed in armor and misguided entertainment 133 **unhaired**
beardless 135 **this** these 138 **take the hatch** jump over the bottom
of a half-door without pausing to open it (cf. 1.1.171) 140 **litter**
bedding 141 **pawns** articles pawned 144 **crow** cock (the Frenchmen were frightened, so the Bastard claims, by the crowing of the
very Gallic cock which symbolizes France) 149 **tow'rs** (hawking
term) mounts up, soars 150 **souse** (1) dive, swoop down on (2)
beat severely 150 **annoyance** any threat 151 **ingrate revolts** ungrateful rebels 152 **Neroes** (among his other crimes, Nero, the
Roman emperor, was said not only to have murdered his mother
but to have torn open her womb)

Like Amazons, come tripping after drums,	*155*
Their thimbles into armèd gauntlets change,
Their needles° to lances, and their gentle hearts
To fierce and bloody inclination.

Lewis. There end thy brave,° and turn thy face in
	peace.
We grant thou canst outscold us: fare thee well;	*160*
We hold our time too precious to be spent
With such a brabbler.°

Pandulph.	Give me leave to speak.

Bastard. No, I will speak.

Lewis.	We will attend to neither.
Strike up the drums, and let the tongue of war
Plead for our interest and our being here.	*165*

Bastard. Indeed, your drums, being beaten, will cry
	out;
And so shall you, being beaten: do but start
An echo with the clamor of thy drum,
And, even at hand, a drum is ready braced°
That shall reverberate° all, as loud as thine.	*170*
Sound but another, and another shall,
As loud as thine, rattle the welkin's ear
And mock the deep-mouthed thunder: for at hand—
Not trusting to this halting° legate here,
Whom he hath used rather for sport than need—	*175*
Is warlike John; and in his forehead sits
A bare-ribbed death, whose office is this day
To feast upon whole thousands of the French.

Lewis. Strike up our drums to find this danger out.

Bastard. And thou shalt find it, Dolphin, do not doubt.	*180*
					Exeunt.

---

157 **needles** (monosyllable, "neels")   159 **brave** bravado, defiant
boasting   162 **brabbler** brawler   169 **braced** stretched taut (the
drumhead)   170 **reverberate** drive back (both the army and the
echo)   174 **halting** imperfect, shifting

Scene 3. [*A battlefield.*]

Alarums. Enter [King] John and Hubert.

King John. How goes the day with us? O, tell me,
   Hubert.

Hubert. Badly, I fear. How fares your Majesty?

King John. This fever, that hath troubled me so long,
   Lies heavy on me: O, my heart is sick!

Enter a Messenger.

Messenger. My lord, your valiant kinsman, Faulcon-
5   bridge,
   Desires your Majesty to leave the field
   And send him word by me which way you go.

King John. Tell him, toward Swinstead,° to the abbey there.

Messenger. Be of good comfort, for the great supply°
10   That was expected by the Dolphin here,
   Are wracked three nights ago on Goodwin sands.°
   This news was brought to Richard but even now:
   The French fight coldly and retire themselves.

King John. Ay me! this tyrant fever burns me up,
15   And will not let me welcome this good news.
   Set on toward Swinstead; to my litter straight:
   Weakness possesseth me, and I am faint.   *Exeunt.*

5.3.8 **Swinstead** (a mistake, historically, for Swineshead Abbey, in
Lincolnshire) 9 **supply** i.e., of men   11 **Goodwin sands** shoals in
the Straits of Dover

Scene 4. [*Elsewhere on the field.*]

Enter Salisbury, Pembroke, and Bigot.

Salisbury. I did not think the King so stored with
 friends.

Pembroke. Up once again: put spirit in the French;
 If they miscarry, we miscarry too.

Salisbury. That misbegotten devil, Faulconbridge,
 In spite of spite,° alone upholds the day.   5

Pembroke. They say King John, sore sick, hath left
 the field.

Enter Melun wounded.

Melun. Lead me to the revolts of England here.

Salisbury. When we were happy, we had other names.

Pembroke. It is the Count Meloone.

Salisbury.   Wounded to death.

Melun. Fly, noble English, you are bought and sold;°   10
 Unthread the rude eye of rebellion,°
 And welcome home again discarded° faith.
 Seek out King John and fall before his feet:
 For if the French be lords of this loud day,
 He° means to recompense the pains you take   15
 By cutting off your heads! Thus hath he sworn,
 And I with him, and many moe° with me,
 Upon the altar at Saint Edmundsbury,

5.4.5 **In spite of spite** despite any opposition   10 **bought and sold**
duped   11 **Unthread … rebellion** (rebellion as a needle into which
they have threaded themselves)   12 **discarded** (1) cast off (2) badly
carded (their faith as ill-made thread)   15 **He** Lewis   17 **moe** more

Even on that altar where we swore to you
20   Dear amity and everlasting love.

Salisbury. May this be possible? May this be true?

Melun. Have I not hideous death within my view,
Retaining but a quantity° of life,
Which bleeds away, even as a form of wax°
25   Resolveth from his figure° 'gainst the fire?
What in the world should make me now deceive,
Since I must lose the use° of all deceit?
Why should I then be false, since it is true
That I must die here, and live hence, by Truth?°
30   I say again, if Lewis do win the day,
He is forsworn° if e'er those eyes of yours
Behold another day break in the east:
But even this night, whose black contagious breath
Already smokes° about the burning crest
35   Of the old, feeble, and day-wearied sun,
Even this ill night, your breathing shall expire,
Paying the fine° of rated° treachery
Even with a treacherous fine of all your lives,
If Lewis by your assistance win the day.
40   Commend me to one Hubert, with your king:
The love of him, and this respect° besides,
For that° my grandsire was an Englishman,
Awakes my conscience to confess all this.
In lieu whereof,° I pray you bear me hence
45   From forth the noise and rumor° of the field,
Where I may think the remnant of my thoughts
In peace, and part this body and my soul
With contemplation and devout desires.

Salisbury. We do believe thee, and beshrew° my soul

23 **quantity** fragment   24 **form of wax** wax image (such, perhaps,
as might be used by a witch to represent her victim)   25 **Resolveth
from his figure** relaxes its form, melts   27 **use** advantage   29 **die
here … by Truth** (only if he dies undissembling and serving God
can he hope for eternal life in heaven)   31 **is forsworn** will be perjured   34 **smokes** spreads like smoke   37 **fine** penalty (but in the
next line "fine" = end)   37 **rated** (1) evaluated (2) chided   41 **respect** consideration   42 **For that** because   44 **lieu whereof** exchange
for which   45 **rumor** tumult   49 **beshrew** a curse upon

But I do° love the favor and the form°   50
Of this most fair occasion, by the which
We will untread° the steps of damnèd flight,
And like a bated° and retirèd flood,
Leaving our rankness° and irregular course,
Stoop low within those bounds we have o'erlooked,°   55
And calmly run on in obedience
Even to our ocean, to our great King John.
My arm shall give thee help to bear thee hence,
For I do see the cruel pangs of death
Right° in thine eye. Away, my friends! New flight,   60
And happy newness,° that intends old right.
                              Exeunt [assisting Melun].

Scene 5. [*The Dauphin's camp.*]

Enter [Lewis, the] Dauphin, and his train.

Lewis. The sun of heaven methought was loath to set,
But stayed and made the western welkin blush,
When English measured backward their own ground
In faint retire!° O, bravely came we off,°
When with a volley of our needless shot,   5
After such bloody toil, we bid good night
And wound our tott'ring colors clearly up,°
Last in the field, and almost lords of it!

---

50 **But I do** if I do not   50 **favor ... form** appearance   52 **untread**
retrace   53 **bated** subsided   54 **rankness** (1) excessive size (2) impetuous violence (3) offensive odor   55 **Stoop ... o'erlooked** (1)
contract within those banks we have overflowed (2) kneel to accept
those obligations we have disregarded   60 **Right** clearly   61 **happy
newness** appropriate and favorable change   5.5.4 **faint retire** cowardly retreat   4 **bravely came we off** (1) fearlessly and (2) worthily
we left the field   7 **wound our tott'ring colors clearly up** rolled up
our (1) tattered (2) flapping banners without interference

Enter a Messenger.

Messenger. Where is my prince, the Dolphin?

Lewis.   Here. What news?

Messenger. The Count Meloone is slain; the English
10   lords
       By his persuasion are again fall'n off,
       And your supply, which you have wished so long,
       Are cast away and sunk on Goodwin sands.

Lewis. Ah, foul, shrewd° news! Beshrew thy very
       heart!
15   I did not think to be so sad tonight
       As this hath made me. Who was he that said
       King John did fly an hour or two before
       The stumbling° night did part our weary pow'rs?

Messenger. Whoever spoke it, it is true, my lord.

Lewis. Well!° keep good quarter and good care to-
20   night:
       The day shall not be up so soon as I
       To try the fair adventure of tomorrow.   *Exeunt.*

Scene 6. [*Near Swinstead.*]

Enter Bastard and Hubert, severally.°

Hubert. Who's there? Speak, ho! speak quickly, or I
       shoot.

Bastard. A friend. What art thou?

Hubert.   Of the part° of England.

14 **shrewd** grievous, cursed 18 **stumbling** stumbling-causing 20
Well! Good! 5.6.s.d. **severally** i.e., from opposite sides 2 **Of the
part** on the side

Bastard. Whither dost thou go?

Hubert. What's that to thee? Why may not I demand
  Of thine affairs as well as thou of mine?   5

Bastard. Hubert, I think?

Hubert.   Thou hast a perfect° thought.
  I will upon all hazards well believe
  Thou art my friend, that know'st my tongue so well.
  Who art thou?°

Bastard.   Who thou wilt: and if thou please,
  Thou mayst befriend me so much as to think   10
  I come one way of the Plantagenets.

Hubert. Unkind remembrance!° thou and endless
    night
  Have done me shame.° Brave soldier, pardon me,
  That any accent breaking from thy tongue
  Should scape the true acquaintance of mine ear.   15

Bastard. Come, come! sans compliment,° what news
    abroad?

Hubert. Why, here walk I, in the black brow° of
    night,
  To find you out.

Bastard.   Brief, then; and what's the news?

Hubert. O, my sweet sir, news fitting to the night,
  Black, fearful, comfortless, and horrible.   20

Bastard. Show me the very wound of this ill news:
  I am no woman; I'll not swound° at it.

Hubert. The King, I fear, is poisoned by a monk:
  I left him almost speechless, and broke out°

6 **perfect** correct 9 **Who art thou?** (given John's weakness and
Arthur's death, this is now a key question) 12 **remembrance**
(1) reminder (2) memory 12–13 **thou ... shame** (the Bastard,
by recognizing Hubert's voice though Hubert did not recognize
his; the night, by concealing his features) 16 **sans compliment**
without courtly flattery 17 **in the black brow** under the threatening countenance 22 **swound** faint 24 **broke out** left abruptly

25   To acquaint you with this evil, that you might
        The better arm you to the sudden time°
        Than if you had at leisure° known of this.

        Bastard. How did he take it? Who did taste to° him?

        Hubert. A monk, I tell you, a resolvèd° villain
30   Whose bowels suddenly burst out.° The King
        Yet speaks, and peradventure° may recover.

        Bastard. Who didst thou leave to tend his Majesty?

        Hubert. Why, know you not? The lords are all come
             back,
        And brought Prince Henry° in their company,
35   At whose request the King hath pardoned them,
        And they are all about his Majesty.

        Bastard. Withhold thine indignation, mighty God,
        And tempt us not to bear above our power!°
        I'll tell thee, Hubert, half my power° this night,
40   Passing these flats,° are taken by the tide;
        These Lincoln Washes have devourèd them;
        Myself, well mounted, hardly have escaped.
        Away before! Conduct me to the King;
        I doubt° he will be dead or ere° I come.   *Exeunt.*

26 **arm you ... time** prepare yourself (both psychologically and materially) for the crisis   27 **at leisure** without haste   28 **taste to** act as taster for (the taster sampled each dish to detect possible poison)   29 **resolvèd** resolute (he poisoned himself, by tasting, in order to poison the King)   30 **Whose bowels ... out** (cf. the death of Judas in Acts 1:18)   31 **peradventure** perhaps   34 **Prince Henry** John's son (this is the first mention of him in the play)   38 **tempt us not ... power** (1) do not tempt us to undertake more than we can accomplish (2) do not test us by imposing more suffering than we can endure   39 **power** army   40 **these flats** the tidal flats at the mouth of the River Welland in The Wash, a large inlet between Lincolnshire and Norfolk   44 **doubt** fear   44 **or ere** before

Scene 7. [*An orchard at Swinstead Abbey.*]

Enter Prince Henry, Salisbury, and Bigot.

Prince Henry. It is too late: the life of all his blood
　Is touched corruptibly,° and his pure° brain,
　Which some suppose the soul's frail dwelling house,
　Doth, by the idle° comments that it makes,
　Foretell the ending of mortality.   5

Enter Pembroke.

Pembroke. His Highness yet doth speak, and holds
　　belief
　That, being brought into the open air,
　It would allay the burning quality
　Of that fell° poison which assaileth him.

Prince Henry. Let him be brought into the orchard
　　here.   10
　Doth he still rage?°

Pembroke.　　　　　　He is more patient
　Than when you left him; even now he sung.
　　　　　　　　　　　　　　　　[*Exit Pembroke.*]

Prince Henry. O, vanity of sickness! fierce extremes
　In their continuance will not feel themselves.°
　Death, having preyed upon the outward parts,   15
　Leaves them invisible,° and his siege is now
　Against the mind, the which he pricks and wounds
　With many legions of strange fantasies,
　Which, in their throng and press to that last hold,°

5.7.2 **touched corruptibly** infected to the point of decomposition
2 **pure** lucid 4 **idle** irrational 9 **fell** cruel 11 **rage** rave 13–14
fierce ... themselves as the sufferings of a dying man continue he
loses awareness of them 16 **invisible** (modifies "Death," but suggests also, as modifying "outward parts," John's present disregard of
his pains) 19 **hold** stronghold

Confound themselves.° 'Tis strange that death
20   should sing!
I am the cygnet to this pale faint swan,
Who chants a doleful hymn to his own death,°
And from the organ-pipe of frailty sings
His soul and body to their lasting rest.

Salisbury. Be of good comfort, Prince, for you are
25   born
To set a form upon that indigest°
Which he hath left so shapeless and so rude.

[*King*] *John brought in.*

King John. Ay, marry, now my soul hath elbow-room,
It would not out at windows, nor at doors;°
30   There is so hot a summer in my bosom
That all my bowels crumble up to dust!
I am a scribbled form, drawn with a pen
Upon a parchment, and against this fire
Do I shrink up.

Prince Henry.   How fares your Majesty?

King John. Poisoned—ill fare!° dead, forsook, cast
35   off,
And none of you will bid the winter come
To thrust his icy fingers in my maw,
Nor let my kingdom's rivers take their course
Through my burned bosom, nor entreat the north
40   To make his bleak winds kiss my parchèd lips
And comfort me with cold. I do not ask you
much—
I beg cold comfort—and you are so strait,°
And so ingrateful, you deny me that.

20 **Confound themselves** defeat or destroy one another (the fantasies
seeking to capture John's mind so get in each other's way that no
one of them succeeds)   22 **Who ... death** (the swan was fabled to
sing only as it died)   26 **indigest** shapeless confusion   28–29 **now ...
doors** either (1) now my soul has room to escape me, which it
did not have inside the Abbey, or (2) now that my soul has room,
it still refuses to leave my body   35 **ill fare** (1) ill fortune (2) bad
food   42 **strait** narrow, severe, stingy

Prince Henry. O, that there were some virtue° in my
    tears
    That might relieve you!

King John.   The salt in them is hot.   *45*
    Within me is a hell, and there the poison
    Is as a fiend confined to tyrannize
    On unreprievable condemnèd blood.

               Enter Bastard.

Bastard. O, I am scalded° with my violent motion
    And spleen° of speed to see your Majesty!   *50*

King John. O cousin, thou art come to set mine eye!°
    The tackle of my heart is cracked and burnt,
    And all the shrouds° wherewith my life should sail
    Are turnèd to one thread, one little hair:
    My heart hath one poor string to stay it by,   *55*
    Which holds but till thy news be utterèd,
    And then all this thou seest is but a clod
    And module° of confounded° royalty.

Bastard. The Dolphin is preparing hitherward,
    Where God He knows° how we shall answer him,   *60*
    For in a night the best part of my pow'r,
    As I upon advantage did remove,°
    Were in the Washes all unwarily°
    Devourèd by the unexpected flood. [*The King dies.*]

Salisbury. You breathe these dead news° in as dead
    an ear.   *65*
    My liege! my lord!—but now a king, now thus!

Prince Henry. Even so must I run on, and even so
    stop.

44 **virtue** healing power   49 **scalded** overheated, covered with hot
liquid (perspiration)   50 **spleen** impetuous violence, eagerness   51
set mine eye close my eyes after I die   53 **shrouds** (1) ropes holding
a mast in place; with a contextually, but not syntactically, appropriate reminder of (2) winding sheets   58 **module** image   58 **confounded** defeated, destroyed   60 **God He knows** God only knows
62 **upon advantage did remove** seizing the chance changed my location   63 **unwarily** without warning   65 **dead news** (1) deadly news
(2) news of death

What surety° of the world, what hope, what stay,°
When this was now a king, and now is clay?

70 *Bastard.* Art thou gone so? I do but stay behind
     To do the office for thee of revenge,
     And then my soul shall wait on thee to heaven,
     As it on earth hath been thy servant still.°
     Now, now, you stars that move in your right
        spheres,°
     Where be your pow'rs?° Show now your mended
75   faiths,
     And instantly return with me again,
     To push destruction and perpetual shame
     Out of the weak door of our fainting land:
     Straight° let us seek, or straight we shall be sought.
80   The Dolphin rages at our very heels.

Salisbury. It seems you know not, then, so much as we:
     The Cardinal Pandulph is within at rest,
     Who half an hour since came from the Dolphin,
     And brings from him such offers of our peace
85   As we with honor and respect may take,
     With purpose presently to leave this war.

Bastard. He will the rather do it when he sees
     Ourselves well sinewèd to our defense.

Salisbury. Nay, 'tis in a manner done already,
90   For many carriages° he hath dispatched
     To the seaside, and put his cause and quarrel
     To the disposing of the Cardinal,
     With whom yourself, myself, and other lords,
     If you think meet, this afternoon will post°
95   To consummate this business happily.

Bastard. Let it be so; and you, my noble prince,
     With other princes that may best be spared,
     Shall wait upon° your father's funeral.

68 **surety** guarantee, certainty   68 **stay** (1) support (2) continuance
73 **still** constantly   74 **stars . . . spheres** noblemen who have returned
to your proper positions   75 **pow'rs** (1) armed troops (2) astral in-
fluences   79 **Straight** immediately   90 **carriages** wagons   94 **post**
hasten   98 **wait upon** escort ceremonially

Prince Henry. At Worcester must his body be interred,
  For so he willed it.

Bastard.   Thither shall it then.   *100*
  And happily° may your sweet self put on
  The lineal state° and glory of the land!
  To whom, with all submission, on my knee,
  I do bequeath my faithful services
  And true subjection everlastingly.   *105*

Salisbury. And the like tender° of our love we make,
  To rest without a spot° for evermore.

Prince Henry. I have a kind soul that would give
    thanks,
  And knows not how to do it but with tears.

Bastard. O, let us pay the time but needful woe,   *110*
  Since it hath been beforehand with our griefs.°
  This England never did, nor never shall,
  Lie at the proud foot of a conqueror
  But when it first did help to wound itself.
  Now these her princes are come home again,   *115*
  Come the three corners° of the world in arms,
  And we shall shock them!° Naught shall make us
    rue
  If England to itself do rest but true!   *Exeunt.*

FINIS

---

101 **happily** fittingly   102 **lineal state** directly inherited rank (as king), or the crown, etc., denoting that rank   106 **tender** offer   107 **spot** stain (of disloyalty)   110–11 **let us pay … griefs** let us weep no more than necessary since time has anticipated our griefs (providing compensation: the French abandonment of the invasion offsetting the English losses; Henry replacing John)   116 **the three corners** (presumably England is the fourth)   117 **shock them** (1) meet them in battle (2) throw them into confusion (3) tie them in bundles like sheaves (?)

Textual Note

Though mentioned by Francis Meres in 1598, *King John* was not printed until 1623, in the Folio. It has usually been thought that it must have been written between 1591, the publication date of *The Troublesome Reign of King John,* upon which many consider Shakespeare's play to have been based, and 1598, when Meres mentioned it. Since, as the note on sources indicates, I am convinced that it preceded *The Troublesome Reign,* I naturally date Shakespeare's play before 1591, somewhere, probably, between 1588 and 1590. I would think that the writing of the three parts of *Henry VI,* certainly, and of *Richard III,* probably, preceded it, and thus I would differ on the dates of composition for all of these plays from those given in the chart at the beginning of this book. *King John* should be seen as belonging with these early plays but, in its conception, a long step forward from them.

To see *The Troublesome Reign* as based upon Shakespeare's play is not to make it a trustworthy quarto. Its author imitates Shakespeare's plot but has little memory for his lines. The Folio remains the only substantive text.

Such inconsistencies as the Folio text contains suggest that the play was printed from author's manuscript and not from a theatrical promptbook. The chief of these inconsistencies is the Act 2 entry of "a Citizen upon the walls" of Angiers, followed by the speech-heading "Cit." for his first four speeches, after which, in midscene, he becomes "Hubert" for one speech, and then "Hub." Presumably this change represents the author's decision, while writing, to develop the anonymous Citizen into a character of importance to the plot, and such confusion of speech-heading would have been removed from the promptbook. To the detriment of the play, most editors have carried the unnamed Citizen through the act, thus introducing Hubert as a new character in 3.2. Hubert's development as a man forced to take a stand is only clear when we recognize his attempt to avoid involvement during Act 2.

The errors in act and scene headings were presumably made by the compositor. His repetition of "Actus Quartus" where he needed "Actus Quintus" may have been carried over from his copy, but a less obvious confusion would seem most simply explained on the basis of his having misunderstood what he found. "Actus Primus, Scaena Prima" is followed by a "Scaena Secunda" covering more than four double-column pages, to be followed in turn by an "Actus Secundus" covering little more than half of one page, which makes for a total first act of more than seven pages, and a second act of less than one. Editors, following Theobald, have generally turned the "Scaena Secunda" into Act 2, and "Actus Secundus" into Act 3, Scene 1, which necessitates considering the Folio's "Actus Tertius, Scaena prima" a further error. Since Constance throws herself to the ground at the conclusion of "Actus Secundus" and is apparently still there at the opening of "Actus Tertius" (in spite of her being listed as entering with the others), editors have felt justified in making those scenes continuous in spite of the indicated division.

It is much more likely, as Honigmann suggests in the Arden edition, that the compositor mistook a simple manuscript *two* (or *2*, or *II*), meaning Act 2, as indicating Scene 2, reversing the process when he came to the next *two* (or *2*, or *II*) and labeling an intended second scene of Act 2 as though it were the whole act. This edition therefore follows Honigmann and differs from other editors by including a 2.2 and thus beginning 3.1 in accordance with the Folio. Given the continuous action of an Elizabethan production, the presence of Constance seated onstage from one act to the next is not a serious challenge to following the Folio at that point.

Several scholars have noted that, at 3.1.81, the Folio prints "heaven" where the context clearly demands the word "God," and they have suggested that censorship intervened at some point between the original manuscript and the Folio. But editors have not considered the implications of this argument.

In only one other history play, *Henry VIII,* does "heaven" appear more frequently than "God" ("heaven" 44 times,

"God" 21); in *1 Henry VI* and *3 Henry VI* they appear an equal number of times (16 times each in the first, 20 times each in the second); in the other five history plays "heaven" appears 115 times to "God's" 270, with the greatest discrepancy in *Richard III* (29 to 79). In all these plays, the lowest frequency of appearance of the word "God" is the 16 times it appears in *1 Henry VI,* and the highest frequency of the word "heaven" is the 44 times in *Henry VIII.* Compare with these figures the fact that "heaven" appears 51 times in the Folio text of *King John,* while "God" appears only 5 times, and the suggestion of censorship is greatly strengthened.

Such being likely, each appearance of the word "heaven" in this play becomes suspect. 5.7.60 is, as clearly as 3.1.81, an instance in which "God" was the original word. In phrases like "heaven and earth" (2.1.173), "clouds of heaven" (2.1.252), or "heaven or hell" (2.1.407), it is obvious that no change should be made. But this leaves a large group of doubtful instances. On the basis of context (verbal, rhythmic, and dramatic) I have made the change from "heaven" to "God" eight times where it seems thoroughly justified, as noted below. Eleven places where I would also prefer to make the change but, in line with the conservative textual policy of this series, have not done so are: 1.1.83, 84, 256; 2.1.373; 3.1.162, 168, 192 (twice); 4.1.55; 4.3.82; and 5.1.29. Eighteen other places where the change would be possible but where, for contextual reasons (with which others might disagree), I would not make it are: 1.1.70; 2.1.35, 86, 170, 171; 3.1.22, 33, 34, 62; 3.2.37, 68; 3.3.48; 4.1.23, 91, 109; and 4.3.10, 145, 159. (In addition to the three instances mentioned previously, I consider "heaven" obviously correct in 2.1.174; 3.2.44; 3.3.77, 87, 158; 4.2.15, 216; 5.2.52; 5.5.1; and 5.7.72.)

Speech-headings in this edition are regularized by spelling them out in full. Spelling and punctuation have been modernized (conservatively), and obvious typographical errors have been corrected. I have changed to *Dauphin* and *Melun* in stage directions, but have left the old spellings, *Dolphin* and *Meloone,* in the speeches for the sake of pronunciation. Other than these changes, departures from the Folio text are listed below, the adopted reading first, in *italics,* followed by the original, in roman.

1.1.1s.d. *with Chatillion* with the Chattylion   43 *God* heauen   62 *God* heauen   147 *I would* It would   203 *Pyrenean* Perennean   208 *smack* smoake   237 *Could he get me* Could get me

2.1. *Act 2* Scaena Secunda s.d. *King Philip . . . Austria and his Attendants* Philip King of France, Lewis, Daulphin, Austria, Constance, Arthur 1 *King Philip* Lewis [the text several times confuses the French king's name]   18 *Ah, noble boy* A noble boy   63 *Ate* Ace   127 *Than thou and John in manners, being as like* Then thou and Iohn, in manners being as like,   149 *Philip* Lewis   150 *King Philip* Lew.   152 *Anjou* Angiers   201s.d. *Hubert* a Citizen [not identified as Hubert until the speech-heading at line 325]   215 *Confronts your* Comfort yours   259 *roundure* rounder   368 *Hubert.* Fra[nce].   487 *Anjou* Angiers [the error—see also 2.1.152—is probably not the author's, for Angiers is the city excepted in line 489; cf. also line 528, where Folio has "Aniow"]

2.2. *Scene 2* Actus Secundus

3.1.36 *day* daies   74 *task* tast   81 *God* heauen   238 *God* heauen

3.3.64 *friends* fiends

4.1.77 *God's* heauen   91 *mote* moth

4.2.1 *again crowned* against crowned   42 *when* then   73 *Does* Do

4.3.33 *man* mans

5. *Act 5* Actus Quartus

5.2.26 *Were* Was   43 *hast thou fought* hast fought   66 *God* heauen   133 *unhaired* vn-heard

5.5.3 *measured* measure

5.6.37 *God* heauen

5.7.17 *mind* winde   21 *cygnet* Symet   42 *strait* straight   60 *God* heauen

The Sources of
The Life and Death of King John

In 1591, one Sampson Clarke published in London an anonymous two-part play, the lengthy title of which begins *The Troublesome Reign of John, King of England . . .*; many, indeed most, editors and scholars assume this to be the source of Shakespeare's play.* The plots are in fact so similar that, in spite of continual, line-by-line differences,** there are only three logically possible relationships between them: either *King John* (*KJ*) is based on *The Troublesome Reign* (*TR*), or *TR* is based on *KJ,* or each is based on some third play, now missing. Missing sources are tantalizing but rarely of any use; though always logically possible, no such third play need be posited to explain the similarities between the two we have. It is sufficient to assume that one is based upon the other.

But which upon which? *TR* is a play of little verbal distinction with a firm anti-Roman-Catholic bias. It is commonly said that Shakespeare improved the verse and cut down on the anti-Catholicism. At the same time he is said to have been careless with his handling of the plot, so that one must read *TR* to understand *KJ*. For example, the Bastard's annoyance at the marriage of Blanch and Lewis is said to be understandable only when we know that in *TR* Elinor had already promised Blanch to the Bastard. One may, however, reverse such an argument and say that, based upon *KJ, TR*

---

*The Troublesome Reign has frequently been reprinted, most recently in *Six Early Plays Related to the Shakespeare Canon,* edited by E. B. Everitt, *Anglistica,* XIV (Copenhagen, 1965), 143–193; this reprint is the basis for the line references in this note.

**Two lines alone appear unchanged in both plays (*King John* 2.1.528 and 5.4.42 are identical with *The Troublesome Reign* 1.862 and 2.793), but there are other lines which are within a word or phrase of exact repetition—e.g., *King John:* "With them a bastard of the king's deceased" (2.1.65); *The Troublesome Reign:* "Next them a bastard of the king's (deceased)" (1.512). Though divided into two parts, each with its own title page, *The Troublesome Reign* is in fact only a few hundred lines longer than *King John.*

supplies the crudest of (misleading) motivation for what is more meaningful thematically in Shakespeare's play. In *KJ*, the Bastard's annoyance is with the blatant political expediency of the marriage; to reduce this to personal jealousy is to confuse the issue and cheapen the play. (It is noteworthy that Elinor's promise is first, and last, mentioned only when the political marriage has been suggested [*TR:* 1.828–30]; the author of *TR* may well be scraping up a motive for something he has failed to understand.) What is taken as "better plotting" in *TR* can be consistently explained as an expansion and cheapening of Shakespeare's implications.*

One may, in addition, indicate many scenes in which *TR* muddles issues, or reproduces the outline of an action while missing the thematic point. The following are examples:

1. Blanch asks Lewis not to forsake his bride on his wedding day, but says nothing of her divided loyalty.
2. Pandulph and Lewis have their private conference after the departure of King Philip and Constance, but little reason for it remains. The Cardinal's Machiavellian exposition of the complex political necessities (*KJ:*3.4.107–83) is reduced to two lines in an eleven-line scene: "Arthur is safe, let John alone with him!/Thy title next is fair'st to England's crown" (*TR:* 1.1232–33).
3. The Bastard comes onstage, bringing Peter of Pomfret to John, *before*—and remains onstage during—John's decision, openly announced to the nobles, to kill Arthur, which announcement itself precedes Hubert's entry with the (mis)information that Arthur is dead. The Bastard is still onstage when Hubert tells John that Arthur is in fact alive. This removes from the Bastard

---

*Major examples would of course be the *TR* scene (written largely in Skeltonics and thus unlike anything else in the play) during which the Bastard, raiding the monasteries, finds a nun hidden in the abbot's chest and a friar in the nun's, and the attention paid to the monk who poisons John, which diverts attention from the Bastard's choice. This scene of the monk and the abbot (supplying a motivation not taken from Holinshed) takes the place, in fact, of the night meeting of Hubert and the Bastard, which does not occur in *TR*. Similarly, though some find *TR* "more effective" because the Bastard chases Austria and captures Richard's lion-skin, here again *TR* may simply bring into the lines what is implied in *KJ*: if the Bastard enters wearing the lion-skin as well as carrying Austria's head, the point is visual and requires no speeches. His complaint of the heat as he enters is a thoroughly effective reference to what he is wearing. To say more is to detract.

any necessity of making up his mind about either John or Hubert and thus drains most of its meaning from the scene in which he is tested by the finding of Arthur's body.

4. In that scene, the nobles find Arthur's body the moment they come on stage, which—along with their having heard John's announcement—supplies them with a sufficient motive for a treachery which in *KJ* is based upon a tangled skein of suspicion and hypocritical self-seeking, rendering doubly ironic Salisbury's reference to "our pure honors" (*KJ*·4.3.25). *TR* is elementary; *KJ* is morally complex and interesting.

5. The Bastard himself boasts that "King Richard's fortune hangs/ Upon the plume of warlike Philip's [i.e., his own] helm" (2.759–60), but John and the Bastard fight alongside each other against Lewis, without John's structurally important conferring of royal power upon the Bastard ("Have thou the ordering of this present time" *KJ*:5.1.77).

6. The dying Melun has two reasons for revealing Lewis' plot to the English nobles, but only one is common to both plays ("For that my grandsire was an Englishman"—the second of the two identical lines). In *TR*, the other reason is his dramatically trite (however relevant) desire to save his soul, "to leave this mansion free of guilt" (2.791); in *KJ* it is the thematic and ironic complexity of "Commend me to one Hubert, with your king:/ The love of him . . . Awakes my conscience to confess all this" (5.4.40–43). Thus *TR* lacks the entire irony of the nobles' being saved for love of the man they have most scorned.

7. John, at his death, asks for "the frozen Alps,/To tumble on, and cool this inward heat" (2.1089–90), without any of the development which, throughout *KJ,* ties heat and cold, fever and cool zeal, blood and eyes into a web of thematic images.

At each of these points, and many others, it is possible to argue that Shakespeare has improved on a *TR* source; but it is equally possible to argue that *TR* has missed the point of the *KJ* scene upon which it is based. It is possible that Shakespeare omitted scenes from *TR* and developed others; it would seem more likely that the author of *TR,* working not from the text of *KJ* but from his memory of performances, invented material to fill out what he considered opportunities too inviting to be missed, and reproduced some actions and stage groupings of which the meaning in *KJ* had quite escaped him. Apart from *KJ,* it is difficult to see why some of these incidents occur in *TR;* drained of their dramatic meaning, they are fragments, implying, like fossils, that they are remnants of a living organism, not that they are random protoplasm which might be blown into future viability.

And yet, if the author of *TR* was remembering performances of *KJ*—if, however he may have misunderstood it, he is reproducing the action as well as he is—how is it possible that he remembered so few of its words, and those few so flat, so peripheral? Why are there no traces of the metaphors or of the forceful lines which strike us as the most obviously Shakespearean element in *KJ*? The absence of all trace of Shakespeare's characteristic language is surely the strongest of arguments against *TR*'s having been based upon *KJ*. To counter it, one is forced to invent a man with no ear for poetry, no memory for lines, who has at the same time a surprisingly good memory for the scene-by-scene progress of the plot. It is possible to conceive such a man, working perhaps some weeks later from a plot outline made immediately after a performance, but he is an unlikely combination, and it is on the basis of this difficulty that one must say that the source question remains open.

For, in terms of plot development, the evidence seems, to me at least, to go strongly the other way. Consider one final relationship in which *TR* is clearer than *KJ:* the question of John's orders to Hubert. The situation is definitely confusing in Shakespeare's play: John hints to Hubert, first obliquely and then directly, to kill Arthur (3.2.69–77). We therefore assume, when we see Hubert preparing instruments with the help of an unspecified number of brutes (labeled, indeed, "Executioners" by the entries and the speech-headings), that he is about to carry out John's wish. However, it turns out that he is going to blind Arthur instead, and he shows the boy written orders to that effect (4.1.33–39). This is the first surprise; the second comes when, having reported Arthur dead, Hubert is defending himself against John's unjustified anger. Nothing is said of blinding in this scene, and Hubert's "Here is your hand and seal for what I did" (4.2.215) apparently refers to written orders to kill Arthur. Whether we are to assume two differing written orders, or a confusion about the contents of one order is not clear.

This is another situation in which we are told that we must go to *TR* if we are to understand what is happening. There, John puts Arthur into Hubert's custody, saying:

> Hubert, keep him safe,
> For on his life doth hang thy sovereign's crown,
> But in his death consists thy sovereign's bliss.
> Then, Hubert, as thou shortly hear'st from me,
> So use the prisoner I have given in charge.   (1.1176–80)

John clearly has conflicting motives, but he gives no such direct hint as we have in Shakespeare. We cannot be sure what the further orders will be. The scene between Hubert and Arthur keeps us in suspense. (The entry calls for "Hubert de Burgh with three men," and the single speech-heading labels them "Attendants.") Hubert is about to commit some form of violence against Arthur, and we expect that he may be going to kill him, but this is first denied in favor of something worse (1.1425–29), and then Hubert reads the words of the order—"put out the eyes of Arthur Plantagenet" (1443). This settles our doubts, and the scene proceeds to Hubert's ultimate decision not to carry out the order. When Hubert returns to John, the King has just informed the nobles that "The brat shall die" (1737), but this is presumably a new decision, and Hubert brings the (false) news that "According to your Highness' strict command/ Young Arthur's eyes are blinded and extinct" (1744–45), adding that he died of the "extreme pain" (1747). This twist is in accordance with Hubert's plan (1520–21), and is presumably a way of covering his failure to obey orders. Whether he is intending to help Arthur escape, or merely to keep him hidden, is not mentioned. Finally, however, when John curses Hubert—"Furies haunt thee still/For killing him whom all the world laments" (1797–98)—Hubert's reply, "Why here's—my lord—your Highness' hand and seal,/ Charging on life's regard to do the deed!" (1799–1800), would seem, as in *KJ*, to refer to an order for Arthur's death and not to the document shown to Arthur at the time. Here is the same confusion; without comparing the scene with *KJ*, however, one might be willing to take "the deed" as blinding.

At any rate, apart from this final detail, the development is logical in *TR,* while it is confused in its major outline in *KJ,* and the argument goes that this is further evidence that *TR* was the original. If so, we have the curious Shakespeare of certain textual scholars, the man who grew toward mastery of his craft through carelessness in handling a perfectly clear source. That Shakespeare was sometimes careless—that he was careless here—there is no doubt; but his carelessness is of a differing kind if he is not following a source which has already solved the problem he then creates. Which is more likely: that an author finding confusion in his source would attempt to straighten it out? or that an author finding clarity would muddle it? It would appear, *prima facie,* more likely that *TR* followed *KJ* than that *KJ* followed *TR. TR'*s improvement at this point is of a piece with its supplying of motivation for the Bastard's resentment of Blanch's marriage, its supplying of a scene in the monastery and a scene dealing with John's poisoner; the author of *TR* was developing what appeared to him faulty or insufficient. The difference is that in the orders to Hubert there was a genuine confusion which, indeed, he only partially resolved.

How then, if I am arguing for the general superiority of Shakespeare's text and the superficiality of *TR'*s "improvements," how then do I account for the confusion of Shakespeare's handling of these scenes? First, it must be clear that any "inferiority" is in the single matter of inconsistent orders; the scenes are vastly superior in every other respect. Only the presence of the inconsistency needs explanation.

It would be difficult to account for the inconsistency if *KJ* were in fact based upon *TR.* However, the contradiction comes right out of Holinshed:

> True it is that great suit was made to have Arthur set at liberty, as well by the French king as by William de Riches, a valiant baron of Poictou, and divers other noblemen of Brittany, who, when they could not prevail in their suit, banded themselves together and, joining in confederacy with Robert, Earl of Alençon, the Viscount Beaumont, William de Fulgiers, and others, they began to levy sharp wars against King John in divers places, insomuch (as it was thought) that so long as Arthur lived there would be no quiet in those parts; whereupon

it was reported that King John, through persuasion of his counselors, appointed certain persons to go to Falais, where Arthur
was kept in prison, under the charge of Hubert de Burgh, and
there to put out the young gentleman's eyes.

The point is that the move from "so long as Arthur lived" to
the order to "put out the young gentleman's eyes" is not logical in Holinshed, which thus provides a basis for the lack
of logic in *KJ*. Furthermore, it is clear that Shakespeare's
attention has been caught less by the illogicality, which he
reproduces, than by the dramatic possibilities, especially the
possibilities for thematic development of both stage and
verse imagery in the attack by the "hot irons" of brute power
upon the helpless eyes of suffering innocence. Shakespeare
would not then be seen as a playwright who carelessly muddled a structure that was clear, as a botcher of someone
else's play, but as an artist creating drama from the raw
material of the chronicle. The structure he gave *KJ*, the structure indicated in my introduction, is his own; it is not in
Holinshed, and it is mangled by *TR*. If he has taken over this
one illogicality from his source, it is because his attention at
that point was focused so firmly on the poetic possibilities.
He was attempting to write a new kind of play, a play with a
dramatic structure, not just a chronicle history; the man who
tried to reproduce it in *TR* quite missed Shakespeare's point.
He thought he was dealing with another play like one of the
parts of *Henry VI*, and indeed the same man may have been
responsible for all three quartos.

For *TR* may be seen as having the same relationship to *KJ*
as *The First part of the Contention betwixt the two famous
Houses of Yorke and Lancaster* and *The True Tragedie of
Richard Duke of Yorke* have to the second and third parts
of *Henry VI*. Long considered to have been the sources of
Shakespeare's plays, these are now generally acknowledged
to have been "bad quartos," versions of Shakespeare's plays
concocted on the basis of some familiarity with performances
of them. *TR* may well be a bad quarto of similar origin; it
need not be Shakespeare's source.

That Holinshed is Shakespeare's source, or one of his
sources, is further attested (to give one or two of a multitude

of examples) by the page in the chronicle at which we last looked. The succeeding paragraph concludes:

> Howbeit, to satisfy his mind for the time and to stay the rage of the Britains [men of Brittany], he [Hubert de Burgh] caused it to be bruited abroad through the country that the King's commandment was fulfilled, and that Arthur also, through sorrow and grief, was departed out of this life. For the space of fifteen days this rumor incessantly ran through both the realms of England and France, and there was ringing for him through the towns and villages as [though] it had been for his funeral.

Two pages earlier in Holinshed is the account of the spectacle of the five moons, but it is given no interpretation. Shakespeare brings these two items together in Hubert's report:

> *King John.* Five moons?
> *Hubert.*   Old men and beldams in the streets
>   Do prophesy upon it dangerously;
>   Young Arthur's death is common in their mouths . . .
>
>   (4.2.185–87)

And the Bastard has already reported: "I find the people strangely fantasied,/Possessed with rumors . . ." (144–45). There is nothing of these rumors in *TR;* had that been Shakespeare's source, he would still have to be seen as having gone also to Holinshed. Similarly, Holinshed probably accounts for Shakespeare's use of the word "commodity." The Bastard has no Commodity soliloquy in *TR.* Just after Holinshed's mention of the fall of Angiers, however, we find:

> The French king all this while conceiving another exploit in his head, more commodious to him than as yet to attempt war against the Englishmen upon so light an occasion, dissembled the matter . . .

It is in this coupling of "commodious" with dissembling that I would see the origin of Shakespeare's use of "commodity." Again, if he were using *TR,* he would still have to be seen as going to Holinshed. That is the position to which some scholars have in fact now arrived. If Shakespeare used Holinshed, however, he had no need of *TR,* while *TR* is difficult to explain on the basis of Holinshed without *KJ*—though its author did refer to some chronicle or other for a few details that Shakespeare had not used (the full name Hubert de Burgh; Chester and Beauchamp as the names of additional barons, etc.). Though neither case has yet been proved, I join Professors Alexander and Honigmann in thinking that the conflicting evidence tends to converge upon Holinshed as Shakespeare's major source and *TR* as a bad quarto.

Here for once we do not need to decide between Holinshed's chronicle and Hall's, for Hall does not deal with the reign of John. However, in inventing the character of the Bastard, based on a brief mention in Holinshed, it is clear that Shakespeare recalled an incident in Hall which he already knew in connection with his writing of *1 Henry VI.* He may have associated the name Faulconbridge with a bastard on the basis of another passage in Hall which he had used in *3 Henry VI.* There he has Margaret say, "Stern Faulconbridge commands the narrow seas" (1.1.239); in Hall, this man is identified as "one Thomas Nevel, bastard son to Thomas, Lord Faulconbridge, the valiant captain, a man of no less courage than audacity (who for [in spite of] his evil conditions was such an apt person that a more meet could not be chosen to set all the world in a broil, and to put the estate of the realm on an ill hazard), had of new begun a great commotion. This bastard was before this time appointed by the Earl of Warwick to be Vice-Admiral of the sea, . . ." Hall describes a foolhardy rebel against Edward IV; in Margaret's speech he is, of course, a faithful partisan of Henry VI. Since we know Shakespeare to have been working with this chronicle material for his preceding plays, we have here additional weight for the argument that he is the one who invented the Bastard of *KJ* as the blunt and dauntless Englishman. (This association in turn probably accounts for his giving the name Faulconbridge to Portia's English suitor, "a proper man's picture" but untaught in other languages, in *The Merchant of Venice* 1.2. Shakespeare used the name elsewhere—Longaville's Maria is "an heir of Faulconbridge" in *Love's Labor's Lost* [2.1.204]—but with no strikingly obvious reason for the choice.)

Though there are possibly other sources from which Shakespeare picked up a detail or two (Bullough reproduces several, as well as *TR,* in volume IV of *Narrative and Dramatic Sources of Shakespeare*), they are not central to the play. *TR* is much more easily available to those who may wish to study the source problem than is the full text of the relevant portion of Holinshed. Where Holinshed has been reproduced, the selections relating to *KJ* have been kept to a minimum. For this reason, and because I have come to consider the case for Shakespeare's use of Holinshed stronger than the case for his use of *TR,* I append here much more of the Holinshed account of John than is elsewhere available in a modern edition. It is presented here in the order in which it occurs in Holinshed, not in the order of the play. The short portion from Hall is also appended, the texts of both having been modernized somewhat in spelling and punctuation.

Though the source question remains unsettled, and a serious investigator must naturally study *TR* also, I consider the material appended here to have been the point of departure for Shakespeare's creative imagination in *KJ.* As in comparing any of his plays with their literary sources—as in comparing the earlier history plays or the later *Macbeth* with other portions of the same chronicles—our interest lies not simply in the source itself as a literary curiosity, but in seeing what Shakespeare used, omitted, modified or invented. It is in understanding his selective approach to a source that we can perhaps come closest to understanding how that creative imagination quickened raw substance into a work of art.

From Chronicles of England, Scotland, and Ireland (1587)

[1190] Now to return to the King [Richard I], who in this meantime was very busy to provide all things necessary to set forward on his journey [to the Holy Land]; his ships which lay in the mouth of the river of Seine being ready to put off, he took order in many points concerning the state of the commonwealth on that side, and chiefly he called to mind that it should be a thing necessary for him to name who should succeed him in the kingdom of England if his chance should not be to return again from so long and dangerous a journey. He therefore named (as some suppose) his nephew Arthur, the son of his brother Geoffrey, Duke of Brittany, to be his successor in the kingdom, a young man of likely proof and princely towardness, but not ordained of God to succeed over this kingdom. . . .

[1193] In the meanwhile, the French king being advertised that King Richard was detained a prisoner, rejoiced not a little thereat, and with all speed by secret messages did send for his [Richard's] brother Earl John, who was ready to come at his call. And being come, he exhorted him not to suffer so convenient an occasion to pass, but to take the government of the realm of England now into his hands, promising him all such aid as he could of him reasonably require, with other like talk still tending to the provocation of the Earl to forsake his allegiance to his brother. And to say the truth, Earl John was easily persuaded so to do. . . .

[1195] . . . Then was a motion made for peace betwixt the two kings [Richard and Philip], being now wearied with long wars: whereof when Earl John was advertised, who (as it should seem by some writers) having tarried with the French king till this present, began now to doubt lest if any agreement were made he might haply be betrayed by the French king by covenants that should pass betwixt them. He determined therefore with himself to commit his whole safety to his natural brother and to no man else, perceiving that the French king made not so great account of him after the loss of his castles in England as he had done before. . . .

But by some writers it should appear that Earl John, immediately upon conclusion of the first truce, came from the French king and submitted himself to his brother, and by mediation of the queen their mother was pardoned, received again into favor, and served ever after against the French king very dutifully, seeking by newly achieved enterprises brought about (to the contentment of his brother) to make a recompense for his former misdemeanor, reputing it mere madness to make means to further mischief. . . .

[1196] About this time also as the Countess of Brittany, the mother of Duke Arthur, came into Normandy to have spoken with King Richard, Ranulph, Earl of Chester, her husband, meeting her at Pontorson, took her as prisoner and shut her up within his castle at S. James de Beumeron. And when her son Arthur could not find means to deliver her out of captivity, he joined the King of France and made great havoc in the lands of his uncle, King Richard, whereupon the King gathered a mighty army and, invading Brittany with great force, cruelly wasted and destroyed the country. . . .

[1199] . . . To be short, feeling himself to wax weaker and weaker, preparing his mind for death, which he perceived now to be at hand, he ordained his testament, or rather reformed and added sundry things to the same which he before had made, at the time of his going forth towards the Holy Land.

To his brother John he assigned the crown of England, and all other his lands and dominions, causing the nobles there present to swear fealty to him. . . .

At length King Richard by force of sickness (increased

with the anguish of his incurable wound) departed this life on the Tuesday before Palm Sunday, being the ninth of April, and the eleventh day after he was hurt, in the year after the birth of our Savior 1199, in the forty-fourth year of his age, and after he had reigned nine years, nine months, and odd days. He left no issue behind him. He was tall of stature and well proportioned, fair and comely of face, so as in his countenance appeared much favor and gravity, of hair bright auburn, as it were betwixt red and yellow, with long arms, and nimble in all his joints; his thighs and legs were of due proportion, and answerable to the other parts of his body.

As he was comely of person, so was he of stomach more courageous and fierce, so that not without cause he obtained the surname of *Coeur de Lion,* that is to say, The Lion's-heart. Moreover he was courteous to his soldiers, and towards his friends and strangers that resorted to him very liberal, but to his enemies hard and not to be entreated, desirous of battle, an enemy to rest and quietness, very eloquent of speech and wise, but ready to enter into jeopardies, and that without fear or forecast in time of greatest perils.

These were his virtuous qualities, but his vices (if his virtues, his age, and the wars which he maintained were thoroughly weighed) were either none at all, or else few in number, and not very notorious. He was noted of the common people to be partly subject to pride, which surely for the most part follows stoutness of mind; of incontinency, to the which his youth might haply be somewhat bent; and of covetousness, into the which infamy most captains and such princes as commonly follow the wars do oftentimes fall, when of necessity they are driven to exact money, as well of friends as enemies, to maintain the infinite charges of their wars. . . .

John, the youngest son of Henry the Second, was proclaimed King of England, beginning his reign the sixth day of April, in the year of our Lord 1199, the first of Philip, Emperor of Rome, and the twentieth of Philip, King of France, King William as yet living in government over the Scots. This man, so soon as his brother Richard was deceased, . . . went to Chinon, where his brother's treasury lay, which was forthwith delivered to him by Robert de Turnham: and therewith all the castle of Chinon and Saumur and divers other places, which were in the custody of the foresaid Robert. But Thomas de Furnes, nephew to the said Robert de Turnham, delivered the city and castle of Angiers to Arthur, Duke of Brittany. For by general consent of the nobles and peers of the countries of Anjou, Maine, and Touraine, Arthur was received as the liege and sovereign lord of the same countries.

For even at this present, and so soon as it was known that King Richard was deceased, divers cities and towns on that side of the sea [English Channel], belonging to the said Richard while he lived, fell at odds among themselves, some of them endeavoring to prefer King John, others laboring rather to be under the governance of Arthur, Duke of Brittany, considering that he seemed by most right to be their chief lord, forsomuch as he was son to Geoffrey, elder brother to John. And thus began the broil in those quarters, whereof in process of time ensued great inconvenience, and finally the death of the said Arthur, as shall be shown hereafter.

Now while King John was thus occupied in recovering his brother's treasury and travailing [or traveling] among his subjects to reduce them to his obedience, Queen Elinor, his mother, by the help of Hubert, Archbishop of Canterbury, and others of the noblemen and barons of the land, travailed [or traveled] as diligently to procure the English people to receive their oath of allegiance to be true to King John. . . .

. . . For she, being bent to prefer her son John, left no stone unturned to establish him in the throne, comparing oftentimes the difference of government between a king that is a man and a king that is but a child. For as John was 32 years old, so Arthur, Duke of Brittany, was but a baby to speak of. In the end, winning all the nobility wholly to her will, and seeing the coast to be clear on every side, without any doubt [fear] of tempestuous weather likely to arise, she signified the whole matter to King John, who forthwith framed all his endeavors to the accomplishment of his business.

Surely Queen Elinor, the King's mother, was sore against her nephew Arthur, rather moved thereto by envy conceived against his mother than upon any just occasion given in the behalf of the child, for she saw, if he were king, how his mother Constance would look to bear most rule within the realm of England, till her son should come to lawful age to govern of himself. . . .

When this doing of the Queen was signified to the said Constance, she, doubting the surety of her son, committed him to the trust of the French king who, receiving him into his tuition, promised to defend him from all his enemies, and forthwith furnished the [strong]holds in Brittany with French soldiers. Queen Elinor, being advertised hereof, stood in doubt by and by of her country of Guienne, and therefore with all possible speed passed over the sea and came to her son John in Normandy, and shortly [there]after they went forth together into the country of Maine, and there took both the city and castle of Mauns, throwing down the walls and turrets thereof, with all the fortifications and stonehouses in and about the same, and kept the citizens as prisoners because they had aided Arthur against his uncle John.

After this, King John, entering into Anjou, held his Easter at Beaufort . . . and from thence went to Rouen, where on the Sunday next after Easter, being Saint Mark's Day, he was girded with the sword of the Duchy of Normandy in the high church there by the hands of Walter, Archbishop of Rouen. And so, being invested Duke of Normandy, received the oath according to the custom, that he should defend the church and maintain the liberties thereof, see justice administered, good laws put into execution, and naughty [evil, worthless] laws and orders abolished. In the meantime his mother, Queen Elinor, together with Captain Marchades, entered into Anjou and wasted [laid waste] the same, because they of that country had received Arthur for their sovereign lord and governor. And amongst other towns and fortresses, they took the city of Angiers, slew many of the citizens, and committed the rest to prison.

This enterprise being thus luckily achieved, the residue of the people in those parts were put in such fear that of their own accord they turned to their wonted obedience, seeming as though they would continue still therein. The French king all this while conceiving another exploit in his head, more commodious to him than as yet to attempt war against the Englishmen upon so light an occasion, dissembled the matter for a time, as though he would know nothing of all that was done, till the King should be otherwise occupied in England about his coronation.

In the mean season, King John having set some stay in his business on the further side of the sea, he left his mother still in Guienne to defend that country against the enemies and, taking the sea, came over himself into England, landing at Shoreham, the 25th day of May. On the next day, being Ascension Eve, he came to London there to receive the crown. . . .

. . . The same day of his coronation also, he invested . . . Geoffrey Fitz Peter with the sword of the Earldom of Essex. . . .

While these things were adoing in England, Philip, King of France, having levied an army, broke into Normandy and took the city of Évreux, the town of Arques, and divers other places from the English. And passing from thence into Maine, he reconquered that country lately before through fear alienated. In another part, an army of Britains [men of Brittany] with great diligence won the towns of Gorney, Butevant, and Gensolin and, following the victory, took the city of Angiers, which King John had won from Duke Arthur in the last year passed. These things being signified to King John, he thought to make provision for the recovery of his losses there with all speed possible. . . .

. . . the two kings . . . came to a communication and took truce for fifty days. . . .

About the same time, King Philip of France made Arthur, Duke of Brittany, knight, and received of him his homage for Anjou, Poictiers, Maine, Touraine, and Brittany. Also somewhat before the time that the truce should expire, to wit, on the morrow after the feast of the Assumption of our Lady, and also the day the next following, the two kings talked by commissioners in a place betwixt the towns of Butevant and Guleton. Within three days after, they came together personally and communed at length of the variance depending between them. But the French king showed himself stiff and hard in this treaty, demanding the whole country of Veulquessine to be restored to him, as that which had been granted by Geoffrey, Earl of Anjou, the father of King Henry the Second, to Lewis le Grosse, to have his aid then against King Stephen. Moreover he demanded that

Poictiers, Anjou, Maine, and Touraine should be delivered and wholly resigned to Arthur, Duke of Brittany.

But these, and divers other requests which he made, King John would not in any wise grant, and so they departed without conclusion of any agreement. . . .

. . . All this while was William de Roches busily occupied about his practice to make King John and his nephew Arthur friends, which thing at length he brought about, and thereupon delivered into King John's hands the city of Mauns, which he had in keeping. . . . But in the night following, upon some mistrust and suspicion gathered in the observation of the covenants on King John's behalf, both the said Arthur and his mother Constance, the said Viscount of Tours, and divers others, fled away secretly from the King and got them to the city of Angiers, where the mother of the said Arthur, refusing her former husband, the Earl of Chester, married herself to the Lord Guy de Tours, brother to the said viscount, by the Pope's dispensation. The same year, Philip, bastard son to King Richard, to whom his father had given the castle and honor of Cognac, killed the Viscount of Limoges, in revenge of his father's death, who was slain (as you have heard) in besieging the castle of Châlus Cheverell. . . .

[1200] . . . Finally upon Ascension Day in the second year of his reign, [John and Philip] came again to a communication betwixt the towns of Vernon and Lisle Dandely, where finally they concluded an agreement, with a marriage to be had betwixt Lewis, the son of King Philip, and the Lady Blanch, daughter to Alfonso, King of Castile, the eighth of that name, and niece to King John by his sister Elinor.

In consideration whereof, King John, besides the sum of thirty thousand marks in silver, as in respect to the dowry assigned to his said niece, resigned his title to the city of Évreux, and also to all those towns which the French king had by war taken from him, the city of Angiers only excepted, which city he received again by covenants of the same agreement. The French king restored also to King John (as Ralph Niger writes) the city of Tours and all the castles and fortresses which he had taken within Touraine: and moreover received of King John his homage for all the lands, fees, and tenements which at any time his brother, King Richard, or his father, King Henry, had held from him, the said King Lewis [Philip?] or any of his predecessors, the quit claims and marriages always excepted. The King of England likewise did homage to the French king for Brittany, and again (as after you shall hear) received homage for the same country, and for the county of Richmont from his nephew Arthur. . . .

By the conclusion of this marriage betwixt the said Lewis and Blanch, the right of King John went away, . . . the right of all which lands, towns, and countries was released to the King of France by King John, who supposed that by his affinity and resignation of his right to those places, the peace now made would have continued forever. And in consideration thereof, he procured furthermore that the foresaid Blanch should be conveyed into France to her husband with all speed. That done he returned into England.

. . . such was the malice of writers in time past, which they bore towards King John, that whatsoever was done in prejudice of him or his subjects, it was still interpreted to chance through his default, so as the blame still was imputed to him, insomuch that though many things he did perhaps in matters of government for the which he might be hardly excused, yet to think that he deserved the tenth part of the blame wherewith writers charge him, it might seem a great lack of advised consideration in them that so should take it. But now to proceed with our purpose.

King John, being now at rest from wars with foreign enemies, began to make war with his subjects' purses at home, emptying them by taxes and tallages to fill his coffers, which alienated the minds of a great number of them from his love and obedience. At length also, when he had got together a great mass of money, he went over again into Normandy, where, by Helias, Archbishop of Bordeaux and the Bishop of Poictiers and Scone, he was divorced from his wife Isabell, that was the daughter of Robert, Earl of Gloucester, because of the nearness of blood, as touching her in the third degree. After that, he married Isabell, the daughter of Amery, Earl of Angoulême, by whom he had two sons,

Henry and Richard, and three daughters, Isabell, Elinor and Jane. . . .

. . . About the same time, King John and Philip, King of France, met together near the town of Vernon, where Arthur, Duke of Brittany (as vassal to his uncle, King John) did his homage to him for the Duchy of Brittany and those other places which he held from him on this side and beyond the river Loire, and afterward still mistrusting his uncle's courtesy, he returned back again with the French king, and would not commit himself to his said uncle, who (as he supposed) did bear him little good will. These things being thus performed, King John returned to England and there caused his newly married wife, Isabell, to be crowned on the Sunday before the feast of Saint Denise, the eighth of October.

At the same time he gave commandment to Hugh Nevill, high justice of his forests, that he should . . . give warning to all the white monks [Benedictines] that . . . they should remove out of his forests all their horses . . . and other cattle under the penalty to forfeit so many of them as after that day chanced to be found within the same forests. The cause that moved the King to deal so hardly with them was that they refused to help him with money when, before his last going over into Normandy, he demanded it of them. . . .

About the month of December there were seen in the province of York five moons, one in the east, the second in the west, the third in the north, the fourth in the south, and the fifth as it were set in the midst of the others, having many stars about it, and [they] went five or six times encompassing the other, as it were the space of one hour, and shortly after vanished away. The winter after was extremely cold, more than the natural course had been aforetime. And in the springtime came a great glutting and continual rain, causing the rivers to rise with higher floods than they had been accustomed. . . .

[In 1201, Philip received John in Paris with great honor, but in 1202 Philip again asserted Arthur's rights and attacked John.]

. . . the young Arthur, being encouraged with this new supply of associates, went first into Touraine, and after[wards] into Anjou, compelling both those countries to submit themselves to him, and proclaimed himself earl of those places, by commission and grant obtained from King Philip.

Queen Elinor, that was regent in those parts, being put in great fear with the news of this sudden stir, got her into Mirabeau, a strong town situated in the country of Anjou, and forthwith dispatched a messenger with letters to King John, requiring his speedy succor in this her present danger. In the meantime, Arthur, following the victory, shortly after[wards] followed her, and won Mirabeau, where he took his grandmother within the same, whom he yet intreated very honorably and with great reverence (as some have reported). But others write far more truly that she was not taken, but escaped into a tower, within which she was straitly besieged. Thither came also to aid Arthur all the nobles and men of arms in Poictou, and namely the foresaid Earl of March, according to the appointment between them, so that by this means Arthur had a great army together in the field.

King John in the meantime, having received his mother's letters and understanding thereby in what danger she stood, was marvelously troubled with the strangeness of the news, and with many bitter words accused the French king as an untrue prince and a fraudulent league-breaker, and in all possible haste he sped forth, continuing his journey for the most part both day and night to come to the succor of his people. To be brief, he used such diligence that he was upon his enemies' necks ere they could understand anything of his coming or guess what the matter meant when they saw such a company of soldiers as he brought with him to approach so near the city. . . .

This their fear being apparent to the Englishmen (by their disorder shown in running up and down from place to place with great noise and turmoil), they set upon them with great violence, and, compassing them round about, they either took them or slew them in a manner at their pleasure. And having thus put them all to flight, they pursued the chase towards the town of Mirabeau, into which the enemies made very great haste to enter; but such speed was used by the English soldiers at that time that they entered and won the said town before their enemies could come near to get into it. Great slaughter was made within Mirabeau itself, and

Arthur, with the residue of the army that escaped with life
from the first bickering, was taken, who being hereupon
committed to prison, first at Falais and after[wards] within
the city of Rouen, lived not long after, as you shall hear. The
other of the prisoners were also committed to safekeeping,
some into castles within Normandy, and some were sent into
England. . . .

The French king, at the same time lying in siege before
Arques, immediately upon the news of this overthrow raised
from thence and returned homewards, destroying all that
came in his way till he was entered into his own country. It
is said that King John caused his nephew Arthur to be
brought before him at Falais, and there went about to persuade him all that he could to forsake his friendship and
alliance with the French king, and to lean and stick to him,
being his natural uncle. But Arthur, like one that wanted
good counsel, and abounding too much in his own willful
opinion, made a presumptuous answer, not only denying so
to do but also commanding King John to restore to him the
realm of England, with all those other lands and possessions
which King Richard had in his hand at the hour of his death.
For since the same appertained to him by right of inheritance, he assured him, except restitution were made the
sooner, he should not long continue quiet. King John, being
sore moved with such words thus uttered by his nephew,
appointed (as before is said) that he should be straitly kept in
prison, at first in Falais, and after at Rouen, within the new
castle there. Thus by means of his good success the countries
of Poictou, Touraine, and Anjou were recovered.

Shortly after[wards], King John, coming over into England, caused himself to be crowned again at Canterbury
by the hands of Hubert, the Archbishop there, on the fourteenth day of April, and then went back again in Normandy,
where, immediately upon his arrival, a rumor was spread
through all France of the death of his nephew Arthur. True it
is that great suit was made to have Arthur set at liberty, as
well by the French king as by William de Riches, a valiant
baron of Poictou, and divers other noblemen of Brittany,
who, when they could not prevail in their suit, banded themselves together and, joining in confederacy with Robert, Earl
of Alençon, the Viscount Beaumont, William de Fulgiers,

and others, they began to levy sharp wars against King John
in divers places, insomuch (as it was thought) that so long as
Arthur lived there would be no quiet in those parts; whereupon it was reported that King John, through persuasion of
his counselors, appointed certain persons to go to Falais,
where Arthur was kept in prison under the charge of Hubert
de Burgh, and there to put out the young gentleman's eyes.

But through such resistance as he made against one of the
tormentors that came to execute the King's commandment
(for the others rather forsook their prince and country than
they would consent to obey the King's authority herein) and
such lamentable words as he uttered, Hubert de Burgh did
preserve him from that injury, not doubting but rather to
have thanks than displeasure at the King's hands for deliv-
ering him from such infamy as would have redounded to his
Highness if the young gentleman had been so cruelly dealt
with. For he considered that King John had resolved upon
this point only in his heat and fury (which moves men to
undertake many an inconvenient enterprise, unbeseeming
the person of a common man, much more reproachful to a
prince, all men in that mood being merely foolish and
furious, and prone to accomplish the perverse conceits of
their ill-possessed hearts . . .) and that afterwards, upon
better advisement, he would both repent himself so to have
commanded, and give them small thank that should see it put
in execution. Howbeit, to satisfy his mind for the time and to
stay the rage of the Britains [men of Brittany], he caused it
to be bruited abroad through the country that the King's
commandment was fulfilled, and that Arthur also, through
sorrow and grief, was departed out of this life. For the space
of fifteen days this rumor incessantly ran through both the
realms of England and France, and there was ringing for him
through towns and villages, as [though] it had been for his
funeral. It was also bruited that his body was buried in the
monastery of Saint Andrews, of the Cistercian order.

But when the Britains were nothing pacified, but rather
kindled more vehemently to work all the mischief they could
devise in revenge of their sovereign's death, there was no
remedy but to signify abroad again that Arthur was as yet
living and in health. Now when the King heard the truth of
all this matter, he was nothing displeased for that his com-

mandment was not executed, since there were divers of his captains which uttered in plain words that he should not find knights to keep his castles if he dealt so cruelly with his nephew. For if it chanced of any of them to be taken by the King of France or others of their adversaries, they should be sure to taste of the like cup.

But now touching the manner in very deed of the end of this Arthur, writers make sundry reports. Nevertheless certain it is that in the year next ensuing he was removed from Falais to the castle or tower of Rouen, out of the which there is not any that would confess that ever he saw him go alive. Some have written that, as he assayed to have escaped out of the prison, and proving [trying] to climb over the walls of the castle, he fell into the river of Seine and so was drowned. Others write that through very grief and langour he pined away and died of natural sickness. But some affirm that King John secretly caused him to be murdered and made away, so that it is not thoroughly agreed upon in what sort he finished his days; but verily King John was had in great suspicion, whether worthily or not, the Lord knows. Yet how extremely soever he dealt with his nephew, he released and set at liberty divers of those lords that were taken prisoners with him. . . .

[1204] King Philip understanding that King John remained still in England, rather occupied in gathering money among his subjects than in making other provision to bring them into the field (to the great offense of his said people) thought now for his part to lose no time, but, assembling a mighty army, he came with the same into Normandy. . . . Thus Normandy, which King Rollo had purchased and gotten 316 years before that present time, was then recovered by the Frenchmen, to the great reproach and dishonor of the English, in this year 1204. About this time Queen Elinor, the mother of King John, departed this life, consumed rather through sorrow and anguish of mind than of any other natural infirmity. . . .

[1206] King John also in this meanwhile, moved with the increase of these new associates and also with desire to revenge so many injuries and losses sustained at the French king's hands, preparing an army of men and a navy of ships, took the sea with them and landed at Rochelle the ninth of July. . . . Finally he entered into Anjou and, coming to the city of Angiers, appointed certain bands of his footmen and all his light horsemen to compass the town about, while he, with the residue of the footmen and all the men of arms, did go to assault the gates. Which enterprise with fire and sword he so manfully executed that, the gates being in a moment broken open, the city was entered and delivered to the soldiers for a prey. So that of the citizens some were taken, some killed, and the walls of the city beaten flat to the ground. . . .

After this it chanced that King John, remembering himself of the destruction of the city of Angiers, which (because he was descended from thence) he had before greatly loved, began now to repent that he had destroyed it, and therefore with all speed he took order to have it again repaired, which was done in most beautiful wise, to his great cost and expense, which he might have saved had not his foolish rashness driven him to attempt that whereof upon sober advisement afterwards he was ashamed. But what will not an ordinary man do in the full tide of his fury; much more princes and great men, whose anger is like the roaring of a lion, even upon light occasions oftentimes, to satisfy their unbridled and brainsick affections, which carry them with a swift and full stream into such follies and dotages as are indecent for their degrees. . . .

[1207] In the meantime the strife depended still in the court of Rome betwixt the two elected archbishops of Canterbury, Reginald and John. But after the Pope was fully informed of the manner of their elections, he disannulled them both and procured by his papal authority the monks of Canterbury (of whom many were come to Rome about that matter) to choose one Stephen Langton, the cardinal of S. Chrysogon, an Englishman born and of good estimation and learning in the court of Rome to be their archbishop. The monks at the first were loath to consent thereto, alleging that they might not lawfully do it without consent of their king and of their covent.

But the Pope, as it were taking the word out of their mouths, said to them, "Do you not consider that we have full authority and power in the church of Canterbury: neither is the assent of kings or princes to be looked for upon elections celebrated in the presence of the Apostolic See. Wherefore I command you by virtue of your obedience and upon pain of cursing, that you being such and so many here as are sufficient for the election, to choose him your archbishop whom I shall appoint to you for father and pastor of your souls." The monks, doubting [fearing] to offend the Pope, consented all of them to gratify him, except Helias de Brantfield, who refused. And so the foresaid Stephen Langton being elected of them was confirmed of the Pope, who signified by letters the whole state thereof to King John, commending the said Stephen as archbishop to him.

The King, sore offended in his mind that the Bishop of Norwich was thus put beside that dignity to which he had advanced him, caused forthwith all the goods of the monks of Canterbury to be confiscated to his use, and after[wards] banished them [from] the realm, as well I mean those at home as those that were at Rome, and herewith wrote his letters to the Pope, giving him to understand for answer that he would never consent that Stephen, which had been brought up and always conversant with his enemies the Frenchmen, should now enjoy the rule of the bishopric and diocese of Canterbury. Moreover, he declared in the same letters that he marveled not a little what the Pope meant, in that he did not consider how necessary the friendship of the King of England was to the See of Rome, since there came more gains to the Roman church out of that kingdom than out of any other realm on this side of the mountains [the Alps]. He added hereto that for the liberties of his crown he would stand to the death if the matter so required. And as for the election of the Bishop of Norwich to the see of Canterbury, since it was profitable to him and to his realm, he meant not to release it.

Moreover he declared that, if he might not be heard and have his mind, he would surely restrain the passages out of this realm, that none should go to Rome, lest his land should be so emptied of money and treasure that he should want sufficient ability to beat back and expel his enemies that might attempt invasion against the same. Lastly of all he concluded, since the archbishops, bishops, abbots and other ecclesiastical persons, as well of his realm of England as of his other lands and dominions, were sufficiently furnished with knowledge, that he would not go for any need that should drive him thereto to seek justice or judgment at the prescript of any foreign persons.

. . . The Pope, being hereof advertised, thought good not to suffer such contempt of his authority, as he interpreted it, namely, in a matter that touched the injurious handling of men within orders of the church. Which example might procure hindrance not to one private person alone but to the whole estate of the spirituality, which he would not suffer in any way to be suppressed. Wherefore he decreed with speed to devise remedy against that large increasing mischief. And though there was no speedier way to redress the same but by excommunication, yet he would not use it at first towards so mighty a prince, but gave him liberty and time to consider his offense and trespass so committed. . . .

Also, upon the first of October, Henry, the son of King John, begotten of his wife, Queen Isabell, was born at Winchester, who after[wards] succeeded his father in the kingdom. But now again to our purpose.

[1208] The Pope perceiving that King John continued still in his former mind (which he called obstinacy) sent over his bulls into England, directed to William, Bishop of London, to Eustace, Bishop of Ely, and to Mauger, Bishop of Worcester, commanding them that, unless King John would suffer peaceably the Archbishop of Canterbury to occupy his see, and his monks their abbey, they should put both him and his land under the sentence of interdiction, denouncing him and his land plainly accursed. . . .

. . . the King in a great rage swore that, if either they or any other presumed to put his land under interdiction, he would incontinently thereupon send all the prelates within the realm out of the same to the Pope, and seize all their goods to his own use. And further he added that what Romans [marginal gloss: "Romans, that is such chaplains strangers as belonged to the Pope"] soever he found within the precinct of any of his dominions, he would put out their eyes and slit their noses and so send them packing to Rome, that by such marks they might be known from all other nations of the world. And herewith he commanded the bishops to pack out of his sight if they loved their own health and preservation.

Hereupon the said bishops departed and, according to the Pope's commission to them sent, upon the eve of the Annunciation of our Lady, denounced both the King and the realm of England accursed, and furthermore caused the doors of churches to be closed up and all other places where divine service was accustomed to be used, first at London and after[wards] in all other places where they came. Then perceiving that the King meant not to stoop for all this which they had done, but rather sought to be revenged upon them, they fled the realm. . . .

It was a miserable time now for priests and churchmen, which were despoiled on every hand without finding remedy against those that offered them wrong. . . .

[1209] It was surely a rueful thing to consider the estate of this realm at that present, when the King neither trusted his peers nor the nobility favored the King; no, there were very few that trusted one another, but each one hid and hoarded up his wealth, looking daily when another should come and enter upon the spoil. The commonality also grew into factions, some favoring and some cursing the King, as they bore affection. The clergy was likewise at dissension, so that nothing prevailed but malice and spite, which brought forth and spread abroad the fruits of disobedience to all good laws and orders, greatly to the disquieting of the whole state. So that herein we have a perfect view of the perplexed state of princes, chiefly when they are overswayed with foreign and profane power and not able to assure themselves of their subjects' allegiance and loyalty. . . .

King John, notwithstanding that the realm was thus wholly interdicted and vexed, so that no priests could be found to say service in churches and chapels, made no great account thereof as touching any offense towards God or the Pope, but, rather mistrusting the hollow hearts of his people, he took a new oath of them for their faithful allegiance. . . .

[In that year and the next, King John was principally occupied in subduing uprisings in Scotland, Ireland and Wales.]

[1211] . . . In the same year also, the Pope sent two legates into England, the one named Pandulph, a lawyer, and the other Durant, a Templar, who, coming to King John, exhorted him with many terrible words to leave his stubborn disobedience to the church and to reform his misdoings. The King for his part quietly heard them and, bringing them to Northampton, being not far distant from the place where he met them upon his return forth of Wales, had much conference with them; but at length, when they perceived that they could not have their purpose, neither for restitution of the goods belonging to priests which he had seized upon, nor of those which appertained to certain other persons, which the King had gotten also into his hands by means of the controversy betwixt him and the Pope, the legates departed, leaving him accursed and the land interdicted as they found it at their coming. . . .

In the meantime, Pope Innocent, after the return of his legates out of England, perceiving that King John would not be ordered by him, determined . . . to deprive King John of his kingly state, and so first absolved all his subjects and vassals of their oaths of allegiance made to the same king, and after[wards] deprived him by solemn protestation of his kingly administration and dignity, and lastly signified his deprivation to the French king and other Christian princes, admonishing them to pursue King John, being thus deprived, forsaken and condemned as a common enemy to God and his church. He ordained furthermore that whosoever employed goods or other aid to vanquish and overcome that disobedient prince should remain in assured peace of the church as well as those which went to visit the sepulcher of our Lord, not only in their goods and persons, but also in suffrages for saving of their souls.

But yet that it might appear to all men that nothing could be more joyful to His Holiness than to have King John to repent his trespasses committed and to ask forgiveness for the same, he appointed Pandulph, which lately before was returned to Rome, with a great number of English exiles, to go into France, together with Stephen, the Archbishop of Canterbury and the other English bishops, giving him in commandment that, repairing to the French king, he should communicate with him all that which he had appointed to be done against King John, and to exhort the French king to make war upon him as a person for his wickedness excommunicated. Moreover this Pandulph was commanded by the Pope, if he saw cause, to go over into England and to deliver to King John such letters as the Pope had written for his better instruction, and to seek by all means possible to draw him from his naughty [wicked] opinion.

In the meantime, when it was bruited through the realm of England that the Pope had released the people and absolved them of their oath of fidelity to the King, and that he was deprived of his government by the Pope's sentence, little by little a great number of soldiers, citizens, burgesses, captains, and constables of castles, leaving their charges, and bishops with a great number of priests, revolting from him and avoiding his company and presence, secretly stole away and got over into France. . . .

[1213] You shall understand, the French king, being requested by Pandulph, the Pope's legate, to take the war in hand against King John, was easily persuaded thereto of an inward hatred that he bore to our king, and thereupon with all diligence made his provision of men, ships, munition, and victual, in purpose to pass over into England; and now was his navy ready rigged at the mouth of [the] Seine and he in greatest forwardness to take his journey. When Pandulph upon good considerations thought first to go again, or at the least to send into England, before the French army should land there, and to assay once again if he might induce the King to show himself reformable to the Pope's pleasure, King John, having knowledge of the French king's purpose and ordinance, assembled his people and lodged them along the coast towards France, that he might resist his enemies and keep them off from landing. . . .

. . . He had also provided a navy of ships, far stronger than the French king's, ready to fight with them by sea if the case so required.

But as he lay thus ready, near to the coast, to withstand

and beat back his enemies, there arrived at Dover two Templars who, coming before the King, declared to him that they were sent from Pandulph, the Pope's legate, who for his profit coveted to talk with him; for he had (as they affirmed) means to propose whereby he might be reconciled both to God and his church, although he were adjudged in the court of Rome to have forfeited all the right which he had to his kingdom.

The King, understanding the meaning of the ministers, sent them back again to bring over the legate who incontinently came over to Dover, upon whose arrival, when the King was advertised, he went thither and received him with all due honor and reverence. Now after they had talked together a little and courteously saluted each other (as the course of humanity required), the legate (as it is reported) uttered these words following:

> The saucy speech of proud Pandulph, the
> Pope's lewd legate, to King John, in the pre-
> sumptuous Pope's behalf.

I DO not think that you are ignorant how that Pope Innocent, to do that which to his duty appertaineth, hath both absolved your subjects of that oath which they made to you at the beginning, and also taken from you the governance of England. . . .

These words being thus spoken by the legate, King John, as then utterly despairing in his matters when he saw himself constrained to obey, was in great perplexity of mind and, as one full of thought, looked about him with a frowning countenance, weighing with himself what counsel were best for him to follow. At length, oppressed with the burden of the imminent danger and ruin, against his will and very loath so to have done, he promised upon his oath to stand to the Pope's order and decree. Wherefore shortly thereafter (in like manner as Pope Innocent had commanded), he took the crown from his own head and delivered the same to Pandulph, the legate, neither he nor his heirs at any time thereafter to receive the same but at the Pope's hands. [Marginal gloss: "King John delivereth his crown unto Pandulph."] Upon this, he promised to receive Stephen, the

Archbishop of Canterbury, into his favor, with all the other bishops and banished men, making to them sufficient amends for all injuries done to them, and so to pardon them that they should not run into any danger because they had rebelled against him.

[Marginal gloss: "Pandulph restoreth the crown again to the King."] Then Pandulph, keeping the crown with him for the space of five days in token of possession thereof, at length (as the Pope's vicar) gave it [to] him again. . . .

Pandulph, having thus reconciled King John, thought it not good to release the excommunication till the King had performed all [the] things which he had promised, and so with all speed, having received eight thousand marks sterling in part of restitution to be made to the archbishop and the other banished men, he sailed back into France and came to Rouen, where he declared to King Philip the effect of his travail and what he had done in England. But King Philip, having in this meanwhile consumed a great mass of money, to the sum of sixty thousand pounds, as he himself alleged, about the furnishing of his journey which he intended to have made into England upon hope to have had no small aid within the realm, by reason of such bishops and other banished men as he had in France with him, was much offended for the reconciliation of King John and determined not so to break off his enterprise lest it might be imputed to him for a great reproach to have been at such charges and great expenses in vain. . . .

[The English navy, however, destroyed the French, which was attacking John's ally the Earl of Flanders.]

There was in this season an hermit, whose name was Peter, dwelling about York [marginal gloss: "An hermit named Peter of Pontfret, or Wakefield as some writers have"], a man in great reputation with the common people because, either inspired with some spirit of prophecy as the people believed, or else having some notable skill in art [of] magic, he was accustomed to tell what should follow after. And for so much as oftentimes his sayings proved true, great credit was given to him as to a very prophet. . . . This Peter, about the first of January last past, had told the King that at the feast of the Ascension it should come to pass that he should be cast out of his kingdom. And (whether to the intent that his words should be the better believed, or upon too much trust of his own cunning) he offered himself to suffer death for it if his prophecy proved not true. Hereupon being committed to prison within the castle of Corfe, when the day by him prefixed came, without any other notable damage to King John, he was by the King's commandment drawn from the said castle to the town of Wareham and there hanged, together with his son.

The people much blamed King John for this extreme dealing because the hermit was supposed to be a man of great virtue and his son nothing guilty of the offense committed by his father (if any were) against the King. Moreover, some thought that he had much wrong to die because the matter fell out even as he had prophesied: for the day before the Ascension Day, King John had resigned the superiority of his kingdom (as they took the matter) to the Pope, and had done to him homage so that he was no absolute king indeed, as authors affirm. One cause, and that not the least, which moved King John the sooner to agree with the Pope rose through the words of the said hermit that did put such a fear of some great mishap in his heart, which should grow through the disloyalty of his people, that it made him yield the sooner. . . .

. . . about the feast of Saint Michael, came Nicholas, the Cardinal of Tusculane, into England, sent from the Pope, to take away the interdiction. . . .

[1214] [King John invaded Brittany but, outnumbered by the French forces under Lewis, the French king's son, he retreated to Angiers. King Philip, meanwhile, defeated the Emperor Otho, John's ally, and John agreed to a five-year truce.] . . . After this, about the 19th day of October, he returned to England to appease certain tumults which began already to shoot out buds of some new civil dissension. And surely the same spread abroad their blossoms so freshly that the fruit was knit before the growth by any timely provision could be hindered. For the people, being set on by divers of the superiors of both sorts, finding themselves grieved that the King kept not promise in restoring the ancient laws of St. Edward, determined from thenceforth to use force, since by request he might not prevail. To appease this fury of the people, not only policy but power also was required. . . .

The nobles, supposing that longer delay therein was not to be suffered, assembled themselves together at the abbey of Bury (under color of going thither to do their devotions to the body of St. Edmund, which lay there enshrined) where they uttered their complaint against the King's tyrannical manners. . . .

. . . And therefore, being thus assembled in the choir of the church of St. Edmund, they received a solemn oath upon the altar there that if the King would not grant to the same liberties [as had been granted by his grandfather, Henry I], with others which he of his own accord had promised to confirm to them, they from thenceforth would make war upon him till they had obtained their purpose and enforced him to grant not only to all these, their petitions, but also yield to the confirmation of them under his seal, forever to remain most steadfast and inviolable. . . .

[1215] . . . The King (though somewhat contrary to his nature), having heard their request, gave them a very gentle answer. For, perceiving them ready with force to constrain him if by gentleness they might not prevail, he thought it should be more safe and easy for him to turn their unquiet minds with soft remedies than to go about to break them of their wills by strong hand, which is a thing very dangerous, especially where both parts are of like force. Therefore he promised them within a few days to have consideration of their request.

And to the intent they might give more credit to his words, he caused the Archbishop of Canterbury and the Bishop of Ely, with William Marshall, Earl of Pembroke (unto whom he had given his daughter Elinor in marriage) to undertake for him and, as it were, to become his sureties: which willingly they did. Herewith the minds of the nobility being somewhat pacified, [they] returned home to their houses. The King soon after[wards] also, to assure himself the more effectually of the allegiance of his people in time to come, caused every man to renew his homage and to take a new oath to be faithful to him against all other persons. And to provide the more surety for himself, on Candlemas Day next

ensuing, he took upon him the cross to go into the Holy
Land, which I think he did rather for fear than any devotion,
as was also thought by others, to the end that he might (under
the protection thereof) remain the more out of danger of
such as were his foes. . . .

[John having refused their demands, the barons rose
against him.]

The barons, having thus gotten possession of the city of
London, wrote letters to all those lords which as yet had not
joined with them in this confederacy, threatening that if they
refused to aid them now in this necessity, they would destroy
their castles, manors, parks and other possessions, making
open war upon them as the enemies of God and rebels to the
church. These were the names of those lords which yet had
not sworn to maintain the foresaid liberties: William Marshall, Earl of Pembroke; Rainulfe, Earl of Chester; Nicholas,
Earl of Salisbury [and nineteen others]. All these, upon
receipt of the barons' letters, or the more part of them, came
to London and joined themselves with the barons, utterly
renouncing to aid King John.

. . . Hereupon he thought good to assay if he might come
to some agreement by way of communication, and incontinently sent his ambassadors to the barons, promising them
that he would satisfy their requests if they would come to
Windsor to talk with him.

Howbeit, the lords having no confidence in his promise
came with their army within three miles of Windsor, and
there pitched down their tents in a meadow betwixt Staines
and Windsor, whither King John also came the 15th day of
June and showed such friendly countenance towards every
one of them that they were put in good hope he meant no
deceit. Being thus met, they fell in consultation about an
agreement to be had. On the King's part (as it were) sat
the Archbishops of Canterbury and Dublin, the Bishops of
London, Winchester, Lincoln, Bath, Worcester, Coventry,
Rochester, and Pandulph, the Pope's Nuncio, with Almeric,
Master of the Knights Templars: the Earls of Pembroke, Salisbury [and eleven others].* On the barons' part, there were

---

*The name Bigot turns up elsewhere on this page (and several other times
in the account), but never this prominently heading a list.

innumerable, for all the nobility of England was in a manner assembled there together.

Finally, when the King, measuring his own strength with the barons', perceived that he was not able to resist them, he consented to subscribe and seal to such articles concerning the liberties demanded, in form for the most part as is contained in the two charters, Magna Charta and Charta de Foresta. . . .

[But John had no intention of living up to his concessions. He appealed to the Pope, who sustained him against the barons. He began besieging the castle of Rochester, a stronghold of the barons.]

Here is to be remembered that, while the siege lay thus at Rochester, Hugh de Boues, a valiant knight but full of pride and arrogancy, a Frenchman born but banished out of his country, came down to Calais with a huge number of men of war and soldiers to come to the aid of King John. But as he was upon the sea with all his people, meaning to land at Dover, by a sudden tempest which rose at that instant, the said Hugh with all his company was drowned by shipwreck. Soon after[wards] the body of the same Hugh with the carcasses of innumerable others, both of men, women, and children, were found not far from Yarmouth and all along that coast. There were of them in all forty thousand, as says Matthew Paris, for of all those which he brought with him, there was (as it is said) not one man left alive. . . .

[The Pope excommunicated the barons and, while they remained in London, John seized or razed their possessions "from the south sea to the borders of Scotland."]

[1216] . . . The barons of the realm being thus afflicted with so many mischiefs all at one time, as both by the sharp and cruel wars which the King made against them on the one side, and by the enmity of the Pope on the other side, they knew not which way to turn them nor how to seek for relief. For by the loss of their accomplices taken in the castle of Rochester they saw not how it should anything avail them to join in battle with the King. Therefore, considering that they were in such extremity of despair, they resolved with themselves to seek for aid at the enemy's hands, and thereupon Saer, Earl of Winchester, and Robert Fitz Walter, with letters under their seals, were sent to Lewis, the son of Philip, the French king, offering him the crown of England, and sufficient pledges for performance of the same and other covenants to be agreed betwixt them, requiring him with all speed to come to their succor. This Lewis had married (as before is said) Blanch, daughter to Alfonso, King of Castile, niece to King John by his sister Elinor.

Now King Philip, the father of Lewis, being glad to have such an occasion to invade the realm of England, which he never loved, promised willingly that his son should come to the aid of the said barons with all convenient speed . . . and herewith he prepared an army and divers ships to transport his son and his army over into England. In the meantime, and to put the barons in comfort, he sent over a certain number of armed men . . . the which, taking the sea, arrived with one and forty ships in the Thames, and so came to London the seven and twentieth of February, where they were received by the barons with great joy and gladness. Moreover the said Lewis wrote to the barons that he purposed by God's assistance to be at Calais by the day appointed, with an army ready to pass over with all speed to their succor. . . .

The King, perceiving that it would not prevail him to attempt the winning of [London] at that time, drew along the coast, fortified his castles and prepared a great navy, meaning to encounter his enemy Lewis by sea: but through tempest the ships which he had got together from Yarmouth, Dunwich Lynn, and other havens, were dispersed asunder and many of them cast away by rage and violence of the outrageous winds. . . .

. . . The Pope, desirous to help King John all that he might (because he was now his vassal), sent his legate Gaulo into France to dissuade King Philip from taking any enterprise in hand against the King of England. But King Philip, though he was content to hear what the legate could say, yet by no means would be turned from the execution of his purpose, alleging that King John was not the lawful King of England, having first usurped and taken it away from his nephew Arthur, the lawful inheritor, and that now, later, as an enemy to his own royal dignity he had given the right of his kingdom away to the Pope (which he could not do without consent of his nobles) and therefore through his own fault he was worthily deprived of all his kingly honor. . . .

Lewis, on the morrow following, being the 26th of April, by his father's procurement came into the council chamber and, with frowning look, beheld the legate, where by his procurator he defended the cause that moved him to take upon him the journey into England, disproving not only the right which King John had to the crown, but also alleging his own interest, not only by his new election by the barons, but also in the title of his wife, whose mother, the queen of Castile, remained alone alive of all the brethren and sisters [sons and daughters] of Henry the Second, late King of England. . . .

[Though warned of excommunication, Lewis came to England and captured many strongholds, including Norwich, where he took prisoner Thomas de Burgh. He failed, however, to take Dover Castle, held for John by Hubert de Burgh.]

In the meantime, Lewis was brought to some good hope through means of Thomas de Burgh, whom he took prisoner (as before you have heard) to persuade his brother Hubert to yield up the castle of Dover, the siege whereof was the next enterprise which he attempted. For his father, King Philip, hearing that the same was kept by a garrison to the benefit of King John, wrote to his son, blaming him that he left behind him so strong a fortress in his enemies' hands. But though Lewis enforced his whole endeavor to win that castle, yet all his travail was in vain. For the said Hubert de Burgh, and Gerard de Sotigam, who were chief captains within, did their best to defend it against him and all his power, so that, despairing to win it by force, he assayed to obtain his purpose by threatening to hang the captain's brother before his face if he would not yield the sooner. But when that would not serve, he sought to win him by large offers of gold and silver. Howbeit, such was the singular constancy of Hubert that he would not give any ear to those flattering inducements. . . .

About the same time, or rather in the year last past, as some hold, it fortuned that the Viscount of Melune, a Frenchman, fell sick at London and, perceiving that death was at hand, he called to him certain of the English barons, which remained in the city upon safeguard thereof, and to them made this protestation: "I lament (said he) your destruction and desolation at hand because you are ignorant of the perils hanging over your heads. For this understand, that Lewis, and with him sixteen earls and barons of France, have secretly sworn (if it shall fortune him to conquer this realm of England and to be crowned king) that he will kill, banish, and confine all those of the English nobility (which now do serve under him and persecute their own king) as traitors and rebels, and furthermore will dispossess all their lineage of such inheritances as they now hold in England. And so that (said he) you shall not have doubt hereof, I which lie here at the point of death do now affirm to you and take it on the peril of my soul that I am one of those sixteen that have sworn to perform this thing: wherefore I advise you to provide for your own safeties and your realm's, which you now destroy, and keep this thing secret which I have uttered to you." After this speech was uttered he straightway died.

When these words of the lord of Melune were opened to the barons, they were, and not without cause, in great doubt of themselves, for they saw how Lewis had already placed and set Frenchmen in most of such castles and towns as he had gotten, the right whereof belonged to them. And again it grieved them much to understand how, besides the hatred of their prince, they were every Sunday and Holy day openly accursed in every church, so that many of them inwardly relented and could have been contented to have returned to King John if they thought that they should thankfully have been received. . . .

[John continued attacking various strongholds of the barons with great success.]

Thus, the country being wasted on each hand, the King hasted forward till he came to Wellstream sands where, passing the washes, he lost a great part of his army, with horses and carriages, so that it was judged to be a punishment appointed by God that the spoil which had been gotten and taken out of churches, abbeys, and other religious houses, should perish and be lost by such means together with the spoilers. Yet the King himself and a few others escaped the violence of the waters by following a good guide. But, as some have written, he took such grief for the loss sustained in this passage that immediately thereupon he fell into an ague, the force and heat whereof, together with his immoderate feeding on raw peaches and drinking new cider, so increased his sickness that he was not able to ride but was fain to be carried in a litter presently made of twigs, with a couch of straw under him, without any bed or pillow, thinking to have gone to Lincoln, but the disease still so raged and grew upon him that he was enforced to stay one night at the castle of Laford, and on the next day, with much pain, caused himself to be carried to Newark, where, in the castle, through anguish of mind rather than through force of sickness, he departed this life the night before the nineteenth day of October, in the year of his age fifty-one, and after he had reigned seventeen years, six months, and twenty-seven days.

There be [some] which have written that, after he lost his army, he came to the abbey of Swineshead, in Lincolnshire, and there understanding the cheapness and plenty of corn, showed himself greatly displeased therewith as he that, for the hatred which he bore to the English people that had so traitorously revolted from him to his adversary Lewis, wished all misery to light upon them, and thereupon said in his anger that he would cause all kind of grain to be at a far higher price ere many days should pass. Whereupon a monk that heard him speak such words, being moved with zeal for the oppression of the country, gave the King poison in a cup of ale, whereof he first took the assay to cause the King not to suspect the matter, and so they both died in manner at one time.

There are [some] that write how one of his own servants did conspire with a convert of that abbey, and that they prepared a dish of pears, which they poisoned, three of the whole number excepted, which dish the said convert presented to him. And when the King suspected them to be poisoned indeed, by reason that such precious stones as he had around him cast forth a certain sweat, as it were betraying the poison, he compelled the said convert to taste and eat some of them, who, knowing the three pears which were not poisoned, took and ate those three, which, when the King had seen, he could no longer abstain but fell to and, eating greedily of the rest, died the same night, no hurt happening to the convert who, through the help of such as bore no good will to the King, found shift to escape and conveyed himself away from danger of receiving due punishment for so wicked a deed. . . .

The men of war that served under his ensigns, being for the more part hired soldiers and strangers, came together and, marching forth with his body, each man with his armor on his back, in warlike order, conveyed it to Worcester, where he was pompously buried in the cathedral church before the high altar, not because he had so appointed (as some write) but because it was thought to be a place of most surety for the lords and others of his friends there to assemble and to take order in their business now after his decease. . . .

Howsoever or wheresoever or whensoever he died, it is not a matter of such moment that it should impeach the credit of the story: but certain it is that he came to his end, let it be by a surfeit or by other means ordained for the shortening of his life. The manner is not so material as the truth is certain. And surely he might be thought to have procured against himself many molestations, many anguishes and vexations, which nipped his heart and gnawed his very bowels with many a sore symptom or passion; all which he might have withstood if fortune had been so favorable that the loyalty of his subjects had remained towards him inviolable; that his nobles with multitude of adherents had not with such shameful apostasy withstood him in open fight, that foreign force had not weakened his dominion or rather robbed him of a main branch of his regiment, that he himself had not sought with the spoil of his own people to please the imaginations of his ill-affected mind; that courtiers and commoners had with one assent performed in duty no less than they pretended in verity, to the preservation of the state and the security of their sovereign: all which presupposed plagues concurring, what happiness could the King arrogate to himself by his imperial title, which was through his own default so embezzled that a small remnant became his in right, when by open hostility and accursed papacy the greater portion was plucked out of his hands.

Here therefore we see the issue of domestic or homebred

broils, the fruits of variance, the gain that rises from dissension, whereas no safer fortification can betide a land than when the inhabitants are all alike minded. By concord many a hard enterprise (in common sense thought impossible) is achieved, many weak things become so defended that without manifold force they cannot be dissolved. From divisions and mutinies do issue (as out of the Trojan horse) ruins of royalties and decays of commonalities. . . .

He was comely of stature, but of look and countenance displeasant and angry, somewhat cruel of nature, as by the writers of his time he is noted, and not so hardy as doubtful [fearful] in time of peril and danger. But this seems to be an envious report uttered by those that were given to speak no good of him whom they inwardly hated. Howbeit some give this witness of him . . . that he was a great and mighty prince, but not yet very fortunate, much like Marius, the noble Roman, tasting of fortune both ways: bountiful and liberal to strangers, but of his own people (for their daily treasons practiced towards him) a great oppressor, so that he trusted more to foreigners than to them, and therefore in the end he was of them utterly forsaken.

Verily, whosoever shall consider the course of the history written of this prince, he shall find that he has been little beholden to the writers of that time in which he lived: for scarcely can they afford him a good word, except when the truth enforces them to come out with it as it were against their wills. The occasion whereof (as some think) was that he was no great friend to the clergy. And yet undoubtedly his deeds show he had a zeal to religion, as it was then accounted. . . .

. . . Certainly it would seem that the man had a princely heart in him and wanted nothing but faithful subjects to have assisted him in revenging such wrongs as were done and offered by the French king and others. . . .

Henry, the third of that name, the eldest son of King John, a child of the age of nine years, began his reign over the realm of England the nineteenth day of October, in the year of our Lord 1216, in the seventh year of the Emperor Frederick the second, and in the 36th year of the reign of Philip the second, King of France.

Immediately after the death of his father, King John, William Marshall, Earl of Pembroke, general of his father's army, brought this young prince with his brother and sisters to Gloucester, and there called a council of all such lords as had taken part with King John. . . . a great number of the lords and chief barons of the realm hasted thither (I mean not only such as had held with King John but also divers others which, upon certain knowledge had of his death, were newly revolted from Lewis) in purpose to aid young King Henry, to whom of right the crown did appertain. . . .

It is reported by writers that among other things, as there were divers which withdrew the hearts of Englishmen from Lewis, the consideration of the confession which the Viscount Melune made at the hour of his death was the principal. . . .

For first they [the lords still following Lewis] considered that the renouncing of their promised faith to Lewis, whom they had sworn to maintain as King of England, would be a great reproach to them; and again they well saw that to continue in their obedience towards him would bring the realm in great danger, since it would be hard for any loving agreement to continue between the French and Englishmen, their natures being so contrary. Thirdly, they stood somewhat in fear of the Pope's curse, pronounced by his legate, both against Lewis and all his partakers. Albeit on the other side, to revolt to King Henry, though the love which they did bear to their country and the great towardness which they saw in him greatly moved them; yet, since by reason of his young years he was not able either to follow the wars himself or to take counsel what was to be done in public government, they judged it a very dangerous case. For, whereas in wars nothing can be more expedient than to have one head by whose appointment all things may be governed, so nothing can be more hurtful than to have many rulers by whose authority things shall pass and be ordered. . . .

. . . divers of the confederates thought that it stood not with their honors so to forsake him till they might have some more honorable color to revolt [for revolting] from their promises. . . .

[Lewis held London and much of eastern England. Not

until 1218, after a defeat of the French forces at Lincoln and the vanquishing of the French fleet by Hubert de Burgh, did Lewis come to an agreement with the Earl of Pembroke, Lord Governor of England, to renounce his claim to the crown and withdraw from England.]

From The Union of the Two Noble and Illustre Families of Lancaster and York (1548)

[1427] After this, in the month of September, he [the Earl of Salisbury] laid his siege [against Orleans] on the one side of the Loire, before whose coming the Bastard of Orleans, and the bishop of the city and a great number of Scots, hearing of the Earl's intent, made divers fortifications about the town. . . .

Here I must a little digress and declare to you what was this Bastard of Orleans, who was not only now captain of the city but also after[wards], by Charles VI made Earl of Dunois, and in great authority in France, and extreme enemy to the English nation, as by this history you shall apparently [clearly] perceive, of whose line and stem descend the Dukes of Longville and the Marquis of Rutylon. Lewis, Duke of Orleans, murdered in Paris by John, Duke of Burgoyne, as you have heard, was owner of the castle of Cauny, on the frontiers of France toward Artois, whereof he made constable the Lord of Cauny, a man not so wise as his wife was fair, and yet she was not so fair but that she was as well beloved of the Duke of Orleans as of her husband. Between the Duke and her husband (I cannot tell who was father) she conceived a child and brought forth a pretty boy called John, which child being of the age of one year, the Duke deceased, and not long after the mother and the Lord of Cauny ended their lives. The next of kin to the Lord Cauny challenged the inheritance, which was worth four thousand crowns a year, alleging that the boy was a bastard; and the kindred of the mother's side, to save her honesty, plainly denied it. In conclusion, this matter was in contention before the presidents of the parliament of Paris, and there hung in controversy until the child came to the age of eight years old. At which time it was demanded of him openly whose son he was: his friends of his mother's side advertised him to require a day to be advised of so great an answer, which he asked and to him it was granted. In the meantime, his said friends persuaded him to claim his inheritance as son to the Lord of Cauny, which was an honorable living and an ancient patrimony, affirming that, if he said contrary, he not only slandered his mother, shamed himself, and stained his blood, but also should have no living nor any thing to take to [depend upon]. The schoolmaster, thinking that his disciple had well learned his lesson and would rehearse it according to his instruction, brought him before the judges at the day assigned, and when the question was repeated to him again, he boldly answered, "My heart gives me, and my noble courage tells me, that I am the son of the noble Duke of Orleans, more glad to be his bastard, with a mean living, than the lawful son of that coward cuckold Cauny, with his four thousand crowns." The justices much marveled at his bold answer, and his mother's cousins [relations] detested him for shaming his mother, and his father's supposed kin rejoiced in gaining the patrimony and possessions. Charles, Duke of Orleans, hearing of this judgment, took him into his family and gave him great offices and fees, which he well deserved for (during his [Charles's] captivity) he defended his lands, expulsed the Englishmen and in conclusion procured his deliverance.

This courageous bastard, after the siege had continued three full weeks, issued out of the gate of the bridge and fought with the Englishmen, but they received him with such fierce and terrible strokes that he was with all his company compelled to retire and fly back into the city. . . .

Commentaries

DONALD A. STAUFFER

From Shakespeare's World of Images*

The isolated play of *King John* serves as prologue to the swelling theme of a triumphant England. It is a restless play, as if it marked the crossroads of many moods and styles in Shakespeare's development. The verse is as formal and regular as in *Love's Labor's Lost* or *Richard II*. Yet the plot is not equally formalized, and historical judgments are rarely developed to conclusions. On the other hand, Shakespeare uses historical situations in order to set up personal dilemmas, in which characters must make a tragic choice between alternatives clearly balanced and stated. The ideal of a united England glimmers but faintly. More memorable are the mad cursings of the bereaved Constance, that lineal descendant (in Shakespeare's art, not in history) of the bitter old Queen Margaret of the Henry VI plays. More memorable also is the pathos of the young Prince Arthur, whose sweet volubility and unboylike forgivingness leads Shakespeare, for perhaps the only time in his career, into sentimentality.

This pathos is intensified, or rendered more implausible, by the hard world around the young prince. The citizens of Angiers will yield their town only to the winner, acknowledging that success constitutes legitimacy. France's claims against

---

England will be abandoned when a projected marriage holds out more profitable opportunities. Self-seeking opportunism, the eye for the main chance, is personified as "that same purpose-changer, that sly devil . . . That smooth-faced gentleman, tickling commodity" (2.1.567, 573). And the speaker who sees so clearly the motivations of the faithless and the cheaters, interrupts his own diatribe to remark: "And why rail I on this commodity?/But for because he hath not wooed me yet" (587–88). For a moment King John seems to stand for an independent commonwealth against the power of Rome as he vows that "no Italian priest/Shall tithe or toll in our dominions" (3.1.79–80)—until we learn that he intends to use the rich ecclesiastical foundations merely as convenient cashboxes and coffers: "the fat ribs of peace/Must by the hungry now be fed upon" (3.2.19–20). On the other hand, the Papal legate Pandulph develops in leisurely logic the conception of ultimate values, warning his pupil to "arm thy constant and thy nobler parts/Against these giddy loose suggestions" (3.1.217–18), and counseling a firm-souled integrity that may stand against "in thyself rebellion to thyself" (215). Action, nevertheless, proves Pandulph's morally unassailable arguments to be special pleading. In a succeeding scene of the same act, this fine philosopher scorns the Dauphin for failing to see the new pattern which Commodity may make of the latest turn of the kaleidoscope of policy; he scoffs at him for not grasping a new opportunity for personal advancement: "How green you are and fresh in this old world!" (3.3.145) The nobles, both French and English, change sides at will; and the play huddles up its end in a series of yieldings, in which the defeated bow to the defeated and dying.

Opposed to this mad mixture of selfish, ephemeral, fearful, greedy striving is the one figure of Philip Faulconbridge, nephew of King John and bastard son of Richard *Coeur de Lion*. He is one of Shakespeare's important experiments. The senseless *Realpolitik* is to be judged *dramatically*—that is, not by wise comments and political adages, but by juxtaposing the free spirit of "a good blunt fellow" next to all the conventions of the chronicles, the romances, the politicians, and the Machiavellians. The invention will be developed even more fully in the person of Falstaff. Philip the Bastard is blood-brother to Berowne—Philip playing his wit, bluntness, and surface cynicism on society and the state, Berowne exercising the same instruments on romantic courtly love and affectations. The moral drama of *King John,* therefore, is the conflict between convention and hypocrisy on the one hand, and clear-eyed humorous reality on the other. It is as if a boon companion whom Shakespeare admired had journeyed almost four hundred years back into the past, to comment from the stage on ancient action in a manner that all contemporaries could understand.

As a moral commentator, the Bastard's great strength is his self-awareness. This manifests itself in his humor and his forthrightness. It is he who not only rails against self-seeking compromises and gainful "Commodity," but is simultaneously aware that he himself may fall a prey to them. His action, rather than his words, shows that he places honor above material possessions: he gives up his estate rather than deny *Coeur de Lion* as his father, "Brother, take you my land, I'll take my chance" (1.1.151). Yet he is humorously aware, even when he makes his decision, of the tricks and affections of "worshipful society," and evaluates his being knighted in terms that show him in no danger of turning into a straw nobleman:

> A foot of honor better than I was,
> But many a many foot of land the worse.   (181–82)

Though he will not practice to deceive, he means to look at the world sharply in order to avoid deceit.

> For he is but a bastard to the time
> That doth not smack of observation.
> And so am I, whether I smack or no.   (207–9)

Observation, then, and the weighing of all possibilities, is to be the safest road to true judgment.* This is strikingly borne out in the ironically accidental death of the young Prince Arthur after he has won his vile-visaged would-be murderer Hubert to compassion. The other lords accuse

---

*For other examples of his realistic choric "observation," compare his comment on the sudden alliance of the two enemies France and England outside Angiers:

Hubert in high-astounding terms. The Bastard is a better
judge that even hideous appearances may be deceitful. He
stops a violent and mistaken vengeance in a line much
admired in its variant in *Othello:* "Your sword is bright, sir;
put it up again." And later he adds in his own idiom:

> Put up thy sword betime,
> Or I'll so maul you and your toasting iron
> That you shall think the devil is come from hell.
> (4.3.98–100)

Irony and the deliberate understatement of emotion keep
him from sentimental hysteria even over the body of the
young prince: "Here's a good world! Knew you of this fair
work?" (116) Though he feels that he may lose his way
"Among the thorns and dangers of this world" (141), though
in the death of Arthur "The life, the right and truth of all this
realm/Is fled to heaven" (144–45), and though dogged war is
now bristling over the bare-picked bone of majesty, signifi-
cantly his immediate decision is to support the King, as he
has always done in the past, among the thousand businesses
that threaten the destruction of the state.

The Bastard, in his practical wisdom, shows a genuine
respect for that which exists, defending the integrity of the
present order against all theories, specious or valid, including
his own; and determined to set the whole above any of its
parts. It is he who unites for a moment the warring French
and British forces against Angiers, when its citizens refuse to
acknowledge the authority of either. He, no less than Salisbury, laments the disfiguring of "the antique and well-noted
face/Of plain old form" (4.2.21–22), and suspects truth when

How like you this wild counsel, mighty states?
Smacks it not something of the policy? (2.1.395–96)

And on the defiance of the Citizen of Angiers:

He speaks plain cannon fire, and smoke, and bounce . . .
Zounds! I was never so bethumped with words
Since I first called my brother's father dad. (462–67)

And on the wooing compliments of the Dauphin (504–9), on the overpow-
ering inevitability of the punishment for evil acts (4.3.116–34), and on the
"bloody Neroes" that rip up the womb of their Mother England (5.2.130–58).

it is decked in "so new a fashioned robe" (27). Tradition and authority are the needed grounds for moral order, and they can be maintained only through obedience to their symbol. This symbol is no other than the King.

King John is not superhuman. His vices, unlike Richard III's, waver into mere velleities. Even the King must leave "the soul's frail dwelling house" (5.7.3). He uses his voice, "the organ-pipe of frailty" (23), in last awareness of the "one thread, one little hair" (54) on which his life hangs, knowing that in one swift moment "all this thou seest is but a clod/And module [= little image] of confounded royalty" (57–58). The new King Henry acknowledges the awful symbol of sovereignty as the foundation of all stability:

> What surety of the world, what hope, what stay,
> When this was now a king, and now is clay?
>
> (68–69)

The King is mortal and weak; but he is also the enduring image, whose subjects "calmly run on in obedience/Even to our ocean, to our great King John" (5.5.56–57). The individual and the state are in conflict; action and ideals; the part and the whole. In this struggle, in order to preserve a stability without which right and wrong are meaningless, Shakespeare takes a stand. With hesitation and misgivings—fully aware of what may be said on the other side, and, indeed, saying it himself—in this rather inchoate play he gives his allegiance to the King. Fealty does not depend upon the person of the King, whose human fallibilities are inexorably magnified by the curse of power; allegiance depends upon the kingly office. The King, then, becomes one of Shakespeare's first serious symbols. He adopts it because without this emblem of authority to which loyalty may attach itself, he has found political thinking to be a tale told by an idiot.

HAROLD C. GODDARD

From The Meaning of Shakespeare*

King John has generally been relegated to a place among
Shakespeare's relatively minor works. It is a mere chronicle,
it is said, just an inconsequence of events. It lacks the orga-
nized unity of a work of art. It is a play at which the author
"perhaps pegged away," a recent commentator suggests,
"when he did not feel in the right mood" for *Richard II,* on
which he may have been working at the same time.

Granted that *King John* is not among Shakespeare's mas-
terpieces, these judgments do the play an injustice. It has a
clear leading idea, marked unity, and such excellent charac-
terization as to put quite out of court the supposition that the
poet took a perfunctory interest in it. It is built around a theme
that Shakespeare never thereafter lost sight of. That theme is
close to the heart of nearly all the other History Plays, both
English and Roman; it is essential to *Hamlet;* it culminates in
King Lear; it echoes through *The Tempest.* This is not the
place to back up these assertions in detail. But if there is truth
in them, *King John* is another extraordinarily seminal work.

The plan of *King John* is simplicity itself. It is centered
around a devastating contrast. In the title role is John himself, about the unkingliest king Shakespeare ever created.
The fact is, John has never grown up. He is mentally dominated by his ambitious mother. When he hears that a foreign
foe has landed in force on his shores, he cries out:

> Where is my mother's care,
> That such an army could be drawn in France,
> And she not hear of it?   (4.2.117–19)

*From *The Meaning of Shakespeare* by Harold C. Goddard (Chicago: The
University of Chicago Press, 1951). Reprinted by permission of The University of Chicago Press.

He is like a bewildered child in the night. And when a moment later he is told that his mother is dead, his repeated exclamation, "What! mother dead! . . . My mother dead!" (127, 181), illuminates him like a flash of lightning. We pity him. Yet it is under that same mother's influence that he has become a liar and a coward. "Weakness possesseth me" (5.3.17) "Within me is a hell" (5.7.46). Those words at the end, though spoken more of his physical than his moral condition, are his own last judgment on himself. They sum him up with justice.

How could a drama be written about such a cipher? It couldn't. And so, quite re-creating a figure he found in his source, Shakespeare puts over against John as upright, downright, forthright a hero as he ever depicted, Philip Faulconbridge. Faulconbridge is everything John is not: truthful, faithful, courageous, humorous, without personal ambition, utterly loyal to his sovereign and to England. He is direct and picturesque in speech to the point of genius. He lacks, if you will, some of the transcendental virtues, but, within his limits, he is a man. "Look at them!" Shakespeare seems to say as he places them side by side, "a man is greater than a king!" But there is another kind of king, and in that sense Faulconbridge is king of *King John*. That is the irony of the title. That is the key to the play. And to make the pill the bitterer to the feudally minded, this king is a bastard. He hasn't even the ordinary title of son. His title is the truth. As the clown was the natural gentleman in *The Two Gentlemen of Verona*, so the bastard is the natural king in *King John*. Here, too, if in quite different senses of the terms, master and man have exchanged places. If ever a play brought the mere name of king, the mere institution of royalty, into disrepute, it is this one. But in behalf of no shallow equalitarianism. For, after all, Faulconbridge had royal blood in his veins. Thoreau once remarked that the life of a great man is the severest satire. The Bastard shows exactly what he meant. But how quietly Shakespeare makes his point.

The fact that Faulconbridge was illegitimate doubtless first suggested the ironic antithesis between him and John. And this antithesis in turn brought the impulse to compose the variations that run through every scene and ramify into every corner of the drama, imparting to it its high degree of unity.

An illegitimate son is likely to react to his birth in one or the other of two opposite ways. "I am a bastard," he may argue. "I was born outside the law. Therefore, I am entitled to revenge myself for the wrong committed against me by setting all law and social conformity at naught whenever it is to my advantage to do so." Don John in *Much Ado about Nothing,* Thersites in *Troilus and Cressida,* and Edmund in *King Lear* are studies in this type. But on the other hand the illegitimate child may reason: "I am a natural son. Instead of becoming a victim of the customs and conventions that reduce most men to slavery, I will be free—true to the best impulses life has implanted in my heart. I will be a son of nature." That was Faulconbridge's reaction. It was the easier for him doubtless because he suspected he was the son of Richard the Lionhearted. When he rejects the Faulconbridge name and inheritance and declares,

> I am I, howe'er I was begot,   (1.1.175)

he shows where he stands on the question with which so much of the play is concerned: which is better, the truth without worldly possessions and position, or worldly possessions and position without the truth? His attitude toward his mother in this matter defines another abysmal difference between himself and the King. John is like a little boy tied to his mother's apron strings. The Bastard dares his mother to reveal his father's name and elicits the truth from her by his very audacity. Thus the first act, which would otherwise be a mere prologue or almost a separate little piece in one act, is perfectly integrated with the rest of the play.

But it is not just John who is foil to Faulconbridge. The play is filled with weaklings, timeservers, turncoats, and traitors. The Bastard's name for the god, or rather the devil, that these worldlings worship is Commodity. There are few if any more important passages in the early works of Shakespeare than the lines at the end of Act 2 of this play in which the Bastard pays his respects to the God of This World to whom all but a few rare characters bow down. Shakespeare's profound agreement with his hero in regard to this object of man's adoration is proved by two of his greatest sonnets, the 123d and 124th, on Time and Policy, which are nothing but the Bastard's soliloquy in another key, or two other keys.

To the Elizabethans, Machiavelli was the father of this god, Commodity. But he is descended from human nature itself. No synonym quite expresses the wealth of meaning that the Bastard compresses into the word. Its derivation suggests a falling-in with, or a taking-up with, the fashion, practice, or advantage of the moment to the neglect of deeper or eternal concerns. The Commodity-server, in Shakespeare's favorite phrase, is the fool of time. Worldliness, compliance, compromise, policy, diplomacy, casuistry, expediency, opportunism: they all are somehow comprehended under the one name. Commodity is intimately related to Langland's Lady Meed, to Bunyan's Worldly Wiseman, to William James's "bitch-goddess, Success." Some of its other names are Mammon, the Main Chance, and The Band-Wagon.

> Commodity, the bias of the world,
> The world, who of itself is peisèd well,
> Made to run even upon even ground,
> Till this advantage, this vile drawing bias,
> This sway of motion, this commodity,
> Makes it take head from all indifferency,
> From all direction, purpose, course, intent.

$$(2.1.574–80)$$

Broker, break-vow, purpose-changer, bawd, cheat, devil, gentleman: Faulconbridge cannot find names strong enough or bad enough to characterize it. Yet he has the modesty and sense of humor to fear that he himself may not be strong enough to resist the wiles of the very tempter he is condemning. So he ironically winds up his diatribe with the couplet:

> Since kings break faith upon commodity,
> Gain, be my lord, for I will worship thee.   (597–98)

This is, of course, the last thing on earth he intends to do or, as the event proves, ever does. But his irony makes dupes of many readers. Indeed, one of the acutest of recent commentators remarks that Faulconbridge "is essentially a crude

person, the successful opportunist and materialist, as one
sees from his 'commodity' speech (2.1.561) with its characteristic ending, 'Gain, be my lord, for I will worship thee.' "
That is getting the Bastard as completely upside down as it
would be to call Iago honest or Desdemona a hypocrite.

There are some earlier words of this man that supply the
key to his attitude. They come just after he has been made
Sir Richard by the King. After some delightful jocosities
about the snobberies his new rank will entitle him to practice, his tone suddenly alters and he adds:

> And not alone in habit and device,
> Exterior form, outward accoutrement,
> But from the inward motion to deliver
> Sweet, sweet, sweet poison for the age's tooth,
> Which, though I will not practice to deceive,
> Yet, to avoid deceit, I mean to learn.   (1.1.210–15)

In more biblical language, what he is saying is that he
intends to live in the world, but, so far as he can, to keep himself unspotted by it. Somehow (if I may repeat what certainly deserves repeating) I cannot escape the conviction
that those words come as directly from Shakespeare's own
heart as from the Bastard's, that he too meant to deliver

> Sweet, sweet, sweet poison for the age's tooth.   (213)

And so the Bastard's dedication of himself to the worship of
Gain is found to be a sort of inverted hypocrisy.

There is nothing inverted about the hypocrisy of the
genuine worshipers of Commodity in the play. King John is
too weak a man to be the perfect representative of this Devil.
That honor falls to Cardinal Pandulph, the papal legate, arch
power-politician of the play, one of the first and one of the
worst of the corrupt ecclesiastics of whom there are so many
in Shakespeare's works. He is a perfect preview of some
of the totalitarians of our time. The contrast between him
and the Bastard is if anything even more striking than that
between the Bastard and John. If ever the style was the
man, and if ever two styles were at opposite poles, it is the
style of the Cardinal and the style of the Bastard. Neither

can utter a line without characterizing himself. A long quotation is needed to give the full flavor of Pandulph's casuistry and verbosity, but these devious and cacophonous sentences from one of his endless, sinuous speeches will have to suffice:

> The better act of purposes mistook
> Is to mistake again; though indirect,
> Yet indirection thereby grows direct,
> And falsehood falsehood cures, as fire cools fire
> Within the scorched veins of one new burned.
> It is religion that doth make vows kept,
> But thou hast sworn against religion
> (By what thou swear'st against the thing thou swear'st)
> And mak'st an oath the surety for thy truth
> (Against an oath the truth); thou art unsure
> To swear—swears only not to be forsworn,
> Else what a mockery should it be to swear!
> But thou dost swear only to be forsworn,
> And most forsworn, to keep what thou dost swear.
>
> (3.1.200–13)

"Zounds!" we are tempted to cry with the Bastard (as he put it on another occasion),

> 'Zounds! I was never so bethumped with words
> Since I first called my brother's father dad.   (2.1.466–67)

lines which may serve as a good example of *his* style: always vernacular, and never a polysyllable where a monosyllable will serve as well.

Interesting as he is, to analyze Pandulph in detail would be superfluous. It is enough to say that he anticipates and rolls into one two of Shakespeare's most famous characters: Polonius and Iago. Iago and Polonius! could there be a more dreadful mixture? Pandulph's profession is turning not only every weakness and slip, but every virtue of other men to his advantage.

> 'tis wonderful
> What may be wrought out of their discontent.
>
> (3.3.178–79)

The gusto of that needs but another turn of the screw to transform it into Iago's

> So will I turn her virtue into pitch,
> And out of her own goodness make the net
> That shall enmesh them all.   (*Othello*, 2.3.380-81)

And the cynicism of

> How green you are and fresh in this old world!   (145)

has the exact accent of Shakespeare's supreme villain when talking with Roderigo. Similarly, the voice, as well as the mental and moral attitude, of Polonius can be caught in

> though indirect,
> Yet indirection thereby grows direct,   (3.1.201-2)

down even to the very words:

> By indirections find directions out.

Almost literally Pandulph may be said to have "split" into Polonius and Iago. It is a good example of what I have called the embryological character of Shakespeare's early works.

Shakespeare carries his central theme into still other parts of his play. The mainspring of *King John* is the rivalry of two jealous women—mothers ambitious for their sons—Elinor for John, who holds the English throne, and Constance for Arthur, who is legitimate heir to it, being the son of John's deceased older brother Geoffrey. The poet sharpens the difference between these two women into one of the high contrasts in which the play abounds. Elinor is a power-politician in her own right, and her ambition is selfish and worldly, not primarily maternal. The completeness with which she has crushed her son's individuality is proof of this. The ambition of Constance, on the other hand, is maternal, the woman's hero-worship of her son. Extravagant as it is, and sentimental or even touched with madness as her grief becomes at Arthur's death, it is human and forgivable, whereas Elinor's machinations are cold and deliberate. Once more, Nature with all her faults looks lovely compared with Commodity.

In addition to the Bastard and the Mother, there is a third representative of Nature in the play, the Child. In spite of a number of conceits that mar his role (touches that a few years later the poet would not have been guilty of), Arthur is one of the most effective portrayals of childhood Shakespeare ever achieved, and the scene in which his innocence and trust overcome Hubert's temptation to do a dastardly deed for the King, who wants Arthur put out of the way, is the emotional climax of the play. Unlike practically all its other characters, who are on the side either of Commodity or of Truth, Hubert trembles for a moment on the brink of the World and then, under the child's influence, turns his back on temptation and is saved. It is a tribute to the Bastard's psychological insight that he accepts Hubert's protestations of innocence in the face of the most damning circumstantial evidence of his guilt.

Emergencies winnow the weak from the strong. At the end of the play, when the French invade England, John, who since Arthur's death by accident has been in a panic, resigns all power to the Bastard:

> Have thou the ordering of this present time,   (5.2.77)

and the latter, almost single-handed, holds the enemy in check until Nature, ever impartial in such conflicts, has her say. The sea swallows half the English force and all the French supplies. Pandulph brings an overture of peace from the French.

> The Cardinal Pandulph is within at rest,
> Who half an hour since came from the Dolphin,
>   (5.7.82–83)

is the way the announcement is made. That nap of the Cardinal's tells us as nothing else could of the pressure he has brought to bear on the previously recalcitrant Lewis and of the assurance he has of its results. The Bastard is wary enough to keep on a war footing while the peace is being arranged.

Meanwhile, King John, poisoned by a monk, has come to

an ignominious end. Yet in his last speeches a kind of
despairing poetry breaks from him that is a measure perhaps
of what nature in vain intended him to be. His last words are
"confounded royalty."

It was the Elizabethan custom to give the final lines of a
play to the man of highest rank. In breaking that custom and
putting the last words of *King John* into the mouth of the
Bastard rather than of Prince Henry, who, save for his formal
coronation, is now King Henry III, Shakespeare clinches the
fact that the Bastard is the king of the play. And in the speech
itself, particularly in its last line, and most particularly in its
last word, he confirms its main theme: Truth or Commodity.
Few, if any, of Shakespeare's plays have a finer ending. It is
like the note of a trumpet:

> Come the three corners of the world in arms,
> And we shall shock them! Naught shall make us rue
> If England to itself do rest but true!   (116–18)

Shakespeare has often been criticized for omitting all reference in this play to what historians and political scientists
consider the main event of John's reign: the granting of
Magna Charta. Yet how trivial the exaction of that compact
from John was compared with the everlasting conflict between Truth and Commodity that Shakespeare records so
powerfully in this drama. Perhaps education will some day
revert to a perception of what was so like an axiom to Shakespeare: that psychology goes deeper than politics and that a
knowledge of man himself must precede any fruitful consideration of the institutions he has created.

MURIEL ST. CLARE BYRNE

From The Shakespeare Season at . . .
Stratford-upon-Avon, 1957*

Everybody, I believe, has his Shakespearian blind spot.
Mine is obviously *King John*. I have seen it six or seven
times at least: have admired individual performances of
John, the Bastard, Elinor, Constance, and Hubert; and can
always be moved by that ringing conclusion and the good
lines scattered up and down the play. I am always shaken by
the fact that many of my actor friends admire it greatly, and
by the frequency with which it is performed nowadays. But
it does not add up to a viable play, for me. Having thus
disabled my own critical judgment in advance, I will add
the rider that I still live in hopes that if anyone will dress it
Elizabethan, perform it on the open stage without lighting
effects, and get rid of what has been called the "Norman-
Nondescript" background, I may come to a better mind. The
Harrow boys did this in 1953, and I warmed to it more than
usual. The flat-topped helms, the gowns and wimples, and
John looking exactly like his effigy in Worcester Cathedral,
drag me inexorably back to the actual historical period, in
which the story has a straight, violent and sinister but not
essentially dramatic and theatrical impact. But to get the
kind of emotional response calculated upon by the author
and evoked from the contemporary audiences in those early
post-Armada years, something quite other than straight
period production seems to me necessary.

This year's *King John* at Stratford has the speed, the
clarity and the vigor of all Douglas Seale's historical productions. The imagery of war and violence which pervades

*From *Shakespeare Quarterly* VIII (1957): 482–85. Reprinted by permission of the Shakespeare Association of America, Inc.

the play was translated into terms of sinister, brooding atmosphere by setting the action either against a background of darkness or else an ominous leaden sky, shot with livid flame during the battle scenes, while silhouetted darkly against these wrathful heavens the fighting armies struggle and swirl around a dark, squat, gray mass of wall and gateway which rears itself in the midst, somber and menacing. For the scenes which moved on a more human level there was a fine spill of light against the darkness, in which the players and the splashes of color made by their costumes stood out in sharp relief. Good as they invariably are, I have never known the opening Faulconbridge scenes come over better, so easy and natural and alive.

Robert Harris' remarkable study of the King, of which I have seen no adequate recognition anywhere, confirms me in the belief that an Elizabethan presentation might put me on better terms with the play. It is sometimes said that the Bastard is the real hero. As I see it, *King John* is a theme without heroes, but with spokesmen. The theme is the interdependence of Tudor nationalism and internal unity; but the material is dramatically recalcitrant, and the author is reduced to forcing a card on us. When the monarch ceases to be a fit spokesman he has to be withdrawn and the Bastard substituted to speak for him. I thought Mr. Harris played the part straight, exactly as Shakespeare wrote it, accepting the fact that the character is composed in three installments which do not add up to a satisfactory whole. To resist the temptation to recompose into a consistent portrait, justified by historical knowledge and popular expectation, argues a rare fidelity to the text on the part of both actor and producer; and this, as I see it, was Mr. Harris' achievement. John is a usurper, as Chatillion and his mother remind him and us in the opening passage; but until the capture of Arthur (3.3) he is, to the Tudor Englishman, the only English king of medieval times who stood out against the Pope, the precursor of the Reformation, the man who calls the Pope's legate "meddling priest" (3.1.89) and announces that though France and everyone may desert him, "Yet I alone, alone do me oppose/ Against the Pope" (96–97). The Bastard may comment ironically upon the game of power politics played by France and England, but King Philip is as ready to sacrifice Arthur's cause to obtain five provinces as the Lady Blanch's dowry as John is to trade them in order to keep his kingdom. The first installment of his character is neither weak nor treacherous: he defies France, is ready to fight, compromises shrewdly, and when he does fight has changed his ground so that he has the emotional support of the Tudor audience. And then, unfortunately, the rest of the story catches up on the author, and John becomes, by intention, the murderer of his nephew.

The three installments of John, as I see them, are: firstly, a build-up of the Tudor "Reformation hero," deriving from Bale, the *Troublesome Raigne,* and Holinshed, combined with a build-up of the monarch as the spokesman or symbol of Tudor nationalism: secondly, in the very center of the play, a brief and brilliant Shakespearian sketch of the evil, cruel, unscrupulous, and unstable nature that was indeed John Lackland—a highly dramatic use of historical truth, as seen by John's contemporaries and by the later historian, but ignored by Tudor writers, which demotes the usurper as spokesman and enables the author to switch the role to a genuinely sympathetic character: thirdly—and this seems to me one of the very trickiest bits of card-forcing in the whole process—a nominal rehabilitation of the royal mystique, factually justified because, Arthur being dead, John is the rightful king, and emotionally boosted by making him the victim of monkish vengeance and by attributing the revolt of the barons not to his tyrannous rule but to the death of Arthur, of which he was not guilty in fact, though in desire, and for which he is allowed at least some show of repentance. Now I do not suggest that Mr. Harris and Mr. Seale went about their job in this crude manner: actors and producers work more directly and intuitively. But I do suggest that Mr. Harris' subtle, human and quite unconventional study, and his refusal to depict John as the villain which in fact he was, is due to a profound fidelity to the Elizabethan play which Shakespeare wrote. The two central scenes of the tempting of Hubert and his subsequent reproaches were brilliantly handled, especially the twists and turns by which his divided mind seeks to evade its own consciousness of guilt.

Elizabethan topicality creates no similar difficulties for the other characters. It is in keeping with the spirit he has shown from the beginning that *Coeur de Lion's* son should take over as spokesman for the national theme and make the monarch the rallying point for national unity, speaking from his royalty of nature the words that should have been the King's, when the political opportunism of the real John invades the Elizabethan play and makes him surrender to the Pope and receive his crown again from the legate's hands. After his admirable Henry V at the Old Vic some years ago, I had expected a bigger performance from Alec Clunes, with more drive to it. He had the humor and the realism, but as Bastards go this was a lightweight conception, lacking in lift and the capacity for something larger than life at the moments when this is needed. He dropped that ringing ending in a way no Elizabethan audience could have forgiven. I thought it was a pity to try to play this character through the mask of a juvenile lead makeup. His own years and his own naturally expressive countenance would have stood him in better stead. And though I am no advocate in general of the Wigs and Beards of the older dispensation, I think perhaps an elder brother's having a beard might have helped.

When I saw the play in the sixteenth week Joan Miller seemed to me to have made Constance her best part in this her first season at Stratford. She was particularly good in that last most difficult scene of all, when, half-crazed with grief for the loss of her son, she has to express it in some of the most elaborately rhetorical writing in Shakespeare. She was not afraid of the emotion, and she had both the power and the pathos needed. As the King of France, Cyril Luckham helped the scene greatly with his gift for sympathetic support. Doreen Aris as Blanch caught and held her moment of real pathos when her newlywedded happiness is abruptly shattered by the declaration of war between France and England. Patrick Wymark was eloquently persuasive as the Citizen of Angiers, and Mark Dignam was an impressive as well as a crafty Pandulph. But it becomes invidious to single out performances when, as always with Mr. Seale's productions, it is the general level of good speaking and the all-round supporting strength that he elicits from his casts which give that overall clarity that makes his interpretations of the histories so solidly satisfying. The formalism of Audrey Cruddas' setting and the austere simplicity of her "correct," dignified medieval costumes fit in admirably with his methods by not attracting attention to themselves. We can, as it were, take them in at first glance and accept them as just what these people would naturally have worn. It is curious to reflect that the opportunity it provided for archaeological spectacle and lavish stage display appears to have been the play's main attraction throughout last century. A comparison of Mr. Seale's text with the severely cut acting editions of the past would be salutary for those rash generalizers who like to say that all our modern producers think about is how to do something different with Shakespeare. The difference, in this case, is that Mr. Seale and his designer and his cast go back to Shakespeare and try to discover what the author meant.

ALAN C. DESSEN

Deborah Warner's Stratford-upon-Avon Production (1988)*

The most rewarding 1988 show for me was Deborah Warner's *King John*. From the outset the spectators, especially those seated below, were enveloped by the actions and interactions that swirled and erupted around them in this boxed-in, highly focused theatrical space. Indeed, the term "high-energy show" might have been coined for this production that seemed at various moments to be about to burst out of the confines of The Other Place. A show-defining action came at the beginning of 2.1 when, to the sound of drums, trumpets, and war cries, nearly the entire cast raced in, singly or in pairs, carrying twenty-four ladders and stacking them up against the wall. This electrifying moment was reminiscent of a high-speed setting up of a circus tent, an impression enhanced when Austria appeared moments later with a full lion's skin (which, with a smug look on his face, he periodically nuzzled). The theatricality of the ladders and of the overall spectacle was exciting and energizing (especially at the outset of a long and difficult sequence) and reminded us vividly that we were watching a play (or actors "at play"). Shakespeare on stage, we were being shown, can be fun.

A great deal of breakneck energy also was provided by David Morrissey's Bastard, never an aloof, witty commentator upon the action, but rather a raw, rude, even anarchic figure, very much involved in the events around him. In the opening scene this Bastard walloped his much smaller

*From Alan C. Dessen, "Shakespeare on Stage: Exciting Shakespeare in 1988," *Shakespeare Quarterly* 40:2 (1989): 205–7. © Folger Shakespeare Library. Reprinted with permission of The Johns Hopkins University Press.

brother in the stomach, whacked Elinor on the back, and, overall, presented a loud, explosive figure that for U.K. play-goers recalled the soccer hooligans much in the news, a link reinforced in Act 2 when he appeared wrapped in a St. George's flag (a visual allusion to the recently arrested British fans at the European soccer championship). Morrissey pro-vided a strong presence in the scenes in France, especially in his taunting of Austria. After the citizen's proposal of the Lewis-Blanche marriage, this Bastard (upstage from the others) first railed against the citizen's rhetoric ("here's a large mouth, indeed") but then stopped in surprise when he saw that the English and French parties huddling in the two doorways were taking the marriage proposal seriously ("our ears are cudgelled"). Thanks to some adept staging, the play-goer could chart this figure's thinking and thereby get a clear glimpse of the Bastard's first insight into Commodity, a moment that then led into his famous speech.

This long and potentially unwieldy 2.1 in front of Angiers was staged adeptly. The first big entrance of the English forces was keyed to Nicholas Woodeson's diminutive but intense John in an oversized greatcoat and helmet, bearing his huge longsword in a sheath and exhibiting a distinctive feisty look (as the shortest figure on stage, he was often looking *up* at others with a mocking belligerence). The action that followed usually kept the key figures (John and Philip) in the center and others in the four corners, except when various figures squared off (e.g., Elinor and Con-stance, Austria and the Bastard). Before our eyes, groupings formed and re-formed so as to produce a choreography that clarified the many confrontations. Added to this mix was the presence of Hubert-citizen above (e.g., eating his French bread while looking out with changing expressions at the battle we could hear but not see). This aloof figure, however, grew increasingly concerned while the Bastard argued in favor of attacking Angiers, then argued effectively for a marriage to Blanche: clearly making it up as he went along, he hesitated, and, in a moment of inspiration, pointed to Lewis as the ideal bridegroom.

Other scenes were equally varied and inventive. In 3.3 John played the solicitous uncle with Arthur, tickling and poking him until Arthur bit John's hand, an action that led to an angry blow and a quick move above with Hubert trailing behind. Hubert's reaction to John's order to kill Arthur was then a potent moment, for, as Hubert looked down at the innocent Arthur below, we could see a gamut of emotions fleet across Robert Demeger's highly expressive face (the siren call of Commodity, a relish for power and violence, a sense of principle or conscience). Demeger's Hubert was equally impressive in his moral dilemma in 4.1 (to blind or not to blind Arthur) and in his confrontation with the nobles and the Bastard in 4.3.

For me, the strongest scene in the show was 4.2. At the outset Pembroke and Salisbury set up some chairs and took down one of the ladders and put it on sawhorses so as to make a "table," thereby "placing" the scene and, by means of the empty chairs, conveying a sense of a council of state. Here the same John who earlier had been sly, cutting, one step ahead of everyone else, the John who could defeat the French and manipulate Arthur, started to come unglued when confronted by his disaffected nobles. This John was then stunned at receiving the news of his mother's death, so that, after the departure of the Bastard, Woodeson put enormous force into the three-word speech that precedes the entrance of Hubert ("My mother dead!"). At this point, in his anger at Hubert and his frustration at his inability to hold on to the allegiance of his nobles, John upended the table and many of the chairs, so that the now chaotic room could signal the disorder of the kingdom, perhaps of John himself. To Woodeson, John's device to get the nobles back (his "way to win their loves again") was to kill Hubert, so he pulled a knife only to be stopped by the warrant that Hubert thrust up between them as a shield and justification, a response reminiscent of the thrusting forth of a cross in a vampire movie. By the end of this scene, we had witnessed a meaningful and well-charted display of both the political and inner collapse of the figure who had dominated the first three acts.

In this show the crown rather than the throne was the pivotal image. The English crown was on John's head in 1.1, then dangled at his waist on a chain in 2.1 (to be whipped on when claiming sovereignty over Angiers), then in 3.3 was placed casually on a ladder above during the interview with

Hubert (almost to be left behind). In 4.2, in his confrontation with his nobles, John was in his shirtsleeves but (after his second coronation) was wearing the crown. The crown then became the central image in a well-wrought 5.1. Here John moved above quickly, with Pandulph following more slowly; John knelt, gave up his crown, got it back quickly, then rose, ready for Pandulph's promised action (to get rid of the French). Obviously, the submission to Rome had been perfunctory, a going-through-the-motions. Then, at the often-cited line at the end of 5.1 ("Have thou the ordering of this present time"), John handed the crown to the Bastard (as if to pass the baton to someone else), but the latter put it back on John's head. The scene was therefore framed by these two moments involving the crown, with John giving it away twice and having it returned twice (though in very different contexts). As Woodeson made clear to us, the reliance upon brute force in the first half of the play now has given way to the weakness and inner turmoil of Act 5 (eventually expressed in the fever that eats away from within). This John, who felt he must kill Arthur to get absolute security, has been surprised by his nobles, stymied by Hubert, undone by the death of his mother, and forced to grasp at straws and twice pass the crown to others. Unable to take out his frustrations on Hubert or in 5.1 to find an answer in Pandulph or the Bastard, John is an increasingly hapless figure who has lost his political base and, as portrayed by Woodeson, is being destroyed by a Macbeth-like moral conscience that cannot be ignored.

Warner and her cast provided many other potent moments and stage images. For example, the quarrel between the Bastard and Austria in 3.1 produced a melee much like a rugby scrum that served as a fine bit of directorial mis-direction so as to cloak Pandulph's entrance. The image of Pandulph at the downstage door facing John and Philip holding hands upstage was then recapitulated in 5.2 when Pandulph again entered in the same spot, this time to confront Lewis holding the hands of the three English nobles. Elsewhere, Susan Engel's Constance was especially powerful in her range of emotions in 3.4, as in her move from an initial high passion to a deliberate, matter-of-fact (and hence chilling) "I am not mad." This Constance stalked Pandulph on some of her lines and grinned so as to show her teeth in a death's-head image during her speech on "amiable, lovely death."

Such thoughtful yet engaging choices are typical of Warner's shows, for, working in small spaces such as the Swan, The Other Place, and The Pit, she manages to get enormous mileage out of her personnel and out of two daunting scripts. The results, moreover, are not caviar for the general, for the audience both times I saw *King John* was composed not of scholars but of "ordinary" people who were quickly caught up in the excitement of a play they did not know (is this going to be about the signing of the Magna Charta?) but, often to their surprise (according to my exit polling), they much enjoyed. What emerged for me as a "specialist" was a tough, unsentimental, thoughtful, and thought-provoking production that proved that this anomalous, neglected, and sometimes maligned play is indeed worthy of our attention and respect. As with her equally telling production of *Titus,* Warner demonstrated once again how a director and a group of talented actors who trust the script can both entertain and enlighten us.

SYLVAN BARNET

King John on Stage and Screen

This is not the place to discuss the alleged defects of *King John*—the usual charges are that the play lacks a central character; that John is inconsistently presented (he is a hero insofar as he defies the Pope, but he is a villain insofar as he is a usurper and a murderer); that Arthur's claim to the throne is unclear; that the Bastard's quarrel with Austria is not adequately accounted for; that the Bastard's language is too frank to be heard by tender ears; that the construction is too episodic, and so on—but it is appropriate to mention that although *King John* has had a moderately respectable stage history, and a few productions have been important, it is among Shakespeare's least frequently staged plays. It gets done, of course, but no production of the twentieth century has managed greatly to excite the public, including those in our day that seek to emphasize the play's relevance by setting it in modern dress (combat fatigues for the battle scenes) in order to suggest that Shakespeare's politicians have their modern equivalents.

Apparently *King John* didn't greatly excite its first audiences either; there is no record of a performance in the seventeenth century, or in the early eighteenth. In 1736, however, Colley Cibber announced that he would present his extensively revised version, which he entitled *Papal Tyranny in the Reign of King John,* but his plan was greeted with such hostility that he withdrew the play while in rehearsal. The first recorded revival of Shakespeare's play took place in the following year, 1737, when *King John* was performed a few times at Covent Garden, in London. An actress played the role of Prince Arthur, thus establishing a tradition that endured, with a few exceptions, until the early twentieth century. The revival of 1737 was successful enough to keep the

play in the repertory, for it was occasionally performed
during the next four seasons. In 1745 Cibber was at last able
to see his play staged at Covent Garden. When he published
his version he explained that he found much in the original
in need of improvement. He expressed his surprise that
Shakespeare "should have taken no more fire" at the "flam-
ing contest between his insolent Holiness and King John"
(Cibber heightened the anti-Catholic element in the play),
and explained: "It was this coldness . . . that first incited the
adapter to inspirit his King John with a resentment that justly
might become an English monarch, and to paint the intoxi-
cated tyranny of Rome in its proper colors." Cibber omitted
the entire (relatively brief) first act, softened the role of
Philip the Bastard, touched up most of the remaining lines,
and added some material that had relevance to contemporary
politics.

   Five days after Cibber's first night, David Garrick produced *King John* at Drury Lane, with Garrick in the role of
John, and Cibber's daughter-in-law, Susannah Cibber, in the
role of Constance. Garrick staged the play eight times in the
Drury Lane season of 1745–46; when he revived it in 1754
he took the role of Philip the Bastard, which he had played
as early as 1745 in a production in Dublin. In 1761 he gave
up acting in *King John,* but as manager of Drury Lane he
kept the play in the repertory until February 1774. Although
Garrick heavily adapted many of Shakespeare's other
texts—not only cutting extensively but also touching up
lines and even writing whole new speeches—he treated
King John with surprising restraint. Of course he made
cuts—almost everyone still cuts Shakespeare's plays, even
the plays more highly esteemed than *King John*—reducing
Shakespeare's 2,570 lines to 1,905; and, on the other hand,
following Alexander Pope's edition of Shakespeare he added
fifteen lines from *The Troublesome Reign of King John;* he
also added a few phrases of his own, chiefly interjections. As
we will see, directors today are still given to clarifying some
passages of *King John* by adding lines from *The Troublesome Reign,* or even lines of their own.

   A word about cutting. The play is not exceptionally
long—it is about average length—but many speeches seem
repetitive. Take, for instance, the speech by Salisbury that

has given us the phrase "To gild the lily." (Oddly, the phrase is a misquotation; it does not appear in the speech.)

> Therefore, to be possessed with double pomp,
> To guard [= ornament] a title that was rich before,
> To gild refined gold, to paint the lily,
> To throw a perfume on the violet,
> To smooth the ice, or add another hue
> Unto the rainbow, or with taper-light
> To seek the beauteous eye of heaven to garnish,
> Is wasteful and ridiculous excess.   (4.2.9–16)

One might think that if Salisbury listened to himself, he would give fewer examples and would cut his speech by half. Confronted with speeches of this sort, there has scarcely been a director who has hesitated to cut *King John* by 500 or more lines.

John Philip Kemble staged the play (or, rather, his version of about 1,690 of Shakespeare's 2,570 lines, with a few additional non-Shakespearean lines) in 1800, though he had already been seen in London as John, and Sara Siddons (his sister) as Constance, as early as 1783. Sara last played Constance in 1812, but Kemble continued to play John (sometimes with his brother Charles as the Bastard) until his final season on the stage, 1817.

Kemble thus kept the play—with a great cast—before the eyes of the public for some thirty years, but he was not the only one in the period to stage *King John*. In 1800 the Reverend Richard Valpy, headmaster of Reading School, produced a "refined" version (the whole of the first act, with its abundant talk about adultery, was eliminated) for his schoolboys; in 1803 this laundered version was done at Covent Garden. More important was the highly researched version that Charles Kemble offered at the same theater in 1823–24. For this production (he had produced the play earlier) he commissioned James Robinson Planché, a noted antiquarian as well as a man of the theater, to design historically accurate costumes. In his rather self-satisfied *Memoir*, Planché gives his account of the origin of the production. Because he gives a good sense of the new "historical" attitude toward staging, he is quoted here at some length, though with ample cuts:

I complained to Mr. [Charles] Kemble that a thousand pounds were frequently lavished on a Christmas pantomime or an Easter spectacle, while the plays of Shakespeare were put upon the stage with make-shift scenery, and, at the best, a new dress or two for the principal characters. That although his brother John, whose classical mind revolted from the barbarisms which even a Garrick had tolerated, had abolished the bag-wig of Brutus and the gold-laced suit of Macbeth, the alterations made in the costumes of the plays founded upon English history in particular, while they rendered them more picturesque, added but little to their propriety. . . . It was not requisite to be an antiquary to see the absurdity of the soldiers before Angiers, at the beginning of the thirteenth century, being clothed precisely the same as those fighting at Bosworth at the end of the fifteenth. If one style of dress was right, the other must be wrong. Mr. Kemble admitted the fact, and perceived the pecuniary advantage that might result from the experiment. It was decided that I should make the necessary researches, design the dresses, and superintend the production of "King John" *gratuitously,* I beg leave to say. . . .

[The actors] had no faith in me, and sulkily assumed their new and strange habiliments, in the full belief that they would be roared at by the audience. They *were* roared at; but in a much more agreeable way than they had contemplated. When the curtain rose, and discovered King John dressed as his effigy appears in Worcester Cathedral, surrounded by his barons sheathed in mail, with cylindrical helmets and correct armorial shields, and his courtiers in the long tunics and mantles of the thirteenth century, there was a roar of applause, so general and so hearty, that the actors were astonished. . . . Receipts of from 400*l.* to 600*l.* nightly soon reimbursed the management for the expense of the production, and a complete reformation of dramatic costume became from that moment inevitable upon the English stage.

A playbill of January 19, 1824, describes Planché's contribution:

Shakespeare's Tragedy of
KING JOHN
With an attention to Costume

Never equalled on the English Stage. Every Character will
appear in the precise
HABIT OF THE PERIOD
The whole of the Dresses and Decorations being executed
from indisputable Authorities such as
Monumental Effigies, Seals, Illumined MSS, &c.

With Charles Kemble as the Bastard, and with Planché's
costumes (which were esteemed as both beautiful and edi-
fying), the version was much praised.

The most important version of the nineteenth century,
and probably still the most important version, was that of
William Charles Macready. Macready first played John in
Charles Kemble's production of 1822–23, i.e. in the production preceding the one for which Planché designed
the costumes and supervised the stage management, and he
occasionally played John in the 1830s, but in 1842–43 he
staged his own production at Drury Lane, and it was this version that he then continued to perform until his farewell
season of 1850. Further, his influence extended even into the
first decade of the twentieth century, for his text and much of
his stage business became standard with his successors. As
Charles Shattuck points out in his invaluable and handsomely illustrated *William Charles Macready's King John,*
although Charles Kean is often given credit for innovations
in *King John,* Kean's text and business are essentially
Macready's. (Kean produced the play in New York in 1846,
and in London in 1852.)

For his 1842 production Macready cut 740 lines (a little
more than Garrick had cut, but less than Kemble); he
omitted some talk about adultery and bastards in the first act,
and he omitted the whole of 5.4, and he trimmed many long
speeches, reducing the play to a running time of about two
and three-quarter hours. Given the fact that there were fourteen scene changes (these took only eighteen minutes) and
vast crowds on the stage (more than two hundred soldiers
might be used in a scene), Macready seems to have been
amazingly adept at keeping the action moving while at the
same time providing elaborate stage pictures.

Something of the excitement of the production can be
gained from a review in the *Times,* quoted by Shattuck:

Mr. Macready has brought before the eyes of his audience an animated picture of those Gothic times which are so splendidly illustrated by the drama. The stage is thronged with the stalwart forms of the middle ages, the clang of battle sounds behind the scenes, massive fortresses bound the horizon. The grouping is admirably managed. The mailed figures now sink into stern tranquillity; now, when the martial fire touches them, they rouse from their lethargy and thirst for action. The sudden interruption in the third act to the temporary peace between John and Philip Augustus was a fine instance of the power of making the stage a living picture. The Englishmen and Frenchmen who had mingled together parted with the rapidity of lightning, the hurried movements, the flashing swords, bespoke the turbulent spirit of the old barons. A quiet mass of glittering accoutrements had suddenly burst into new combinations of animation and energy.

It should be mentioned, too, that the cast (as well as the costumes and stage management) of this production was noteworthy: Macready himself played John, Samuel Phelps played Hubert, Helen Faucit played Constance, and James Anderson played the Bastard. A Miss Newcombe—a small girl—played Arthur.

Despite this mid-century success, first by Macready and then by Kean, the play virtually disappeared from the stage in the later decades of the nineteenth century, though in 1899 Herbert Beerbohm Tree mounted a revival that gained favorable comment. Like the earlier productions of the nineteenth century, this one was rich in spectacle. Tree arranged the play into three acts, and began the third act with a splendid dumb show of the granting of Magna Charta. (This of course was an interpolation; perhaps the most conspicuous thing about Shakespeare's *King John* is that it makes no reference to what we take to be the the most important happening during John's reign.) The nineteenth-century theatrical interest in historically accurate costume, and in pageantry, of course is rooted in larger matters, such as the rise of realism in literature, and the interest in scientific history, but one should not forget that drama from the time of Aeschylus has made use of spectacle. Readers of *King John* may let their eyes glide over such stage directions as "Enter

King John, Queen Elinor, Pembroke, Essex, and Salisbury, with Chatillion of France" (1.1), "Enter before Angiers, King Philip of France, Lewis the Dauphin, Constance, Arthur, and their Attendants and, from the other side, Austria and his Attendants" (2.1), and "Alarums, excursions. Enter Bastard, with Austria's head" (3.2), but even in Shakespeare's day the spectators probably saw impressive displays of banners, costumes, and swordsmanship. The play that we read is not the play that the Elizabethans experienced when they attended the theater, and readers need not feel guilty if they find the theater preferable to the library. Max Beerbohm, in a review of Beerbohm Tree's production, said he found reading the play "insufferably tedious"; "drama had seemed to me absolutely lacking. That was because I have not much imagination. . . . I feel that I owe a great debt of gratitude to the management which has brought out the latent possibilities." Two further details of Tree's production may be mentioned. First, of John in the scene in which he instigates Hubert to kill Arthur, Hesketh Pearson in *Beerbohm Tree* writes:

> There was a bed of flowers, the heads of which he flicked off with his sword as he mused, and at the close of the episode he fell on his knees at a prie-dieu before a stained-glass window, an ironic touch that must have amused him.

(By the way, Tree's performance of this scene—3.3 in Shakespeare, but 1.5 in Tree's rearrangement—was filmed in 1899; it was the first movie ever made from a play by Shakespeare.) The second point to be mentioned is that a spectacular dawn effect at the end of the play, suggesting the hope associated with a new reign, was much liked.

In terms of numbers of productions, the play has had a moderately respectable history in the twentieth century, and eminent actors and directors have been involved. For instance, in 1920 and 1924 Ernest Milton played John, in 1931 Ralph Richardson played the Bastard, in 1941 Tyrone Guthrie directed an Old Vic production that included Sybil Thorndike (Constance), Lewis Casson (Pandulph), and Ernest Milton (John), in 1945 Peter Brook directed the Birmingham Repertory production (with Paul Scofield as the Bastard), in 1948 Robert Helpmann played John, and in 1953 the Old Vic production included Richard Burton (the Bastard), Michael Hordern (John), and Fay Compton (Constance). In America, John Houseman directed it at Stratford, Connecticut, with Mildred Dunnock as Constance. None of these productions, however, aroused great enthusiasm, though Douglas Seale's at Stratford-upon-Avon in 1957 was well-received. In 1960 Seale staged the play again, this time at Stratford, Ontario, and again he received generally favorable notices. A 1970 production of the Royal Shakespeare Company, directed by Buzz Goodbody—this was the first RSC production directed by a woman—was universally dismissed as a failure. It was played for laughs—apparently the idea was that the scheming politicians were all incompetent—but reviewers found it puerile. Another RSC production, this one by John Barton in 1974, irked reviewers even more. Barton believed that some of the uncertainties in *King John*—for instance Arthur's claim to the throne—are clarified by passages in *The Troublesome Reign of King John* and by passages in an even older morality-like play, Bishop Bale's *King Johan*. So he added portions of these, as well as some lines of his own. The rewriting irked the critics, and so did much of the stage business. Richard David, in *Shakespeare in the Theatre,* complained at some length. The following short extract, heavily ironic, is fairly typical of the response to Barton's production:

> We begin with the entombment, by monks (how splendid!) of Richard Coeur de Lion, which will be balanced by the entombment of John at the end of the play. There follows a reading of one of Richard's wills, imported from a historical source (Constance will read a rival will at the beginning of the next scene) while John makes damnable faces on the forestage. He is crowned and announces his just purposes, as in Bale's Morality. Queen Elinor exhorts his nobles to support her son—this is from *The Troublesome Reign.*

Writing in the middle of the twentieth century, in *Shakespeare and the Actors* (1945), Arthur Colby Sprague said that *King John* is "now almost unknown as an acting play." We have glanced at a few productions, but Sprague was right, and his comment continues to apply at the outset of the twenty-first century. Still, the second half of the twentieth century did see a few productions that stimulated considerable interest, the most effective of which—and it probably was the most important production of the play in the century—was staged by the Royal Shakespeare Company, directed by Deborah Warner, at Stratford-upon-Avon in 1988 and in London in 1989. The Stratford production was in a converted storage shed, The Other Place, where the audience sat on three sides of the stage, and the simplicity of the place seemed admirably suited to the production. (This theater was demolished in 1990 and rebuilt in the following year.) The uncut text of the play was presented much as a play, theatrically rather than realistically, but not theatrical in the sense of offering the historical spectacles—we might say not the archaeological specimens—of Macready, Kean, and Beerbohm Tree in the nineteenth century. It was, at least in part, about theater as well as about history, and thus, to use a fairly new word, it was metatheatrical, i.e., a self-conscious examination of theater, a sort of experiment in or test of the genre. In Warner's version, some actors doubled, sets were minimal, changes of locale were indicated by changes in lighting, and costumes ("timeless modern," a reviewer said) seemed to have come from the local secondhand clothing shop. Viewers in The Other Place were very much aware that the play (like, say, a Hollywood film on an historical subject) was not history but merely a theatrical interpretation of what allegedly was history. Given the fact that *King John* is entirely in verse, and the highly rhetorical verse often seems unconnected with the character of the speaker, such a production is entirely reasonable. For a detailed comment on this production, see Alan C. Dessen's review, reprinted in this book.

The Royal Shakespeare Company in 2001–02 staged another effective *King John,* this one directed by Greg Doran. The stage was bare, except for a simple wooden throne that later (in 4.1) served as a chair to which Arthur was bound when he is threatened with being blinded. Russell Jackson, reviewing the production in *Shakespeare Quarterly* (53:4; 2002), says that it effectively moved "from pathos to comedy and back." He summarized the ending thus:

In a refusal of closure consistent with the production's overall
skepticism, the Bastard's final speech was followed by the
new king's turning away from him, as if his clear-sighted but
cynical views were no longer welcome, despite their patriotic
fervor. Such a qualified expression of hope ("*If* England . . .")
was not for the new regime.

Finally, a word about the BBC television production
(1984), with Claire Bloom as Constance. Much of the play
was realistic, but some of the sets—for instance the set representing the tower and battlements of Angiers—are highly
stylized with cardboard cutouts. The effect of the stylization
is, for the most part, to diminish the characters, to suggest
their childishness, their pettiness, and although one can
argue that the decorative scenery is often appropriate, it
sometimes seems utterly inappropriate, as in the scene when
Arthur leaps to his death.

Bibliographic Note: Many of the titles listed below in the
Suggested References, Section 4 ("Shakespeare on Stage
and Screen") include brief discussions of productions of
King John.

Shakespeare Quarterly is a good source for reviews of
productions—not only in the English-speaking world but
also elsewhere—since the middle of the twentieth century.
Shakespeare Survey, an annual, includes reviews of British
productions of the same period. On Macready's version, see
Shattuck's magisterial volume, *William Macready's King
John* (1962). For *King John* in the mid-nineteenth century,
see Eugene Waith in *Shakespeare Quarterly* 29 (1978):
192–211. On Herbert Beerbohm Tree's silent film, see Robert Hamilton Ball's article in *Shakespeare Quarterly* 24
(1973):455–59—a note that supersedes his earlier discussions of the film. For extracts from reviews of the BBC
television production (1984), see J. C. Bulman and H. R.
Coursen, *Shakespeare on Television* (1988), pp. 31–32.
Nicholas Woodeson discusses his performance as King John
in Deborah Warner's acclaimed 1988 production in *Players
of Shakespeare,* ed. Russell Jackson and Robert Smallwood

(1993), pp. 87–98. We include in the present volume Alan C. Dessen's review of Warner's production.

A small book, in a series called "Shakespeare in Performance," is devoted to the stage history of the play: Geraldine Cousin, in *King John* (1994), surveys productions up through the middle of the twentieth century, and then concentrates on Royal Shakespeare Company productions of the 1970s, the BBC television production of 1984, and Deborah Warner's Stratford-upon-Avon production of 1988 (and London, 1989).

The Famous History
of the Life of
KING HENRY
the
EIGHTH

Introduction
to *Henry VIII*

Although *Henry VIII* has for over a century given rise to vigorous, sometimes heated, discussion, it has received much less interpretative consideration than any other of Shakespeare's dramatizations of English history; the two best-known books on the subject, Lily B. Campbell's *Shakespeare's Histories* and E. M. W. Tillyard's *Shakespeare's History Plays*, ignore it. Attention has focused instead on a single great problem unrelated in any direct fashion to the play's meaning or worth. In the title of his celebrated essay, first published in 1850, James Spedding asked, "Who Wrote Shakespeare's *Henry VIII*?", and scholars have raised the same question ever since.* Indeed, the dean of living Shakespeareans, John Dover Wilson, has confessed with engaging candor that the chief interest of the play for him lies in the authorship problem. That problem is the most vexing to face the editor of *Henry VIII*. While he may be permitted to regret the disproportionate attention lavished on a single specialized issue of scholarship, he must nevertheless recognize that it can scarcely be disregarded in a responsible Introduction. He will do well to confront it straightaway.

Spedding argued that *Henry VIII* represents not Shakespeare's unaided work but, rather, a collaborative effort in which he was joined by an inferior writer who composed the greater part and was responsible for the general design, which Spedding found incoherent. This inferior playwright

---

*The essay, which first appeared in *The Gentleman's Magazine* (August 1850), is more conveniently accessible in *Transactions of the New Shakspere Society* (London, 1874). For my discussion of the authorship question in this Introduction I am obliged to Northwestern University Press for permission to include materials from my book, *Internal Evidence and Elizabethan Dramatic Authorship* (Evanston, 1966), in which the principal contributions to the controversy are evaluated.

he identified as John Fletcher. Although some earlier scholars had expressed doubts about the homogeneity of *Henry VIII,* no one had previously developed a reasoned case for Fletcherian part-authorship. Spedding's evidence is internal. In the scenes attributed to Shakespeare he finds vigor, reality, impassioned language, and figurative richness; the Fletcher portions are conventional, diffuse, and languid. These stylistic impressions Spedding reinforces with metrical statistics: the scenes assigned to Fletcher are distinguished by a preponderance of feminine endings (an extra unstressed syllable terminating the blank-verse line) normal for Fletcher but excessive for Shakespeare. Spedding's argument was not universally accepted— Swinburne early demurred—but it has proved enormously influential: so influential that the theory of Shakespeare-Fletcher collaboration is even today not infrequently stated as a fact.

The great drawback to stylistic evidence is its subjectivity, which resides to a degree even in the seemingly mechanical metrical tests that Spedding, along with most nineteenth-century scholars, found persuasive. But additional evidence of a more objective nature has been forthcoming. In an important monograph, *The Problem of Henry VIII Reopened* (1949), A. C. Partridge offered linguistic data based on the use of expletive *do* in affirmative statements (favored by Shakespeare), *-th* inflectional endings in the third-person singular present indicative of notional and auxiliary verbs (also favored by Shakespeare), and colloquial clippings of personal pronouns (favored by Fletcher). These linguistic characteristics essentially confirm Spedding's division of the play. Partridge's evidence has been supplemented by Cyrus Hoy in his recent painstaking investigation of the entire Fletcher canon. Hoy finds in the Folio text of *Henry VIII* "two distinct linguistic patterns: one [Fletcher's] marked by the occurrence of *ye* in eleven of the play's sixteen scenes, to a total of 71 times, and a distinct preference for the contraction *'em* to the expanded pronominal form *them;* the second pattern [Shakespeare's] is marked by the absence of *ye,* a preference for *them* to *'em,* and the frequent use of *hath* which, with one exception (1.1) is never found in a scene containing *ye*."* (The present edition differs from most modern-spelling texts in retaining contracted forms as they appear in the Folio.)

For the reader's convenience, the customary scene allocation made by those who view the play as a Fletcher-Shakespeare collaboration is summarized in the following table:

Prologue	Fletcher
Act 1, sc. 1–2	Shakespeare
sc. 3–4	Fletcher
Act 2, sc. 1–2	Fletcher
sc. 3–4	Shakespeare
Act 3, sc. 1	Fletcher
sc. 2 (lines 1–203)	Shakespeare
sc. 2 (remainder)	Fletcher
Act 4, sc. 1–2	Fletcher
Act 5, sc. 1	Shakespeare
sc. 2–5	Fletcher
Epilogue	Fletcher

The dual-authorship hypothesis is, moreover, attractive on other than linguistic or stylistic grounds. Around 1609, Shakespeare's company began performing in the enclosed Blackfriars theater, the lease to which it had recently acquired. Although the open-air Globe remained in use (indeed *Henry VIII* was written for that house), it was gradually supplanted in importance by the new theater, which catered to a select, well-to-do clientele. At about the same time as this crucial change in operations, the premier theatrical company of the age was faced with the problem of the imminent retirement of the playwright largely responsible for its overwhelming preeminence. How, after all, does one go about replacing Shakespeare? The King's Men could not very well avoid pondering this unenviable question. Their crisis was resolved—successfully by the criterion of box-office receipts—when the company arranged for Fletcher to suc-

---

*Cyrus Hoy, "The Shares of Fletcher and His Collaborators in the Beaumont and Fletcher Canon (VII)," *Studies in Bibliography* XV (1962): 77. Hoy's discussion of the play occupies pp. 76–85; a statistical table of his findings appears on p. 90.

ceed Shakespeare as their principal dramatist. And what could be a more natural procedure during the transitional phase than that Shakespeare should collaborate with the brilliant young playwright destined to replace him?*

Yet it is an hypothesis, not a certainty, that *Henry VIII* is the end product of such a partnership. A distinguished minority of scholars—among them Peter Alexander, Hardin Craig, R. A. Foakes, G. Wilson Knight, and Geoffrey Bullough—have remained unconvinced despite the cumulative weight of stylistic, linguistic, and historical probabilities. They have, furthermore, discerned in the play an organic unity which they regard as more compatible with single than with divided authorship. The concrete evidence for collaboration is, after all, entirely internal and, in the nature of things, inconclusive without external support. Even the welcome linguistic data do not always provide so clear-cut a pattern as one might wish, and there is always the danger that scribes or compositors did not consistently follow such minutiae in the manuscripts which they transmitted. It is a fact that Heminges and Condell, the earliest editors of Shakespeare, printed *Henry VIII* in the First Folio without any hint that another writer had a share in the play. Whether they did or did not know the circumstances of composition we cannot definitively say; but, as they were Shakespeare's friends and professional colleagues at the time, the likelihood is that they did. But would they have omitted the work from the Folio even if they understood it to be in large measure another's? Again we cannot positively say. It is also a fact, though, that they failed to include *Sir Thomas More, Pericles,* and *The Two Noble Kinsmen:* works of collaborative or doubtful status. It is true, too, that they printed a text of *Macbeth* with the non-Shakespearean Hecate scenes; but these amount only to a small portion of the whole play. The external evidence thus points to single jurisdiction, yet not with such force as to dismay those maintaining the contrary view.

After working closely with the text of *Henry VIII* over a

*For an excellent discussion of these questions see Gerald Eades Bentley, "Shakespeare and the Blackfriars Theatre," *Shakespeare Survey* 1 (Cambridge, England, 1948): 38–50; reprinted in the Signet Classic Shakespeare edition of *The Two Noble Kinsmen,* edited by Clifford Leech (1966).

period of some time, and after weighing the arguments of his predecessors, the present editor is personally satisfied that two styles indeed coexist in the play, that Shakespeare and Fletcher are the authors indicated by those styles, and that the traditional distribution of scenes is by and large correct. He also believes, however, that Hoy may be right in detecting Shakespeare's presence in several scenes usually attributed to Fletcher alone (2.2, 3.2.203–459, and 4.2), although he would not venture upon any line-by-line allocation.* Because the Prologue and Epilogue are such short passages, he doubts that a persuasive case can be made for ascription to either Shakespeare or Fletcher. The view, maintained by the anticollaborationists, that *Henry VIII* possesses a structure of imagery and other features reflecting careful planning does not for this reader carry any great evidential significance as regards authorship. Such interpretative considerations inevitably have a subjective aspect: there are competent critics who do not find in the work the unity claimed for it by other competent critics. And even granting the existence of such unity, it does not necessarily follow that it could have been achieved only by an artist working on his own. There are sufficient instances of dramatists who have pooled their talents to produce integrated works, sometimes attaining (as in the case of Jonson, Chapman, and Marston's *Eastward Ho*) remarkable consistency of texture; just as there are instances of totally incoherent plays composed by one individual. The hypothesis of Shakespeare-Fletcher collaboration on *Henry VIII* is reasonable and better supported by tangible evidence than most such hypotheses, and it is probable that the majority of students will continue to support it. At the same time it remains an hypothesis, and there will probably always be some dissenters. For better or for worse, this editor is unstirred by the partisan fervor that the debate has aroused; his firmest conviction is that the problem admits of no ultimate solution.

If the authorship question presents notorious difficulties, the very existence of the play is in some respects awkward. For many, one suspects, it would have been much more

---

*This editor would not, however, join Hoy in also crediting Shakespeare with a share in 2.1 and 4.1.

satisfying had Shakespeare concluded his playwriting career
with *The Tempest,* a drama as magically evocative as the
island on which its action takes place. The great themes of
forgiveness and reconciliation achieve (so it seems) final
form: it is the culmination of the artist's vision. Understand-
ably, readers and audiences have found irresistible the temptation to identify the creator with his creation, and to see in
Prospero's abjuration of his magic the dramatist's farewell
to the stage:

> I'll break my staff,
> Bury it certain fathoms in the earth,
> And deeper than did ever plummet sound
> I'll drown my book.
>
> (5.1.54–57)

And then how anticlimactic, after the revels have been
declared ended, for their master to return a couple of years
later with yet another revel! To complicate matters further,
the play in which the timeless artificer now had at least a
hand was quite possibly topical in its inspiration, and certainly it was spectacular (in the showy theatrical sense) in its
design. If the composition of *Henry VIII* testifies to anything, it is to the committed professionalism of its author: the
supreme poet was yet a shareholder in a company of players
and not unwilling to emerge from semiretirement in Stratford to provide his London colleagues with a vehicle
admirably suited to catching the popular fancy in a moment
of national rejoicing.

The occasion for rejoicing was the marriage on St. Valen-
tine's Day, 1613, of Princess Elizabeth, daughter of James I,
to Prince Frederick, the Elector Palatine and champion
of the Protestant cause in Germany. During the previous
autumn Prince Henry, the heir to the throne, had died, and
the nation had been plunged into grief; now the period of
mourning was over, and the lavish wedding celebrations—
including masques, feasts, and fireworks—signalized the
change of mood. A play extolling the reign of England's first
Protestant defender of the faith, and doing so in scenes of
pomp and pageantry, would be in harmony with the occasion. Act 5 of *Henry VIII* celebrates the birth of Princess

Elizabeth of glorious memory, and (as R. A. Foakes has observed) the identity of name between the young bride and the great Queen did not escape notice at the time. "How much are we, the inhabitants of this whole isle, bound unto our good God, that hath lent us such a princess," declared George Webbe in *The Bride Royal* (1613), "and in her hath renewed and revived the name and nature of our late deceased, ever to be remembered, happy Queen Elizabeth!" Cranmer's speech (5.5.14–62), prophesying the peace and prosperity of Elizabeth's reign and alluding flatteringly to their continuance under James, resembles in phrasing and imagery what was being said in the marriage tracts and sermons.*

To suggest, however, that *Henry VIII* was composed specifically for the royal festivities would be to stretch the evidence, for no court performance of the play is mentioned in the Lord Treasurer's accounts for this period, although we know that five other works of Shakespeare were acted before the newlyweds. Possibly *Henry VIII* was the "stage play to be acted in the Great Hall by the King's players" which aroused "much expectation" on February 16, but which was canceled in favor of a masque; but this is mere speculation.

In identifying *Henry VIII* with *All Is True,* a play about the same monarch's reign known only from a single contemporary reference, we are on surer ground: *All Is True* would be an appropriate alternative title for *Henry VIII,* in view of the Prologue emphasis on "our chosen truth" (18). A performance of *All Is True* at the Globe Theatre on June 29, 1613, was the occasion of the most sensational occurrence in the history of that playhouse. The event is described in a letter, dated July 2, 1613, written by Sir Henry Wotton to Sir Edmund Bacon:

> The King's players had a new play called *All Is true,* representing some principal pieces of the reign of Henry VIII, which was set forth with many extraordinary circumstances of pomp and majesty, even to the matting of the stage; the Knights of the Order with their Georges and

---

*The correspondences are described and documented by R. A. Foakes in his Introduction to the new Arden edition of *Henry VIII* (London, 1957), pp. xxxi–xxxii. I owe my reference to *The Bride Royal* to this edition (p. xxx).

garters, the Guards with their embroidered coats, and the like: sufficient in truth within a while to make greatness very familiar, if not ridiculous. Now, King Henry making a masque at the Cardinal Wolsey's house, and certain chambers being shot off at his entry, some of the paper, or other stuff, wherewith one of them was stopped, did light on the thatch, where being thought at first but an idle smoke, and their eyes more attentive to the show, it kindled inwardly, and ran round like a train, consuming within less than an hour the whole house to the very grounds.

This was the fatal period of that virtuous fabric, wherein yet nothing did perish but wood and straw, and a few forsaken cloaks; only one man had his breeches set on fire, that would perhaps have broiled him, if he had not by the benefit of a provident wit put it out with bottle ale.*

Thus did the Globe perish; but (as Stow's *Annals,* 1631 ed., records) "the next spring it was new builded in far fairer manner than before."

We need feel no surprise that the patrician Wotton should express tolerant disapproval at the public staging of the ceremonies and pastimes of the great before the heterogeneous multitude that frequented the Globe. More suggestive is his tacit admission that he has been impressed, if reluctantly, by "the many extraordinary circumstances of pomp and majesty"—impressed at second-hand, for he was not an eye-witness to the performance he recounts. Whatever deeper resonances are implied, *Henry VIII* on the stage was the super-spectacle of its own day. In an Introduction to the play this aspect calls for special emphasis, as it is least likely to come through adequately on the printed page: the life of a spectacle, appealing as it does directly to eye and ear, is in the presentation.

How deliberately does the play dwell on awesome princely occasions! Sometimes these are depicted through the resources of language alone, as in Norfolk's description of the Field of the Cloth of Gold (1.1), or in the account by the two Gentlemen of the trial of "the great Duke of

---

The Life and Letters of Sir Henry Wotton, edited by L. Pearsall Smith (Oxford, 1907), II, 32–33.

Buckingham" by his peers at Westminster Hall (2.1), or in the third Gentleman's narration of the solemn ritual at the coronation of Queen Anne in Westminster Abbey (4.1). But, where possible, stirring events are dramatized. We attend Wolsey's splendid banquet and masque; we witness Katherine's vision of dancing, white-robed spirits; we become bystanders when Anne returns with her retinue from the Abbey. The *dramatis personae* for *Henry VIII* is the largest for any play in the canon, and for such episodes as the procession in Act 4 the company must have pressed into service all of its available personnel. The extended stage directions, authorial in origin, show an unusual regard for the proper disposition of the players in the big scenes. For Katherine's trial

> *The King takes place under the cloth of state; the two Cardinals sit under him as judges. The Queen takes place some distance from the King. The Bishops place themselves on each side the court in manner of a consistory; below them, the Scribes. The Lords sit next the Bishops. The rest of the Attendants stand in convenient order about the stage.*
>
> (2.4.s.d.)

The gorgeous costumes of princes, prelates, and functionaries contributed to the visual magnificence of these scenes, as did the impressive assortment of stage properties, including the purse with the Great Seal, the silver cross, silver mace, and silver pillars, the gold scepter and collars of S's, the gilt copper crown, gold crown, and gold coronals and demicoronals.

These visual effects were complemented and enhanced by sound, which is called for throughout. Patience, Queen Katherine's woman, sings of the miraculous powers of "sweet music" as she accompanies herself on the lute. Such soothing moments, however, are rare: on other occasions we hear the blended voices of the choristers, the sound of oboes and cornets, the sterner notes of drum and trumpet, the roar of the cannon. *Henry VIII* is an unabashedly noisy play, guaranteed to keep even the drowsiest spectator awake. "Some come to take their ease," the Epilogue declares,

> And sleep an act or two; but those, we fear,
> W'have frighted with our trumpets . . .
>
>   (3–4)

Of the several companies performing in London at the time, only the King's Men had the resources to do justice to such a play. The destruction of the theater during what was possibly the premier performance is not without a certain ironic fitness: it was the spectacular effect to end (literally) all spectacular effects.

In the most notable modern revival of *Henry VIII*, produced by Tyrone Guthrie at Stratford-on-Avon in 1949–50, the director fully exploited the opportunities for processional pageantry, display, and crowd movement. For such exploitation the earliest theatrical precedents and the text itself (as we have noted) afford ample warrant. These features of the play have contributed to the dissatisfaction with it expressed by some commentators: spectacle, being nonverbal, has always prompted condescension or worse on the part of critics whose orientation is literary or philosophical rather than theatrical. "The Spectacle," Aristotle observed in the *Poetics,* "has, indeed, an emotional attraction of its own, but, of all the parts, it is the least artistic, and connected least with the art of poetry." Even granting the validity of the judgment, the propriety of applying to another genre the criteria Aristotle formulated for tragedy may be doubtful. For although *Henry VIII* dramatizes several individual tragedies—Buckingham's, Katherine's, Wolsey's—it is not itself a tragedy but a history play concerned more with the public conduct of its personages than with their buried lives; its intention is to stage, in Wotton's words, "some principal pieces of the reign of Henry VIII."

Clowning and buffoonery of the kind found in Samuel Rowley's *When You See Me You Know Me* (1605), which deals with the same reign, are rejected in favor of an appropriate seriousness and dignity of tone, although the rejection is fortunately not so sweeping as to exclude humor altogether: witness the bawdry of the old Lady (2.3) and the low comedy of the Porter and his man (5.4). The repeated stress in the Prologue is on the historical genuineness of the play's people and events, their reality:

> Think ye see
> The very persons of our noble story
> As they were living.
>
> (25–27)

The pursuit of historical verisimilitude (whether achieved or not) obviously limits the playwright's freedom to select, shape, and explore events. It cannot be claimed that the genre represents the highest form to which dramatic art may aspire, but there can be no denying its perennial appeal to theatergoers; of plays produced in recent years, Peter Shaffer's spectacular dramatization of Pizarro's conquest of Peru, *The Royal Hunt of the Sun,* perhaps most closely approximates the type. *Henry VIII* is best understood—and appreciated—on its own terms.

Those terms are not, however, confined to spectacle. Again the Prologue helpfully gives a clue to purpose. The audience is instructed in how to respond to the calamities befalling the eminent personages whose careers will unfold before it:

> Think you see them great,
> And followed with the general throng and sweat
> Of thousand friends. Then, in a moment, see
> How soon this mightiness meets misery;
> And if you can be merry then, I'll say
> A man may weep upon his wedding day.
>
> (27–32)

These lines suggest the evanescence of worldly glory. Fortune, the blind goddess, raises her favorites high upon her wheel, then capriciously flings them to earth. It is an old theme; in the permutations of Fortune's wheel medieval writers discerned the quintessential tragic pattern. According to Chaucer's Monk, in *The Canterbury Tales,*

> Tragedie is to seyn a certeyn storie,
> As olde bookes maken us memorie,
> Of hym that stood in greet prosperitee,
> And is yfallen out of heigh degree
> Into myserie, and endeth wrecchedly.
>
> (Prologue, Monk's Tale, 1973–77)

Henry VIII presents, in the context of Renaissance court life, a trio of such falls from high degree.

The victims, so different in their characters and lives, share not only a common fortune but also, at the last, a common pathos, which they fully savor. Buckingham's stoic forbearance in the face of death gives place in his final words to a self-pitying note, however sober and controlled:

> All good people,
> Pray for me! I must now forsake ye; the last hour
> Of my long weary life is come upon me.
> Farewell!
> And when you would say something that is sad,
> Speak how I fell. I have done, and God forgive me.
>
> (2.1.131–36)

No sooner has he departed the scene than the two Gentlemen, having lamented his passing, discuss the impending fall of Katherine in almost identical terms (" 'Tis woeful"). The discarded Queen, "sick to death," is granted a dream of eternal happiness to come. In a last assertion of regal greatness, she dismisses an unintentionally negligent messenger, then prepares for the end. "I must to bed," she cries to Patience;

> Call in more women. When I am dead, good wench,
> Let me be used with honor. Strew me over
> With maiden flowers, that all the world may know
> I was a chaste wife to my grave. Embalm me,
> Then lay me forth. Although unqueened, yet like
> A queen and daughter to a king, inter me.
> I can no more.
>
> (4.2.167–73)

It is perhaps the play's most affecting moment.

The most stunning of the three downfalls, however, is that of Wolsey. For a suitable epitaph we may turn to a contemporary of Shakespeare who suffered a fate analogous to that of the Cardinal. "The rising unto place is laborious," Francis Bacon wrote in his essay "Of Great Place," and by pains men come to greater pains; and it is sometimes base; and by indignities men come to dignities. The standing is slippery, and the regress is either a downfall or at least an eclipse, which is a melancholy thing.

Although the Cardinal is not the play's protagonist, his cold presence dominates the first three acts. Somehow he must be humanized in defeat, and in the space of a hundred lines the arrogant prince of the church is humbled and reconciled to his new condition. Like Katherine and Buckingham, he prays for his King. He also shows solicitude for the future of his servant Cromwell, and for the first time we do not suspect a selfish motive lurking behind the apparent altruism. Wolsey weeps—the scene is frankly sentimental—and repents (a trifle smugly) his worldliness:

> O Cromwell, Cromwell,
> Had I but served my God with half the zeal
> I served my King, he would not in mine age
> Have left me naked to mine enemies.
>
> (3.2.454–57)

There is only slight foreshadowing (in 2.2) of Wolsey's fall, and the transformation itself, read in the study, seems somewhat abrupt; but in a spectacular drama of comparatively external nature, subtle nuances of character portrayal are hardly required. The scene has worked superbly well on the stage, as is attested by the fact that the rôle of Wolsey has attracted a number of great actors, among them Kemble, Macready, and Kean.

If the three successive falls from greatness are well contrived to move an audience to generous sympathy, they do not engage the deeper tragic emotions, nor were they intended to do so, as the larger pattern of the play makes clear. Scenes of calamity alternate throughout with happier occasions. The splendid festivities in York Place (1.4), for example, follow hard upon the Surveyor's devastating testimony against Buckingham; the gaiety of the masque is in turn succeeded by the somber episode of the Duke's entry after his arraignment. At the same time that Katherine's misfortunes press in upon her, we watch Ann Bullen's star rise.

And so on. Such juxtapositions are not unusual in Elizabethan plays, nor, for that matter, in dramatic art generally,
but in this case the total effect is of a complex tonal and thematic orchestration.

In the concluding movement of *Henry VIII,* in which the
grand design stands fully revealed, the joyous strain triumphs. The fourth—and last—of the threatened falls does
not come to pass. Cranmer, who never aspired to greatness,
is tested in the crucible of courtly intrigue. Like his predecessors, he is the object of plots, but he undergoes special
humiliations: the Archbishop of Canterbury is made to cool
his heels outside the council chamber door with grooms and
lackeys. Yet he emerges unscathed, and no heads roll as a
result. Instead there is forgiveness and reconciliation, in
which Cranmer, his accusers, and the King all participate.
The Archbishop can then go on to officiate at the christening
of Princess Elizabeth and to utter the speeches of prophetic
rapture in the final scene. Machinations have ceased. Some
private individuals, most notably Katherine, have in the
course of the drama suffered unjust deprivations, but the
commonwealth has prospered. A newborn infant symbolizes happier days to come.

Henry VIII is unique among Shakespeare's histories in
not depicting an England at war or under the threat of war.
Thematically the play has closer links with the immediately
preceding romances than with the two historical tetralogies
of a previous decade. We are not so far removed after all
from the world of *The Tempest,* in which sinister plots are
thwarted, enemies are reconciled, and hopeful auguries
attend a younger generation. In the character of Henry, who
presides over the action by exercising the quasi-magical pre-
rogatives of kingship, we have a figure in some ways analogous to Prospero.*

The destinies of all the principal personages lie in Henry's
hands. A Buckingham or a Wolsey or a Katherine may absorb
attention for a time, but they all pass from the stage, not to
return; Henry abides, and his presence gives a measure of

---

*The relationship of *Henry VIII* to Shakespeare's last plays is explored
with penetrating subtlety (occasionally oversubtlety) by Foakes in the new
Arden edition, Introduction, pp. xxxvii–lxii. Foakes also deals perceptively
with the themes and structure of the play.

narrative unity to heterogeneous events. Yet his actual rôle is limited—he speaks fewer than 450 lines—and the King makes no appearance whatever in Act 4. No very searching portrayal of him is attempted in the play that bears his name. For a modern audience he must present difficulties: the figure cut by Shakespeare's Henry differs so strikingly from the popular image derived from more recent histories or from films and stage plays. In the Jacobean Henry we do not see the insatiable thirster after sovereignty or the profligate who squandered his parsimonious father's treasure in pursuit of the sport of kings. Nor do we see the gourmand and sensualist, the devourer of drumsticks and wives. Great events associated with Henry's reign lie outside the scope of the action: the Reformation and the dissolution of the monasteries, the martyrdom of Sir Thomas More, the execution of Anne Boleyn three brief years after the christening celebrated in the play.

The Henry of *The Famous History* wears the mantle of royalty securely. At first, it is true, his exalted position shields him from knowledge of the intrigues in his own court; he has never heard of Wolsey's oppressive tax scheme for which (as a matter of historical fact) Henry himself was responsible. But as the action unfolds, his awareness, and hence his authority, increase. Once he knows about Wolsey's perfidy, he rejects the Cardinal decisively. In the Cranmer episode, Henry controls all the strings, but the manipulation serves national interests rather than any need for self-aggrandizement. Thus he would appear to approximate closely enough the popular patriot-monarch lauded by Holinshed and the other Tudor apologists.

But what are we to make of the divorce? Much attention is given in the play to the King's conscientious scruple—after over twenty years of wedlock!—about the propriety of his marriage to the widow of his own brother. On this issue of a wounded conscience Henry meditates privately, expatiates at length in public, and seeks counsel from the most learned scholars in Christendom. Yet before any divorce is bruited, we see him evidently attracted to the woman who will become his next wife. And before Katherine's trial— the results of which are a foregone conclusion—there is Suffolk's cynically revealing aside:

   Chamberlain. It seems the marriage with his brother's
      wife
   Has crept too near his conscience.
   Suffolk. [*Aside*]   No, his conscience
   Has crept too near another lady.

                                      (2.2.16–18)

Historically Henry's reasons for a divorce were several, but
the overriding consideration was his need to continue the
succession with a male heir, which Katherine had failed to
produce and was no longer capable of producing. This
motive is not glossed over in the play—indeed Henry dwells
on it at length (2.4.186–99)—but the force of the point is
blunted by the weight given to the King's scruple.

   The problem is further complicated by the fact that the
dramatists provide Henry with no self-revelatory soliloquies
and by the related fact that his public pronouncements
cannot always be taken at face value. In open court he
declares:

     Prove but our marriage lawful, by my life
     And kingly dignity, we are contented
     To wear our mortal state to come with her,
     Katherine our queen, before the primest creature
     That's paragoned o' th' world.

                                      (226–30)

This does not sound insincere, but hard upon Henry's tribute
to his sweet bedfellow comes an aside (235–40) in which he
expresses impatience with the "dilatory sloth and tricks of
Rome" that hinder the divorce; and in the next scene we
have Katherine's complaint that he has long ceased to love
her. It is as though the dramatists, having set out to extol
Henry and, through him, England, were nevertheless unable—
or unwilling—entirely to suppress undercurrents of motive
and policy inconsistent with so simplified a view of him. The
effect is of a disturbing ambiguity of character.

   It is not the play's only ambiguity. Buckingham presents
a similar problem, although to a lesser degree. Is he in fact a
traitor or is he a wholly innocent sacrifice to Wolsey's
malice? Our first inclination is to regard the Duke simply as

the victim of a frame-up, and certainly much weight is given
to his wrongs. In the sympathetically conceived Katherine
he has a stalwart defender. The chief witness against him
bears, we know, a personal grudge, and Buckingham
protests his innocence in moving terms as he goes to the
block. Yet the King's anger in 1.2 has a righteous accent,
and if he is responsible, however unwittingly, for a judicial
murder, he is not afterwards disturbed by it. The Surveyor's
testimony is never rebutted. Buckingham himself admits
that, "upon the premises," he has been justly tried by his
peers, and the Second Gentleman's last remark about him
has a proviso: "If the Duke be guiltless . . ." After Buckingham's last exit, fairly early in the play, little is made of
the matter apart from an inconclusive exchange between
Surrey and Wolsey in 3.2. The "woefulness" of Buckingham's fall we do not question, but his degree of actual
guilt—if any—remains in doubt. A faint unease persists in
the reader's mind.*

Such puzzlements, which have prompted reservations
about the play on the part of some critics, loom larger in the
study than on the stage. In the theater attention focuses first
on the splendor and fanfare of the grand processional entries
and the ceremonies of public life. The contrastingly intimate
scenes, in which a young maid of honor is shown royal favor
while her defeated elders confront isolation and imminent
death, appeal more directly to the emotions, if on no very
profound level. Then there are the great set speeches: we are
stirred by the eloquence—impassioned or elegiac—of
Buckingham's apologia, Katherine's defense of the sanctity
of her marriage, and Wolsey's long farewell to all his greatness. And finally, along with the multitude on the stage and
in the audience, we are swept up in the visionary ecstasy of
the ritualistic episode of the christening. *Henry VIII* is
Shakespeare's festive history. It is appropriate that the play
was chosen for performance at the Old Vic in London in
1953 to celebrate the coronation of Queen Elizabeth II.

—S. SCHOENBAUM
Northwestern University

*Compare the treatment of this question in the source, below, pp. 372–77.

The Famous History
of the Life of
KING HENRY
the
EIGHTH

[Dramatis Personae

King Henry the Eighth
Cardinal Wolsey
Cardinal Campeius
Capucius, ambassador from the Emperor Charles V
Cranmer, Archbishop of Canterbury
Duke of Norfolk
Duke of Buckingham
Duke of Suffolk
Earl of Surrey
Lord Chamberlain
Lord Chancellor
Gardiner, Bishop of Winchester
Bishop of Lincoln
Lord Abergavenny
Lord Sands
Sir Henry Guildford
Sir Thomas Lovell
Sir Anthony Denny
Sir Nicholas Vaux
Secretaries to Wolsey
Cromwell, servant to Wolsey
Griffith, gentleman usher to Queen Katherine
Three Gentlemen
Doctor Butts, physician to the King
Garter King-at-Arms
Surveyor to the Duke of Buckingham
Brandon, and a Sergeant-at-Arms
Door-keeper of the Council-chamber
Page to Gardiner. A Crier
Porter, and his Man

Queen Katherine, wife to King Henry, afterward
   divorced
Anne Bullen, her Maid of Honor, afterward Queen
An old Lady, friend to Anne Bullen
Patience, woman to Queen Katherine

Several Lords and Ladies in the Dumb Shows;
   Women attending upon the Queen; Scribes, Officers, Guards, and other Attendants; Spirits

Scene: London; Westminster; Kimbolton]

The Famous History
of the Life of
KING HENRY
the
EIGHTH

THE PROLOGUE

I come no more to make you laugh.° Things now
That bear a weighty and a serious brow,
Sad, high, and working,° full of state° and woe,
Such noble scenes as draw the eye to flow,
We now present. Those that can pity, here   5
May, if they think it well, let fall a tear:
The subject will deserve it. Such as give
Their money out of hope they may believe
May here find truth° too. Those that come to see
Only a show or two, and so agree   10
The play may pass, if they be still and willing,
I'll undertake may see away their shilling°

Prologue 1 **no more to make you laugh** (the previous play was
presumably a comedy) 3 **Sad, high, and working** serious, elevated,
and moving 3 **state** dignity 9 **truth** (possibly alluding to the play's
alternative title, *All Is True*) 12 **shilling** (the admission price for
an expensive seat near the stage)

Richly in two short hours.° Only they
That come to hear a merry bawdy play,
15   A noise of targets,° or to see a fellow
In a long motley coat guarded with yellow,°
Will be deceived;° for, gentle hearers, know,
To rank our chosen truth with such a show
As fool and fight is, beside forfeiting
20   Our own brains and the opinion that we bring
To make that only true we now intend,°
Will leave us never an understanding friend.°
Therefore, for goodness' sake, and as you are known
The first and happiest hearers of the town,°
25   Be sad, as we would make ye. Think ye see
The very persons of our noble story
As° they were living. Think you see them great,
And followed with the general throng and sweat
Of thousand friends. Then, in a moment, see
30   How soon this mightiness meets misery;
And if you can be merry then, I'll say
A man may weep upon his wedding day.

13 **two short hours** (a conventional reference to performance duration; not to be taken literally)   15 **targets** shields   16 **In a long
... yellow** i.e., in the parti-colored costume of the professional
fool, trimmed ("guarded") in yellow   17 **deceived** disappointed
19–21 **beside forfeiting ... intend** besides abandoning any claims
to intelligence and our reputation for aiming to present only the
truth   22 **an understanding friend** (perhaps alluding to the groundlings—spectators standing under the stage—who were sometimes
ironically praised for their "understanding")   24 **first and happiest hearers of the town** i.e., the best and most favorably disposed
audience in London   27 **As** as if

ACT 1

Scene 1. [*London. An antechamber in the palace.*]

*Enter the Duke of Norfolk at one door; at the other
the Duke of Buckingham and the Lord Abergavenny.*

Buckingham. Good morrow, and well met. How have
    ye done
Since last we saw° in France?

Norfolk.   I thank your Grace,
Healthful, and ever since a fresh° admirer
Of what I saw there.

Buckingham.   An untimely ague°
Stayed me a prisoner in my chamber when   5
Those suns of glory,° those two lights of men,
Met in the vale of Andren.

Norfolk.   'Twixt Guynes and Arde.°
I was then present; saw them salute on horseback;
Beheld them when they lighted,° how they clung
In their embracement, as° they grew together;   10
Which had they, what four throned ones could
    have weighed°
Such a compounded one?

1.1.2 **saw** saw one another 3 **fresh** ready, eager 4 **ague** fever 6
suns of glory i.e., Henry VIII and Francis I (with perhaps a quibble on "suns"=sons) 7 **Guynes and Arde** (towns in Picardy lying
on either side of the valley of Andren; Guynes was in English, Arde
in French hands) 9 **lighted** alighted 10 **as** as if 11 **weighed**
equalled in weight.

241

Buckingham.   All the whole time
    I was my chamber's prisoner.°

Norfolk.   Then you lost
    The view of earthly glory. Men might say,
15 Till this time pomp was single,° but now married
    To one above itself.° Each following day
    Became the next day's master,° till the last
    Made former wonders its. Today the French,
    All clinquant,° all in gold, like heathen gods,
20 Shone down the English; and tomorrow they
    Made Britain India:° every man that stood
    Showed like a mine. Their dwarfish pages were
    As cherubins, all gilt. The madams° too,
    Not used to toil, did almost sweat to bear
25 The pride° upon them, that their very labor
    Was to them as a painting.° Now this masque°
    Was cried° incomparable, and th' ensuing night
    Made it a fool and beggar. The two kings,
    Equal in luster, were now best, now worst,
30 As presence° did present them: him in eye
    Still him in praise;° and being present both,
    'Twas said they saw but one, and no discerner
    Durst wag his tongue in censure.° When these suns
    (For so they phrase° 'em) by their heralds chal-
        lenged
35 The noble spirits to arms, they did perform
    Beyond thought's compass, that former fabulous
        story,°

12–13 **All the whole ... prisoner** (historically, he was in fact
present, whereas Norfolk was in England at the time) 15 **single**
i.e., relatively modest 15–16 **married/To one above itself** united
to constitute a greater pomp 16–17 **Each following ... master**
each day taught something to the next, which superseded it ("master"
= teacher) 19 **clinquant** glittering 21 **India** (probably not India
but the New World, whose gold mines yielded fabulous wealth)
23 **madams** ladies 25 **pride** finery 25–26 **their very labor ...
painting** their very exertion made them flushed, as if rouged 26
masque courtly spectacle 27 **cried** declared 30 **presence** being in
public 30–31 **him in eye ... praise** the one seen was always the
one praised 32–33 **no discerner ... censure** i.e., no beholder dared
choose one above the other 34 **phrase** describe 36 **that former
fabulous story** so that stories formerly thought incredible

    Being now seen possible enough, got credit,
    That Bevis° was believed.

Buckingham.   O, you go far.

Norfolk. As I belong to worship,° and affect
    In honor honesty,° the tract of everything   40
    Would by a good discourser lose some life
    Which action's self was tongue to.° All was royal;
    To the disposing of it nought rebelled.°
    Order gave each thing view;° the office° did
    Distinctly° his full function.

Buckingham.   Who did guide—   45
    I mean, who set the body and the limbs
    Of this great sport° together, as you guess?

Norfolk. One, certes,° that promises no element°
    In such a business.

Buckingham.   I pray you, who, my lord?

Norfolk. All this was ord'red° by the good discretion   50
    Of the right reverend Cardinal of York.

Buckingham. The devil speed him!° No man's pie
    is freed
    From his ambitious finger. What had he
    To do in these fierce° vanities? I wonder
    That such a keech° can with his very bulk   55
    Take up° the rays o' th' beneficial sun,°
    And keep it from the earth.

---

38 **Bevis** Bevis of Hampton, the legendary Saxon knight celebrated in medieval romance   39 **worship** the nobility   39–40 **affect/In honor honesty** love truth as a point of honor   40–42 **the tract ... tongue to** the course of all these events, however well narrated, would in the description lose some of the color and spark of the actuality   43 **rebelled** jarred   44 **Order gave each thing view** everything was arranged so that it could easily be viewed   44 **office** official, or officials as a group   45 **Distinctly** i.e., without confusion   47 **sport** entertainment   48 **certes** certainly   48 **promises no element** would not be expected to share   50 **ord'red** arranged   52 **The devil speed him** the Devil, i.e., rather than God, prosper him   54 **fierce** extravagant   55 **keech** animal fat rolled into a lump (with a sneer at Wolsey's reputed origin as a butcher's son; cf. line 120)   56 **Take up** obstruct   56 **sun** i.e., the King

Norfolk.   Surely, sir,
  There's in him stuff° that puts him to these ends;
  For, being not propped by ancestry, whose grace
60 Chalks successors their way,° nor called upon
  For high feats done to th' crown,° neither allied
  To eminent assistants,° but spider-like,
  Out of his self-drawing° web, 'a gives us note,°
  The force of his own merit makes his way°—
65 A gift° that heaven gives for him, which buys
  A place next to the King.

Abergavenny.   I cannot tell
  What heaven hath given him: let some graver eye
  Pierce into that. But I can see his pride
  Peep through each part of him. Whence has he
    that?
70 If not from hell, the devil is a niggard,°
  Or has given all before, and he begins
  A new hell in himself.

Buckingham.   Why the devil,
  Upon this French going out,° took he upon him
  (Without the privity° o' th' King) t' appoint
75 Who should attend on him? He makes up the file°
  Of all the gentry, for the most part such
  To whom as great a charge° as little honor
  He meant to lay upon; and his own letter,
  The honorable board of council out,°
  Must fetch him in he papers.°

80 *Abergavenny.*   I do know
  Kinsmen of mine, three at the least, that have

---

58 **stuff** qualities, capabilities   59–60 **whose grace ... way** whose
special excellence marks a path for followers   60–61 **called ...
crown** chosen in recognition of lofty exploits in behalf of the crown
62 **assistants** (1) public officials (2) supporters   63 **self-drawing**
self-spinning   63 **'a gives us note** he lets us know   64 **makes his
way** wins him preferment   65 **gift** i.e., merit   70 **If not ... niggard**
(the devil is the source of pride, the sin for which Lucifer fell and
hell was created)   73 **going out** expedition   74 **privity** confiden-
tial participation   75 **file** list   77 **charge** expense   79 **out** uncon-
sulted   80 **fetch him in he papers** fetch in whom he puts on his list

By this so sickened their estates that never
They shall abound° as formerly.

Buckingham.   O, many
Have broke their backs with laying manors on 'em°
For this great journey. What did this vanity°   85
But minister communication of
A most poor issue?°

Norfolk.   Grievingly I think,
The peace between the French and us not values°
The cost that did conclude it.

Buckingham.   Every man,
After the hideous storm that followed, was   90
A thing inspired, and, not consulting,° broke
Into a general prophecy:° that this tempest,
Dashing the garment of this peace, aboded°
The sudden breach on't.

Norfolk.   Which is budded out;
For France hath flawed the league, and hath at-
    tached°   95
Our merchants' goods at Bordeaux.

Abergavenny.   Is it therefore
Th' ambassador is silenced?

Norfolk.   Marry,° is't.

Abergavenny. A proper title of a peace,° and pur-
    chased
At a superfluous rate!°

Buckingham.   Why, all this business
Our reverend Cardinal carried.°

83 **abound** prosper   84 **broke … manors on 'em** ruined themselves
by pawning their estates to outfit themselves   85 **vanity** extravagance   86–87 **minister … issue** furnish occasion for unproductive
talk (with a possible quibble, "poor issue"=impoverished heirs)
88 **not values** is not worth   91 **not consulting** i.e., one another   92
a general prophecy i.e., all prophesied the same   93 **aboded** foretold
95 **flawed the league, and hath attached** broken the treaty and
confiscated   97 **Marry** (a mild oath, from the name of the Virgin
Mary)   98 **A proper title of a peace** an excellent contract of peace
(ironic)   99 **superfluous rate** excessive cost   100 **carried** managed

100 *Norfolk.*   Like it° your Grace,
The state takes notice of the private difference°
Betwixt you and the Cardinal. I advise you
(And take it from a heart that wishes towards you
Honor and plenteous° safety) that you read°
105 The Cardinal's malice and his potency°
Together; to consider further that
What his high hatred would effect wants not
A minister° in his power. You know his nature,
That he's revengeful, and I know his sword
110 Hath a sharp edge. It's long and 't may be said
It reaches far, and where 'twill not extend,°
Thither he darts it. Bosom up° my counsel;
You'll find it wholesome.° Lo, where comes that
    rock
That I advise your shunning.

*Enter Cardinal Wolsey, the purse° borne before him,
certain of the Guard, and two Secretaries with papers.
The Cardinal in his passage fixeth his eye on Buckingham, and Buckingham on him, both full of disdain.*

115 *Wolsey.* The Duke of Buckingham's surveyor,° ha?
Where's his examination?°

First Secretary.   Here, so please you.

Wolsey. Is he in person ready?

First Secretary.   Aye, please your Grace.

Wolsey. Well, we shall then know more, and Buck-
    ingham
Shall lessen this big° look.
                                Exeunt Cardinal and his train.

---

100 **Like it** if it please (a courteous formula for volunteering un-
asked information) 101 **difference** disagreement 104 **plenteous**
ample 104 **read** construe 105 **potency** power 107–08 **wants not/
A minister** does not lack an agent 111 **extend** reach 112 **Bosom
up** conceal within your bosom 113 **wholesome** sound 114s.d.
purse bag containing the Great Seal that is the insignia of the Lord
Chancellor's office 115 **surveyor** overseer of an estate; Charles
Knyvet, Buckingham's cousin 116 **examination** deposition 119
big haughty

Buckingham. This butcher's cur° is venomed-mouthed,
    and I   *120*
  Have not the power to muzzle him. Therefore best
  Not wake him in his slumber. A beggar's book
  Outworths a noble's blood.°

Norfolk.   What, are you chafed?°
  Ask God for temp'rance; that's th' appliance only°
  Which your disease requires.

Buckingham.   I read in's looks   *125*
  Matter against me, and his eye reviled
  Me as his abject object.° At this instant
  He bores° me with some trick. He's gone to th' King;
  I'll follow and outstare him.

Norfolk.   Stay, my lord,
  And let your reason with your choler question°   *130*
  What 'tis you go about. To climb steep hills
  Requires slow pace at first. Anger is like
  A full hot° horse who, being allowed his way,
  Self-mettle° tires him. Not a man in England
  Can advise me like you; be to yourself   *135*
  As you would to your friend.

Buckingham.   I'll to the King,
  And from a mouth of honor° quite cry down
  This Ipswich° fellow's° insolence, or proclaim
  There's difference in no persons.°

Norfolk.   Be advised.°
  Heat not a furnace for your foe so hot   *140*
  That it do singe yourself. We may outrun
  By violent swiftness that which we run at,

---

120 **butcher's cur** (referring to Wolsey's parentage) 122–23 **A
beggar's ... blood** a beggar's book-learning is more esteemed than
nobility of descent 123 **chafed** angry 124 **appliance only** only
remedy 127 **abject object** object of contempt 128 **bores** cheats
130 **with your choler question** dispute with your anger 133 **full
hot** high-spirited 134 **Self-mettle** his own natural vigor 137 **from
a mouth of honor** speaking as a nobleman 138 **Ipswich** (Wolsey's
birthplace) 138 **fellow's** (usually applied to inferiors; cf. 3.2.279
and 4.2.100) 139 **There's ... persons** distinctions of rank no
longer matter 139 **Be advised** take care

And lose by overrunning.° Know you not
The fire that mounts the liquor° till't run o'er
145   In seeming to augment it wastes it? Be advised.
I say again there is no English soul
More stronger° to direct you than yourself,
If with the sap° of reason you would quench,
Or but allay, the fire of passion.

Buckingham.   Sir,
150   I am thankful to you, and I'll go along
By your prescription; but this top-proud° fellow
(Whom from the flow of gall I name not, but
From sincere motions)° by intelligence°
And proofs as clear as founts in July° when
155   We see each grain of gravel, I do know
To be corrupt and treasonous.

Norfolk.   Say not "treasonous."

Buckingham. To th' King I'll say't, and make my
         vouch° as strong
As shore of rock. Attend.° This holy fox,
Or wolf, or both (for he is equal rav'nous
160   As he is subtle, and as prone to mischief
As able to perform't, his mind and place°
Infecting one another, yea, reciprocally)
Only to show his pomp° as well in France
As here at home, suggests° the King our master
165   To this last costly treaty, th' interview,°
That swallowed so much treasure, and like a glass
Did break i' th' wrenching.°

143 **overrunning** running beyond   144 **mounts the liquor** causes the
liquor to rise   147 **More stronger** better qualified (double comparatives, and also superlatives, are frequent in Shakespeare)   148
sap juice, fluid   151 **top-proud** excessively proud   152–53 **Whom . . .
motions** of whom I thus speak not out of spite but from sincere
motives   153 **intelligence** intelligence reports   154 **founts in July**
i.e., streams no longer muddied by spring floods (the accent in "July"
is on the first syllable)   157 **vouch** allegation   158 **Attend** listen
161 **mind and place** inclinations and position   163 **pomp** magnificence   164 **suggests** prompts (used of the devil)   165 **interview** "ceremonial meeting of princes" (Foakes)   167 **wrenching**
rinsing

Norfolk.　　　　　　　　　　　　Faith, and so it did.

Buckingham. Pray give me favor,° sir. This cunning
　　Cardinal
　　The articles o' th' combination drew°
　　As himself pleased; and they were ratified　　　　　*170*
　　As he cried, "Thus let be," to as much end
　　As give a crutch to th' dead. But our count-cardinal
　　Has done this, and 'tis well; for worthy Wolsey,
　　Who cannot err, he did it. Now this follows
　　(Which, as I take it, is a kind of puppy　　　　　*175*
　　To th' old dam,° treason) Charles the Emperor,
　　Under pretense to see the Queen his aunt
　　(For 'twas indeed his color,° but he came
　　To whisper Wolsey) here makes visitation.°
　　His fears were that the interview betwixt　　　　　*180*
　　England and France might through their amity
　　Breed him some prejudice, for from this league
　　Peeped harms that menaced him. He privily°
　　Deals with our Cardinal; and, as I trow°
　　(Which I do well, for I am sure the Emperor　　　*185*
　　Paid ere he promised, whereby his suit was granted
　　Ere it was asked) but when the way was made
　　And paved with gold, the Emperor thus desired,
　　That he would please to alter the King's course
　　And break the foresaid peace. Let the King know, *190*
　　As soon he shall by me, that thus the Cardinal
　　Does buy and sell° his honor as he pleases,
　　And for his own advantage.

Norfolk.　　　　　　　　　　　I am sorry
　　To hear this of him, and could wish he were
　　Something mistaken° in 't.

Buckingham.　　　　　　　　No, not a syllable:　　*195*

168 **Pray give me favor** please hear me out　169 **articles o' th'
combination drew** drew up the terms of the peace treaty　176 **dam**
mother　178 **color** pretext　179 **makes visitation** pays a visit　183
privily secretly　184 **as I trow** as I believe (the principal clause
required after the parenthetical comment does not appear; grammar has yielded to the speaker's emotion, but the sense of the
passage is clear)　192 **buy and sell** traffic in　195 **Something
mistaken** to some extent misinterpreted

I do pronounce° him in that very shape
He shall appear in proof.°

*Enter Brandon, a Sergeant-at-Arms before him, and
two or three of the Guard.*

Brandon. Your office, sergeant: execute it.

Sergeant.   Sir,
My lord the Duke of Buckingham, and Earl
200   Of Hereford, Stafford, and Northampton, I
Arrest thee of high treason, in the name
Of our most sovereign King.

Buckingham.   Lo you,° my lord,
The net has fall'n upon me! I shall perish
Under device and practice.°

Brandon.   I am sorry
205   To see you ta'en from liberty, to look on
The business present.° 'Tis his Highness' pleasure
You shall to th' Tower.°

Buckingham.   It will help me nothing
To plead mine innocence, for that dye is on me
Which makes my whit'st part black. The will of
          heav'n
210   Be done in this and all things! I obey.
O my Lord Aberga'ny, fare you well!

Brandon. Nay, he must bear you company.
       [*To Abergavenny*] The King
Is pleased you shall to th' Tower, till you know
How he determines further.

Abergavenny.   As the Duke said,
215   The will of heaven be done, and the King's pleasure
By me obeyed!

Brandon.   Here is a warrant from

196 **pronounce** declare   197 **He shall appear in proof** experience
will reveal him   202 **Lo you** behold   204 **device and practice**
plots and intrigues   205–6 **to look ... present** (1) and to see
what is now happening (2) to be involved in the present affair   207
Tower the Tower of London (where suspected traitors were imprisoned)

The King t' attach° Lord Montacute, and the bodies°
Of the Duke's confessor, John de la Car,
One Gilbert Parke, his councillor—

Buckingham.　　　　　　　　　　　So, so;
These are the limbs o' th' plot. No more, I hope.　220

Brandon. A monk o' th' Chartreux.°

Buckingham.　　　　　　　　　O, Nicholas Hopkins?

Brandon.　　　　　　　　　　　　　　　　　　He.

Buckingham. My surveyor is false; the o'er-great
　　Cardinal
Hath showed him gold. My life is spanned° already.
I am the shadow of poor Buckingham,
Whose figure even this instant cloud puts on,　225
By dark'ning my clear sun.° My lord, farewell.
　　　　　　　　　　　　　　　　　　Exeunt.

Scene 2. [*The same. The council-chamber.*]

*Cornets. Enter King Henry, leaning on the Cardinal's
shoulder; the Nobles, [a Secretary of the Cardinal's,]
and Sir Thomas Lovell. The Cardinal places himself
under the King's feet° on his right side.*

King. My life itself, and the best heart° of it,
Thanks you for this great care. I stood i' th' level°
Of a full-charged confederacy,° and give thanks
To you that choked it. Let be called before us

---

217 **attach** arrest 217 **bodies** persons 221 **Chartreux** Charter-
house (i.e., a Carthusian) 223 **spanned** measured out 225–26
Whose figure ... sun whose form is at this instant clouded by misfortune that dims my glory and alienates me from my King ("sun"
may refer to both Buckingham and Henry) 1.2.s.d. **under the King's
feet** at the feet of the King, who is seated on a raised and canopied
"state," or throne 1 **best heart** very core 2 **i' th' level** in direct
range 3 **full-charged confederacy** fully-loaded conspiracy

5   That gentleman of Buckingham's.° In person
       I'll hear him his confessions justify,°
       And point by point the treasons of his master
       He shall again relate.

       A noise within, crying "Room for the Queen!"
       [Katherine, who is] ushered by the Duke of Norfolk.
       Enter the Queen, [Duke of] Norfolk and [Duke of]
       Suffolk. She kneels. King riseth from his state, takes
       her up, kisses and placeth her by him.

       Queen Katherine. Nay, we must longer kneel: I am
       a suitor.

10 *King.* Arise, and take place° by us. Half your suit
       Never name to us: you have half our power.
       The other moiety° ere you ask is given.
       Repeat your will,° and take it.

       Queen Katherine.   Thank your Majesty.
       That you would love yourself, and in that love
15   Not unconsiderèd leave your honor nor
       The dignity of your office, is the point
       Of my petition.

       King.   Lady mine, proceed.

       Queen Katherine. I am solicited,° not by a few,
       And those of true condition,° that your subjects
20   Are in great grievance. There have been commissions
       Sent down among 'em, which hath flawed° the heart
       Of all their loyalties; wherein although,
       My good Lord Cardinal, they vent reproaches
       Most bitterly on you as putter-on°
25   Of these exactions, yet the King our master—
       Whose honor heaven shield from soil!—even he
       escapes not
       Language unmannerly; yea, such which breaks

       5 **That gentleman of Buckingham's** (the surveyor referred to at
       1.1.222) 6 **justify** confirm 10 **take place** be seated 12 **moiety** half
       13 **Repeat your will** state your wish 18 **solicited** informed by peti-
       tioners 19 **true condition** loyal disposition 21 **flawed** broken 24
       putter-on instigator

The sides of loyalty, and almost appears
In loud rebellion.

Norfolk.   Not almost appears—
It doth appear. For, upon these taxations,   30
The clothiers all, not able to maintain
The many to them 'longing,° have put off
The spinsters, carders, fullers,° weavers, who,
Unfit for other life, compelled by hunger
And lack of other means, in desperate manner   35
Daring th' event to th' teeth,° are all in uproar,
And danger serves among them.°

King.   Taxation?
Wherein? And what taxation? My Lord Cardinal,
You that are blamed for it alike with us,
Know you of this taxation?

Wolsey.   Please you, sir,   40
I know but of a single part° in aught
Pertains to th' state, and front but in that file
Where others tell steps with me.°

Queen Katherine.   No, my lord?
You know no more than others? But you frame
Things that are known alike,° which are not whole-
    some   45
To° those which would not know them, and yet must
Perforce be their acquaintance.° These exactions
(Whereof my sovereign would have note),° they
    are
Most pestilent° to th' hearing; and to bear 'em
The back is sacrifice to th' load. They say   50

---

32 **to them 'longing** employed by them   33 **spinsters, carders,
fullers** "spinsters" = spinners (usually female); carders combed out
impurities from the wool; fullers cleansed the cloth by beating
36 **Daring th' event to th' teeth** defiantly daring the worst   37
serves among them is welcomed as a comrade   41 **a single part**
i.e., my own individual share   42–43 **front ... with me** only march
in the front rank of those who keep in step with me, i.e., share
my responsibility   44–45 **frame ... alike** devise measures known to
all alike (in the council)   45–46 **wholesome/To** (1) beneficial to
(2) approved by   47 **their acquaintance** acquainted with them   48
note knowledge   49 **pestilent** offensive

They are devised by you, or else you suffer
Too hard an exclamation.°

King.   Still exaction!
The nature of it? In what kind, let's know,
Is this exaction?

Queen Katherine. I am much too venturous
55   In tempting of your patience, but am boldened
Under your promised pardon. The subject's grief°
Comes through commissions, which compels from
         each
The sixth part of his substance, to be levied
Without delay; and the pretense° for this
Is named your wars in France. This makes bold
60   mouths.
Tongues spit their duties out, and cold hearts freeze
Allegiance° in them. Their curses now
Live where their prayers did, and it's come to pass,
This tractable obedience is a slave
65   To each incensèd will.° I would your Highness
Would give it quick consideration, for
There is no primer baseness.°

King.   By my life,
This is against our pleasure.

Wolsey.   And for me,
I have no further gone in this than by
70   A single voice,° and that not passed me but
By learned approbation of the judges. If I am
Traduced by ignorant tongues, which neither know
My faculties° nor person, yet will be
The chronicles of my doing, let me say
75   'Tis but the fate of place,° and the rough brake°
That virtue must go through. We must not stint
Our necessary actions in the fear

52 **exclamation** reproach 56 **grief** grievance 59 **pretense** pretext
62 **Allegiance** (four syllables) 64–65 **This tractable ... will** this
willing obedience of theirs has given way to angry passion 67
primer baseness "mischief more urgently in need of redress"
(Foakes) 70 **voice** vote 73 **faculties** qualities 75 **place** high office 75 **brake** thicket

To cope° malicious censurers, which ever,
As rav'nous fishes, do a vessel follow
That is new-trimmed,° but benefit no further　　　80
Than vainly longing. What we oft do best,
By sick° interpreters (once° weak ones) is
Not ours or not allowed;° what worst, as oft,
Hitting a grosser quality,° is cried up
For our best act. If we shall stand still,　　　85
In fear our motion° will be mocked or carped at,
We should take root here where we sit,
Or sit state-statues only.°

King.　　　　　　　　　　Things done well,
And with a care, exempt themselves from fear.
Things done without example,° in their issue°　　　90
Are to be feared. Have you a precedent
Of this commission? I believe, not any.
We must not rend° our subjects from our laws,
And stick them in our will.° Sixth part of each?
A trembling° contribution! Why, we take　　　95
From every tree lop,° bark, and part o' th' timber,
And though we leave it with a root, thus hacked,°
The air will drink the sap. To every county
Where this is questioned° send our letters with
Free pardon to each man that has denied　　　100
The force° of this commission. Pray look to't;
I put it to your care.

Wolsey.　　　　　[*To the Secretary*] A word with you.
Let there be letters writ to every shire
Of the King's grace and pardon. The grievèd com-
mons

---

78 **cope** encounter　80 **new-trimmed** newly made seaworthy　82
sick unsound　82 **once** in short　83 **Not ours or not allowed** denied
us or condemned　84 **Hitting a grosser quality** appealing to the baser
sort　86 **motion** (1) movement (2) proposal　88 **state-statues only**
mere replicas of statesmen　90　**example** precedent　90 **issue** consequences　93 **rend** pluck　94 **stick them in our will** i.e., make them
creatures of our arbitrary power　95 **trembling** accompanied by,
or causing, trembling　96 **lop** smaller branches and twigs　97 **thus
hacked** when it is thus hacked　99 **questioned** disputed　101 **force**
validity

105 Hardly conceive° of me: let it be noised
    That through our° intercession this revokement
    And pardon comes. I shall anon° advise you
    Further in the proceeding.   *Exit Secretary.*

              Enter Surveyor.

Queen Katherine. I am sorry that the Duke of
        Buckingham
    Is run in° your displeasure.

110 *King.*   It grieves many.
    The gentleman is learned and a most rare° speaker;
    To nature none more bound;° his training such
    That he may furnish and instruct great teachers,
    And never seek for aid out of° himself. Yet see,
115 When these so noble benefits° shall prove
    Not well disposed,° the mind growing once corrupt,
    They turn to vicious forms, ten times more ugly
    Than ever they were fair. This man so complete,
    Who was enrolled 'mongst wonders, and when we,
120 Almost with ravished listening,° could not find
    His hour of speech a minute—he, my lady,
    Hath into monstrous habits° put the graces
    That once were his, and is become as black
    As if besmeared in hell. Sit by us. You shall hear—
125 This was his gentleman in trust°—of him
    Things to strike honor sad. Bid him recount
    The fore-recited practices,° whereof
    We cannot feel too little, hear too much.

Wolsey. Stand forth, and with bold spirit relate what°
        you,
130 Most like a careful subject, have collected°
    Out of the Duke of Buckingham.

105 **Hardly conceive** (1) think harshly (2) scarcely have any conception 106 **our** (note his use of the royal pronoun) 107 **anon** soon 110 **Is run in** has incurred 111 **rare** accomplished 112 **bound** indebted (for his endowments) 114 **out of** from outside 115 **benefits** natural gifts 116 **disposed** applied 120 **Almost with ravished listening** listening almost spellbound 122 **habits** garments 125 **in trust** trusted 127 **fore-recited practices** already revealed plots 129 **what** i.e., what information 130 **collected** gathered (by spying)

King.   Speak freely.

Surveyor. First, it was usual with him—every day
   It would infect his speech—that if the King
   Should without issue die, he'll carry it° so
   To make the scepter his. These very words   135
   I've heard him utter to his son-in-law,
   Lord Aberga'ny, to whom by oath he menaced
   Revenge upon the Cardinal.

Wolsey.   Please your Highness, note
   This dangerous conception° in this point.
   Not friended by his wish,° to your high person   140
   His will is most malignant, and it stretches
   Beyond you to your friends.

Queen Katherine.   My learned Lord Cardinal,
   Deliver all with charity.

King.   Speak on.
   How grounded he his title to the crown
   Upon our fail?° To this point hast thou heard him 145
   At any time speak aught?

Surveyor.   He was brought to this
   By a vain prophecy of Nicholas Henton.°

King. What was that Henton?

Surveyor.   Sir, a Chartreux friar,
   His confessor, who fed him every minute
   With words of sovereignty.°

King.   How know'st thou this? 150

Surveyor. Not long before your Highness sped to°
      France,
   The Duke being at the Rose,° within the parish
   Saint Lawrence Poultney, did of me demand

134 **carry it** manage things 139 **conception** design 140 **Not friended
by his wish** not granted his wish (that the King should die child-
less) 145 **fail** (1) failure to beget an heir (2) death 147 **Henton**
(his name was in fact Nicholas Hopkins, Henton being the name
of his priory) 150 **sovereignty** i.e., relating to his accession to the
throne 151 **sped to** set out for 152 **the Rose** a manor house
belonging to Buckingham

What was the speech° among the Londoners
155 Concerning the French journey. I replied
     Men feared the French would prove perfidious,
     To the King's danger. Presently° the Duke
     Said 'twas the fear indeed and that he doubted°
     'Twould prove the verity of certain words
160 Spoke by a holy monk "that oft," says he,
     "Hath sent to me, wishing me to permit
     John de la Car, my chaplain, a choice° hour
     To hear from him a matter of some moment;
     Whom after under the confession's seal
165 He solemnly had sworn that what he spoke
     My chaplain to no creature living but
     To me should utter, with demure° confidence
     This pausingly ensued: 'Neither the King nor's heirs
     (Tell you the Duke) shall prosper. Bid him strive
170 To win the love o' th' commonalty.° The Duke
     Shall govern England.' "

Queen Katherine.   If I know you well,
     You were the Duke's surveyor, and lost your office
     On the complaint o' th' tenants. Take good heed
     You charge not in your spleen° a noble person,
175 And spoil° your nobler soul.° I say, take heed;
     Yes, heartily beseech you.

King.   Let him on.
     Go forward.

Surveyor.   On my soul, I'll speak but truth.
     I told my lord the Duke, by th' devil's illusions
     The monk might be deceived, and that 'twas
          dangerous
180 To ruminate on this so far, until
     It forged him° some design, which,° being believed,
     It was much like to do. He answered, "Tush,

154 **speech** report 157 **Presently** instantly 158 **doubted** suspected
162 **choice** suitable 167 **demure** solemn 170 **commonalty** common people 174 **spleen** malice 175 **spoil** destroy 175 **nobler soul**
(moral nobility taking precedence over the nobility of rank mentioned in the previous line) 181 **forged him** caused him to fashion
181 **which** i.e., the monk's words

It can do me no damage"; adding further,
That, had the King in his last sickness failed,°
The Cardinal's and Sir Thomas Lovell's heads   *185*
Should have gone off.

King.   Ha! What, so rank?° Ah, ha!
There's mischief in this man. Canst thou say
   further?

Surveyor. I can, my liege.

King.   Proceed.

Surveyor.   Being at Greenwich,
After your Highness had reproved the Duke
About Sir William Bulmer—

King.   I remember   *190*
Of such a time: being my sworn° servant,
The Duke retained him his. But on. What hence?

Surveyor. "If" (quoth he), "I for this had been
   committed,
As to the Tower I thought, I would have played
The part my father meant to act upon   *195*
Th' usurper Richard, who, being at Salisbury,
Made suit to come in's presence; which if granted,
As he made semblance° of his duty, would
Have put his knife into him."

King.   A giant traitor!

Wolsey. Now, madam, may his Highness live in
   freedom,   *200*
And this man out of prison?

Queen Katherine.   God mend all!

King. There's something more would out of thee.
   What say'st?

Surveyor. After "the Duke his father," with the
   "knife,"

184 **failed** died 186 **rank** (1) corrupt (2) full grown (the plot)
191 **sworn** (two syllables) 198 **semblance** pretense

He stretched him,° and with one hand on his
    dagger,
205 Another spread on's breast, mounting° his eyes,
He did discharge a horrible oath whose tenor
Was, were he evil used,° he would outgo
His father by as much as a performance
Does an irresolute° purpose.

King.   There's his period,°
210 To sheathe his knife in us. He is attached.°
Call him to present° trial. If he may
Find mercy in the law, 'tis his; if none,
Let him not seek't of us. By day and night!
He's traitor to th' height.°

                                Exeunt.

Scene 3. [*An antechamber in the palace.*]

Enter Lord Chamberlain and Lord Sands.

Chamberlain. Is't possible the spells of France should
    juggle
Men into such strange mysteries?°

Sands.   New customs,
Though they be never so ridiculous
(Nay, let 'em be unmanly) yet are followed.

5 *Chamberlain.* As far as I see, all the good our English
Have got by the late voyage is but merely
A fit or two o' th' face;° but they are shrewd° ones,
For when they hold 'em,° you would swear directly

204 **stretched him** i.e., stretched himself to his full height 205
mounting raising 207 **evil used** badly treated 209 **irresolute** un-
fulfilled 209 **period** goal 210 **attached** arrested 211 **present** immediate 214 **height** utmost degree 1.3.1–2 **juggle ... mysteries** trick men into such oddly mysterious behavior 7 **A fit or
two o' th' face** a grimace or two 7 **shrewd** nasty 8 **hold 'em** i.e.,
screw up their faces in this way

Their very noses had been counsellors
To Pepin or Clotharius,° they keep state° so.   *10*

Sands. They have all new legs,° and lame ones; one
     would take it,
That never saw 'em pace° before, the spavin
Or springhalt° reigned among 'em.

Chamberlain.   Death! My lord,
Their clothes are after such a pagan cut to't,°
That, sure, th' have worn out Christendom.°   *15*

         Enter Sir Thomas Lovell.

                       How now?
What news, Sir Thomas Lovell?

Lovell.   Faith, my lord,
I hear of none but the new proclamation
That's clapped° upon the court gate.

Chamberlain.   What is't for?

Lovell. The reformation of our traveled gallants
That fill the court with quarrels, talk, and tailors.   *20*

Chamberlain. I'm glad 'tis there. Now I would pray
     our monsieurs
To think an English courtier may be wise,
And never see the Louvre.°

Lovell.   They must either
(For so run the conditions) leave those remnants
Of fool and feather° that they got in France,   *25*
With all their honorable points of ignorance°
Pertaining thereunto, as fights and fireworks,°

10 **Pepin or Clotharius** sixth- and seventh-century kings of the
Franks   10 **keep state** affect grandeur   11 **new legs** new fashions
in walking or bowing   12 **pace** walk (suggesting horse references
that follow)   12–13 **spavin/Or springhalt** diseases affecting horses'
legs   14 **to't** as well   15 **worn out Christendom** used up Christian
fashions   18 **clapped** fastened   23 **Louvre** palace of the French
kings in Paris; now the art museum   25 **fool and feather** foolish
fashions (alluding to the feathers worn by some gallants in their
hats)   26 **honorable points of ignorance** ignorant conceptions of
honorable conduct   27 **fights and fireworks** i.e., duelling and whor-
ing (with a possible reference to venereal disease as the outcome)

Abusing° better men than they can be
Out of a foreign wisdom, renouncing clean
30   The faith they have in tennis and tall stockings,
Short blist'red° breeches, and those types° of travel,
And understand° again like honest men,
Or pack° to their old playfellows. There, I take it,
They may, *cum privilegio,*° "oui" away
35   The lag-end° of their lewdness, and be laughed at.

Sands. 'Tis time to give 'em physic,° their diseases
Are grown so catching.

Chamberlain.   What a loss our ladies
Will have of these trim vanities!°

Lovell.   Aye, marry,
There will be woe indeed, lords. The sly whoresons
40   Have got a speeding° trick to lay down ladies.
A French song and a fiddle has no fellow.°

Sands. The devil fiddle 'em! I am glad they are going,
For, sure, there's no converting of 'em. Now
An honest country lord, as I am, beaten
45   A long time out of play, may bring his plain-song,°
And have an hour of hearing; and, by'r lady,°
Held current music° too.

Chamberlain.   Well said, Lord Sands.
Your colt's tooth° is not cast yet?

Sands.   No, my lord,
Nor shall not while I have a stump.°

Chamberlain.   Sir Thomas,
Whither were you agoing?

28 **Abusing** (goes with "points of ignorance," and is not parallel with "renouncing" in the next line which continues the thought indicated by "leave" in line 24) 31 **blist'red** puffed 31 **types** insignia 32 **understand** comprehend things, in general (with a possible quibble on "stand under" [i.e., clothes]) 33 **pack** clear out 34 **cum privilegio** with license 35 **lag-end** latter part 36 **physic** medical treatment 38 **trim vanities** spruce fops 40 **speeding** effective 41 **fellow** equal 45 **plain-song** simple melody 46 **by'r lady** i.e., by the Virgin Mary (a mild oath) 47 **Held current music** have it accepted as good music 48 **colt's tooth** i.e., youthful lustiness 49 **stump** (with a bawdy double meaning)

Lovell.   To the Cardinal's.   50
  Your lordship is a guest too.

Chamberlain.   O, 'tis true.
  This night he makes a supper, and a great one,
  To many lords and ladies. There will be
  The beauty of this kingdom, I'll assure you.

Lovell. That churchman bears a bounteous mind
    indeed,   55
  A hand as fruitful as the land that feeds us.
  His dews fall everywhere.

Chamberlain.   No doubt he's noble.
  He had a black° mouth that said other of him.

Sands. He may, my lord; has wherewithal. In him
  Sparing° would show a worse sin than ill doctrine.   60
  Men of his way° should be most liberal;
  They are set here for examples.

Chamberlain.   True, they are so,
  But few now give so great ones. My barge stays;
  Your lordship shall along. Come, good Sir Thomas,
  We shall be late else, which I would not be,   65
  For I was spoke to,° with Sir Henry Guildford
  This night to be comptrollers.°

Sands.   I am your lordship's. *Exeunt.*

58 **black** evil 60 **Sparing** frugality 61 **way** i.e., of life 66 **spoke
to** asked 67 **comptrollers** household officers in charge of the
festivities

Scene 4. [*A Hall in York Place.*]

Hautboys.° A small table under a state° for the Car-
dinal, a longer table for the guests. Then enter Anne
Bullen and divers other Ladies and Gentlemen as
guests, at one door; at another door, enter Sir Henry
Guildford.

Guildford. Ladies, a general welcome from his Grace
       Salutes ye all. This night he dedicates
       To fair content and you. None here, he hopes,
       In all this noble bevy,° has brought with her
5   One care abroad. He would have all as merry
       As, first, good company, good wine, good welcome,
       Can make good people.

              Enter Lord Chamberlain, Lord Sands, and
                   [*Sir Thomas*] *Lovell.*

                                    O, my lord, y'are tardy.
       The very thought of this fair company
       Clapped wings to me.

Chamberlain. You are young, Sir Harry Guildford.

10   *Sands.* Sir Thomas Lovell, had the Cardinal
       But half my lay thoughts in him, some of these
       Should find a running banquet,° ere they rested,
       I think would better please 'em. By my life,
       They are a sweet society° of fair ones.

15   *Lovell.* O, that your lordship were but now confessor
       To one or two of these!

Sands.   I would I were;
       They should find easy penance.

1.4.s.d. **Hautboys** oboes s.d. **state** canopy 4 **bevy** company (of
ladies) 12 **running banquet** hasty repast (with a bawdy double
meaning) 14 **society** assembly

Lovell.   Faith, how easy?

Sands. As easy as a down bed would afford it.

Chamberlain. Sweet ladies, will it please you sit? Sir
   Harry,
   Place you° that side; I'll take the charge of this.   20
   His Grace is ent'ring. Nay, you must not freeze.
   Two women placed together makes cold weather.
   My Lord Sands, you are one will keep 'em waking:
   Pray, sit between these ladies.

Sands.   By my faith,
   And thank your lordship. By your leave, sweet
      ladies.   25
   If I chance to talk a little wild, forgive me;
   I had it from my father.

Anne.   Was he mad, sir?

Sands. O, very mad, exceeding mad, in love too;
   But he would bite none. Just as I do now,
   He would kiss you twenty with a breath.°

                              [*Kisses her.*]

Chamberlain.   Well said,° my lord.   30
   So, now y'are fairly° seated. Gentlemen,
   The penance lies on you if these fair ladies
   Pass away° frowning.

Sands.   For my little cure,°
   Let me alone.

         *Hautboys. Enter Cardinal Wolsey, and takes
                  his state.°*

Wolsey. Y'are welcome, my fair guests. That noble
   lady   35
   Or gentleman that is not freely merry

---

20 **Place you** i.e., place the guests   30 **kiss you twenty with a
breath** kiss twenty in one breath   30 **said** done   31 **fairly** properly
33 **Pass away** leave   33 **cure** (1) charge, parish (continuing the ecclesiastical metaphor of lines 15ff.) (2) remedy   34s.d. **state** chair of
state

Is not my friend. This, to confirm my welcome;
And to you all, good health.   [*Drinks.*]

Sands.   Your Grace is noble.
Let me have such a bowl may hold my thanks,
And save me so much talking.

40 *Wolsey.*   My Lord Sands,
I am beholding° to you. Cheer your neighbors.
Ladies, you are not merry. Gentlemen,
Whose fault is this?

Sands.   The red wine first must rise
In their fair cheeks, my lord. Then we shall have
    'em
Talk us to silence.

45 *Anne.*   You are a merry gamester,°
My Lord Sands.

Sands.   Yes, if I make my play.°
Here's to your ladyship; and pledge it, madam,
For 'tis to such a thing—

Anne.   You cannot show me.

Sands. I told your Grace they would talk anon.
          Drum and trumpet; chambers° discharged.

Wolsey.   What's that?

Chamberlain. Look out there, some° of ye.
                    [*Exit Servant.*]

50 *Wolsey.*   What warlike voice,
And to what end, is this? Nay, ladies, fear not;
By all the laws of war y'are privileged.°

          [*Re*]*enter a Servant.*

Chamberlain. How now, what is't?

Servant.   A noble troop of strangers,

---

41 **beholding** beholden   45 **gamester** playful person   46 **make my play** win my game   49s.d. **chambers** small cannon used for cere-monial purposes   50 **some** some one (cf. also line 60)   52 **privileged** entitled to immunity

For so they seem. Th' have left their barge, and
   landed,
And hither make,° as great ambassadors   *55*
From foreign princes.

Wolsey.   Good Lord Chamberlain,
  Go, give 'em welcome: you can speak the French
    tongue;
  And pray receive 'em nobly and conduct 'em
  Into our presence, where this heaven of beauty
  Shall shine at full upon them. Some attend him.   *60*
         [*Exit Chamberlain, attended.*] *All rise,*
                     and tables removed.
  You have now a broken° banquet, but we'll mend
    it.
  A good digestion to you all; and once more
  I show'r a welcome on ye: welcome all.

Hautboys. Enter King and others, as masquers,°
habited° like shepherds, ushered by the Lord Cham-
berlain. They pass directly before the Cardinal, and
gracefully salute him.

  A noble company! What are their pleasures?

Chamberlain. Because they speak no English,
    thus they prayed   *65*
  To tell your Grace: that, having heard by fame°
  Of this so noble and so fair assembly
  This night to meet here, they could do no less
  (Out of the great respect they bear to beauty)
  But leave their flocks and, under your fair conduct,° *70*
  Crave leave to view these ladies and entreat
  An hour of revels with 'em.

Wolsey.   Say, Lord Chamberlain,
  They have done my poor house grace; for which I
    pay 'em

---

55 **make** make their way 61 **broken** interrupted, with a possible
pun on "poor remains" (of a feast) 63s.d. **masquers** i.e., disguised
and vizarded as for a court masque 63s.d. **habited** dressed 66
fame report 70 **under your fair conduct** with your kind permission

A thousand thanks and pray 'em take their
    pleasures.   *Choose ladies; King and Anne Bullen.*

75 *King.* The fairest hand I ever touched! O beauty,
    Till now I never knew thee!   *Music. Dance.*

Wolsey. My lord!

Chamberlain.   Your Grace?

Wolsey.   Pray tell 'em thus much from me:
    There should be one amongst 'em, by his person,
    More worthy this place than myself, to whom
80   (If I but knew him) with my love and duty
    I would surrender it.°

Chamberlain.   I will, my lord.
               Whisper[s with the masquers].

Wolsey. What say they?

Chamberlain.   Such a one, they all confess,
    There is indeed, which they would have your Grace
    Find out, and he will take it.

Wolsey.   Let me see then.
85 By all your good leaves, gentlemen; here I'll make
    My royal choice.°

King. [*Unmasking*] Ye have found him, Cardinal.
    You hold a fair assembly; you do well, lord.
    You are a churchman, or, I'll tell you, Cardinal,
    I should judge now unhappily.°

Wolsey.   I am glad
    Your Grace is grown so pleasant.°

90 *King.*   My Lord Chamberlain,
    Prithee come hither. What fair lady's that?

Chamberlain. An't please your Grace, Sir Thomas
    Bullen's daughter,
    The Viscount Rochford, one of her Highness'
    women.

---

81 **it** i.e., the place of honor   86 **royal choice** choice of a king   89
unhappily unfavorably   90 **pleasant** merry

King. By heaven, she is a dainty one. Sweetheart,
　　I were unmannerly to take you out°   95
　　And not to kiss you.° A health, gentlemen!
　　Let it go round.

Wolsey. Sir Thomas Lovell, is the banquet ready
　　I' th' privy chamber?

Lovell.　　　　　　　　Yes, my lord.

Wolsey.　　　　　　　　　　　Your Grace,
　　I fear, with dancing is a little heated.   100

King. I fear, too much.

Wolsey.　　　　　　There's fresher air, my lord,
　　In the next chamber.

King. Lead in your ladies, every one. Sweet partner,
　　I must not yet forsake you. Let's be merry,
　　Good my Lord Cardinal. I have half a dozen healths 105
　　To drink to these fair ladies, and a measure°
　　To lead 'em once again; and then let's dream
　　Who's best in favor.° Let the music knock it.°
　　　　　　　　　　　　Exeunt with trumpets.

---

95 **to take you out** i.e., to invite you to dance 96 **to kiss you**
(customary following a dance) 106 **measure** stately dance 108
best in favor (1) prettiest (2) most favored (by the ladies) 108
knock it strike up

ACT 2

Scene 1. [*Westminster. A street.*]

Enter two Gentlemen at several° doors.

First Gentleman. Whither away so fast?

Second Gentleman.   O, God save ye!
Ev'n to the Hall,° to hear what shall become
Of the great Duke of Buckingham.

First Gentleman.   I'll save you
That labor, sir. All's now done but the ceremony
Of bringing back the prisoner.

5   *Second Gentleman.*   Were you there?

First Gentleman. Yes, indeed was I.

Second Gentleman.   Pray speak what has happened.

First Gentleman. You may guess quickly what.

Second Gentleman.   Is he found guilty?

First Gentleman. Yes, truly is he, and condemned
upon't.

Second Gentleman. I am sorry for't.

First Gentleman.   So are a number more.

2.1.s.d. **several** different   2 **Hall** Westminster Hall

Second Gentleman. But, pray, how passed it?°   10

First Gentleman. I'll tell you in a little.° The great
   Duke
  Came to the bar, where to his accusations
  He pleaded still not guilty, and allegèd°
  Many sharp reasons to defeat° the law.
  The King's attorney° on the contrary°   15
  Urged on° the examinations, proofs,° confessions
  Of divers witnesses; which the Duke desired
  To him brought *viva voce* to his face;
  At which appeared against him his surveyor;
  Sir° Gilbert Parke, his councillor; and John Car,   20
  Confessor to him; with that devil monk,
  Hopkins, that made this mischief.

Second Gentleman.   That was he
  That fed him with his prophecies?

First Gentleman.   The same.
  All these accused him strongly, which° he fain°
  Would have flung from him; but indeed he could
    not.   25
  And so his peers upon this evidence
  Have found him guilty of high treason. Much
  He spoke, and learnedly, for life, but all
  Was either pitied in him or forgotten.°

Second Gentleman. After all this, how did he bear
  himself?   30

First Gentleman. When he was brought again to th'
  bar, to hear
  His knell rung out, his judgment,° he was stirred
  With such an agony he sweat extremely

---

10 **how passed it** i.e., what happened at the trial   11 **in a little**
in brief   13 **allegèd** put forward   14 **defeat** frustrate   15 **King's
attorney** John Fitz-James, afterward Chief Justice of the King's
Bench   15 **contrary** contrary side   16 **Urged on** (1) argued on the
evidence of (intransitive) (2) pressed the evidence of (transitive)
16 **examinations, proofs** depositions, statements   20 **Sir** (a courtesy title for a cleric)   24 **which** i.e., which accusations   24 **fain**
gladly   29 **Was ... forgotten** either aroused only unavailing pity
or had no effect   32 **judgment** sentence (also in line 58)

And something spoke in choler, ill and hasty.
35 But he fell to himself again, and sweetly
In all the rest showed a most noble patience.

Second Gentleman. I do not think he fears death.

First Gentleman.   Sure,° he does not;
He never was so womanish. The cause
He may a little grieve at.

Second Gentleman.   Certainly
The Cardinal is the end° of this.

40 *First Gentleman.*   'Tis likely,
By all conjectures: first, Kildare's attainder,°
Then Deputy of Ireland, who removed,
Earl Surrey was sent thither, and in haste too,
Lest he should help his father.°

Second Gentleman.   That trick of state
Was a deep envious° one.

45 *First Gentleman.*   At his return
No doubt he will requite it. This is noted,
And generally:° whoever the King favors,
The Card'nal instantly will find employment,
And far enough from court too.

Second Gentleman.   All the commons
50 Hate him perniciously,° and, o' my conscience,
Wish him ten fathom deep. This Duke as much
They love and dote on; call him bounteous Buck-
    ingham,
The mirror of all courtesy—

*Enter Buckingham from his arraignment, tipstaves°
before him, the ax with the edge towards him,
halberds° on each side, accompanied with Sir Thomas*

37 **Sure** surely 40 **the end** at the root 41 **attainder** disgrace
44 **father** father-in-law (cf. 3.2.260–64) 45 **envious** malicious 47 **generally** by all 50 **perniciously** mortally 53s.d. **tipstaves** bailiffs, so
called because they carried silver-tipped staffs 53s.d. **halberds** hal-
berdiers (officers bearing long-handled weapons with blade-and-spear
points)

Lovell, Sir Nicholas Vaux, Sir Walter Sands,° and
common people, etc.

First Gentleman.   Stay there, sir,
And see the noble ruined man you speak of.

Second Gentleman. Let's stand close,° and behold him.

Buckingham.   All good people,   55
You that thus far have come to pity me,
Hear what I say, and then go home and lose° me.
I have this day received a traitor's judgment,
And by that name must die. Yet, heaven bear wit-
    ness,
And if I have a conscience, let it sink° me   60
Even as the ax falls, if I be not faithful!
The law I bear no malice for my death:
'T has done, upon the premises,° but justice.
But those that sought it I could wish more° Chris-
    tians.
Be what they will,° I heartily forgive 'em.   65
Yet let 'em look° they glory not in mischief
Nor build their evils° on the graves of great men,°
For then my guiltless blood must cry against 'em.
For further life in this world I ne'er hope,
Nor will I sue, although the King have mercies   70
More than I dare make faults. You few that loved
    me
And dare be bold to weep for Buckingham,
His noble friends and fellows, whom to leave
Is only bitter° to him, only dying,
Go with me like good angels to my end;   75
And as the long divorce of steel° falls on me,
Make of your prayers one sweet sacrifice,°
And lift my soul to heaven. Lead on, o' God's name.

53s.d. **Sir Walter Sands** (Sir William Sands in Holinshed) 55
close (1) out of view (2) silent 57 **lose** forget 60 **sink** destroy
63 **premises** (1) circumstances (2) proceedings 64 **more** i.e., more
sincere 65 **Be what they will** whoever they may be 66 **look** look
to it 67 **evils** privies (?) 67 **great men** noblemen 74 **only bitter**
the only bitterness 76 **divorce of steel** separation of body and soul
caused by the ax 77 **sacrifice** offering

Lovell. I do beseech your Grace, for charity,
80   If ever any malice in your heart
      Were hid against me, now to forgive me frankly.°

Buckingham. Sir Thomas Lovell, I as free forgive you
      As I would be forgiven. I forgive all.
      There cannot be those numberless offenses
      'Gainst me that I cannot take° peace with. No black
85   envy°
      Shall mark my grave. Commend me to his Grace,
      And if he speak of Buckingham, pray tell him
      You met him half in heaven. My vows and prayers
      Yet are the King's and, till my soul forsake,°
90   Shall cry for blessings on him. May he live
      Longer than I have time to tell° his years!
      Ever beloved and loving may his rule be,
      And when old time shall lead him to his end,
      Goodness and he fill up one monument!°

95 *Lovell.* To th' waterside I must conduct your Grace,
      Then give my charge up to Sir Nicholas Vaux,
      Who undertakes° you to your end.

Vaux.   Prepare there;
      The Duke is coming. See the barge be ready,
      And fit it with such furniture° as suits
      The greatness of his person.

100 *Buckingham.*   Nay, Sir Nicholas,
      Let it alone; my state now will but mock me.
      When I came hither, I was Lord High Constable
      And Duke of Buckingham; now, poor Edward
          Bohun.°
      Yet I am richer than my base accusers
105   That never knew what truth meant. I now seal° it,
      And with that blood will make 'em one day groan
          for't.

81   **frankly** freely (for Lovell's reference see 1.2.185–86)   85 **take**
make   85 **envy** malice   89 **forsake** i.e., part from my body   91 **tell**
count   94 **monument** grave   97 **undertakes** has charge of   99
furniture equipment   103 **Bohun** (his family name was actually
Stafford, although in the female line he was descended from the
Bohuns)   105 **seal** ratify

My noble father, Henry of Buckingham,
Who first raised head° against usurping Richard,°
Flying for succor to his servant Banister,
Being distressed, was by that wretch betrayed,   *110*
And without trial fell. God's peace be with him!
Henry the Seventh succeeding, truly pitying
My father's loss, like a most royal prince,
Restored me to my honors, and out of ruins
Made my name once more noble. Now his son,   *115*
Henry the Eighth, life, honor, name, and all
That made me happy, at one stroke has taken
Forever from the world. I had my trial,
And must needs say a noble one; which makes me
A little happier than my wretched father.   *120*
Yet thus far we are one in fortunes: both
Fell by our servants, by those men we loved most—
A most unnatural and faithless service!
Heaven has an end° in all. Yet, you that hear me,
This from a dying man receive as certain: *125*
Where you are liberal of your loves and counsels
Be sure you be not loose.° For those you make
  friends
And give your hearts to, when they once perceive
The least rub° in your fortunes, fall away
Like water from ye, never found again   *130*
But where they mean to sink° ye. All good people,
Pray for me! I must now forsake ye; the last hour
Of my long weary life° is come upon me.
Farewell!
And when you would say something that is sad,   *135*
Speak how I fell. I have done, and God forgive me.
                    Exeunt Duke and Train.

First Gentleman. O, this is full of pity! Sir, it calls,
I fear, too many curses on their heads
That were the authors.°

Second Gentleman.   If the Duke be guiltless,

---

108 **raised head** gathered troops   108 **Richard** Richard III   124 **end**
purpose   127 **loose** careless   129 **rub** check   131 **sink** destroy
133 **long weary life** (he was forty-three)   139 **authors** originators

140   'Tis full of woe. Yet I can give you inkling
           Of an ensuing evil, if it fall,
           Greater than this.

    First Gentleman.   Good angels keep it from us!
           What may it be? You do not doubt my faith,° sir?

    Second Gentleman. This secret is so weighty, 'twill re-
           quire
           A strong faith to conceal it.

145 *First Gentleman.*   Let me have it;
           I do not talk much.

    Second Gentleman.   I am confident;°
           You shall,° sir. Did you not of late days hear
           A buzzing° of a separation
           Between the King and Katherine?

    First Gentleman.   Yes, but it held°
           not;
150   For when the King once heard it, out of anger
           He sent command to the Lord Mayor straight
           To stop the rumor and allay° those tongues
           That durst disperse it.

    Second Gentleman.   But that slander, sir,
           Is found a truth now, for it grows again
155   Fresher than e'er it was, and held for certain
           The King will venture at it. Either the Cardinal
           Or some about him near have, out of malice
           To the good Queen, possessed him with a scruple°
           That will undo her. To confirm this too,
160   Cardinal Campeius is arrived, and lately;°
           As all think, for this business.

    First Gentleman.   'Tis the Cardinal;
           And merely to revenge him on the Emperor°

143 **faith** trustworthiness 146 **confident** i.e., of your discretion
147 **shall** i.e., shall have it 148 **buzzing** rumor 149 **held** lasted
152 **allay** silence 158 **possessed him with a scruple** put a doubt in
his mind 160 **Cardinal ... lately** (Lorenzo Campeggio, or Campeius, did not actually arrive from Rome until 1528, seven years
after Buckingham's execution) 162 **Emperor** (Charles V, Holy
Roman Emperor and King of Spain; nephew to Katherine. See
1.1.176–90 and 2.2.25)

For not bestowing on him at his asking
The archbishopric of Toledo, this is purposed.

Second Gentleman. I think you have hit the mark. But
is't not cruel   165
That she should feel the smart of this? The Cardinal
Will have his will, and she must fall.

First Gentleman.   'Tis woeful.
We are too open° here to argue this;
Let's think in private more.

                                        Exeunt.

Scene 2. [*An antechamber in the palace.*]

Enter Lord Chamberlain, reading this letter.

Chamberlain. "My lord, the horses your lordship sent
    for, with all the care I had, I saw well chosen,
    ridden,° and furnished.° They were young and hand-
    some, and of the best breed in the north. When they
    were ready to set out for London, a man of my   5
    Lord Cardinal's, by commission and main power,°
    took 'em from me, with this reason: his master
    would be served before a subject, if not before the
    King; which stopped our mouths, sir."
I fear he will indeed. Well, let him have them.   10
He will have all, I think.

*Enter to the Lord Chamberlain, the Dukes of
Norfolk and Suffolk.*

Norfolk. Well met, my Lord Chamberlain.

Chamberlain. Good day to both your Graces.

---

168 **open** (1) public (2) indiscreet 2.2.3 **ridden** broken in 3
furnished outfitted 6 **commission and main power** warrant and
sheer force

Suffolk. How is the King employed?

Chamberlain.   I left him private,°
    Full of sad° thoughts and troubles.

15 *Norfolk.*   What's the cause?

Chamberlain. It seems the marriage with his brother's
        wife
    Has crept too near his conscience.

Suffolk. [*Aside*]   No, his conscience
    Has crept too near another lady.

Norfolk.   'Tis so.
    This is the Cardinal's doing; the king-cardinal,
20 That blind priest, like the eldest son of Fortune,
    Turns what he list.° The King will know° him one
        day.

Suffolk. Pray God he do! He'll never know himself
    else.

Norfolk. How holily he works in all his business,
    And with what zeal! For, now he has cracked the
        league
    Between us and the Emperor, the Queen's great
25   nephew,
    He dives into the King's soul, and there scatters
    Dangers, doubts, wringing° of the conscience,
    Fears and despairs; and all these for° his marriage.
    And out of all these to restore the King,
30 He counsels a divorce, a loss of her
    That like a jewel has hung twenty years
    About his neck, yet never lost her luster;
    Of her that loves him with that excellence
    That angels love good men with, even of her
35 That, when the greatest stroke of fortune falls,
    Will bless the King. And is not this course pious?

---

14 **private** alone   15 **sad** grave (also in lines 57, 62)   20–21 **That
blind … list** i.e., he takes after Fortune in his disregard for
others and his capriciousness (Fortune was depicted as blind and
turning a wheel; eldest sons had special privileges)   21 **know** understand (also in next line)   27 **wringing** torture   28 **for** because of

Chamberlain. Heaven keep me from such counsel! 'Tis
    most true
    These news are everywhere; every tongue speaks
      'em,
    And every true heart weeps for't. All that dare
    Look into these affairs see this main end,   40
    The French King's sister.° Heaven will one day
      open
    The King's eyes, that so long have slept upon°
    This bold bad man.

Suffolk.   And free us from his slavery.

Norfolk. We had need pray,
    And heartily, for our deliverance,   45
    Or this imperious man will work us all
    From princes into pages. All men's honors
    Lie like one lump° before him, to be fashioned
    Into what pitch° he please.

Suffolk.   For me, my lords,
    I love him not, nor fear him—there's my creed.   50
    As I am made without him, so I'll stand,
    If the King please. His curses and his blessings
    Touch me alike; th'are breath I not believe in.
    I knew him, and I know him; so I leave him
    To him that made him proud—the Pope.°

Norfolk.   Let's in,   55
    And with some other business put the King
    From these sad thoughts that work too much upon
      him.
    My lord, you'll bear us company?

Chamberlain.   Excuse me,
    The King has sent me otherwise. Besides,
    You'll find a most unfit time to disturb him.   60
    Health to your lordships.

41 **The French King's sister** the Duchess of Alençon (see 3.2.
85–86) 42 **slept upon** been blind to 48 **lump** i.e., of clay (cf.
Romans 9:21) 49 **pitch** height (figurative), i.e., rank or degree
of dignity 55 **the Pope** (the expected reference would be to the
devil)

Norfolk.   Thanks, my good Lord Chamberlain.

*Exit Lord Chamberlain, and the King draws
the curtain° and sits reading pensively.*

Suffolk. How sad he looks; sure, he is much afflicted.°

King. Who's there, ha?

Norfolk.   Pray God he be not angry.

King. Who's there, I say? How dare you thrust yourselves
65   Into my private meditations?
Who am I, ha?

Norfolk. A gracious king that pardons all offenses
Malice ne'er meant. Our breach of duty this way°
Is business of estate,° in which we come
To know your royal pleasure.

70 *King.*   Ye are too bold.
Go to;° I'll make ye know your times of business.
Is this an hour for temporal affairs, ha?

Enter Wolsey and Campeius, with a commission.

Who's there? My good Lord Cardinal? O my
Wolsey,
The quiet of my wounded conscience,
Thou art a cure fit for a king. [*To Campeius*] You're
75   welcome,
Most learnèd reverend sir, into our kingdom:
Use us and it. [*To Wolsey*] My good lord, have
great care
I be not found a talker.°

Wolsey.   Sir, you cannot.
I would your Grace would give us but an hour
Of private conference.

61s.d. **King draws the curtain** (he is thus revealed seated within a cur-
tained booth or recess; see Overview, p. xxix   62 **afflicted** disturbed
68 **this way** in this respect   69 **estate** state   71 **Go to** (an exclamation
of impatience or disapproval)   78 **talker** i.e., rather than a doer

King. [*To Norfolk and Suffolk*] We are busy; go.	*80*

Norfolk. [*Aside to Suffolk*] This priest has no pride in
    him?

Suffolk. [*Aside to Norfolk*] Not to speak of.
    I would not be so sick though for his place.°
    But this cannot continue.

Norfolk. [*Aside to Suffolk*] If it do,
    I'll venture one have-at-him.°

Suffolk. [*Aside to Norfolk*]	I another.
                    Exeunt Norfolk and Suffolk.

Wolsey. Your Grace has given a precedent of wisdom	*85*
    Above all princes, in committing freely
    Your scruple to the voice of Christendom.
    Who can be angry now? What envy° reach you?
    The Spaniard,° tied by blood and favor to her,
    Must now confess, if they have any goodness,	*90*
    The trial just and noble. All the clerks°
    (I mean the learnèd ones) in Christian kingdoms
    Have their free voices.° Rome, the nurse of judg-
        ment,
    Invited by your noble self, hath sent
    One general tongue° unto us, this good man,	*95*
    This just and learnèd priest, Card'nal Campeius,
    Whom once more I present unto your Highness.

King. And once more in mine arms I bid him welcome,
    And thank the holy conclave° for their loves.
    They have sent me such a man I would have wished
        for.	*100*

Campeius. Your Grace must needs deserve all strang-
        ers'° loves,

82 **so sick though for his place** so sick with pride even if it meant
having his position 84 **have-at-him** thrust (the phrase "have at
you," meaning "here goes!" or "watch out!" signaled an attack)
88 **envy** malice 89 **Spaniard** Spaniards (Katherine was daughter
to Ferdinand of Spain) 91 **clerks** scholars 93 **Have their free
voices** may freely express their opinions 95 **One general tongue**
one spokesman for all 99 **holy conclave** College of Cardinals
101 **strangers'** foreigners'

You are so noble. To your Highness' hand
I tender my commission; by whose virtue,
The court of Rome commanding, you, my Lord
105 Cardinal of York, are joined with me their servant
In the unpartial° judging of this business.

King. Two equal° men. The Queen shall be acquainted
Forthwith for what you come. Where's Gardiner?

Wolsey. I know your Majesty has always loved her
110 So dear in heart not to deny her that°
A woman of less place might ask by law:
Scholars allowed freely to argue for her.

King. Aye, and the best she shall have, and my favor
To him that does best—God forbid else. Cardinal,
115 Prithee call Gardiner to me, my new secretary;
I find him a fit fellow.

[*Wolsey beckons.*]

Enter Gardiner.

Wolsey. [*Aside to Gardiner*] Give me your hand:
much joy and favor to you.
You are the King's now.

Gardiner. [*Aside to Wolsey*] But to be commanded
Forever by your Grace, whose hand has raised me.

120 *King.* Come hither, Gardiner.

Walks and whispers.

Campeius. My Lord of York, was not one Doctor
Pace
In this man's place before him?

Wolsey.   Yes, he was.

Campeius. Was he not held a learnèd man?

Wolsey.   Yes, surely.

---

106 **unpartial** impartial 107 **equal** just, impartial 110 **that** that
which

Campeius. Believe me, there's an ill opinion spread
   then,
   Even of yourself, Lord Cardinal.

Wolsey.   How? Of me?   *125*

Campeius. They will not stick° to say you envied him
   And, fearing he would rise (he was so virtuous),
   Kept him a foreign man still;° which so grieved him
   That he ran mad and died.°

Wolsey.   Heaven's peace be with him!
   That's Christian care enough. For living murmurers°   *130*
   There's places of rebuke. He was a fool,
   For he would needs be virtuous. That good fellow,
   If I command him, follows my appointment;°
   I will have none so near else. Learn this, brother,
   We live not to be griped° by meaner persons.   *135*

King. Deliver° this with modesty to th' Queen.
                                   Exit Gardiner.
   The most convenient place that I can think of
   For such receipt° of learning is Blackfriars;°
   There ye shall meet about this weighty business.
   My Wolsey, see it furnished.° O, my lord,   *140*
   Would it not grieve an able° man to leave
   So sweet a bedfellow? But, conscience, conscience!
   O, 'tis a tender place, and I must leave her.
                                   Exeunt.

126 **stick** scruple   128 **a foreign man still** continually on missions
abroad   129 **died** (Pace in fact outlived Wolsey by six years)
130 **murmurers** grumblers   133 **appointment** direction   135 **griped**
clutched   familiarly   136 **Deliver** relate   138 **receipt** accommodation   138 **Blackfriars** Dominican monastery buildings in London
140 **furnished** fitted up   141 **able** vigorous

Scene 3. [*An antechamber of the Queen's
apartments.*]

Enter Anne Bullen and an old Lady.

Anne. Not for that neither. Here's the pang that
    pinches:°
His Highness having lived so long with her, and she
So good a lady that no tongue could ever
Pronounce° dishonor of her—by my life,
5   She never knew harmdoing—O, now, after
So many courses of the sun° enthronèd,
Still growing in a majesty and pomp, the which
To leave a thousandfold more bitter than
'Tis sweet at first t' acquire—after this process,°
10   To give her the avaunt,° it is a pity
Would move a monster.

Old Lady.   Hearts of most hard temper
Melt and lament for her.

Anne.   O, God's will! Much better
She ne'er had known pomp; though't be temporal,°
Yet, if that quarrel,° Fortune, do divorce
15   It from the bearer, 'tis a sufferance panging°
As soul and body's severing.

Old Lady.   Alas, poor lady!
She's a stranger° now again.

Anne.   So much the more
Must pity drop upon her. Verily,
I swear, 'tis better to be lowly born

2.3.1 **pinches** torments 4 **Pronounce** utter 6 **courses of the sun**
years 9 **this process** what has passed 10 **give her the avaunt**
order her to go 13 **temporal** worldly 14 **quarrel** quarreler (abstract for concrete) 15 **sufferance panging** suffering as agonizing
17 **stranger** foreigner

   And range with humble livers° in content   20
   Than to be perked up° in a glist'ring° grief
   And wear a golden sorrow.

Old Lady.   Our content
   Is our best having.°

Anne.   By my troth and maidenhead,
   I would not be a queen.

Old Lady.   Beshrew me,° I would,
   And venture maidenhead for't; and so would you,   25
   For all this spice° of your hypocrisy.
   You that have so fair parts° of woman on you,
   Have too a woman's heart, which ever yet
   Affected° eminence, wealth, sovereignty;
   Which, to say sooth,° are blessings; and which gifts   30
   (Saving your mincing)° the capacity
   Of your soft cheveril° conscience would receive,
   If you might please to stretch it.

Anne.   Nay, good troth.°

Old Lady. Yes, troth, and troth. You would not be
   a queen?

Anne. No, not for all the riches under heaven.   35

Old Lady. 'Tis strange. A threepence bowed° would
   hire me,
   Old as I am, to queen° it. But, I pray you,
   What think you of a duchess? Have you limbs
   To bear that load of title?

Anne.   No, in truth.

Old Lady. Then you are weakly made. Pluck off° a
   little;   40

20 **range with humble livers** rank with humble folk   21 **perked up**
decked out   21 **glist'ring** glittering   23 **having** possession   24 **Beshrew me** may evil befall me! (a mild imprecation)   26 **spice** dash,
sample   27 **parts** qualities (of mind and person)   29 **Affected**
aspired to   30 **say sooth** tell the truth   31 **Saving your mincing**
despite your coyness   32 **cheveril** kidskin   33 **troth** faith   36
bowed bent (and therefore worthless); with a possible quibble on
"bawd"   37 **queen** (with a pun on "quean"=bawd)   40 **Pluck off**
come down in rank

I would not be a young count° in your way,°
For more than blushing comes to. If your back
Cannot vouchsafe° this burden, 'tis too weak
Ever to get a boy.

Anne.   How you do talk!
45   I swear again, I would not be a queen
For all the world.

Old Lady.   In faith, for little England°
You'd venture an emballing.° I myself
Would for Caernarvonshire,° although there 'longed
No more to th' crown but that. Lo, who comes
here?

Enter Lord Chamberlain.

Chamberlain. Good morrow, ladies. What were't worth
50   to know
The secret of your conference?°

Anne.   My good lord,
Not your demand; it values not° your asking.
Our mistress' sorrows we were pitying.

Chamberlain. It was a gentle business, and becoming
55   The action of good women. There is hope
All will be well.

Anne.   Now, I pray God, amen!

Chamberlain. You bear a gentle mind, and heav'nly
blessings
Follow such creatures. That you may, fair lady,
Perceive I speak sincerely, and high note's
60   Ta'en of your many virtues, the King's Majesty
Commends his good opinion of you,° and

---

41 **count** (with a bawdy double meaning) 41 **way** (1) path (2) virginal condition 43 **vouchsafe** deign to accept 46 **little England** (perhaps with a reference to Pembrokeshire, called "little England beyond Wales"; word follows [line 63] of Anne's promotion to Marchioness—historically, to Marquess—of Pembroke) 47 **emballing** investment with the ball as emblem of sovereignty (with a bawdy pun) 48 **Caernarvonshire** a poor Welsh county 51 **conference** conversation 52 **values not** is not worth 61 **Commends his good opinion of you** presents his compliments

Does purpose honor to you no less flowing°
Than Marchioness of Pembroke; to which title
A thousand pound a year, annual support,
Out of his grace he adds.

Anne.   I do not know   65
What kind° of my obedience I should tender.
More than my all is nothing; nor my prayers
Are not° words duly hallowed, nor my wishes
More worth than empty vanities. Yet prayers and
    wishes
Are all I can return. Beseech your lordship,   70
Vouchsafe° to speak my thanks and my obedience,
As from a blushing handmaid, to his Highness,
Whose health and royalty I pray for.

Chamberlain.   Lady,
I shall not fail t' approve the fair conceit°
The King hath of you. [*Aside*] I have perused her
    well.   75
Beauty and honor in her are so mingled
That they have caught the King; and who knows
    yet
But from this lady may proceed a gem
To lighten all this isle?—I'll to the King,
And say I spoke with you.

Anne.   My honored lord.   80
                    Exit Lord Chamberlain.

Old Lady. Why, this it is:° see, see!
I have been begging sixteen years in court,
Am yet a courtier beggarly,° nor could
Come pat betwixt too early and too late
For any suit of pounds;° and you (O fate!)   85
A very fresh fish here—fie, fie, fie upon
This compelled° fortune!—have your mouth filled up
Before you open it.

62 **flowing** abundant 66 **kind** expression 67–68 **nor ... not** (the
double negative lends emphasis) 71 **Vouchsafe** be good enough
74 **approve the fair conceit** confirm the good opinion 81 **this it is** so
it goes 83 **beggarly** (1) poor (2) begging 85 **suit of pounds**
i.e., petition for money 87 **compelled** i.e., forced upon her

Anne.   This is strange to me.

Old Lady. How tastes it? Is it bitter? Forty pence, no.
90   There was a lady once ('tis an old story)
      That would not be a queen, that would she not,
      For all the mud in Egypt.° Have you heard it?

Anne. Come, you are pleasant.

Old Lady.   With your theme, I could
      O'ermount° the lark. The Marchioness of Pem-
         broke?
95   A thousand pounds a year for pure respect?°
      No other obligation? By my life,
      That promises moe° thousands: honor's train
      Is longer than his foreskirt. By this time
      I know your back will bear a duchess. Say,
      Are you not stronger than you were?

100 *Anne.*   Good lady,
      Make yourself mirth with your particular fancy,
      And leave me out on't. Would I had no being,
      If this salute my blood° a jot. It faints me°
      To think what follows.
105   The Queen is comfortless, and we forgetful
      In our long absence. Pray, do not deliver°
      What here y'have heard to her.

Old Lady.   What do you think me?——
                                        Exeunt.

92 **mud in Egypt** riches of Egypt (the mud being the source of its
fertility)   94 **O'ermount** fly higher than   95 **for pure respect** simply out of esteem   97 **moe** more   103 **salute my blood** exhilarates
me   103 **faints me** makes me faint   106 **deliver** report

Scene 4. [*A hall in Blackfriars.*]

*Trumpets, sennet,° and cornets. Enter two Vergers,
with short silver wands; next them, two Scribes, in the
habit of doctors;° after them, the [Arch]bishop of
Canterbury alone; after him, the Bishops of Lincoln,
Ely, Rochester, and Saint Asaph. Next them, with
some small distance, follows a Gentleman bearing the
purse, with the Great Seal, and a cardinal's hat; then
two Priests, bearing each a silver cross; then a Gentleman Usher bareheaded, accompanied with a Sergeant
at Arms bearing a silver mace; then two Gentlemen
bearing two great silver pillars;° after them, side by
side, the two Cardinals; two Noblemen with the sword
and mace. The King takes place° under the cloth of
state;° the two Cardinals sit under him as judges. The
Queen takes place some distance from the King. The
Bishops place themselves on each side the court, in
manner of a consistory;° below them, the Scribes. The
Lords sit next the Bishops. The rest of the Attendants
stand in convenient order about the stage.*

Wolsey. Whilst our commission from Rome is read,
　Let silence be commanded.

King.　　　　　　　　　　What's the need?
　It hath already publicly been read,
　And on all sides th' authority allowed.
　You may then spare that time.

Wolsey.　　　　　　　　　Be't so. Proceed.　　　5

Scribe. Say "Henry King of England, come into the
　court."

2.4.s.d. **sennet** trumpet fanfare **habit of doctors** i.e., capped and
gowned as doctors of law **two great silver pillars** Wolsey's insignia **takes place** takes his seat **cloth of state** canopy **consistory** College of Cardinals

Crier. Henry King of England, etc.

King. Here.

10　*Scribe.* Say "Katherine Queen of England, come into the court."

Crier. Katherine Queen of England, etc.

> *The Queen makes no answer, rises out of her chair,*
> *goes about the court, comes to the King,*
> *and kneels at his feet; then speaks.*

Queen Katherine. Sir, I desire you do me right and
　　　justice,
　　And to bestow your pity on me; for
15　I am a most poor woman and a stranger,
　　Born out of your dominions; having here
　　No judge indifferent,° nor no more assurance
　　Of equal friendship and proceeding.° Alas, sir,
　　In what have I offended you? What cause
20　Hath my behavior given to your displeasure
　　That thus you should proceed to put me off°
　　And take your good grace° from me? Heaven
　　　witness,
　　I have been to you a true and humble wife,
　　At all times to your will conformable,
25　Ever in fear to kindle your dislike,
　　Yea, subject to your countenance, glad or sorry
　　As I saw it inclined. When was the hour
　　I ever contradicted your desire,
　　Or made it not mine too? Or which of your friends
30　Have I not strove to love, although I knew
　　He were mine enemy? What friend of mine
　　That had to him derived° your anger did I
　　Continue in my liking? Nay, gave° notice
　　He was from thence discharged? Sir, call to mind
35　That I have been your wife in this obedience
　　Upward of twenty years, and have been blessed

---

17 **indifferent** unbiased　18 **equal friendship and proceeding** impartial friendship and proceedings　21 **put me off** discard me　22 **grace** (1) self (2) favor　32 **derived** incurred　33 **gave** i.e., gave not

With many children by you. If, in the course
And process of this time, you can report,
And prove it too, against mine honor aught,
My bond to wedlock or my love and duty,   *40*
Against° your sacred person, in God's name,
Turn me away, and let the foul'st contempt
Shut door upon me, and so give me up
To the sharp'st kind of justice. Please you, sir,
The King, your father, was reputed for   *45*
A prince most prudent, of an excellent
And unmatched wit° and judgment. Ferdinand,
My father, King of Spain, was reckoned one
The wisest° prince that there had reigned by many
A year before. It is not to be questioned   *50*
That they had gathered a wise council to them
Of every realm, that did debate this business,
Who deemed our marriage lawful. Wherefore I humbly
Beseech you, sir, to spare me, till I may
Be by my friends in Spain advised, whose counsel   *55*
I will implore. If not, i' th' name of God,
Your pleasure be fulfilled!

Wolsey.   You have here, lady,
And of your choice, these reverend fathers, men
Of singular integrity and learning,
Yea, the elect o' th' land, who are assembled   *60*
To plead your cause. It shall be therefore bootless°
That longer you desire the court,° as well
For your own quiet,° as to rectify
What is unsettled in the King.

Campeius.   His Grace
Hath spoken well and justly. Therefore, madam,   *65*
It's fit this royal session do proceed,
And that without delay their arguments
Be now produced and heard.

41 **Against** (1) i.e., or aught against (?) (2) toward (?)   47 **wit** intelligence   48–49 **one/The wisest** the very wisest   61 **bootless** profitless   62 **longer you desire the court** longer you draw out the business of the court (by pleading for a postponement)   63 **quiet** i.e., of mind

Queen Katherine.   Lord Cardinal,
 To you I speak.

Wolsey.   Your pleasure, madam?

Queen Katherine.   Sir,
70 I am about to weep; but, thinking that
 We are a queen, or long have dreamed so, certain°
 The daughter of a king, my drops of tears
 I'll turn to sparks of fire.

Wolsey.   Be patient yet.

Queen Katherine. I will, when you are humble; nay,
 before,
75 Or God will punish me. I do believe
 (Induced by potent circumstances)° that
 You are mine enemy, and make my challenge°
 You shall not be my judge; for it is you
 Have blown this coal° betwixt my lord and me—
80 Which God's dew quench! Therefore I say again,
 I utterly abhor,° yea, from my soul
 Refuse you for my judge, whom, yet once more,
 I hold my most malicious foe, and think not
 At all a friend to truth.

Wolsey.   I do profess
85 You speak not like yourself, who ever yet
 Have stood to° charity and displayed th' effects
 Of disposition gentle and of wisdom
 O'ertopping woman's pow'r. Madam, you do me
 wrong:
 I have no spleen° against you, nor injustice
90 For you or any. How far I have proceeded,
 Or how far further shall, is warranted
 By a commission from the consistory,
 Yea, the whole consistory of Rome. You charge me
 That I have blown this coal. I do deny it.

---

71 **certain** certainly 76 **Induced by potent circumstances** persuaded by strong reasons 77 **challenge** objection (legal term) 79 **blown this coal** stirred up this strife (proverbial) 81 **abhor** protest against (legal term) 86 **stood to** supported 89 **spleen** malice

The King is present. If it be known to him   95
That I gainsay my deed,° how may he wound,
And worthily, my falsehood—yea, as much
As you have done my truth. If he know
That I am free of your report,° he knows
I am not of your wrong.° Therefore in him   100
It lies to cure me, and the cure is to
Remove these thoughts from you; the which before
His Highness shall speak in,° I do beseech
You, gracious madam, to unthink your speaking
And to say so no more.

Queen Katherine.   My lord, my lord,   105
I am a simple woman, much too weak
T' oppose your cunning. Y' are meek and
    humble-mouthed.
You sign your place and calling, in full seeming,
With meekness and humility,° but your heart
Is crammed with arrogancy, spleen, and pride.   110
You have by fortune and his Highness' favors
Gone slightly° o'er low steps, and now are mounted
Where pow'rs° are your retainers, and your words
(Domestics to you) serve your will as 't please
Yourself pronounce their office.° I must tell you,   115
You tender° more your person's honor than
Your high profession spiritual; that again
I do refuse you for my judge, and here,
Before you all, appeal unto the Pope,
To bring my whole cause 'fore his Holiness,   120
And to be judged by him.
          She curtsies to the King, and offers to depart.

Campeius.   The Queen is obstinate,
    Stubborn° to justice, apt to accuse it,° and

96 **gainsay my deed** now deny what I have done   99 **free of your
report** innocent of your charges   100 **I am not of your wrong** i.e.,
I have been wronged by you   103 **in** regarding   108–9 **You sign
... humility** to all outward appearances you set a stamp of meekness and humility on your high spiritual office   112 **slightly** easily
113 **pow'rs** those in power   113–15 **your words ... office** i.e., your
words are your servants, and you need only speak in order for your
will to be done   116 **tender** value   122 **Stubborn** unpliant   122
apt to accuse it prone to call it in question

Disdainful to be tried by't. 'Tis not well.
She's going away.

125 *King.* Call her again.

Crier. Katherine Queen of England, come into the
court.

Gentleman Usher. Madam, you are called back.

Queen Katherine. What need you note it? Pray you
keep your way;°
When you are called, return. Now the Lord help!
130 They vex me past my patience. Pray you, pass on.
I will not tarry; no, nor ever more
Upon this business my appearance make
In any of their courts.

Exit Queen, and her Attendants.

King.   Go thy ways, Kate.
That man i' th' world who shall report he has
135 A better wife, let him in naught be trusted,
For speaking false in that. Thou art, alone°—
If thy rare qualities, sweet gentleness,
Thy meekness saint-like, wife-like government,°
Obeying in commanding,° and thy parts
140 Sovereign and pious else, could speak thee out°—
The queen of earthly queens. She's noble born,
And like her true nobility she has
Carried herself towards me.

Wolsey.   Most gracious sir,
In humblest manner I require° your Highness,
145 That it shall please you to declare in hearing
Of all these ears—for where I am robbed and
bound,
There must I be unloosed, although not there
At once and fully satisfied—whether ever I
Did broach this business to your Highness, or

---

128 **keep your way** keep going   136 **alone** without rival   138 **government** self-control   139 **Obeying in commanding** self-restrained when giving orders   139–40 **thy parts ... out** your other excellent and pious qualities could describe you fully   144 **require** beg

Laid any scruple in your way which might   *150*
Induce you to the question on't? Or ever
Have to you, but with thanks to God for such
A royal lady, spake one the least° word that might
Be to the prejudice of her present state,
Or touch° of her good person?

King.   My Lord Cardinal,   *155*
I do excuse you; yea, upon mine honor,
I free you from't. You are not to be taught°
That you have many enemies that know not
Why they are so, but, like to village curs,
Bark when their fellows do. By some of these   *160*
The Queen is put in anger. Y'are excused.
But will you be more justified? You ever
Have wished the sleeping of this business, never
  desired
It to be stirred, but oft have hind'red, oft,
The passages° made toward it. On my honor   *165*
I speak° my good Lord Cardinal to this point,
And thus far clear him. Now, what moved me to't,
I will be bold with time and your attention.
Then mark th' inducement. Thus it came; give heed
  to't:
My conscience first received a tenderness,   *170*
Scruple, and prick, on certain speeches uttered
By th' Bishop of Bayonne, then French ambassador,
Who had been hither sent on the debating
A marriage 'twixt the Duke of Orleans and
Our daughter Mary. I' th' progress of this business, *175*
Ere a determinate resolution,° he
(I mean the bishop) did require a respite,
Wherein he might the King his lord advertise°
Whether our daughter were legitimate,
Respecting this our marriage with the dowager,   *180*
Sometimes° our brother's wife. This respite shook

---

153 **one the least** a single   155 **touch** sullying   157 **You are not
to be taught** you do not have to be told   165 **passages** proceedings
166 **speak** bear witness for   176 **determinate resolution** final decision   178 **advertise** inform (accent on second syllable)   181
Sometimes formerly

The bosom of my conscience, entered me,
Yea, with a spitting° power, and made to tremble
The region of my breast; which forced such way
185   That many mazed considerings° did throng,
And pressed in with this caution. First, methought
I stood not in the smile of heaven, who had
Commanded nature that my lady's womb,
If it conceived a male child by me, should
190   Do no more offices of life to't than
The grave does to th' dead; for her male issue
Or° died where they were made, or shortly after
This world had aired them. Hence I took a thought
This was a judgment on me, that my kingdom,
195   Well worthy the best heir o' th' world, should not
Be gladded in't by me. Then follows that
I weighed the danger which my realms stood in
By this my issue's fail,° and that gave to me
Many a groaning throe. Thus hulling° in
200   The wild sea of my conscience, I did steer
Toward this remedy whereupon we are
Now present here together. That's to say,
I meant to rectify° my conscience, which
I then did feel full sick, and yet° not well,
205   By all the reverend fathers of the land
And doctors learned. First I began in private
With you, my Lord of Lincoln. You remember
How under my oppression° I did reek,°
When I first moved° you.

Lincoln.   Very well, my liege.

210 *King.* I have spoke long. Be pleased yourself to say
How far you satisfied me.

Lincoln.   So please your Highness,
The question did at first so stagger me,

---

183 **spitting** as though impaled on a spit, transfixing   185 **mazed considerings** perplexed thoughts   192 **Or** either   198 **issue's fail** i.e., failure to have a son   199 **hulling** drifting with sail furled   203 **rectify** set right (cf. line 63)   204 **yet** now still   208 **oppression** heavy burden   208 **reek** sweat (literally smoke with heat)   209 **moved** proposed the matter

Bearing a state of mighty moment in't
And consequence of dread, that I committed
The daring'st counsel which I had to doubt,°   *215*
And did entreat your Highness to this course
Which you are running here.

King.   I then moved you,
My Lord of Canterbury, and got your leave
To make this present summons.° Unsolicited
I left no reverend person in this court,   *220*
But by particular consent proceeded
Under your hands and seals.° Therefore, go on;
For no dislike i' th' world against the person
Of the good Queen, but the sharp thorny points
Of my allegèd° reasons, drives this forward.   *225*
Prove but our marriage lawful, by my life
And kingly dignity, we are contented
To wear our mortal state to come with her,
Katherine our queen, before the primest° creature
That's paragoned° o' th' world.

Campeius.   So please your Highness, *230*
The Queen being absent, 'tis a needful fitness
That we adjourn this court till further° day.
Meanwhile must be an earnest motion°
Made to the Queen to call back her appeal
She intends unto his Holiness.

King. [Aside]   I may perceive   *235*
These cardinals trifle with me. I abhor
This dilatory sloth and tricks of Rome.
My learned and well-belovèd servant, Cranmer,
Prithee return; with thy approach, I know,
My comfort comes along.—Break up the court;   *240*
I say, set on.

                    Exeunt, in manner as they entered.

213–15 **Bearing ... doubt** concerning so momentous a state of affairs, with consequences so dreadful to contemplate, that I did not
trust myself to give the boldest advice (i.e., that the marriage be
dissolved) 219 **summons** i.e., of the Queen 222 **Under your hands
and seals** with your signed and sealed consent 225 **allegèd** stated
229 **primest** foremost 230 **paragoned** held up as a paragon 232
further a more distant 233 **motion** appeal

ACT 3

Scene 1. [*London. The Queen's apartments.*]

Enter Queen and her Women, as at work.

Queen Katherine. Take thy lute, wench. My soul
   grows sad with troubles;
Sing and disperse 'em, if thou canst. Leave°
   working.

Song

Orpheus° with his lute made trees,
And the mountain tops that freeze,
   Bow themselves when he did sing.
To his music plants and flowers
Ever sprung, as sun and showers
   There had made a lasting spring.

Everything that heard him play,
Even the billows of the sea,
   Hung their heads, and then lay by.°
In sweet music is such art,
Killing care and grief of heart
   Fall asleep, or hearing die.

Enter a Gentleman.

5

10

15   *Queen Katherine.* How now?

3.1.2 **Leave** leave off   3 **Orpheus** (in mythology the music of his
lyre tamed wild beasts and entranced even inanimate nature)   11
lay by subsided

Gentleman. And't please your Grace, the two great
　　cardinals
　　Wait in the presence.°

Queen Katherine. 　　　　Would they speak with me?

Gentleman. They willed me say so, madam.

Queen Katherine. 　　　　　　Pray their Graces
　　To come near. [*Exit Gentleman.*] What can be their
　　　business
　　With me, a poor weak woman, fall'n from favor?　　　　20
　　I do not like their coming, now I think on't.
　　They should be good men, their affairs as
　　　righteous;°
　　But all hoods make not monks.

Enter the two Cardinals, Wolsey and Campeius.

Wolsey. 　　　　　　Peace to your Highness!

Queen Katherine. Your Graces find me here part of° a
　　housewife.
　　I would be all, against the worst may happen.°　　　　25
　　What are your pleasures with me, reverend lords?

Wolsey. May it please you, noble madam, to withdraw
　　Into your private chamber, we shall give you
　　The full cause of our coming.

Queen Katherine. 　　　　　Speak it here;
　　There's nothing I have done yet, o' my conscience,　　30
　　Deserves a corner. Would all other women
　　Could speak this with as free a soul as I do!
　　My lords, I care not (so much I am happy
　　Above a number) if my actions
　　Were tried by every tongue, every eye saw 'em,　　　35
　　Envy and base opinion° set against 'em,
　　I know my life so even.° If your business

---

17 **presence** presence chamber　22 **their affairs as righteous** i.e.,
their business should be as righteous as they themselves good　24
part of to some extent (because she is sewing)　25 **I would ...
happen** I would like to be a complete one, in preparation for the
worst (i.e., in case I am divorced and left nothing else)　36 **Envy
and base opinion** malice and unworthy gossip　37 **even** equable

　　　　Seek me out, and that way I am wife in,°
　　　　Out with it boldly: truth loves open dealing.

40　*Wolsey. Tanta est erga te mentis integritas, regina*
　　　serenissima°—

　　　Queen Katherine. O, good my lord, no Latin;
　　　　I am not such a truant since my coming,
　　　　As not to know the language I have lived in.
　　　　A strange tongue makes my cause more strange,
45　　　　　suspicious;°
　　　　Pray speak in English. Here are some will thank
　　　　　you,
　　　　If you speak truth, for their poor mistress' sake.
　　　　Believe me, she has had much wrong. Lord Car-
　　　　　dinal,
　　　　The willing'st° sin I ever yet committed
　　　　May be absolved in English.

50　*Wolsey.*　　　　　　　　　Noble lady,
　　　　I am sorry my integrity should breed
　　　　(And service to his Majesty and you)
　　　　So deep suspicion, where all° faith was meant.
　　　　We come not by the way of accusation,
55　　　To taint that honor every good tongue blesses,
　　　　Nor to betray you any way to sorrow—
　　　　You have too much, good lady—but to know
　　　　How you stand minded in the weighty difference
　　　　Between the King and you, and to deliver,
60　　　Like free and honest men, our just opinions
　　　　And comforts to your cause.

　　　Campeius.　　　　　　　Most honored madam,
　　　　My Lord of York, out of his noble nature,
　　　　Zeal and obedience he still bore° your Grace,
　　　　Forgetting, like a good man, your late censure
65　　　Both of his truth and him (which was too far)°

38 **Seek ... wife in** concerns me, and my behavior as a wife　40–41
Tanta ... serenissima so unprejudiced are we toward you, most
serene Queen　45 **strange, suspicious** foreign, and hence suspicious
49 **willing'st** most deliberate　53 **all** only　63 **still bore** has always borne　65 **far** extreme

Offers, as I do, in° a sign of peace,
His service and his counsel.

Queen Katherine. [*Aside*] To betray me.—
  My lords, I thank you both for your good wills.
  Ye speak like honest men; pray God ye prove so!
  But how to make ye suddenly° an answer,   70
  In such a point of weight, so near° mine honor,
  More near my life, I fear, with my weak wit,°
  And to such men of gravity and learning,
  In truth I know not. I was set° at work
  Among my maids, full little, God knows, looking   75
  Either for such men or such business.
  For her sake that I have been°—for I feel
  The last fit° of my greatness—good your Graces,
  Let me have time and counsel for my cause.
  Alas, I am a woman friendless, hopeless!   80

Wolsey. Madam, you wrong the King's love with these
    fears.
  Your hopes and friends are infinite.

Queen Katherine.   In England
  But little for my profit. Can you think, lords,
  That any Englishman dare give me counsel
  Or be a known friend, 'gainst his Highness' plea-
    sure—   85
  Though he be grown so desperate to be honest°—
  And live a subject? Nay, forsooth, my friends,
  They that must weigh out° my afflictions,
  They that my trust must grow to, live not here.
  They are, as all my other comforts, far hence   90
  In mine own country, lords.

Campeius.   I would your Grace
  Would leave your griefs, and take my counsel.

Queen Katherine.   How, sir?

66 **in** as   70 **suddenly** on the spur of the moment   71 **near** closely
affecting   72 **wit** intelligence   74 **set** seated   77 **For her sake that
I have been** for what I once was   78 **fit** seizure (as in an illness)
86 **so desperate to be honest** i.e., so reckless as to come out hon-
estly in my support   88 **weigh out** attach full weight to

Campeius. Put your main cause into the King's protec-
    tion;
    He's loving and most gracious. 'Twill be much
95 Both for your honor better and your cause,°
    For if the trial of the law o'ertake ye,
    You'll part away° disgraced.

Wolsey.   He tells you rightly.

Queen Katherine. Ye tell me what ye wish for both—
    my ruin.
    Is this your Christian counsel? Out upon ye!
100 Heaven is above all yet; there sits a judge
    That no king can corrupt.

Campeius.   Your rage mistakes us.

Queen Katherine. The more shame for ye. Holy men
    I thought ye,
    Upon my soul, two reverend cardinal virtues;°
    But cardinal sins° and hollow hearts I fear ye.
    Mend 'em, for shame, my lords. Is this your com-
105   fort?
    The cordial that ye bring a wretched lady,
    A woman lost among ye, laughed at, scorned?
    I will not wish ye half my miseries:
    I have more charity. But say I warned ye.
    Take heed, for heaven's sake, take heed, lest at
110   once°
    The burden of my sorrows fall upon ye.

Wolsey. Madam, this is a mere distraction.°
    You turn the good we offer into envy.°

Queen Katherine. Ye turn me into nothing. Woe upon
    ye,
115   And all such false professors!° Would you have me

95 **Both ... cause** better for both your honor and your cause   97
part away depart   103 **cardinal virtues** the essential virtues (com-
prising fortitude, justice, prudence, and temperance); with a pun
on the visitors' station   104 **cardinal sins** (alluding to the seven
deadly sins; with pun on "carnal," the Elizabethan pronunciation
of "cardinal")   110 **at once** all at once   112 **mere distraction**
sheer madness   113 **envy** malice   115 **professors** i.e., of Christianity

(If you have any justice, any pity,
If ye be anything but churchmen's habits)°
Put my sick cause into his hands that hates me?
Alas, has banished me his bed already;
His love, too long ago! I am old,° my lords,   *120*
And all the fellowship I hold now with him
Is only my obedience. What can happen
To me above this wretchedness? All your studies
Make me a curse like this!°

Campeius.   Your fears are worse.°

Queen Katherine. Have I lived thus long (let me
     speak° myself,   *125*
Since virtue finds no friends) a wife, a true one?
A woman, I dare say without vainglory,
Never yet branded with suspicion?
Have I with all my full affections
Still met the King? Loved him next heaven? Obeyed
     him?   *130*
Been, out of fondness, superstitious to him?°
Almost forgot my prayers to content him?
And am I thus rewarded? 'Tis not well, lords.
Bring me a constant woman° to her husband,
One that ne'er dreamed a joy beyond his pleasure,° *135*
And to that woman, when she has done most,
Yet will I add an honor: a great patience.

Wolsey. Madam, you wander from the good we aim at.

Queen Katherine. My lord, I dare not make myself so
     guilty
To give up willingly that noble title   *140*
Your master wed me to. Nothing but death
Shall e'er divorce my dignities.

Wolsey.   Pray hear me.

---

117 **habits** garb   120 **old** (she was forty-three)   123–24 **All ...
this** i.e., let all your learned efforts make my life any more wretched
than it already is   124 **worse** i.e., than your actual situation   125
speak describe   131 **superstitious to him** his idolator   134 **constant
woman** woman faithful   135 **pleasure** (1) enjoyment (2) wishes

Queen Katherine. Would I had never trod this English
    earth,
    Or felt the flatteries that grow upon it!
    Ye have angels' faces, but heaven knows your
145   hearts.°
    What will become of me now, wretched lady!
    I am the most unhappy woman living.
    Alas, poor wenches, where are now your fortunes?
    Shipwracked upon a kingdom, where no pity,
150   No friends, no hope; no kindred weep for me;
    Almost no grave allowed me. Like the lily,
    That once was mistress of the field, and flourished,
    I'll hang my head and perish.

Wolsey.   If your Grace
    Could but be brought to know our ends are
    honest,°
    You'd feel more comfort. Why should we, good
155   lady,
    Upon what cause, wrong you? Alas, our places,
    The way of our profession is against it.
    We are to cure such sorrows, not to sow 'em.
    For goodness' sake, consider what you do;
160   How you may hurt yourself, aye, utterly
    Grow° from the King's acquaintance, by this car-
    riage.°
    The hearts of princes kiss obedience,
    So much they love it; but to stubborn spirits
    They swell, and grow as terrible as storms.
165   I know you have a gentle, noble temper,
    A soul as even as a calm. Pray think us
    Those we profess, peacemakers, friends, and ser-
    vants.

Campeius. Madam, you'll find it so. You wrong your
    virtues
    With these weak women's fears. A noble spirit,
170   As yours was put into you, ever casts

145 **Ye have ... hearts** (alluding to the proverbial "Fair face, foul
heart")   154 **ends are honest** intentions are honorable   161 **Grow**
be estranged   161 **carriage** conduct

Such doubts, as false coin, from it. The King loves
　　you;
Beware you lose it not. For us, if you please
To trust us in your business, we are ready
To use our utmost studies° in your service.

Queen Katherine. Do what ye will, my lords; and pray
　　forgive me.　　　　　　　　　　　　　　　　　　*175*
If I have used myself° unmannerly,
You know I am a woman, lacking wit
To make a seemly answer to such persons.
Pray do my service° to his Majesty.
He has my heart yet, and shall have my prayers　　*180*
While I shall have my life. Come, reverend fathers,
Bestow your counsels on me. She now begs
That little thought, when she set footing° here,
She should have bought her dignities so dear.
　　　　　　　　　　　　　　　　　　　　　　Exeunt.

Scene 2. [*Antechamber to the King's apartment.*]

*Enter the Duke of Norfolk, Duke of Suffolk,
Lord Surrey, and Lord Chamberlain.*

Norfolk. If you will now unite in your complaints
And force them with a constancy,° the Cardinal
Cannot stand under them. If you omit
The offer of this time,° I cannot promise
But that you shall sustain moe new disgraces,　　*5*
With these you bear already.

Surrey.　　　　　　　　　　I am joyful
To meet the least occasion that may give me

---

174 **studies** endeavors　176 **used myself** behaved　179 **do my service**
offer my respects　183 **footing** foot　3.2.2 **force them with a
constancy** urge them with determination　3–4 **omit . . . time** neglect
this opportunity

Remembrance of my father-in-law, the Duke,°
To be revenged on him.

Suffolk.　　　　　　　　　　　　Which of the peers
10　Have uncontemned° gone by him, or at least°
Strangely neglected? When did he regard
The stamp of nobleness in any person
Out of° himself?

Chamberlain.　　　My lords, you speak your plea-
sures.°　　　•
What he deserves of you and me I know;
15　What we can do to him, though now the time
Gives way° to us, I much fear.° If you cannot
Bar his access to th' King, never attempt
Anything on him, for he hath a witchcraft
Over the King in's tongue.

Norfolk.　　　　　　　　　　　O, fear him not;
20　His spell in that is out.° The King hath found
Matter against him that forever mars
The honey of his language. No, he's settled,
Not to come off, in his displeasure.°

Surrey.　　　　　　　　　　　　　　Sir,
I should be glad to hear such news as this
Once every hour.

25　*Norfolk.*　　　　　　　Believe it, this is true.
In the divorce his contrary proceedings°
Are all unfolded; wherein he appears
As I would wish mine enemy.

Surrey.　　　　　　　　　　　　How came
His practices° to light?

8 **my father-in-law, the Duke** (Buckingham; see 2.1.43–44) 10 **un-
contemned** undespised 10 **at least** i.e., have not at least been
13 **Out of** besides 13 **speak your pleasures** are free to say what
you care to 16 **way** scope 16 **fear** doubt 20 **His spell in that
is out** his influence that way is finished 22–23 **he's settled …
displeasure** i.e., he (Wolsey) is fixed, not to escape, in his (the
King's) displeasure (but "he" could possibly refer to the King, in
which case "come off" = desist) 26 **contrary proceedings** (1) proceedings contradicting their outward appearance (2) adverse proceedings 29 **practices** plots

Suffolk.   Most strangely.

Surrey.   O, how? How?

Suffolk. The Cardinal's letters to the Pope miscar-
   ried,   30
  And came to th' eye o' th' King; wherein was read
  How that the Cardinal did entreat his Holiness
  To stay the judgment o' th' divorce. For if
  It did take place, "I do" (quoth he), "perceive
  My king is tangled in affection to   35
  A creature° of the Queen's, Lady Anne Bullen."

Surrey. Has the King this?

Suffolk.   Believe it.

Surrey.   Will this work?

Chamberlain. The King in this perceives him how he
   coasts
  And hedges his own way.° But in this point
  All his tricks founder, and he brings his physic   40
  After his patient's death: the King already
  Hath married the fair lady.

Surrey.   Would he had!

Suffolk. May you be happy in your wish, my lord!
  For, I profess, you have it.

Surrey.   Now, all my joy
  Trace the conjunction!°

Suffolk.   My amen to't!

Norfolk.   All men's!   45

Suffolk. There's order given for her coronation.
  Marry, this is yet but young, and may be left
  To some ears unrecounted. But, my lords,
  She is a gallant creature and complete°

---

36 **creature** dependent 38–39 **coasts ... way** moves circuitously
and stealthily (i.e., as by coasts and hedgerows) toward his own
goals 44–45 **all ... conjunction** all the joy I can wish follow
the marriage 49 **complete** fully endowed

50   In mind and feature. I persuade me, from her
        Will fall some blessing to this land, which shall
        In it be memorized.°

        Surrey.   But will the King
            Digest° this letter of the Cardinal's?
            The Lord forbid!

        Norfolk.   Marry, amen!

        Suffolk.   No, no.
55   There be moe wasps that buzz about his nose
        Will make this sting the sooner. Cardinal Campeius
        Is stol'n away to Rome; hath ta'en no leave;
        Has left the cause o' th' King unhandled, and
        Is posted° as the agent of our Cardinal
60   To second all his plot. I do assure you
        The King cried "Ha!" at this.

        Chamberlain.   Now God incense him,
            And let him cry "Ha!" louder!

        Norfolk.   But, my lord,
            When returns Cranmer?

        Suffolk. He is returned in his opinions,° which
65   Have satisfied the King for his divorce,
        Together with all famous colleges
        Almost in Christendom. Shortly, I believe,
        His second marriage shall be published,° and
        Her coronation. Katherine no more
70   Shall be called Queen, but Princess Dowager
        And widow to Prince Arthur.

        Norfolk.   This same Cranmer's
            A worthy fellow, and hath ta'en much pain
            In the King's business.

        Suffolk.   He has, and we shall see him
            For it an archbishop.

52 **memorized** made memorable   53 **Digest** stomach   59 **posted**
hastened   64 **returned in his opinions** i.e., not in person, but in
that the opinions have been received from him   68 **published**
proclaimed

Norfolk.   So I hear.

Suffolk.   'Tis so.

                    Enter Wolsey and Cromwell.

   The Cardinal!

Norfolk. Observe, observe, he's moody.   75

Wolsey. The packet,° Cromwell,
   Gave't you the King?

Cromwell.   To his own hand, in's bedchamber.

Wolsey. Looked he o' th' inside of the paper?°

Cromwell.   Presently°
   He did unseal them, and the first he viewed,
   He did it with a serious mind; a heed   80
   Was in his countenance. You he bade
   Attend him here this morning.

Wolsey.   Is he ready
   To come abroad?

Cromwell.   I think by this he is.

Wolsey. Leave me awhile.

                                    Exit Cromwell.

   [*Aside*] It shall be to the Duchess of Alençon,   85
   The French King's sister; he shall marry her.
   Anne Bullen? No. I'll no Anne Bullens for him;
   There's more in't than fair visage. Bullen?
   No, we'll no Bullens. Speedily I wish
   To hear from Rome. The Marchioness of Pem-
      broke!°   90

Norfolk. He's discontented.

Suffolk.   Maybe he hears the King
   Does whet his anger to° him.

---

76 **packet** parcel of state papers 78 **paper** wrapper 78 **Presently**
immediately 90 **Marchioness of Pembroke** (Anne did not in fact
receive the title until 1532, three years after the events of this
scene) 92 **to** against

Surrey.   Sharp enough,
　　Lord, for thy justice!

Wolsey. [*Aside*] The late queen's gentlewoman, a
　　knight's daughter,
95　　To be her mistress' mistress? The Queen's queen?
　　This candle burns not clear. 'Tis I must snuff it;
　　Then out it goes.° What though I know her virtuous
　　And well deserving? Yet I know her for
　　A spleeny° Lutheran, and not wholesome to
100　　Our cause that she should lie i' th' bosom of
　　Our hard-ruled° King. Again, there is sprung up
　　An heretic, an arch one, Cranmer, one
　　Hath° crawled into the favor of the King,
　　And is his oracle.

Norfolk.   He is vexed at something.

　　Enter King, reading of a schedule[*, and Lovell*].

Surrey. I would 'twere something that would fret the
105　　string,°
　　The master-cord on's° heart.

Suffolk.   The King, the King!

King. What piles of wealth hath he accumulated
　　To his own portion! And what expense by th' hour
　　Seems to flow from him! How, i' th' name of thrift,
110　　Does he rake this together? Now, my lords,
　　Saw you the Cardinal?°

Norfolk.   My lord, we have
　　Stood here observing him. Some strange commotion°
　　Is in his brain. He bites his lip, and starts;
　　Stops on a sudden, looks upon the ground,
115　　Then lays his finger on his temple; straight

96–97 **This candle ... goes** i.e., I will be called on to clear away
the impediments to this marriage, but instead will use the opportunity to quash it altogether ("snuff" = trim the wick) 99
spleeny (1) staunch (2) splenetic   101 **hard-ruled** difficult to manage   103 **Hath** that hath   105 **fret the string** gnaw through the
tendon   106 **on's** of his   111 **Saw you the Cardinal** (the King,
engrossed in the schedule [see s.d.], has not noticed Wolsey's
presence)   112 **commotion** turmoil, mutiny (see line 120)

Springs out into fast gait; then stops again,
Strikes his breast hard, and anon he casts
His eye against° the moon. In most strange postures
We have seen him set himself.

King.　　　　　　　　　　　　It may well be
There is a mutiny in's mind. This morning　　　　　*120*
Papers of state he sent me to peruse,
As I required. And wot° you what I found
There, on my conscience, put unwittingly?
Forsooth, an inventory, thus importing:°
The several parcels° of his plate,° his treasure,　　*125*
Rich stuffs,° and ornaments of household, which
I find at such proud rate° that it outspeaks
Possession of a subject.°

Norfolk.　　　　　　　　It's heaven's will;
Some spirit put this paper in the packet
To bless your eye withal.

King.　　　　　　　　　　　If we did think　　*130*
His contemplation were above the earth,
And fixed on spiritual object,° he should still
Dwell in his musings; but I am afraid
His thinkings are below the moon,° not worth
His serious considering.

　　　　　　　King takes his seat; whispers Lovell, who
　　　　　　　　　　　　goes to the Cardinal.

Wolsey.　　　　　　　Heaven forgive me!　　*135*
Ever God bless your Highness!

King.　　　　　　　　　　Good my lord,
You are full of heavenly stuff,° and bear the in-
　　ventory
Of your best graces in your mind; the which

118 **against** toward　122 **wot** know　124 **thus importing** conveying
this information　125 **several parcels** various particulars　125 **plate**
gold and silver household plate　126 **stuffs** cloths　127 **proud rate**
high value　127–28 **outspeaks ... subject** describes more than a
subject should own　132 **spiritual object** a spiritual objective
134 **below the moon** worldly　137 **stuff** concerns (with a possible
quibble on the household stuff referred to in line 126)

You were now running o'er. You have scarce time
140 To steal from spiritual leisure° a brief span
To keep your earthly audit. Sure, in that
I deem you an ill husband,° and am glad
To have you therein my companion.

Wolsey.   Sir,
For holy offices I have a time; a time
145 To think upon the part of business which
I bear i' th' state; and Nature does require
Her times of preservation, which perforce
I, her frail son, amongst my brethren mortal,°
Must give my tendance° to.

King.   You have said well.

150 *Wolsey.* And ever may your Highness yoke together,
As I will lend you cause, my doing well
With my well saying!

King.   'Tis well said again,
And 'tis a kind of good deed to say well.
And yet words are no deeds. My father loved you;
155 He said he did, and with his deed did crown°
His word upon you. Since I had my office
I have kept you next my heart; have not alone
Employed you where high profits might come home,
But pared my present havings,° to bestow
My bounties upon you.

160 *Wolsey.* [*Aside*]   What should this mean?

Surrey. [*Aside*] The Lord increase this business!

King.   Have I not made you
The prime man of the state? I pray you tell me
If what I now pronounce you have found true;
And, if you may confess it, say withal,
165 If you are bound to us or no. What say you?

---

140 **spiritual leisure** religious occupations   142 **husband** manager
148 **amongst my brethren mortal** i.e., in my human (as distinguished
from divine) capacity   149 **tendance** attention   155 **crown** confirm
159 **havings** possessions

Wolsey. My sovereign, I confess your royal graces,
　Showered on me daily, have been more than could
　My studied purposes requite,° which went
　Beyond all man's endeavors. My endeavors
　Have ever come too short of my desires,	170
　Yet filed° with my abilities. Mine own ends
　Have been mine so that° evermore they pointed
　To th' good of your most sacred person and
　The profit of the state. For your great graces
　Heaped upon me, poor undeserver, I	175
　Can nothing render but allegiant° thanks,
　My prayers to heaven for you, my loyalty,
　Which ever has and ever shall be growing
　Till death, that winter, kill it.

King.　　　　　　　　　　Fairly answered;
　A loyal and obedient subject is	180
　Therein illustrated. The honor of it
　Does pay the act of it, as, i' th' contrary,
　The foulness is the punishment.° I presume
　That, as my hand has opened bounty to you,
　My heart dropped love, my pow'r rained honor,
　　more	185
　On you than any,° so your hand and heart,
　Your brain and every function of your power,
　Should, notwithstanding that° your bond of duty,
　As 'twere in love's particular,° be more
　To me, your friend, than any.

Wolsey.　　　　　　　　I do profess	190
　That for your Highness' good I ever labored
　More° than mine own; that am, have,° and will
　　be—
　Though all the world should crack their duty to you

167–68 **more ... requite** more than I could with diligent endeavors
repay　171 **filed** kept pace　172 **so that** only to the extent that
176 **allegiant** loyal　181–83 **The honor ... punishment** i.e., virtue
is its own reward, just as evil is its own punishment　186 **any** on
anyone　188 **notwithstanding that** over and above　189 **in love's
particular** out of personal affection　192 **More** (as in Buckingham's speech, 1.1.184ff., the speaker's emotion overcomes the re-
straints of normal syntax in the rest of this speech, but the sense
is clear)　192 **have** have been

And throw it from their soul; though perils did
195 Abound as thick as thought could make 'em, and
Appear in forms more horrid—yet my duty,
As doth a rock against the chiding° flood,
Should the approach of this wild river break,°
And stand unshaken yours.

King.   'Tis nobly spoken.
200 Take notice, lords, he has a loyal breast,
For you have seen him open't. [*Giving him papers.*]
    Read o'er this;
And after, this; and then to breakfast with
What appetite you have.

        *Exit King, frowning upon the Cardinal; the nobles
        throng after him, smiling and whispering.*

Wolsey.   What should this mean?
What sudden anger's this? How have I reaped it?
205 He parted frowning from me, as if ruin
Leaped from his eyes. So looks the chafèd° lion
Upon the daring huntsman that has galled° him,
Then makes him nothing.° I must read this paper;
I fear, the story of his anger. 'Tis so;
210 This paper has undone me. 'Tis th' account
Of all that world of wealth I have drawn together
For mine own ends; indeed, to gain the popedom,
And fee my friends in Rome. O negligence,
Fit for a fool to fall by! What cross° devil
215 Made me put this main° secret in the packet
I sent the King? Is there no way to cure this?
No new device to beat this from his brains?
I know 'twill stir him strongly; yet I know
A way, if it take right,° in spite of fortune
Will bring me off° again. What's this? "To th'
220   Pope"?
The letter, as I live, with all the business
I writ to's Holiness. Nay then, farewell!

197 **chiding** tumultuous 198 **break** check 206 **chafèd** angry 207
galled wounded 208 **makes him nothing** annihilates him 214 **cross**
thwarting, perverse 215 **main** crucial 219 **take right** succeed
220 **bring me off** rescue me

I have touched the highest point of all my greatness,
And from that full meridian° of my glory
I haste now to my setting. I shall fall   225
Like a bright exhalation° in the evening,
And no man see me more.

*Enter to Wolsey the Dukes of Norfolk and Suffolk,
the Earl of Surrey, and the Lord Chamberlain.*

Norfolk. Hear the King's pleasure, Cardinal, who
    commands you
To render up the Great Seal° presently°
Into our hands, and to confine yourself   230
To Asher House, my Lord of Winchester's,°
Till you hear further from his Highness.

Wolsey.   Stay:
Where's your commission, lords? Words cannot carry
Authority so weighty.

Suffolk.   Who dare cross° 'em,
Bearing the King's will from his mouth expressly?   *235*

Wolsey. Till I find more than will or words to do it°—
I mean your malice—know, officious lords,
I dare, and must deny it. Now I feel
Of what coarse metal ye are molded—envy;
How eagerly ye follow my disgraces,   240
As if it fed ye! And how sleek and wanton°
Ye appear in everything may bring my ruin!
Follow your envious courses, men of malice;
You have Christian warrant° for 'em, and no doubt
In time will find their fit rewards. That seal   245
You ask with such a violence, the King,
Mine and your master, with his own hand gave me;
Bade me enjoy it, with the place and honors,

224 **meridian** (a star's highest point) 226 **exhalation** meteor 229 **Great Seal** (insignia of the Lord Chancellor's office; see 1.1.114s.d.n.) 229 **presently** at once 231 **Lord of Winchester's** (as Wolsey was himself still Bishop of Winchester, we are perhaps meant to think of his successor, Stephen Gardiner) 234 **cross** oppose 236 **do it** (1) "render up the Great Seal" (line 229) (2) carry such great authority 241 **wanton** unrestrained 244 **Christian warrant** justification by Christian principles (ironical)

During my life; and, to confirm his goodness,
250 Tied it by letters-patents.° Now, who'll take it?

Surrey. The King, that gave it.

Wolsey.   It must be himself, then.

Surrey. Thou art a proud traitor, priest.

Wolsey.   Proud lord, thou liest.
Within these forty hours Surrey durst better
Have burnt that tongue than said so.

Surrey.   Thy ambition,
255 Thou scarlet sin,° robbed this bewailing land
Of noble Buckingham, my father-in-law.
The heads of all thy brother cardinals,
With thee and all thy best parts° bound together,
Weighed° not a hair of his. Plague of your policy!
260 You sent me Deputy for Ireland;°
Far from his succor, from the King, from all
That might have mercy on the fault thou gav'st him,
Whilst your great goodness, out of holy pity,
Absolved him with an ax.

Wolsey.   This, and all else
265 This talking lord can lay upon my credit,°
I answer, is most false. The Duke by law
Found his deserts. How innocent I was
From any private malice in his end,
His noble jury and foul cause can witness.
270 If I loved many words, lord, I should tell you
You have as little honesty as honor,
That° in the way of loyalty and truth
Toward the King, my ever royal master,
Dare mate° a sounder man than Surrey can be,
And all that love his follies.

275 *Surrey.*   By my soul,

250 **Tied it by letters-patents** confirmed it by documents of formal
conveyance 255 **scarlet sin** (referring to the color of his cassock,
and also the traditional idea of scarlet sins, as in Isaiah 1:18) 258
parts qualities 259 **weighed** equalled in weight 260 **Ireland**
(three syllables) 265 **credit** reputation 272 **That** (the antecedent
is "I," line 270) 274 **mate** match

Your long coat, priest, protects you; thou shouldst
    feel
My sword i' th' lifeblood of thee else. My lords,
Can ye endure to hear this arrogance?
And from this fellow? If we live thus tamely,
To be thus jaded° by a piece of scarlet,   280
Farewell nobility. Let his Grace go forward,
And dare us with his cap, like larks.°

Wolsey.   All goodness
Is poison to thy stomach.

Surrey.   Yes, that goodness
Of gleaning all the land's wealth into one,
Into your own hands, Card'nal, by extortion;   285
The goodness of your intercepted packets
You writ to th' Pope against the King. Your good-
    ness,
Since you provoke me, shall be most notorious.
My Lord of Norfolk,° as you are truly noble,
As you respect the common good, the state   290
Of our despised nobility, our issues,°
Who, if he live, will scarce be gentlemen,
Produce the grand sum of his sins, the articles°
Collected from his life. I'll startle you
Worse than the sacring bell,° when the brown
    wench   295
Lay kissing in your arms, Lord Cardinal.

Wolsey. How much, methinks, I could despise this
    man,
But that I am bound in charity against it!

Norfolk. Those articles, my lord, are in the King's
    hand;
But, thus much,° they are foul ones.

---

280 **jaded** intimidated   282 **dare us with his cap, like larks** i.e.,
dazzle us with his cardinal's hat, as larks were dazed and caught
by means of a mirror and piece of red cloth   289 **Lord of Norfolk**
(Norfolk was actually Surrey's father)   291 **issues** children   293
articles charges in an indictment   295 **sacring bell** the consecrating
bell rung at the elevation of the Host, the most solemn portion of
the Mass   300 **thus much** i.e., so much I can say

300 *Wolsey*.   So much fairer
And spotless shall mine innocence arise,
When the King knows my truth.

Surrey.   This cannot save you.
I thank my memory I yet remember
Some of these articles, and out they shall.
305 Now, if you can blush and cry "guilty," Cardinal,
You'll show a little honesty.

Wolsey.   Speak on, sir;
I dare your worst objections. If I blush,
It is to see a nobleman want° manners.

Surrey. I had rather want those than my head. Have
    at you!°
310 First that, without the King's assent or knowledge,
You wrought to be a legate;° by which power
You maimed the jurisdiction of all bishops.

Norfolk. Then that in all you writ to Rome, or else
To foreign princes, *"Ego et Rex meus"*°
315 Was still inscribed; in which you brought the King
To be your servant.

Suffolk.   Then, that without the knowledge
Either of King or Council, when you went
Ambassador to the Emperor,° you made bold
To carry into Flanders the Great Seal.°

320 *Surrey*. Item, you sent a large commission
To Gregory de Cassado, to conclude,
Without the King's will or the state's allowance,
A league between his Highness and Ferrara.

308 **want** lack   309 **Have at you** here goes; cf. 2.2.84 (the six
charges that follow are the most serious of the nine leveled
against Wolsey; see appendix on sources)   311 **legate** i.e., the
papal representative in England   314 **Ego et Rex meus** my King
and I (the normal Latin word order, although Shakespeare followed
the chroniclers in taking it to imply that Wolsey put himself before
the King)   318 **Emperor** Charles V; see 1.1.176–90   319 **To carry . . .
Seal** (the Seal, and thus the Lord Chancellor, were not supposed to leave the country)

Suffolk. That out of mere° ambition you have caused
   Your holy hat to be stamped on the King's coin.° 325

Surrey. Then that you have sent innumerable sub-
      stance°
   (By what means got, I leave to your own con-
      science)
   To furnish° Rome and to prepare the ways
   You have for dignities, to the mere undoing
   Of all the kingdom. Many more there are,   *330*
   Which, since they are of you and odious,
   I will not taint my mouth with.

Chamberlain.   O my lord,
   Press not a falling man too far: 'tis virtue.°
   His faults lie open to the laws; let them,
   Not you, correct him. My heart weeps to see him *335*
   So little of his great self.

Surrey.   I forgive him.

Suffolk. Lord Cardinal, the King's further pleasure
      is—
   Because all those things you have done of late,
   By your power legative,° within this kingdom,
   Fall into th' compass of a præmunire°—   *340*
   That therefore such a writ be sued° against you:
   To forfeit all your goods, lands, tenements,
   Chattels, and whatsoever, and to be
   Out of the King's protection. This is my charge.

Norfolk. And so we'll leave you to your meditations *345*
   How to live better. For your stubborn answer
   About the giving back the Great Seal to us,
   The King shall know it, and no doubt shall thank
      you.
   So fare you well, my little good Lord Cardinal.
                         Exeunt all but Wolsey.

---

324 **mere** sheer 325 **Your holy ... coin** (a usurpation of royal pre-
rogative) 326 **innumerable substance** countless treasure 328 **furnish** supply 333 **virtue** i.e., to relent 339 **legative** as a papal
legate 340 **Fall ... præmunire** i.e., come within the penalties—
forfeiture of goods and outlawry—prescribed by the Statute of
Præmunire, which limited papal authority in England 341 **sued**
moved

350 *Wolsey.* So farewell to the little good you bear me.
　　　Farewell! A long farewell to all my greatness!
　　　This is the state of man: today he puts forth
　　　The tender leaves of hopes; tomorrow blossoms,
　　　And bears his blushing honors thick upon him.
355　　The third day comes a frost, a killing frost,
　　　And, when he thinks, good easy° man, full surely
　　　His greatness is aripening, nips his root,
　　　And then he falls, as I do. I have ventured,
　　　Like little wanton° boys that swim on bladders,
360　　This many summers in a sea of glory,
　　　But far beyond my depth. My high-blown pride
　　　At length broke under me and now has left me,
　　　Weary and old with service, to the mercy
　　　Of a rude° stream that must forever hide me.
365　　Vain pomp and glory of this world, I hate ye.
　　　I feel my heart new opened. O, how wretched
　　　Is that poor man that hangs on princes' favors!
　　　There is betwixt that smile we would aspire to,
　　　That sweet aspect of princes, and their ruin,°
370　　More pangs and fears than wars or women have.
　　　And when he falls, he falls like Lucifer,°
　　　Never to hope again.

　　　　　　Enter Cromwell, standing amazed.

　　　　　　　　　　Why, how now, Cromwell?

Cromwell. I have no power to speak, sir.

Wolsey.　　　　　　　　　　　　What, amazed
　　　At my misfortunes? Can thy spirit wonder
375　　A great man should decline? Nay, and° you weep,
　　　I am fall'n indeed.

Cromwell.　　　　　How does your Grace?

Wolsey.　　　　　　　　　　　　　　Why, well;
　　　Never so truly happy, my good Cromwell.

356 **easy** easygoing 359 **wanton** playful **364 rude** turbulent 369
their ruin the ruin they cause 371 **he falls like Lucifer** (cf. Isaiah
14:12: "How art thou fallen from Heaven, O Lucifer, son of the
morning") 375 **and** if

I know myself° now, and I feel within me
A peace above all earthly dignities,
A still and quiet conscience. The King has cured me,   *380*
I humbly thank his Grace; and from these shoulders,
These ruined pillars, out of pity, taken
A load would sink a navy—too much honor.
O, 'tis a burden, Cromwell, 'tis a burden
Too heavy for a man that hopes for heaven!   *385*

Cromwell. I am glad your Grace has made that right
    use of° it.

Wolsey. I hope I have. I am able now, methinks,
  Out of a fortitude of soul I feel,
  To endure more miseries and greater far
  Than my weak-hearted enemies dare offer.   *390*
  What news abroad?

Cromwell.   The heaviest and the worst
  Is your displeasure° with the King.

Wolsey.   God bless him!

Cromwell. The next is, that Sir Thomas More is
    chosen
  Lord Chancellor in your place.

Wolsey.   That's somewhat sudden.
  But he's a learnèd man. May he continue   *395*
  Long in his Highness' favor and do justice
  For truth's sake and his conscience, that his bones,
  When he has run his course and sleeps in blessings,
  May have a tomb of orphans' tears wept on him!
  What more?

Cromwell. That Cranmer is returned with welcome,
  Installed Lord Archbishop of Canterbury.   *400*

Wolsey. That's news indeed.

Cromwell.   Last, that the Lady Anne,
  Whom the King hath in secrecy long married,

378 **know myself** i.e., "recognize my limitations and my sins and
am able to transcend them" (Foakes)   386 **made that right use of**
derived that benefit from   392 **displeasure** loss of favor

This day was viewed in open as his queen,
405   Going to chapel; and the voice° is now
Only about her coronation.

Wolsey. There was the weight that pulled me down.
    O Cromwell,
The King has gone beyond° me. All my glories
In that one woman I have lost forever.
410   No sun shall ever usher forth mine honors,
Or gild again the noble troops that waited
Upon my smiles. Go get thee from me, Cromwell;
I am a poor fall'n man, unworthy now
To be thy lord and master. Seek the King
415   (That sun I pray may never set!)—I have told him
What and how true thou art. He will advance thee;
Some little memory of me will stir him
(I know his noble nature) not to let
Thy hopeful service perish too. Good Cromwell,
420   Neglect him not; make use° now, and provide
For thine own future safety.

Cromwell.   O my lord,
Must I then leave you? Must I needs forgo°
So good, so noble, and so true a master?
Bear witness, all that have not hearts of iron,
425   With what a sorrow Cromwell leaves his lord.
The King shall have my service, but my prayers
Forever and forever shall be yours.

Wolsey. Cromwell, I did not think to shed a tear
In all my miseries, but thou hast forced me,
430   Out of thy honest truth,° to play the woman.
Let's dry our eyes—and thus far hear me, Cromwell,
And when I am forgotten, as I shall be,
And sleep in dull° cold marble where no mention
Of me more must be heard of, say I taught thee,
435   Say, Wolsey, that once trod the ways of glory,
And sounded all the depths and shoals of honor,

405 **voice** talk   408 **gone beyond** overreached   420 **make use** take
advantage   422 **forgo** forsake   430 **truth** faith   433 **dull** (1) inanimate (2) cheerless

Found thee a way, out of his wrack, to rise in:
A sure and safe one, though thy master missed it.
Mark but my fall and that that ruined me.
Cromwell, I charge thee, fling away ambition.   *440*
By that sin fell the angels. How can man then,
The image of his Maker, hope to win° by it?
Love thyself last; cherish those hearts that hate thee;
Corruption wins not more than honesty.
Still° in thy right hand carry gentle peace   *445*
To silence envious tongues. Be just, and fear not.
Let all the ends thou aim'st at be thy country's,
Thy God's, and truth's. Then if thou fall'st, O
      Cromwell,
Thou fall'st a blessed martyr.° Serve the King;
And prithee, lead me in.   *450*
There take an inventory of all I have
To the last penny; 'tis the King's. My robe,°
And my integrity to heaven, is all
I dare now call mine own. O Cromwell, Cromwell,
Had I but served my God with half the zeal   *455*
I served my King, he would not in mine age
Have left me naked to mine enemies.

Cromwell. Good sir, have patience.

Wolsey.   So I have. Farewell
The hopes of court! My hopes in heaven do dwell.
                                              Exeunt.

---

442 **win** profit   445 **Still** always   447–49 **Let ... martyr** (after
becoming Earl of Essex and Lord Great Chamberlain, Cromwell
fell from favor and was beheaded in 1540)   452 **robe** i.e., cardinal's
habit

ACT 4

Scene 1. [*A street in Westminster.*]

Enter two Gentlemen, meeting one another.

First Gentleman. Y'are well met once again.°

Second Gentleman.   So are you.

First Gentleman. You come to take your stand here,
    and behold
The Lady Anne pass from her coronation?

Second Gentleman. 'Tis all my business. At our last
    encounter

5   The Duke of Buckingham came from his trial.

First Gentleman. 'Tis very true. But that time offered
    sorrow;
This, general joy.

Second Gentleman.   'Tis well. The citizens,
    I am sure, have shown at full their royal° minds—
    As, let 'em have their rights, they are ever for-
    ward°—

4.1.1 **again** (they met previously in 2.1)   8 **royal** i.e., well disposed
to the King   9 **let 'em have their rights, they are ever forward**
to give them their due, they are always eager to do

324

In celebration of this day with shows,   10
Pageants, and sights of honor.

First Gentleman.   Never greater,
Nor, I'll assure you, better taken,° sir.

Second Gentleman. May I be bold to ask what that
     contains,
That paper in your hand?

First Gentleman.   Yes. 'Tis the list
Of those that claim their offices this day   15
By custom° of the coronation.
The Duke of Suffolk is the first, and claims
To be High Steward; next, the Duke of Norfolk,
He to be Earl Marshal. You may read the rest.

Second Gentleman. I thank you, sir; had I not known
     those customs,   20
I should have been beholding° to your paper.
But, I beseech you, what's become of Katherine,
The Princess Dowager? How goes her business?

First Gentleman. That I can tell you too. The Arch-
     bishop
Of Canterbury, accompanied with other   25
Learnèd and reverend fathers of his order,
Held a late° court at Dunstable, six miles off
From Ampthill, where the Princess lay; to which
She was often cited° by them, but appeared not.
And, to be short, for not appearance and   30
The King's late scruple, by the main assent°
Of all these learnèd men she was divorced,
And the late marriage made of none effect;°
Since which she was removed to Kimbolton,
Where she remains now sick.

Second Gentleman.   Alas, good lady!   35
                              [*Trumpets.*]

12 **taken** received   16 **By custom** i.e., in accordance with hereditary
privilege   21 **beholding** beholden   27 **late** recent   29 **cited** summoned
31 **main assent** general agreement   33 **late marriage made of none
effect** former marriage annulled

The trumpets sound: stand close, the Queen is
coming.

Hautboys.

THE ORDER OF THE CORONATION.

1. *A lively flourish° of trumpets.*
2. *Then two judges.*
3. *Lord Chancellor, with purse and mace before him.*
4. *Choristers, singing.*   Music.°
5. *Mayor of London, bearing the mace. Then Garter,°
   in his coat of arms, and on his head he wore a gilt
   copper crown.*
6. *Marquess Dorset, bearing a scepter of gold, on his
   head a demicoronal° of gold. With him, the Earl
   of Surrey, bearing the rod of silver with the dove,
   crowned with an earl's coronet. Collars of S's.°*
7. *Duke of Suffolk, in his robe of estate,° his coronet
   on his head, bearing a long white wand, as High
   Steward. With him, the Duke of Norfolk, with the
   rod of marshalship, a coronet on his head. Collars
   of S's.*
8. *A canopy borne by four of the Cinque-ports;°
   under it, the Queen in her robe, in her hair,°
   richly adorned with pearl, crowned. On each side
   her, the Bishops of London and Winchester.*
9. *The old Duchess of Norfolk, in a coronal of gold,
   wrought with flowers, bearing the Queen's train.*
10. *Certain Ladies or Countesses, with plain circlets
    of gold without flowers.*

*Exeunt, first passing over the stage in order and state,
and then a great flourish of trumpets. [As the procession passes, the two Gentlemen comment upon it.]*

36s.d. **flourish** fanfare **Music** musicians **Garter** i.e., Garter King-
at-Arms **demicoronal** small coronet **Collars of S's** gold chains
of office fashioned of S-shaped links **estate** state **four of the
Cinque-ports** i.e., four barons of the channel ports (the ports,
five in all, were Dover, Hastings, Hythe, Romney, and Sandwich)
in her hair with her hair hanging loosely (the custom for brides)

Second Gentleman. A royal train,° believe me. These
    I know.
Who's that that bears the scepter?

First Gentleman.   Marquess Dorset;
    And that the Earl of Surrey, with the rod.

Second Gentleman. A bold brave gentleman. That
    should be   40
The Duke of Suffolk?

First Gentleman.   'Tis the same: High Steward.

Second Gentleman. And that my Lord of Norfolk?

First Gentleman.   Yes.

Second Gentleman. [*Looking on the Queen*] Heaven
    bless thee!
Thou hast the sweetest face I ever looked on.
Sir, as I have a soul, she is an angel;
Our King has all the Indies° in his arms,   45
And more and richer, when he strains° that lady.
I cannot blame his conscience.

First Gentleman.   They that bear
The cloth of honor over her, are four barons
Of the Cinque-ports.

Second Gentleman. Those men are happy, and so are
    all are near her.   50
I take it, she that carries up the train
Is that old noble lady, Duchess of Norfolk.

First Gentleman. It is, and all the rest are countesses.

Second Gentleman. Their coronets say so. These are
    stars indeed.

First Gentleman. And sometimes falling° ones.

Second Gentleman.   No more of that. 55

---

37 **train** retinue   45 **all the Indies** i.e., the East and the West (the
Indies were celebrated for their riches)   46 **strains** clasps   55 **falling** (with a double entendre; "falling" = surrendering chastity)

[*The last of the procession exits; trumpets sound.*]

Enter a third Gentleman.

First Gentleman. God save you, sir! Where have you
been broiling?

Third Gentleman. Among the crowd i' th' abbey,
where a finger
Could not be wedged in more: I am stifled
With the mere rankness° of their joy.

Second Gentleman.   You saw
The ceremony?

Third Gentleman. That I did.

60 *First Gentleman.*   How was it?

Third Gentleman. Well worth the seeing.

Second Gentleman.   Good sir, speak° it to us.

Third Gentleman. As well as I am able. The rich
stream
Of lords and ladies, having brought the Queen
To a prepared place in the choir, fell off°
65 A distance from her, while her Grace sat down
To rest awhile, some half an hour or so,
In a rich chair of state, opposing° freely
The beauty of her person to the people.
Believe me, sir, she is the goodliest woman
70 That ever lay by man; which when the people
Had the full view of, such a noise arose
As the shrouds° make at sea in a stiff tempest,
As loud and to as many tunes; hats, cloaks—
Doublets,° I think—flew up, and had their faces
75 Been loose, this day they had been lost. Such joy
I never saw before. Great-bellied° women

59 **mere rankness** sheer stink   61 **speak** describe   64 **off** back   67
opposing exposing   72 **shrouds** sail-ropes   74 **Doublets** men's close-
fitting garments, with or without sleeves   76 **Great-bellied** pregnant

That had not half a week to go, like rams°
In the old time of war, would shake the press,°
And make 'em reel before 'em. No man living
Could say "This is my wife" there, all were woven   80
So strangely in one piece.

Second Gentleman.   But what followed?

Third Gentleman. At length her Grace rose, and with
     modest paces
Came to the altar, where she kneeled and saint-like
Cast her fair eyes to heaven and prayed devoutly;
Then rose again and bowed her to the people;   85
When by the Archbishop of Canterbury
She had all the royal makings of° a queen,
As° holy oil, Edward Confessor's crown,
The rod, and bird of peace, and all such emblems
Laid nobly on her; which performed, the choir,   90
With all the choicest music° of the kingdom,
Together sung "Te Deum." So she parted,°
And with the same full state° paced back again
To York Place, where the feast is held.°

First Gentleman.   Sir,
You must no more call it York Place; that's past.   95
For, since the Cardinal fell, that title's lost:°
'Tis now the King's, and called Whitehall.

Third Gentleman.   I know it,
But 'tis so lately altered that the old name
Is fresh about me.

Second Gentleman. What two reverend bishops
Were those that went on each side of the Queen?   100

Third Gentleman. Stokesly and Gardiner; the one of
     Winchester,
Newly preferred from° the King's secretary,
The other, London.

77 **rams** battering rams   78 **press** crowd   87 **makings of** things that
go to make   88 **As** namely   91 **music** musicians   92 **parted** departed   93 **state** pomp   94 **To York ... held** (it was in fact held
in Westminster Hall; the change permits the reference to Wolsey
which follows)   96 **lost** erased   102 **preferred from** promoted from
being

Second Gentleman. He of Winchester
    Is held no great good lover of the Archbishop's,
    The virtuous Cranmer.

105 *Third Gentleman.*   All the land knows that;
    However, yet there is no great breach. When it
        comes,
    Cranmer will find a friend will° not shrink from
        him.

Second Gentleman. Who may that be, I pray you?

Third Gentleman.   Thomas Cromwell,
    A man in much esteem with th' King, and truly
110 A worthy friend. The King has made him Master
    O' th' Jewel House,
    And one, already, of the Privy Council.

Second Gentleman. He will deserve more.

Third Gentleman.   Yes, without all doubt.
    Come, gentlemen, ye shall go my way,
    Which is to th' court, and there ye shall be my
        guests;
115 Something° I can command. As I walk thither,
    I'll tell ye more.

Both.   You may command us, sir.
                                                Exeunt.

Scene 2. [*Kimbolton.*]

*Enter Katherine, Dowager, sick; led between
    Griffith, her Gentleman Usher, and
        Patience, her woman.*

Griffith. How does your Grace?

Katherine.   O Griffith, sick to death.
    My legs like loaden branches bow to th' earth,

107 **will** who will   116 **Something** to some extent

Willing to leave their burden. Reach a chair.
So—now, methinks, I feel a little ease.
Didst thou not tell me, Griffith, as thou led'st me,   5
That the great child of honor, Cardinal Wolsey,
Was dead?°

Griffith.   Yes, madam; but I think your Grace,
Out of the pain you suffered, gave no ear to't.

Katherine. Prithee, good Griffith, tell me how he
    died.
If well, he stepped before me happily°   10
For my example.

Griffith.   Well, the voice goes,° madam.
For after the stout Earl Northumberland
Arrested him at York, and brought him forward,
As a man sorely tainted,° to his answer,
He fell sick suddenly, and grew so ill   15
He could not sit his mule.

Katherine.   Alas, poor man!

Griffith. At last, with easy roads,° he came to Leices-
    ter,
Lodged in the abbey; where the reverend abbot,
With all his covent,° honorably received him;
To whom he gave these words: "O father abbot,   20
An old man broken with the storms of state
Is come to lay his weary bones among ye;
Give him a little earth for charity."
So went to bed, where eagerly° his sickness
Pursued him still; and three nights after this,   25
About the hour of eight, which he himself
Foretold should be his last, full of repentance,
Continual meditations, tears, and sorrows,
He gave his honors to the world again,
His blessèd part° to heaven, and slept in peace.   30

4.2.7 **dead** (Wolsey died in 1530, Katherine in 1536) 10 **happily**
(1) appropriately (2) perhaps 11 **the voice goes** people say 14
sorely tainted severely disgraced 17 **roads** stages 19 **covent** convent (used of religious companies of either sex) 24 **eagerly**
sharply 30 **blessèd part** soul

Katherine. So may he rest. His faults lie gently on
  him!
  Yet thus far, Griffith, give me leave to speak° him,
  And yet with charity. He was a man
  Of an unbounded stomach,° ever ranking
35 Himself with princes; one that by suggestion
  Tied° all the kingdom. Simony° was fair play;
  His own opinion was his law. I' th' presence°
  He would say untruths and be ever double°
  Both in his words and meaning. He was never,
40 But where he meant to ruin, pitiful.
  His promises were, as he then was, mighty,
  But his performance, as he is now, nothing.
  Of his own body he was ill,° and gave
  The clergy ill example.

Griffith.   Noble madam,
45 Men's evil manners live in brass; their virtues
  We write in water. May it please your Highness
  To hear me speak his good° now?

Katherine.   Yes, good Griffith;
  I were malicious else.

Griffith.   This Cardinal,
  Though from an humble stock, undoubtedly
50 Was fashioned to much honor from his cradle.
  He was a scholar, and a ripe and good one;
  Exceeding wise, fair-spoken, and persuading;
  Lofty and sour to them that loved him not,
  But to those men that sought him, sweet as summer.
55 And though he were unsatisfied in getting,°
  Which was a sin, yet in bestowing, madam,
  He was most princely: ever witness for him
  Those twins of learning that he raised in you,°

---

32 **speak** describe 34 **stomach** arrogance 35–36 **by suggestion/
Tied** by underhand dealing brought into bondage 36 **Simony** the
buying and selling of ecclesiastical preferment 37 **presence** presence chamber, i.e., before the King 38 **double** deceitful 43 **Of
his own body he was ill** i.e., he was depraved in his sexual conduct 47 **speak his good** describe his good qualities 55 **unsatisfied in getting** insatiably acquisitive 58 **raised in you** i.e., erected
in your cities

   Ipswich and Oxford; one of which fell with him,
   Unwilling to outlive the good° that did it;   60
   The other,° though unfinished, yet so famous,
   So excellent in art,° and still so rising,
   That Christendom shall ever speak his virtue.
   His overthrow heaped happiness upon him,
   For then, and not till then, he felt himself,°   65
   And found the blessedness of being little.
   And, to add greater honors to his age
   Than man could give him, he died fearing God.

Katherine. After my death I wish no other herald,
   No other speaker of my living actions,°   70
   To keep mine honor from corruption,
   But such an honest chronicler as Griffith.
   Whom° I most hated living, thou hast made me,
   With thy religious truth and modesty,°
   Now in his ashes honor. Peace be with him!   75
   Patience, be near me still, and set me lower:
   I have not long to trouble thee. Good Griffith,
   Cause the musicians play me that sad note°
   I named my knell, whilst I sit meditating
   On that celestial harmony° I go to.   80
                        Sad and solemn music.

Griffith. She is asleep. Good wench, let's sit down
   quiet,
   For fear we wake her. Softly, gentle Patience.

                The Vision.

Enter, solemnly tripping° one after another, six per-
sonages, clad in white robes, wearing on their heads
garlands of bays,° and golden vizards° on their faces;

---

60 **good** goodness   61 **other** i.e., Christ Church, Oxford   62 **art**
learning   65 **felt himself** truly knew himself   70 **living actions** actions during my life   73 **Whom** (object of "hated"; also of "honor" in
line 75)   74 **religious truth and modesty** strict truth and moderation
78 **note** tune   80 **celestial harmony** (the heavenly spheres in their revo-
lutions were thought to produce a music accessible only to the liberated
soul)   82s.d. **tripping** with light steps   **bays** bay leaves (symbolic of
triumph)   **vizards** masks (probably to indicate that they are spirits)

*branches of bays or palm in their hands. They first
congee°   unto   her,   then   dance;   and,   at   certain
changes,° the first two hold a spare garland over her
head; at which the other four make reverent curtsies.
Then the two that held the garland deliver the same to
the   other   next   two,   who   observe   the   same   order   in
their changes, and holding the garland over her head;
which done, they deliver the same garland to the last
two, who likewise observe the same order; at which,
as it were by inspiration, she makes in her sleep signs
of rejoicing, and holdeth up her hands to heaven. And
so in their dancing vanish, carrying the garland with
them. The music continues.*

Katherine. Spirits of peace, where are ye? Are ye all
  gone,
 And leave me here in wretchedness behind ye?

Griffith. Madam, we are here.

85 *Katherine.*   It is not you I call for.
 Saw ye none enter since I slept?

Griffith.   None, madam.

Katherine. No? Saw you not even now a blessèd troop
 Invite me to a banquet, whose bright faces
 Cast thousand beams upon me, like the sun?
90 They promised me eternal happiness,
 And brought me garlands, Griffith, which I feel
 I am not worthy yet to wear. I shall, assuredly.

Griffith. I am most joyful, madam, such good dreams
 Possess your fancy.

Katherine.   Bid the music leave;°
 They are harsh and heavy to me. *Music ceases.*

95 *Patience.*   Do you note
 How much her Grace is altered on the sudden?
 How long her face is drawn? How pale she looks,
 And of an earthy cold? Mark her eyes.

82s.d. **congee** bow ceremoniously **changes** movements in the dance
94 **music leave** musicians stop

Griffith. She is going, wench. Pray, pray.

Patience. Heaven comfort her!

Enter a Messenger.

Messenger. And't like° your Grace—

Katherine. You are a saucy fellow! 100
Deserve we no more reverence?

Griffith. You are to blame,
Knowing she will not lose° her wonted greatness,
To use so rude behavior. Go to, kneel.

Messenger. I humbly do entreat your Highness' pardon:
My haste made me unmannerly. There is staying° 105
A gentleman, sent from the King, to see you.

Katherine. Admit him entrance, Griffith; but this fellow
Let me ne'er see again. *Exit Messenger.*

Enter Lord Capucius.°
If my sight fail not,
You should be Lord Ambassador from the Emperor,
My royal nephew, and your name Capucius. 110

Capucius. Madam, the same. Your servant.

Katherine. O, my lord,
The times and titles now are altered strangely
With me since first you knew me. But I pray you,
What is your pleasure with me?

Capucius. Noble lady,
First, mine own service to your Grace; the next, 115
The King's request that I would visit you,
Who grieves much for your weakness, and by me

100 **And't like** if it please 102 **lose** give up 105 **staying** waiting
108s.d. **Exit ... Capucius** (most editors have Griffith exit with the
messenger and reenter with Capucius, but he need not leave the
stage in order to usher in the visitor)

Sends you his princely commendations,°
And heartily entreats you take good comfort.

Katherine. O my good lord, that comfort comes too
120   late;
'Tis like a pardon after execution.°
That gentle physic,° given in time, had cured me,
But now I am past all comforts here° but prayers.
How does his Highness?

Capucius.   Madam, in good health.

125 *Katherine.* So may he ever do, and ever flourish,
When I shall dwell with worms, and my poor name
Banished the kingdom! Patience, is that letter
I caused you write yet sent away?

Patience.   No, madam.
                    [*Giving it to Katherine.*]

Katherine. Sir, I most humbly pray you to deliver
This to my lord the King.

130 *Capucius.*   Most willing, madam.

Katherine. In which I have commended to his good-
          ness
The model° of our chaste loves, his young daugh-
          ter°—
The dews of heaven fall thick in blessings on her!—
Beseeching him to give her virtuous breeding°—
135   She is young, and of a noble modest nature;
I hope she will deserve well—and a little
To love her for her mother's sake that loved him
Heaven knows how dearly. My next poor petition
Is that his noble Grace would have some pity
140   Upon my wretched women that so long
Have followed both my fortunes° faithfully;
Of which there is not one, I dare avow

118 **commendations** greetings 121 **execution** ("-tion" two syllables) 122 **physic** healing art 123 **here** i.e., in this world 132
model image 132 **daughter** Mary, afterward Queen (1553–58) 134
breeding upbringing 141 **both my fortunes** i.e., my good fortune
and bad

(And now° I should not lie), but will deserve,
For virtue and true beauty of the soul,
For honesty and decent carriage,   *145*
A right good husband, let him be° a noble;
And, sure, those men are happy that shall have 'em.
The last is, for my men—they are the poorest,
But poverty could never draw 'em from me—
That they may have their wages duly paid 'em,   *150*
And something over to remember me by.
If heaven had pleased to have given me longer life
And able° means, we had not parted thus.
These are the whole contents; and, good my lord,
By that you love the dearest in this world,   *155*
As you wish Christian peace to souls departed,
Stand these poor people's friend, and urge the King
To do me this last right.

Capucius.   By heaven, I will,
Or let me lose the fashion° of a man!

Katherine. I thank you, honest lord. Remember me   *160*
In all humility unto his Highness.
Say his long trouble now is passing
Out of this world. Tell him in death I blessed him,
For so I will. Mine eyes grow dim. Farewell,
My lord. Griffith, farewell. Nay, Patience,   *165*
You must not leave me yet. I must to bed;
Call in more women. When I am dead, good wench,
Let me be used with honor. Strew me over
With maiden flowers,° that all the world may know
I was a chaste wife to my grave. Embalm me,   *170*
Then lay me forth. Although unqueened, yet like
A queen and daughter to a king, inter me.
I can° no more.   *Exeunt, leading Katherine.*

---

143 **now** i.e., at the point of death   146 **let him be** i.e., even   153
able sufficient   159 **fashion** form, nature   169 **maiden flowers** i.e.,
flowers appropriate to one who was chaste   173 **can** i.e., can do

ACT 5

Scene 1. [*London. A gallery in the palace.*]

Enter Gardiner, Bishop of Winchester,
a Page with a torch before him,
met by Sir Thomas Lovell.

Gardiner. It's one o'clock, boy, is't not?

Boy. It hath struck.

Gardiner. These should be hours for necessities,
Not for delights; times to repair our nature
With comforting repose, and not for us
To waste these times. Good hour of night, Sir
Thomas!
Whither so late?

Lovell. Came you from the King, my lord?

Gardiner. I did, Sir Thomas, and left him at primero°
With the Duke of Suffolk.

Lovell. I must to him too
Before he go to bed. I'll take my leave.

Gardiner. Not yet, Sir Thomas Lovell. What's the
matter?
It seems you are in haste; and if there be

No great offense belongs to't, give your friend
Some touch° of your late business. Affairs that walk
(As they say spirits do) at midnight have
In them a wilder nature than the business   *15*
That seeks dispatch by day.

Lovell.   My lord, I love you,
And durst commend a secret to your ear
Much weightier than this work. The Queen's in labor,
They say, in great extremity, and feared
She'll with the labor end.

Gardiner.   The fruit she goes with   *20*
I pray for heartily, that it may find
Good time,° and live; but for the stock,° Sir Thomas,
I wish it grubbed up now.

Lovell.   Methinks I could
Cry thee amen,° and yet my conscience says
She's a good creature and, sweet lady, does   *25*
Deserve our better wishes.

Gardiner.   But, sir, sir,
Hear me, Sir Thomas. Y'are a gentleman
Of mine own way;° I know you wise, religious;
And, let me tell you, it will ne'er be well—
'Twill not, Sir Thomas Lovell, take't of me—   *30*
Till Cranmer, Cromwell (her two hands)° and she
Sleep in their graves.

Lovell.   Now, sir, you speak of two
The most remarked° i' th' kingdom. As for Cromwell,
Beside that of the Jewel House, is made Master
O' th' Rolls,° and the King's secretary; further, sir,   *35*
Stands in the gap and trade° of moe preferments,

13 **touch** inkling 22 **Good time** i.e., a safe delivery 22 **stock** trunk (of a tree), i.e., the Queen 24 **Cry thee amen** i.e., second you 28 **way** i.e., religious persuasion (anti-Lutheran) 31 **hands** supporters 33 **remarked** in the public eye 34–35 **Master/O' th' Rolls** Keeper of the Records 36 **gap and trade** entrance and beaten path

With which the time° will load him. Th' Archbishop
Is the King's hand and tongue, and who dare speak
One syllable against him?

Gardiner.   Yes, yes, Sir Thomas,
40   There are that dare, and I myself have ventured
To speak my mind of him. And indeed this day,
Sir, I may tell it you, I think I have
Insensed° the lords o' th' council that he is
(For, so I know he is, they know he is)°
45   A most arch heretic, a pestilence
That does infect the land; with which they moved°
Have broken with° the King, who hath so far
Given ear to our complaint, of his great grace
And princely care foreseeing those fell° mischiefs
50   Our reasons° laid before him, hath° commanded
Tomorrow morning to the council board
He be convented.° He's a rank weed, Sir Thomas,
And we must root him out. From your affairs
I hinder you too long. Good night, Sir Thomas.
                              Exit Gardiner and Page.

55   *Lovell.* Many good nights, my lord; I rest your servant.

                    Enter King and Suffolk.

King. Charles, I will play no more tonight.
My mind's not on't; you are too hard for me.

Suffolk. Sir, I did never win of you before.

King. But little, Charles,
60   Nor shall not, when my fancy's on my play.
Now, Lovell, from the Queen what is the news?

Lovell. I could not personally deliver to her
What you commanded me, but by her woman
I sent your message; who° returned her thanks

37 **time** i.e., the trend of the times 43 **Insensed** (1) informed (2)
stirred up ("insensed" = incensed) 44 **For ... they know he is**
i.e., for if I know he is, then I can make them know 46 **moved**
angered 47 **broken with** broken the information to 49 **fell** terrible 50 **reasons** account, explanation 50 **hath** i.e., that he has
52 **convented** summoned 64 **who** and who (i.e., the Queen)

In the great'st humbleness, and desired your High-
    ness   65
Most heartily to pray for her.

King.   What say'st thou, ha?
To pray for her? What, is she crying out?

Lovell. So said her woman, and that her suff'rance°
    made
Almost each pang a death.

King.   Alas, good lady!

Suffolk. God safely quit° her of her burden, and   70
With gentle travail, to the gladding of
Your Highness with an heir!

King.   'Tis midnight, Charles;
Prithee, to bed, and in thy prayers remember
Th' estate° of my poor queen. Leave me alone,
For I must think of that which company   75
Would not be friendly to.°

Suffolk.   I wish your Highness
A quiet night, and my good mistress will
Remember in my prayers.

King.   Charles, good night. *Exit Suffolk.*

              Enter Sir Anthony Denny.

Well, sir, what follows?

Denny. Sir, I have brought my lord the Archbishop,   80
As you commanded me.

King.   Ha? Canterbury?

Denny. Aye, my good lord.

King.   'Tis true: where is he, Denny?

Denny. He attends your Highness' pleasure.

---

68 **suff'rance** suffering   70 **quit** release   74 **estate** condition   75–76
that which … friendly to i.e., matters for which company would
not be helpful

King.   Bring him to us.
                                          [*Exit Denny.*]

  Lovell. [*Aside*] This is about that which the bishop°
      spake;
85   I am happily° come hither.

                    Enter Cranmer and Denny.

  King. Avoid° the gallery. (*Lovell seems to stay.*) Ha!
      I have said.° Be gone.
      What!   *Exeunt Lovell and Denny.*

  Cranmer. [*Aside*] I am fearful.° Wherefore frowns he
      thus?
      'Tis his aspect° of terror. All's not well.

  King. How now, my lord? You do desire to know
      Wherefore I sent for you.

90   *Cranmer.* [*Kneeling*]   It is my duty
      T' attend your Highness' pleasure.

  King.   Pray you, arise,
      My good and gracious Lord of Canterbury.
      Come, you and I must walk a turn together;
      I have news to tell you. Come, come, give me
          your hand.
95   Ah, my good lord, I grieve at what I speak,
      And am right sorry to repeat what follows.
      I have, and most unwillingly, of late
      Heard many grievous, I do say, my lord,
      Grievous complaints of you; which, being consid-
          ered,
100   Have moved° us and our council, that you shall
      This morning come before us; where I know
      You cannot with such freedom purge° yourself
      But that, till further trial in those charges
      Which will require your answer, you must take
105   Your patience to you and be well contented

84 **bishop** Gardiner   85 **happily** opportunely   86 **Avoid** leave   86
said spoken   87 **fearful** afraid   88 **aspect** expression (accent on
second syllable)   100 **moved** persuaded   102 **purge** i.e., of guilt

 To make your house our Tow'r.° You a brother of
   us,°
 It fits we thus proceed, or else no witness
 Would come against you.

Cranmer. [*Kneeling*] I humbly thank your Highness,
   And am right glad to catch this good occasion
   Most throughly° to be winnowèd, where my chaff   *110*
   And corn° shall fly asunder; for I know
   There's none stands under° more calumnious
     tongues
   Than I myself, poor man.

King.   Stand up, good Canterbury;
   Thy truth and thy integrity is rooted
   In us, thy friend. Give me thy hand; stand up.   *115*
   Prithee, let's walk. Now, by my holidame,°
   What manner of man are you? My lord, I looked
   You would have given me your petition, that
   I should have ta'en some pains to bring together
   Yourself and your accusers, and to have heard you, *120*
   Without indurance further.°

Cranmer.   Most dread liege,
   The good I stand on is my truth and honesty.
   If they shall fail, I with mine enemies
   Will triumph o'er my person; which I weigh not,
   Being of those virtues vacant.° I fear nothing°   *125*
   What can be said against me.

King.   Know you not
   How your state stands i' th' world, with the whole
     world?
   Your enemies are many, and not small. Their prac-
     tices

106 **make your house our Tow'r** be housed in the Tower (cf.1.1.207)
106 **You a brother of us** i.e., you being a member of the council
10 **throughly** thoroughly   111 **corn** wheat   112 **stands under** subject to   116 **by my holidame** by my holiness (a formula of protestation)   121 **indurance further** (1) imprisonment in addition (2)
further hardship   124–25 **I weigh ... vacant** I do not value if
it is devoid of those virtues (i.e., truth and honesty)   125 **nothing**
not at all

         Must bear the same proportion,° and not ever°
130   The justice and the truth o' th' question carries
         The due° o' th' verdict with it. At what ease°
         Might corrupt minds procure knaves as corrupt
         To swear against you? Such things have been done.
         You are potently opposed, and with a malice
135   Of as great size. Ween you of° better luck—
         I mean, in perjured witness°—than your master,°
         Whose minister you are, whiles here he lived
         Upon this naughty° earth? Go to, go to;
         You take a precipice for no leap of danger,
         And woo your own destruction.

140 *Cranmer.*   God and your Majesty
         Protect mine innocence, or I fall into
         The trap is° laid for me!

         King.   Be of good cheer;
         They shall no more prevail than we give way° to.
         Keep comfort to you, and this morning see
145   You do appear before them. If they shall chance,
         In charging you with matters, to commit you,°
         The best persuasions to the contrary
         Fail not to use, and with what vehemency
         Th' occasion shall instruct you. If entreaties
150   Will render you no remedy, this ring
         Deliver them, and your appeal to us
         There make before them. Look, the good man
            weeps!
         He's honest, on mine honor. God's blest mother,
         I swear he is true-hearted, and a soul
155   None better in my kingdom. Get you gone,
         And do as I have bid you. (*Exit Cranmer.*) He has
            strangled
         His language in his tears.

128–29 **Their practices ... proportion** their plots must correspond
in number and scope 129 **ever** always 131 **due** fit reward 131
At what ease how easily 135 **Ween you of** do you reckon on 136
witness evidence 136 **master** i.e., Christ 138 **naughty** wicked
142 **is** that is 143 **way** scope 146 **commit you** i.e., to imprisonment in the Tower

Enter Old Lady[; Lovell following].

Gentleman. *(Within.)* Come back: what mean you?

Old Lady. I'll not come back; the tidings that I bring
    Will make my boldness manners. Now, good angels
    Fly o'er thy royal head, and shade thy person   *160*
    Under their blessed wings!

King.   Now by thy looks
    I guess thy message. Is the Queen delivered?
    Say "aye," and of a boy.

Old Lady.   Aye, aye, my liege,
    And of a lovely boy. The God of heaven
    Both now and ever bless her! 'Tis a girl   *165*
    Promises boys hereafter. Sir, your Queen
    Desires your visitation, and to be
    Acquainted with this stranger. 'Tis as like you
    As cherry is to cherry.

King.   Lovell!

Lovell.   Sir?

King. Give her an hundred marks.° I'll to the Queen. *170*
                         Exit King.

Old Lady. An hundred marks? By this light, I'll ha'
    more.
    An ordinary groom is for° such payment.
    I will have more, or scold it out of him.
    Said I for this, the girl was like to him? I'll
    Have more, or else unsay't; and now, while 'tis hot,   *175*
    I'll put it to the issue.   [*Exeunt.*]

---

170 **an hundred marks** (one mark = 13s.4d. [two-thirds of a pound];
a hundred marks = £66.13s.4d., a substantial sum)   172 **for** entitled to

Scene 2. [*Before the entrance to the
council-chamber.*]

Enter Cranmer, Archbishop of Canterbury; [*pursuivants,° pages, etc., attending at the door*].

Cranmer. I hope I am not too late; and yet the gentleman
    That was sent to me from the council prayed me
    To make great haste. All fast?° What means this?
Ho!
    Who waits there? Sure, you know me?

Enter Keeper.

Keeper.   Yes, my lord,
5   But yet I cannot help you.

Cranmer. Why?

Keeper. Your Grace must wait till you be called for.

Enter Doctor Butts.

Cranmer.   So.

Butts. [*Aside*] This is a piece of malice. I am glad
    I came this way so happily. The King
    Shall understand it presently.°   *Exit Butts.*

10 *Cranmer.* [*Aside*]   'Tis Butts,
    The King's physician. As he passed along,
    How earnestly he cast his eyes upon me.
    Pray heaven he sound° not my disgrace! For cer-
tain,
    This is of purpose laid by some that hate me

5.2.s.d. **pursuivants** junior officers attendant upon the heralds 3
fast shut 10 **understand it presently** know about it at once 13
sound (1) fathom (2) make known

(God turn° their hearts! I never sought their
    malice)   15
To quench mine honor. They would shame to make
    me
Wait else at door, a fellow-councillor,
'Mong boys, grooms, and lackeys. But their plea-
    sures
Must be fulfilled, and I attend with patience.

Enter the King and Butts at a window above.°

Butts. I'll show your Grace the strangest sight—

King.   What's that, Butts?   20

Butts. I think your Highness saw this many a day.

King. Body o' me, where is it?

Butts.   There, my lord:
The high promotion of his Grace of Canterbury,
Who holds his state° at door 'mongst pursuivants,
Pages, and footboys.

King.   Ha? 'Tis he, indeed.   25
Is this the honor they do one another?
'Tis well there's one above 'em yet. I had thought
They had parted so much honesty° among 'em,
At least good manners, as not thus to suffer
A man of his place and so near our favor   30
To dance attendance on their lordships' pleasures,
And at the door too, like a post with packets.°
By holy Mary, Butts, there's knavery.
Let 'em alone, and draw the curtain close;
We shall hear more anon.   35

[*They retire behind the curtain; Cranmer remains
                    waiting outside.*]

---

15 **turn** convert 19s.d. **above** (i.e., on the upper stage; note the
reference to a curtain, line 34) 24 **holds his state** maintains the
dignity of his position 28 **parted so much honesty** shared enough
decency 32 **post with packets** courier with letters

Scene 3. [*The council-chamber.*]

*A council-table brought in with chairs and stools, and
placed under the state.° Enter Lord Chancellor, places
himself at the upper end of the table on the left hand;
a seat being left void° above him, as for Canterbury's
seat. Duke of Suffolk, Duke of Norfolk, Surrey, Lord
Chamberlain, Gardiner, seat themselves in order on
each side. Cromwell at lower end, as secretary.
[Keeper at the door.]*

Chancellor. Speak to the business, master secretary.
  Why are we met in council?

Cromwell.   Please your honors,
  The chief cause concerns his Grace of Canterbury.

Gardiner. Has he had knowledge° of it?

Cromwell.   Yes.

Norfolk.   Who waits there?

Keeper. Without,° my noble lords?

Gardiner.   Yes.

5 *Keeper.*   My Lord Archbishop;
  And has done half an hour, to know your pleasures.

Chancellor. Let him come in.

Keeper.   Your Grace may enter now.

Cranmer [*enters and*] *approaches the council-table.*

Chancellor. My good Lord Archbishop, I'm very sorry
  To sit here at this present° and behold
10 That chair stand empty. But we all are men,

5.3.s.d. **state** canopy **void** empty 4 **had knowledge** been informed 5 **Without** outside the door 9 **at this present** now

In our own natures frail and capable
Of° our flesh; few are angels: out of which frailty
And want of wisdom, you, that best should teach
    us,
Have misdemeaned yourself, and not a little,
Toward the King first, then his laws, in filling   15
The whole realm, by your teaching and your chap-
    lains'—
For so we are informed—with new opinions,
Divers and dangerous; which are heresies,
And, not reformed, may prove pernicious.°

Gardiner. Which reformation must be sudden too,   20
    My noble lords; for those that tame wild horses
    Pace 'em not in their hands° to make 'em gentle,
    But stop their mouths with stubborn° bits and spur
        'em
    Till they obey the manage.° If we suffer,
    Out of our easiness and childish pity   25
    To one man's honor, this contagious sickness,
    Farewell all physic. And what follows then?
    Commotions, uproars, with a general taint°
    Of the whole state; as of late days our neighbors,
    The upper Germany,° can dearly witness,   30
    Yet freshly pitied in our memories.

Cranmer. My good lords, hitherto, in all the progress
    Both of my life and office, I have labored,
    And with no little study, that my teaching
    And the strong course of my authority   35
    Might go one way, and safely; and the end
    Was ever to do well. Nor is there living
    (I speak it with a single heart,° my lords)
    A man that more detests, more stirs° against,
    Both in his private conscience and his place,   40

11–12 **capable/Of** i.e., susceptible to the weaknesses of 19 **pernicious** ruinous 22 **Pace 'em not in their hands** do not lead them by hand through their paces 23 **stubborn** stiff, inflexible 24 **manage** training 28 **taint** corruption 30 **upper Germany** (possibly referring to the peasants' uprising in Saxony in 1521–22 or to other insurrections in 1524 and 1535) 38 **with a single heart** i.e., without duplicity 39 **stirs** bestirs himself

Defacers of a public peace, than I do.
Pray heaven, the King may never find a heart
With less allegiance in it! Men that make
Envy and crookèd malice nourishment°
45   Dare bite the best. I do beseech your lordships
That, in this case of° justice, my accusers,
Be what they will, may stand forth face to face,
And freely urge° against me.

Suffolk.   Nay, my lord,
That cannot be. You are a councillor,
50   And, by that virtue,° no man dare accuse you.

Gardiner. My lord, because we have business of more
    moment,
We will be short with you. 'Tis his Highness' plea-
    sure,
And our consent,° for better trial of you,
From hence you be committed to the Tower;
55   Where, being but a private man° again,
You shall know many dare accuse you boldly,
More than, I fear, you are provided for.

Cranmer. Ah, my good Lord of Winchester, I thank
    you;
You are always my good friend. If your will pass,°
60   I shall both find your lordship° judge and juror,
You are so merciful. I see your end:
'Tis my undoing. Love and meekness, lord,
Become a churchman better than ambition.
Win straying souls with modesty° again;
65   Cast none away. That I shall clear myself,
Lay all the weight ye can upon my patience,
I make as little doubt as you do conscience°
In doing daily wrongs. I could say more,
But reverence to your calling makes me modest.

43–44 **make ... nourishment** ("make nourishment" = feed on)   46
of involving   48 **urge** press their charges   50 **that virtue** virtue of
that   53 **our consent** what we have consented to   55 **private man**
i.e., without public office   59 **pass** prevail   60 **both find your lordship** find your lordship both   64 **modesty** moderation   67 **I make ...
conscience** I have as little doubt as you have scruples

Gardiner. My lord, my lord, you are a sectary;°   70
 That's the plain truth. Your painted gloss dis-
    covers,°
 To men that understand you, words° and weakness.

Cromwell. My Lord of Winchester, y'are a little,
 By your good favor, too sharp. Men so noble,
 However faulty, yet should find respect   75
 For what they have been; 'tis a cruelty
 To load° a falling man.

Gardiner.   Good master secretary,
 I cry your honor mercy;° you may, worst°
 Of all this table, say so.

Cromwell.   Why, my lord?

Gardiner. Do not I know you for a favorer   80
 Of this new sect? Ye are not sound.°

Cromwell.   Not sound?

Gardiner. Not sound, I say.

Cromwell.   Would you were half so honest!
 Men's prayers then would seek you, not their fears.

Gardiner. I shall remember this bold language.

Cromwell.   Do.
 Remember your bold life too.

Chancellor.   This is too much;   85
 Forbear, for shame, my lords.

Gardiner.   I have done.

Cromwell.   And I.

Chancellor. Then thus for you, my lord: it stands
    agreed,
 I take it, by all voices, that forthwith

70 **sectary** follower of a (heretical) sect   71 **painted gloss discovers**
deceitful appearance (or speech) reveals   72 **words** i.e., rather than
content   77 **load** oppress   78 **cry your honor mercy** beg your
honor's pardon   78 **worst** with least justification   81 **sound** loyal

You be conveyed to th' Tower a prisoner,
90   There to remain till the King's further pleasure
Be known unto us. Are you all agreed, lords?

All. We are.

Cranmer.   Is there no other way of mercy,
But I must needs to th' Tower, my lords?

Gardiner.   What other
Would you . expect? You are strangely° trouble-
some.
Let some o' th' guard be ready there.

Enter the Guard.

95   *Cranmer.*   For me?
Must I go like a traitor thither?

Gardiner.   Receive him,
And see him safe i' th' Tower.

Cranmer.   Stay, good my lords,
I have a little yet to say. Look there, my lords.
By virtue of that ring, I take my cause
100   Out of the gripes° of cruel men, and give it
To a most noble judge, the King my master.

Chamberlain. This is the King's ring.

Surrey.   'Tis no counterfeit.

Suffolk. 'Tis the right ring, by heaven. I told ye all,
When we first put this dangerous stone arolling,
'Twould fall upon ourselves.

105   *Norfolk.*   Do you think, my lords,
The King will suffer but° the little finger
Of this man to be vexed?

Chamberlain.   'Tis now too certain.
How much more is his life in value with° him?
Would I were fairly out on't!

94 **strangely** uncommonly   100 **gripes** clutches   106 **suffer but** allow even   108 **in value with** esteemed by

Cromwell.　　　　　　　　　　　My mind gave° me,
　In seeking tales and informations　　　　　　　　　110
　Against this man, whose honesty the devil
　And his disciples only envy at,°
　Ye blew the fire that burns ye. Now have at ye!

　Enter King, frowning on them; takes his seat.

Gardiner. Dread sovereign, how much are we bound
　　to heaven
　In daily thanks, that gave us such a prince,　　　　115
　Not only good and wise, but most religious;
　One that in all obedience makes the church
　The chief aim of his honor, and, to strengthen
　That holy duty, out of dear respect,°
　His royal self in judgment comes to hear　　　　　120
　The cause betwixt her and this great offender.

King. You were ever good at sudden commenda-
　　tions,°
　Bishop of Winchester. But know, I come not
　To hear such flattery now, and in my presence
　They are too thin and bare to hide offenses.　　　125
　To me you cannot reach. You play the spaniel,
　And think with wagging of your tongue to win me;
　But, whatsoe'er thou tak'st me for, I'm sure
　Thou hast a cruel nature and a bloody.
　[*To Cranmer*] Good man, sit down. Now let me see
　　the proudest,　　　　　　　　　　　　　　　130
　He that dares most, but wag his finger at thee.
　By all that's holy, he had better starve°
　Than but once think this place becomes thee not.

Surrey. May it please your Grace—

King.　　　　　　　　No, sir, it does not please me.
　I had thought I had had men of some understand-
　　ing
　And wisdom of my council, but I find none.　　　135

109 **gave** told　112 **envy at** hate　119 **dear respect** heartfelt care
(for the church)　122 **sudden commendations** extemporaneous compliments　132 **starve** die

　　　Was it discretion, lords, to let this man,
　　　This good man—few of you deserve that title—
　　　This honest man, wait like a lousy° footboy
140　At chamber door? And one as great as you are?
　　　Why, what a shame was this! Did my commission
　　　Bid ye so far forget yourselves? I gave ye
　　　Power as he was a councillor to try him,
　　　Not as a groom. There's some of ye, I see,
145　More out of malice than integrity,
　　　Would try him to the utmost, had ye mean;°
　　　Which ye shall never have while I live.

　　　Chancellor.　　　　　　　　　　　　Thus far,
　　　My most dread sovereign, may it like° your Grace
　　　To let my tongue excuse all. What was purposed
150　Concerning his imprisonment was rather,
　　　If there be faith in men, meant for his trial
　　　And fair purgation° to the world, than malice,
　　　I'm sure, in me.

　　　King.　　　　　　　Well, well, my lords, respect him.
　　　Take him and use him well; he's worthy of it.
155　I will say thus much for him, if a prince
　　　May be beholding to a subject, I
　　　Am, for his love and service, so to him.
　　　Make me no more ado, but all embrace him.
　　　Be friends, for shame, my lords! My Lord of Can-
　　　　　terbury,
160　I have a suit which you must not deny me:
　　　That is, a fair young maid that yet wants° baptism;
　　　You must be godfather, and answer for her.

　　　Cranmer. The greatest monarch now alive may glory
　　　In such an honor. How may I deserve it,
165　That am a poor and humble subject to you?

　　　King. Come, come, my lord, you'd spare your
　　　spoons.° You shall have two noble partners° with

139 **lousy** lice infested　146 **mean** means　148 **like** please　152
purgation vindication　161 **wants** lacks　166–67 **spare your spoons**
save the expense of giving spoons (traditional christening gifts)
167 **partners** cosponsors

you: the old Duchess of Norfolk, and Lady
Marquess Dorset. Will these please you?
Once more, my Lord of Winchester, I charge you,   170
Embrace and love this man.

Gardiner.   With a true heart
And brother-love I do it.

Cranmer.   And let heaven
Witness how dear I hold this confirmation.

King. Good man, those joyful tears show thy true
    heart.
The common voice,° I see, is verified   175
Of thee, which says thus: "Do my Lord of Can-
    terbury
A shrewd° turn, and he's your friend forever."
Come, lords, we trifle time away. I long
To have this young one made a Christian.
As I have made ye one, lords, one remain;   180
So I grow stronger, you more honor gain.   *Exeunt.*

Scene 4. [*The palace yard.*]

Noise and tumult within. Enter Porter and his Man.

Porter. You'll leave your noise anon, ye rascals. Do
you take the court for Parish Garden?° Ye rude°
slaves, leave your gaping.°

(Within.) Good master porter, I belong to th' larder.°

Porter. Belong to th' gallows, and be hanged, ye   5
rogue! Is this a place to roar in? Fetch me a dozen
crab-tree staves, and strong ones: these are but

---

175 **common voice** popular report   177 **shrewd** nasty   5.4.2 **Parish
Garden** Paris Garden, a boisterous bear-baiting arena on the Bank-
side   2 **rude** uncivilized   3 **leave your gaping** stop your bawling
4 **belong to th' larder** am employed in the (palace) pantry

switches to 'em.° I'll scratch your heads. You must
be seeing christenings? Do you look for ale and
10 cakes° here, you rude rascals?

Man. Pray, sir, be patient. 'Tis as much impossible,
Unless we sweep 'em from the door with cannons,
To scatter 'em, as 'tis to make 'em sleep
On May-Day° morning, which will never be.
15 We may as well push against Paul's° as stir 'em.

Porter. How got they in, and be hanged?

Man. Alas, I know not. How gets the tide in?
As much as one sound cudgel of four foot
(You see the poor remainder) could distribute,
I made no° spare, sir.

20 *Porter.*   You did nothing, sir.

Man. I am not Samson, nor Sir Guy, nor Colbrand,°
To mow 'em down before me; but if I spared any
That had a head to hit, either young or old,
He or she, cuckold or cuckold-maker,
25 Let me ne'er hope to see a chine° again;
And that I would not for a cow, God save her!°

(Within.) Do you hear, master porter?

Porter. I shall be with you° presently, good master
puppy. Keep the door close, sirrah.°

30 *Man.* What would you have me do?

Porter. What should you do, but knock 'em down by
th' dozens? Is this Moorfields° to muster in? Or

8 **switches to 'em** twigs in comparison   9–10 **ale and cakes** (traditional fare at christenings and other celebrations)   14 **May-Day**
(a holiday the celebration of which began before sunrise)   15
Paul's St. Paul's Cathedral   20 **made no** did not   21 **Samson, nor
Sir Guy, nor Colbrand** (all three possessed legendary strength;
Guy of Warwick was celebrated in romance for slaying the Danish
Giant Colbrand)   25 **see a chine** i.e., eat beef   26 **for a cow, God
save her** (a current expression of doubtful import; perhaps meaningless)   28 **I shall be with you** I'll trounce you (Maxwell)   29
sirrah (term of address used to inferiors)   32 **Moorfields** a recreation field on the London outskirts

have we some strange Indian with the great tool°
come to court, the women so besiege us? Bless me,
what a fry of fornication° is at door! On my Chris-   *35*
tian conscience, this one christening will beget a
thousand; here will be father, godfather, and all together.

Man. The spoons° will be the bigger, sir. There is
a fellow somewhat near the door, he should be a   *40*
brazier by his face,° for, o' my conscience, twenty
of the dog days° now reign in's nose. All that stand
about him are under the line;° they need no other
penance. That firedrake° did I hit three times on
the head, and three times was his nose discharged   *45*
against me; he stands there, like a mortarpiece,° to
blow us.° There was a haberdasher's wife of small
wit near him, that railed upon me till her pinked
porringer° fell off her head, for kindling such a
combustion in the state. I missed the meteor once,   *50*
and hit that woman, who cried out "Clubs!"° when
I might see from far some forty truncheoners° draw
to her succor, which were the hope o' th' Strand,°
where she was quartered. They fell on; I made
good° my place. At length they came to th' broom-   *55*
staff° to me. I defied 'em still; when suddenly a
file° of boys behind 'em, loose shot,° delivered such
a show'r of pebbles, that I was fain° to draw mine

---

33 **some strange Indian with the great tool** (American Indians were
exhibited at court; "tool" = penis) 35 **fry of fornication** (1)
swarm of would-be fornicators (2) swarming offspring of fornication 39 **spoons** (cf. 5.3.166–67) 41 **brazier by his face** brassworker
by his (red) face 42 **dog days** (the period from about July
3 to August 15, when Sirius, the Dog Star, rises at almost the
same time as the sun; regarded as the hottest and most unwhole-
some season of the year) 43 **line** equator 44 **firedrake** (1) fiery
dragon (2) meteor 46 **mortarpiece** squat cannon with a large bore
47 **blow us** blow us up 48–49 **pinked porringer** round cap with scal-
loped edge or ornamental perforations 51 **Clubs** (the rallying cry
of the London apprentices) 52 **truncheoners** truncheon (or cudgel)
bearers 53 **were the hope o' th' Strand** i.e., belonged to the shops
in the Strand, in Jacobean times a fashionable street 54–55 **They
fell on; I made good** they attacked; I defended 55–56 **to th' broom-
staff** i.e., to close quarters 57 **file** small company 57 **loose shot**
unaffiliated marksmen 58 **fain** obliged

honor in and let 'em win the work.° The devil was
60   amongst 'em, I think, surely.

Porter. These are the youths that thunder at a playhouse and fight for bitten apples; that no audience
but the tribulation° of Tower Hill° or the limbs° of
Limehouse,° their dear brothers, are able to en-
65   dure. I have some of 'em in Limbo Patrum,° and
there they are like to dance these three days; besides the running banquet of two beadles° that is
to come.

Enter Lord Chamberlain.

Chamberlain. Mercy o' me, what a multitude are here!
70   They grow still too; from all parts they are coming,
As if we kept a fair here. Where are these porters,
These lazy knaves? Y'have made a fine hand, fel-
lows;
There's a trim° rabble let in. Are all these
Your faithful friends o' th' suburbs?° We shall have
75   Great store of room, no doubt, left for the ladies,
When they pass back from the christening.

Porter.   And't please your honor,
We are but men; and what so many may do,
Not being torn apieces, we have done.
An army cannot rule 'em.

Chamberlain.   As I live,
80   If the King blame me for't, I'll lay ye all
By th' heels, and suddenly;° and on your heads
Clap round° fines for neglect. Y'are lazy knaves,
And here ye lie baiting of bombards° when
Ye should do service. Hark! The trumpets sound;

---

59 **work** fort   63 **tribulation** troublemakers   63 **Tower Hill** an un-
ruly district   63 **limbs** inhabitants, with a possible reference to
the limbs of the devil   64 **Limehouse** the rough dockyard area   65
Limbo Patrum i.e., prison (literally the underworld abode of the
souls of the just who died before Christ's coming)   67 **running
banquet of two beadles** i.e., a public whipping, as a dessert to the
"feast" of their confinement   73 **trim** fine   74 **suburbs** disreputable
districts outside City jurisidiction   80–81 **I'll lay ... suddenly** I'll
have you all put straightaway into fetters   82 **round** stiff   83 **baiting of bombards** drinking from leather jugs

Th'are come already from the christening.   85
Go, break among the press,° and find a way out
To let the troop pass fairly, or I'll find
A Marshalsea° shall hold ye play these two months.

Porter. Make way there for the Princess.

Man.   You great fellow,
Stand close up, or I'll make your head ache.   90

Porter. You i' th' camlet,° get up o' th' rail;
I'll peck you o'er the pales° else.   *Exeunt.*

Scene 5. [*The palace.*]

*Enter trumpets, sounding; then two Aldermen, Lord
Mayor, Garter,° Cranmer, Duke of Norfolk with his
marshal's staff, Duke of Suffolk, two Noblemen bearing great standing-bowls° for the christening gifts;
then four Noblemen bearing a canopy, under which
the Duchess of Norfolk, godmother, bearing the child
richly habited in a mantle, etc., train borne by a
Lady. Then follows the Marchioness Dorset, the other
godmother, and Ladies. The troop pass once about
the stage, and Garter speaks.*

Garter. Heaven, from thy endless goodness, send
   prosperous life, long, and ever happy, to the high
   and mighty Princess of England, Elizabeth!

   Flourish. Enter King and Guard.

Cranmer. [*Kneeling*] And to your royal Grace and the
   good Queen.

---

86 **press** throng 88 **Marshalsea** prison in Southwark 91 **camlet**
a rich fabric made of Angora wool and other materials 92 **peck
you o'er the pales** pitch you over the palings 5.5.s.d. **Garter** (see
4.1.36s.d., and note) **standing-bowls** i.e., bowls with supporting
legs or base

5   My noble partners° and myself thus pray:
       All comfort, joy, in this most gracious lady
       Heaven ever laid up to make parents happy
       May hourly fall upon ye!

   King.   Thank you, good Lord Archbishop.
       What is her name?

   Cranmer.   Elizabeth.

   King.   Stand up, lord.
                            [*The King kisses the child.*]
10   With this kiss take my blessing: God protect thee!
       Into whose hand I give thy life.

   Cranmer.   Amen.

   King. My noble gossips,° y'have been too prodigal.°
       I thank ye heartily; so shall this lady,
       When she has so much English.

   Cranmer.   Let me speak, sir,
15   For heaven now bids me; and the words I utter
       Let none think flattery, for they'll find 'em truth.
       This royal infant—heaven still° move about her!—
       Though in her cradle, yet now promises
       Upon this land a thousand thousand blessings,
20   Which time shall bring to ripeness. She shall be
       (But few now living can behold that goodness)
       A pattern to all princes living with her
       And all that shall succeed. Saba° was never
       More covetous of wisdom and fair virtue
25   Than this pure soul shall be. All princely graces
       That mold up such a mighty piece° as this is,
       With all the virtues that attend the good,
       Shall still be doubled on her. Truth shall nurse her,
       Holy and heavenly thoughts still counsel her.
       She shall be loved and feared. Her own° shall bless
30   her;

5 **partners** cosponsors   12 **gossips** godparents   12 **prodigal** generous with gifts   17 **still** always   23 **Saba** the Queen of Sheba   26
mold up such a mighty piece go to form so great a personage
30 **own** i.e., own people

Her foes shake like a field of beaten corn,°
And hang their heads with sorrow. Good grows
   with her;
In her days every man shall eat in safety
Under his own vine what he plants, and sing
The merry songs of peace to all his neighbors.   35
God shall be truly known, and those about her
From her shall read° the perfect ways of honor,
And by those claim their greatness, not by blood.
Nor shall this peace sleep with her; but as when
The bird of wonder dies, the maiden phoenix,°   40
Her ashes new create another heir
As great in admiration° as herself,
So shall she leave her blessedness to one°
(When heaven shall call her from this cloud of
   darkness)
Who from the sacred ashes of her honor   45
Shall star-like rise, as great in fame as she was,
And so stand fixed.° Peace, plenty, love, truth,
   terror,
That were the servants to this chosen infant,
Shall then be his, and like a vine grow to him.
Wherever the bright sun of heaven shall shine,   50
His honor and the greatness of his name
Shall be, and make new nations. He shall flourish,
And like a mountain cedar reach his branches
To all the plains about him.° Our children's chil-
   dren
Shall see this, and bless heaven.

King.   Thou speakest wonders.   55

Cranmer. She shall be, to the happiness of England,
   An agèd princess; many days shall see her,
   And yet no day without a deed to crown it.

31 **corn** wheat   37 **read** learn   40 **phoenix** the fabled Arabian bird
—unique in all the world—that after a life of 660 years rises anew
from the ashes in which it has consumed itself   42 **admiration**
"ability to excite wonder" (Foakes)   43 **one** i.e., James I   47 **fixed**
i.e., as a fixed star   50–54 **Wherever ... about him** (inspired by
a prophecy in Genesis 17:4–6 which was often cited in connection
with Princess Elizabeth's marriage in 1613 [Foakes]; the "new
nations" may allude to the colonization of Virginia)

Would I had known no more! But she must die:
60   She must, the saints must have her. Yet a virgin,
    A most unspotted lily, shall she pass
    To th' ground, and all the world shall mourn her.

    King. O Lord Archbishop,
        Thou hast made me now a man; never before
65   This happy child did I get° anything.
    This oracle of comfort has so pleased me
    That when I am in heaven I shall desire
    To see what this child does, and praise my Maker.
    I thank ye all. To you, my good Lord Mayor,
70   And your good brethren, I am much beholding;
    I have received much honor by your presence,
    And ye shall find me thankful. Lead the way, lords.
    Ye must all see the Queen, and she must thank ye;
    She will be sick else. This day, no man think°
75   Has° business at his house; for all shall stay:°
    This little one shall make it holiday.   *Exeunt.*

THE EPILOGUE

    'Tis ten to one this play can never please
    All that are here. Some come to take their ease,
    And sleep an act or two; but those, we fear,
    W'have frighted with our trumpets; so, 'tis clear,
5   They'll say 'tis naught;° others, to hear the city
    Abused extremely, and to cry "That's witty!"°
    Which we have not done neither; that,° I fear,
    All the expected good w'are like to hear
    For this play at this time, is only in
10   The merciful construction° of good women,
    For such a one we showed 'em. If they smile
    And say 'twill do, I know, within a while
    All the best men are ours; for 'tis ill hap°
    If they hold when their ladies bid 'em clap.

FINIS

65 **get** beget   74 **no man think** let no man think   75 **Has** he has   75
stay stop   Epilogue   5 **naught** worthless   5–6 **others ... witty** (a
glance at the vogue for satirical comedies of London life)   7 **that**
so that   10 **construction** interpretation   13 **hap** luck

Textual Note

The Famous History of the Life of King Henry the Eighth did not achieve publication until seven years after Shakespeare's death, when it appeared in the collected First Folio of his works as the last of the history plays. The 1623 Folio furnishes the only authoritative early edition of *Henry VIII*. Fortunately it is a very good one: behind the Folio text apparently lies a careful scribal transcription of the authors'—or author's—own manuscript. To the playwright(s), rather than the prompter, we presumably owe the very full stage directions called for by a spectacular historical drama. With few exceptions, entrances and exits are fully indicated. Speech prefixes are throughout correct and unambiguous, except for confusion of the First and Second Gentleman at 4.1.20–23 and 55, and of the Lord Chamberlain with the Lord Chancellor at 5.3.85 and 87. Indeed the text as a whole is very clean and straightforward, with relatively little corruption or error of any kind, although the language—often complex in Shakespeare's mature manner—not surprisingly presents a number of interpretative problems.

The Folio text directly or indirectly provides the basis for all subsequent editions of *Henry VIII*. Wherever possible the present edition reproduces it, modernizing spelling, and altering punctuation and verse lineations where the editor's sense of literary and dramatic fitness dictated. The Latin act and scene divisions of the Folio have been translated, and a new division (as in the Globe text) is introduced after 5.2.35. Consequently, in the fifth act the Folio's *Scena Tertia* and *Scena Quarta* are rendered as 5.4 and 5.5 respectively. Abbreviations have been expanded and speech prefixes regularized. Stage directions have been amplified where necessary, such additions being printed within square brackets. Obvious typographical errors have been corrected and eccentric spellings regularized where appropriate without notice, but all significant emendations are noted below. In this list the adopted reading is given in italics and is followed

by the rejected Folio reading in roman type or a note of the
Folio's omission within square brackets.

1.1.42–45 *All . . . function* [F assigns to Buckingham]   47 *as you guess*
[F assigns to Norfolk]   63 *web, 'a* Web. O   69–70 *that? . . . hell,* that, . . .
Hell?   183 *He* [F omits]   200 *Hereford* Hertford   219 *Parke* Pecke
221 *Nicholas* Michaell   226 *lord* Lords

1.2.156 *feared* feare   164 *confession's* Commissions   170 *win* [F omits]
180 *To* For this to   190 *Bulmer* Blumer

1.3.12 *saw* see   13 *Or* A   59 *wherewithal. In him* wherewithall in him;

2.1.20 *Parke* Pecke   86 *mark* make

2.3.14 *quarrel,* quarrell.   61 *you* you, to you

2.4.174 *A* And   219 *summons. Unsolicited* Summons vnsolicited.

3.1.21 *coming, now I think on't.* comming; now I thinke on't,   23s.d.
Campeius Campian   61 *your* our

3.2.142 *glad* gald   171 *filed* fill'd   292 *Who* Whom   343 *Chattels* Castles

4.1.20–23 *I thank . . . business?* [F assigns to First Gentleman]   34 *Kimbolton* Kymmalton   55 *And sometimes falling ones.* [F assigns to Second
Gentleman]   101 *Stokesly* Stokeley

4.2.7 *think* thanke   50 *honor from* Honor. From

5.1.24 *thee* the   37 *time* Lime   139 *precipice* Precepit   176s.d. [*Exeunt.*]
Exit Ladie.

5.2.8 *piece* Peere

5.3.85–86 *This . . . lords.* [F assigns to Lord Chamberlain]   87–91 *Then . . .
agreed, lords?* [F assigns to Lord Chamberlain]   125 *bare* base   133 *this*
his   174 *heart* hearts

5.5.37 *ways* way   70 *your* you

The Sources of
Henry VIII

The chief sources for the play, as for Shakespeare's great earlier cycle of historical dramas on the reigns of the English monarchs from Richard II through Richard III, is Raphael Holinshed's *Chronicles of England, Scotland, and Ireland* (2nd ed., 1587). It is depended upon throughout, except for the story of the plot against Cranmer, and his vindication, in Act 5; here the authority, closely followed, is John Foxe's *Acts and Monuments,* the enlarged 1570 version of which went through a number of editions before the close of the century. Whether the playwright(s) also profited from other narrative chronicles is matter for speculation: the phraseological parallels adduced by scholars are often less than striking, and it is well known that the chroniclers themselves borrowed from one another freely. But Edward Hall's *Union of the Two Noble and Illustre Families of Lancaster and York* (1542) may have been consulted, and it is possible—although not demonstrable—that Wolsey's images of the star past its meridian and of the bladder of pride (3.2.222–27, 359–62) derive from John Speed's *History of Great Britain* (1611). More persuasive is the evidence that the author(s) knew Samuel Rowley's boisterously farcical and blithely anachronistic drama on Henry's reign, *When You See Me You Know Me,* printed in 1605 and perhaps revived before being reprinted in 1613—the probable year of first performance for *Henry VIII.* The sneering references in the latter to "a merry bawdy play" consisting of "fool and fight" (Prologue 14–19) may allude to *When You See Me,* which nevertheless seems to have provided some minor inspiration, most notably in Henry's persistent ejaculation, "Ha!", used in both works. A significant indirect source is George Cavendish's *Life of Wolsey,* which, although not published until 1641, was utilized by the chroniclers from Stow (1565) onwards.

But of the direct and continuous dependence on Holinshed in *Henry VIII* there can be no question. The historical events of the play, from the Field of the Cloth of Gold in 1520 to the christening of Princess Elizabeth in 1533, cover roughly a third of Henry's long reign (1509–47). Four great episodes dominate this segment of Holinshed's narrative: Buckingham's fall, the divorce, Wolsey's disgrace, and the King's remarriage, culminating in the christening of the future queen. So too do they dominate the play. The source was evidently read with great care. At times, as in Katherine's long speech (2.4.12–57), the dramatic blank verse is the prose of the *Chronicles* paraphrased (although even here there are significant additions). Holinshed is levied upon also for the elaborate stage directions for the ceremonial entries and processions in 2.4, 4.1, and 5.5.

If adherence to the source was close, it was not, however, slavish. The abundant material of the *Chronicles* is winnowed, rearranged, and combined in accordance with the necessities of the dramatic design. Certain changes were dictated by limitations of stage personnel: the pageantry of the coronation, calling for a multitude of supernumeraries, had to be reduced. Other alterations are more substantive. Holinshed's account of the unfortunate Bishop of Durham who mistakenly sent the King a book documenting his private affairs, and thus enabled Wolsey to destroy him, is transferred to the Cardinal himself (3.2.120ff.). In the play the first hint of the King's attraction to Anne Bullen precedes Buckingham's execution, and is manifested at a feast which, with nice artistic economy, also illustrates the lavish scale on which Wolsey lives (1.4). Historically, the King set his affections on Anne eight years after the execution, and she does not appear in Holinshed's description of the revel at York Place that provides the basis for this scene.

Perhaps the most interesting transformations involve the portrayal of character. It is true that the King remains, in play as in chronicle, the exemplary monarch whose motives, unlike those of lesser mortals, are never critically examined. But on the stage his moments of anger or of withdrawal into pensiveness reveal facets of the smiling or stern public figure that Holinshed does not attempt to suggest. So, too, the Henry of the play gains in authority in the course of the action; hoodwinked by Wolsey in the earlier scenes, he is nobody's fool in Act 5. Again the source offers no precedent. In the play the fallen Wolsey is invested with a pathos and dignity only barely hinted at in the chronicle. Katherine is endowed by the dramatist(s) with greater strength and regality than she displays in Holinshed, an effect in part achieved by such devices as her fearless—if unavailing—defense of Buckingham and accusations against the Cardinal in the King's presence (1.2.9ff.).

These and other instances of the means by which prosaic historical narrative is transformed into complex poetic drama may be seen in the copious extracts from the relevant passages of Holinshed and Foxe which follow.

RAPHAEL HOLINSHED

From Chronicles of England, Scotland, and Ireland (1587)

[3.2.120–30] This year [1508] was Thomas Ruthall made Bishop of Durham. . . .

To whom . . . the King gave in charge to write a book of the whole estate of the kingdom. . . .

Afterwards the King commanded Cardinal Wolsey to go to this bishop, and to bring the book away with him to deliver to his Majesty. But see the mishap! That a man in all other things so provident should now be so negligent. . . . For this bishop, having written two books (the one to answer the King's command, and the other intreating of [i.e., dealing with] his own private affairs), did bind them both after one sort in vellum, . . . as the one could not by any especial note be discerned from the other. . . .

Now when the Cardinal came to demand the book due to the King, the Bishop unadvisedly commanded his servant to bring him the book bound in white vellum. . . . The servant . . . brought forth . . . the book intreating of the state of the Bishop, and delivered the same unto his master, who . . . gave it to the Cardinal to bear unto the King. The Cardinal . . . , understanding the contents thereof, he greatly rejoiced, having now occasion . . . to bring the Bishop into the King's disgrace.

Wherefore he went forthwith to the King, delivered the book into his hands, and briefly informed the King of the contents thereof; putting further into the King's head, that if at any time he were destitute of a mass of money, he should not need to seek further therefore than to the coffers of the Bishop, who by the tenor of his own book had accompted his

proper riches and substance to the value of a hundred thousand
pounds. Of all which when the Bishop had intelligence . . . he
was stricken with such grief . . . that he shortly through
extreme sorrow ended his life at London. . . .

[2.1.5–41] During this time [of the delivery of Tournai to
the French king in 1520] remained in the French court divers
young gentlemen of England, and they with the French king
rode daily disguised through Paris, throwing eggs, stones,
and other foolish trifles at the people; which light demeanor
of a king was much discommended and jested at. And when
these young gentlemen came again into England, they were
all French in eating, drinking, and apparel, yea, and in
French vices and brags, so that all the estates of England
were by them laughed at. The ladies and gentlewomen were
dispraised, so that nothing by them was praised, but if it
were after the French turn, which after turned them to displeasure, as you shall hear. . . .

Then the King's council caused the Lord Chamberlain to
call before them divers of the privy chamber, which had
been in the French court, and banished them the court for
divers considerations, laying nothing particularly to their
charges . . . which discharge out of court grieved sore the
hearts of these young men, which were called the King's
minions. . . .

[1.2.189–92] . . . the King specially rebuked Sir William Bulmer, Kt., because he, being his servant sworn, refused the King's service, and became servant to the Duke of
Buckingham. . . .

[1.1.1ff.] The French king, desirous to continue the
friendship lately begun betwixt him and the king of England,
made means unto the Cardinal that they might in some convenient place come to an interview together. . . . But the
fame went that the Cardinal desired greatly, of himself, that
the two kings might meet, who, measuring by his will what
was convenient, thought it should make much with his glory
if in France also at some high assembly of noblemen he should
be seen in his vain pomp and show of dignity . . . and thus
with his persuasions the King began to conceive an earnest
desire to see the French king, and thereupon appointed to go
over to Calais, and so in the marches of Guisnes to meet with
him. . . .

Herewith were letters written to all such lords, ladies, gentlemen, and gentlewomen, which should give their attendance on the King and Queen, which incontinently put themselves in a readiness after the most sumptuous sort. Also it was appointed that the king of England and the French king, in a camp between Ard and Guisnes, with eighteen aides, should in June next ensuing abide all comers, being gentlemen, at the tilt, at tourney, and at barriers. . . .

. . . both the kings committed the order and manner of their meeting, and how many days the same should continue, and what preëminence each should give to other, unto the Cardinal of York, which, to set all things in a certainty, made an instrument containing an order and direction concerning the premises by him devised and appointed. . . .

The peers of the realm—receiving letters to prepare themselves to attend the King in this journey, and no apparent necessary cause expressed, why nor wherefore—seemed to grudge that such a costly journey should be taken in hand to their importunate charges and expenses, without consent of the whole board of the council. But namely the Duke of Buckingham, being a man of a lofty courage but not most liberal, sore repined that he should be at so great charges for his furniture forth at this time, saying that he knew not for what cause so much money should be spent about the sight of a vain talk to be had, and communication to be ministered of things of no importance; wherefore he sticked not to say that it was an intolerable matter to obey such a vile and importunate person. . . .

Now such grievous words as the Duke thus uttered against him came to the Cardinal's ear, whereupon he cast beforehand all ways possible to have him in a trip, that he might cause him to leap headless. But because he doubted his friends, kinsmen, and allies, and chiefly the Earl of Surrey, Lord Admiral, which had married the Duke's daughter, he thought good first to send him some whither out of the way, lest he might cast a trump in his way. . . .

At length there was occasion offered him to compass his purpose, by occasion of the Earl of Kildare his coming out of Ireland. . . . Such accusations were framed against him . . . that he was committed to prison, and then by the Cardinal's good preferment the Earl of Surrey was sent into

Ireland as the King's deputy, in lieu of the said Earl of Kildare, there to remain rather as an exile than as lieutenant to
the King, even at the Cardinal's pleasure, as he himself well
perceived. . . .

[1.2.171–76] Now it chanced that the Duke . . . went . . .
into Kent unto a manor place which he had there. And whilst
he stayed in that country . . . , grievous complaints were
exhibited to him by his farmers and tenants against Charles
Knevet, his surveyor, for such bribing as he had used there
amongst them; whereupon the Duke took such displeasure
against him that he deprived him of his office, not knowing
how that in so doing he procured his own destruction, as
after appeared. . . .

[1.1.176–93] [The Emperor Charles V visited England to
see his aunt, the Queen, "of whom ye may be sure he was
most joyfully received and welcomed."] The chief cause
that moved the Emperor to come thus on land at this time
was to persuade that, by word of mouth, which he had before
done most earnestly by letters; which was, that the King
should not meet with the French king at any interview: for
he doubted lest if the king of England and the French king
should grow into some great friendship and faithful bond of
amity, it might turn him to displeasure.

But now that he perceived how the King was forward on
his journey, he did what he could to procure that no trust
should be committed to the fair words of the Frenchmen;
and that, if it were possible, the great friendship that
was now in breeding betwixt the two kings might be dissolved.
And forsomuch as he knew the Lord Cardinal to be won with
rewards, as a fish with a bait, he bestowed on him great gifts,
and promised him much more, so that he would be his friend,
and help to bring his purpose to pass. The Cardinal . . .
promised to the Emperor that he would so use the matter as
his purpose should be sped. . . .

[1.1.6–45] The day of the meeting [of the Field of the
Cloth of Gold] was appointed to be on the Thursday, the seventh of June, upon which day the two kings met in the vale
of Andren, accompanied with such a number of the nobility
of both realms, so richly appointed in apparel and costly
jewels, as chains, collars of S's, and other the like ornaments
to set forth their degrees and estates, that a wonder it was to

behold and view them in their order and rooms, which every man kept according to his appointment.

The two kings meeting in the field, either saluted other in most loving wise, first on horseback, and after alighting on foot eftsoons embraced with courteous words, to the great rejoicing of the beholders; and after they had thus saluted each other, they went both together into a rich tent of cloth of gold, . . . till it drew toward the evening, and then departed for that night, the one to Guisnes, the other to Ard. . . . [A description of the tilting follows.]

Thus, course after course each with other, his counter party, did right valiantly, but the two kings surmounted all the rest in prowess and valiantness. . . .

[1.1.89–94] On Monday, the eighteenth of June, was such an hideous storm of wind and weather, that many conjectured it did prognosticate trouble and hatred shortly after to follow between princes.

[1.1.212–26, 1.2.129–214] [In 1521] the Cardinal, boiling in hatred against the Duke of Buckingham and thirsting for his blood, devised to make Charles Knevet, that had been the Duke's surveyor, . . . an instrument to bring the Duke to destruction. This Knevet, being had in examination before the Cardinal, disclosed all the Duke's life. And first he uttered, that the Duke was accustomed, by way of talk, to say how he meant so to use the matter, that he would attain to the crown if King Henry chanced to die without issue; and that he had talk and conference of that matter on a time with George Nevill, Lord of Abergavenny, unto whom he had given his daughter in marriage; and also that he threatened to punish the Cardinal for his manifold misdoings, being without cause his mortal enemy.

The Cardinal, having gotten that which he sought for, . . . procured Knevet, with many comfortable words and great promises, that he should with a bold spirit and countenance object and lay these things to the Duke's charge, with more if he knew it when time required. Then Knevet, partly provoked with desire to be revenged and partly moved with hope of reward, openly confessed that the Duke had once fully determined to devise means how to make the King away, being brought into a full hope that he should be king by a vain prophecy which one Nicholas Hopkins, a monk of an house of the Chartreux order beside Bristow, called Henton, sometime his confessor, had opened unto him.

The Cardinal, having thus taken the examination of Knevet, went unto the King and declared unto him that his person was in danger by such traitorous purpose as the Duke of Buckingham had conceived in his heart, . . . wherefore he exhorted the King to provide for his own surety with speed. The King . . . enforced to the uttermost by the Cardinal, made this answer: "If the Duke have deserved to be punished, let him have according to his deserts." The Duke . . . was straightways attached, and brought to the Tower by Sir Henry Marney, Captain of the Guard. . . . There was also attached the foresaid Chartreux monk, Master John de la Car *alias* de la Court, the Duke's confessor, and Sir Gilbert Perke, priest, the Duke's chancellor.

. . . inquisitions were taken in divers shires of England of him, so that by the knights and gentlemen he was indicted of high treason, for certain words spoken . . . by the same Duke . . . to the Lord of Abergavenny; and therewith was the same lord attached for concealment, and so likewise was the Lord Montacute, and both led to the Tower. . . . [There follows a listing of the "divers points of high treason" in the indictment against Buckingham.]

. . . the same Duke . . . said unto one Charles Knevet, Esq., after that the King had reproved the Duke for retaining William Bulmer, Kt., into his service, that if he had perceived that he should have been committed to the Tower . . . he would have played the part which his father intended to have put in practice against King Richard the Third at Salisbury, who made earnest suit to have come unto the presence of the same King Richard; which suit if he might have obtained, he having a knife secretly about him, would have thrust it into the body of King Richard, as he had made semblance to kneel down before him. And, in speaking these words, he maliciously laid his hand upon his dagger, and said that, if he were so evil used, he would do his best to accomplish his pretensed purpose, swearing to confirm his word by the blood of our Lord.

Beside all this, the same Duke . . . at London in a place called the Rose, within the parish of St. Lawrence Poultney . . . demanded of the said Charles Knevet, Esq., what was the talk amongst the Londoners concerning the King's journey beyond the seas? And the said Charles told him that many stood in doubt of that journey, lest the Frenchmen meant some deceit towards the King. Whereto the Duke answered, that it was to be feared, lest it would come to pass, according to the words of a certain holy monk: "For there is" (saith he), "a Chartreux monk that divers times hath sent to me, willing me to send unto him my chancellor; and I did send unto him John de la Court, my chaplain, unto whom he would not declare anything till de la Court had sworn unto him to keep all things secret, and to tell no creature living what he should hear of him, except it were to me.

"And then the said monk told de la Court that neither the King nor his heirs should prosper, and that I should endeavor myself to purchase the good wills of the commonalty of England, for I, the same Duke, and my blood should prosper, and have the rule of the realm of England." Then said Charles Knevet, "The monk may be deceived through the devil's illusion," and that it was evil to meddle with such matters. "Well," said the Duke, "it cannot hurt me," and so (saith the indictment) the Duke seemed to rejoice in the monk's words. And further, at the same time, the Duke told the said Charles that, if the King had miscarried now in his last sickness, he would have chopped off the heads of the Cardinal, of Sir Thomas Lovell, Kt., and of others; and also said that he had rather die for it than to be used as he had been. . . .

[2.1.1–140] . . . the Cardinal chiefly procured the death of this nobleman, no less favored and beloved of the people of this realm in that season than the Cardinal himself was hated and envied; which thing caused the Duke's fall the more to be pitied and lamented, sith he was the man of all other that chiefly went about to cross the Cardinal in his lordly demeanor and heady proceedings. . . . Shortly after that the Duke had been indicted . . . he was arraigned in Westminster Hall. . . .

When the lords had taken their place, the Duke was brought to the bar, and upon his arraignment pleaded not guilty, and put himself upon his peers. Then was his indictment read, which the Duke denied to be true, and (as he was an eloquent man) alleged reasons to falsify the indictment; pleading the matter for his own justification very pithily and earnestly. The King's attorney against the Duke's reasons alleged the examinations, confessions, and proofs of witnesses.

The Duke desired that the witnesses might be brought forth. And then came before him Charles Knevet, Perke, de la Court, and Hopkins the monk . . . which like a false hypocrite had induced the Duke to the treason with his false, forged prophecies. Divers presumptions and accusations were laid unto him by Charles Knevet, which he would fain have covered. The depositions were read, and the deponents delivered as prisoners to the officers of the Tower. . . .

[The peers conferred.] The Duke was brought to the bar sore chafing, and sweat marvellously; and after he had made his reverence, he paused a while. The Duke of Norfolk, as judge, said: "Sir Edward, you have heard how you be indicted of high treason. You pleaded thereto not guilty, putting yourself to the peers of the realm, which have found you guilty." Then the Duke of Norfolk wept and said, "You shall be led to the King's prison and there laid on a hurdle, and so drawn to the place of execution, and there be hanged. . . ."

The Duke of Buckingham said: "My lord of Norfolk, you have said as a traitor should be said unto, but I was never any; but my lords I nothing malign for that you have done to me, but the eternal God forgive you my death, and I do. I shall never sue to the King for life, howbeit he is a gracious prince, and more grace may come from him than I desire. I desire you my lords, and all my fellows, to pray for me." Then was the edge of the ax turned towards him, and he led into a barge. Sir Thomas Lovell desired him to sit on the cushions and carpet ordained for him. He said, "Nay: for when I went to Westminster I was Duke of Buckingham; now I am but Edward Bohun, the most caitiff of the world." Thus they landed at the Temple, where received him Sir Nicholas Vaux and Sir William Sands, Bts., and led him through the city, who desired ever the people to pray for him, of whom some wept and lamented. . . .

[The Duke was led to the scaffold,] where he said he had offended the King's Grace through negligence and lack of grace, and desired all noblemen to beware by him, and all men to pray for him, and that he trusted to die the King's true man. Thus meekly with an ax he took his death. . . .

[There follows "A convenient collection concerning the High Constables of England," an office which Buckingham and his father were the last to hold.]

[1.1.200; 2.1.53, 107–24] Henry Stafford . . . was High Constable of England, and Duke of Buckingham. This man, raising war against Richard the Third usurping the crown, was in the first year of the reign of the said Richard . . . betrayed by his man Humphrey Banister (to whom being in distress he fled for succor) and . . . was beheaded without arraignment or judgment. . . .

Edward Stafford, son to Henry . . . , being also Duke of Buckingham after the death of his father, was Constable of England, Earl of Hereford, Stafford, and Northampton. . . . He is termed . . . the flower and mirror of all courtesy. This man . . . was by Henry the Seventh restored to his father's inheritance, in recompense of the loss of his father's life. . . .

[1.2.20–108] The King [in 1525] being determined . . . to make wars in France, . . . by the Cardinal there was devised strange commissions, and sent . . . into every shire, . . . that the sixth part of every man's substance should be paid in money or plate to the King without delay, for the furniture of his war. Hereof followed such cursing, weeping, and exclamation against both King and Cardinal, that pity it was to hear. . . .

The Duke of Suffolk, sitting in commission about this subsidy in Suffolk, persuaded by courteous means the rich clothiers to assent thereto; but when they came home, and went about to discharge and put from them their spinners, carders, fullers, weavers, and other artificers, . . . the people began to assemble in companies. . . . The rage of the people increased. . . . And herewith there assembled together after the manner of rebels four thousand men. . . .

The King . . . assembled . . . a great council, in the which he openly protested that his mind was never to ask anything of his commons which might sound to the breach of his laws, wherefore he willed to know by whose means the commissions were so strictly given forth. . . .

The Cardinal excused himself, and said that . . . by the consent of the whole council it was done. . . . The King indeed was much offended. . . . Therefore he . . . caused letters to be sent into all shires, that the matter should no further be talked of; and he pardoned all them that had denied the demand openly or secretly. The Cardinal, to deliver himself of the evil will of the commons, . . . caused it to be bruited abroad that through his intercession the King had pardoned and released all things. . . .

[2.1.147–67; 2.2.89–106; 3.2.85–86; 2.4] There rose [1527] a secret bruit in London that the King's confessor, Dr. Longland, and divers other great clerks had told the King that the marriage between him and the Lady Katherine, late wife to his brother Prince Arthur, was not lawful; whereupon the King should sue a divorce, and marry the Duchess of Alençon, sister to the French king. . . . The King was offended with those tales, and sent for Sir Thomas Seymour, Mayor of the city of London, secretly charging him to see that the people ceased from such talk. . . .

The truth is that, whether this doubt was first moved by the Cardinal or by the said Longland, . . . the King was . . . determined to have the case examined, cleared, and adjudged by learning, law, and sufficient authority. The Cardinal verily was put in most blame for this scruple now cast into the King's conscience, for the hate he bare to the Emperor, because he would not grant to him the archbishopric of Toledo, for the which he was a suitor. And therefore he did not only procure the king of England to join in friendship with the French king, but also sought a divorce betwixt the King and the Queen that the King might have had in marriage the Duchess of Alençon. . . .

. . . the King . . . thus troubled in conscience . . . , to have the doubt clearly removed, he called together the best learned of the realm, which were of several opinions; wherefore he thought to know the truth by indifferent judges, lest peradventure the Spaniards and other also in favor of the Queen would say that his own subjects were not indifferent judges in this behalf. And therefore he wrote his cause to Rome, and also sent . . . to the great clerks of all christendom, to know their opinions, and desired the court of Rome to send into his realm a legate, which should be indifferent, and of a great and profound judgment, to hear the cause debated; at whose request the whole consistory of the College of Rome sent thither Laurence Campeius, a priest cardinal, a man of great wit and experience, . . . and with him was joined in commission the Cardinal of York and legate of England. . . .

The place where the cardinals should sit to hear the cause of matrimony . . . was ordained to be at the Blackfriars in London, where in the great hall was preparation made of seats, tables, and other furniture, according to such a solemn session and royal appearance. The court was platted in tables and benches in manner of a consistory, one seat raised higher for the judges to sit in. Then, as it were in the midst of the said judges, aloft above them three degrees high, was a cloth of estate hanged, with a chair royal under the same, wherein sat the King; and besides him, some distance from him sat the Queen, and under the judges' feet sat the scribes and other officers. . . .

Then before the King and the judges within the court sat the Archbishop of Canterbury, Warham, and all the other bishops. . . . The judges commanded silence whilst their commission was read, both to the court and to the people assembled. That done, the scribes commanded the crier to call the King by the name of "King Henry of England, come into the court," etc. With that the King answered and said, "Here." Then called he the Queen by the name of "Katherine, Queen of England, come into the court," etc.; who made no answer, but rose out of her chair.

And because she could not come to the King directly, for the distance severed between them, she went about by the court and came to the King, kneeling down at his feet, to whom she said in effect as followeth: "Sir" (quoth she), "I desire you to do me justice and right, and take some pity upon me, for I am a poor woman, and a stranger, born out of your dominion, having here no indifferent counsel, and less assurance of friendship. Alas, sir, what have I offended you, or what occasion of displeasure have I showed you, intending thus to put me from you after this sort? I take God to my judge, I have been to you a true and humble wife, ever conformable to your will and pleasure, that never contraried or gainsaid anything thereof, and being always contented with all things wherein you had any delight, whether little or much. Without grudge or displeasure, I loved for your sake all them whom you loved, whether they were my friends or enemies.

"I have been your wife these twenty years and more, and you have had by me divers children. If there be any just cause that you can allege against me, either of dishonesty, or matter lawful to put me from you, I am content to depart to my shame and rebuke; and if there be none, then I pray you to let me have justice at your hand. The King your father was in his time of excellent wit, and the king of Spain, my father Ferdinando, was reckoned one of the wisest princes that reigned in Spain many years before. It is not to be doubted but that they had gathered as wise counsellors unto them of every realm as to their wisdoms they thought meet, who deemed the marriage between you and me good and lawful (etc.). Wherefore, I humbly desire you to spare me, until I may know what counsel my friends in Spain will advertise me to take, and if you will not, then your pleasure be fulfilled." With that she arose up, making a low curtsy to the King, and departed from thence.

The King, being advertised that she was ready to go out of the house, commanded the crier to call her again, who called her by these words: "Katherine, Queen of England, come into the court." With that, quoth Master Griffith, "Madam, you be called again." "On, on" (quoth she), "it maketh no matter, I will not tarry; go on your ways." And thus she departed, without any further answer at that time or any other, and never would appear after in any court. The King, perceiving she was departed, said these words in effect: "Forasmuch . . . as the Queen is gone, I will in her absence declare to you all, that she hath been to me as true, as obedient, and as conformable a wife as I would wish or desire. She hath all the virtuous qualities that ought to be in a woman of her dignity, or in any other of a baser estate. She is also surely a noblewoman born: her conditions will well declare the same."

With that quoth Wolsey the Cardinal: "Sir, I most humbly require your Highness to declare before all this audience whether I have been the chief and first mover of this matter unto your Majesty or no, for I am greatly suspected herein." "My Lord Cardinal" (quoth the King), "I can well excuse you in this matter; marry, . . . you have been rather against me in the tempting hereof than a setter forward or mover of the same. The special cause that moved me unto this matter was a certain scrupulosity that pricked my conscience, upon certain words spoken at a time when it was, by the Bishop of Bayonne, the French ambassador, who had been hither sent, upon the debating of a marriage to be concluded between our daughter, the Lady Mary, and the Duke of Orleans, second son to the king of France.

"Upon the resolution and determination whereof, he desired respite to advertise the King his master thereof, whether our daughter Mary should be legitimate in respect of this my marriage with this woman, being sometimes my brother's wife; which words, once conceived within the secret bottom of my conscience, engendered such a scrupulous doubt that my conscience was incontinently accombered, vexed, and disquieted; whereby I thought myself to be greatly in danger of God's indignation—which appeared to be (as me seemed) the rather, for that He sent us no issue male, and all such issues male as my said wife had by me died incontinent after they came into the world, so that I doubted the great displeasure of God in that behalf.

"Thus my conscience being tossed in the waves of a scrupulous mind, and partly in despair to have any other issue than I had already by this lady now my wife, it behooved me further to consider the state of this realm and the danger it stood in for lack of a prince to succeed me, I thought it good in release of the weighty burden of my weak conscience, and also the quiet estate of this worthy realm, to attempt the law therein, whether I may lawfully take another wife ... by whom God may send me more issue, ... not for any displeasure or misliking of the Queen's person and age, with whom I would be as well contented to continue, if our marriage may stand with the laws of God, as with any woman alive.

"In this point consisteth all this doubt that we go about now to try, by the learning, wisdom, and judgment of you our prelates and pastors ..., to whose conscience and learning I have committed the charge and judgment. ... After that I perceived my conscience so doubtful, I moved it in confession to you, my Lord of Lincoln, then ghostly father. And forsomuch as then you yourself were in some doubt, you moved me to ask the counsel of all these my lords; whereupon I moved you, my Lord of Canterbury, first to have your license . . . to put this matter in question. And so I did of all you, my lords; to which you granted, under your seals, here to be showed." "That is truth," quoth the Archbishop of Canterbury. After that the King rose up, and the court was adjourned until another day.

Here is to be noted that the Queen, in presence of the whole court, most grievously accused the Cardinal of untruth, deceit, wickedness, and malice, which had sown dissension betwixt her and the King her husband; and therefore openly protested that she did utterly abhor, refuse, and forsake such a judge, as was not only a most malicious enemy to her, but also a manifest adversary to all right and justice; and therewith did she appeal unto the Pope, committing her whole cause to be judged of him. But notwithstanding this appeal, the legates sat weekly, . . . and still they assayed if they could by any means procure the Queen to call back her appeal, which she utterly refused to do. The King would gladly have had an end in the matter, but when the legates drave time and determined upon no certain point, he conceived a suspicion, that this was done of purpose, that their doings might draw to none effect or conclusion. . . .

[2.1] And thus this court passed from . . . day to day, till at certain of their sessions the King sent the two cardinals to the Queen . . . to persuade with her by their wisdoms and to advise her to surrender the whole matter into the King's hands by her own consent and will; which should be much better to her honor than to stand to the trial of law, and thereby to be condemned. . . .

. . . the gentleman usher advertised the Queen that the cardinals were come to speak with her. With that she rose up, and with a skein of white thread about her neck, came into her chamber of presence, where the cardinals were attending. At whose coming, quoth she, "What is your pleasure with me?" "If it please your Grace" (quoth Cardinal Wolsey), "to go into your privy chamber, we will show you the cause of our coming." "My lord" (quoth she), "if ye have anything to say, speak it openly before all these folk, for I fear nothing that ye can say against me, but that I would all the world should hear and see it, and therefore speak your mind." Then began the Cardinal to speak to her in Latin. "Nay, good my lord" (quoth she), "speak to me in English."

"Forsooth" (quoth the Cardinal), "good madam, if it please you, we come both to know your mind how you are disposed to do in this matter between the King and you, and also to declare secretly our opinions and counsel unto you; which we do only for very zeal and obedience we bear unto your Grace." "My lord" (quoth she), "I thank you for your good will, but to make you answer in your request I cannot so suddenly, for I was set among my maids at work, thinking full little of any such matter, wherein there needeth a longer deliberation and a better head than mine to make answer; for I need counsel in this case which toucheth me so near, and for any counsel or friendship that I can find in England, they are not for my profit. What think you, my lords, will any Englishman counsel me, or be friend to me against the King's pleasure that is his subject? Nay, forsooth. And as for my council in whom I will put my trust, they be not here, they be in Spain in my own country.

"And, my lords, I am a poor woman, lacking wit, to answer to any such noble persons of wisdom as you be, in so weighty a matter. Therefore I pray you be good to me, poor woman, destitute of friends here in a foreign region, and your counsel also I will be glad to hear." And therewith she took the Cardinal by the hand, and led him into her privy chamber with the other cardinal, where they tarried a season talking with the Queen. . . .

[2.4.230–37] . . . the King's counsel at the bar called for judgment. . . . Quoth Cardinal Campeius: "I . . . will adjourn this court for this time, according to the order of the court of Rome." And with that the court was dissolved. . . . This protracting of the conclusion of the matter, King Henry took very displeasantly. . . .

[3.2] Whilst these things were thus in hand, the Cardinal of York was advised that the King had set his affection upon a young gentlewoman named Anne, the daughter of Sir Thomas Bullen, Viscount Rochford, which did wait upon the Queen. This was a great grief unto the Cardinal, as he that perceived aforehand that the King would marry the said gentlewoman if the divorce took place; wherefore he began with all diligence to disappoint that match, which by reason of the misliking that he had to the woman, he judged ought to be avoided more than present death. . . . The Cardinal required the Pope by letters and secret messengers that in any wise he should defer the judgment of the divorce till he might frame the King's mind to his purpose.

Howbeit he went about nothing so secretly but that the same came to the King's knowledge, who took so high displeasure with such his cloaked dissimulation that he determined to abase his degree. . . . When the nobles of the realm perceived the Cardinal to be in displeasure, they began to accuse him of such offenses as they knew might be proved against him, and thereof they made a book containing certain articles, to which divers of the King's council set their hands. The King, understanding more plainly by those articles the great pride, presumption, and covetousness of the Cardinal, was sore moved against him; but yet kept his purpose secret for a while. . . .

In the meantime the King, being informed that all those things that the Cardinal had done by his power legantine within this realm were in the case of the præmunire and provision, caused his attorney, Christopher Hales, to sue out a writ of præmunire against him. . . . And further . . . the King sent the two dukes of Norfolk and Suffolk to the Cardinal's place at Westminster, who . . . , finding the Cardinal there, they declared that the King's pleasure was that he should surrender up the Great Seal into their hands, and to depart simply unto Asher, which was an house situate nigh unto Hampton Court, belonging to the bishopric of Winchester. The Cardinal demanded of them their commission that gave them such authority; who answered again, that they were sufficient commissioners and had authority to do no less by the King's mouth. Notwithstanding, he would in no wise agree in that behalf without further knowledge of their authority, saying that the Great Seal was delivered him by the King's person, to enjoy the ministration thereof, with the room of the chancellor for the term of his life, whereof for his surety he had the King's letters patents.

This matter was greatly debated between them . . . insomuch that the dukes were fain to depart again without their purpose . . . ; but the next day they returned again, bringing with them the King's letters. Then the Cardinal delivered unto them the Great Seal. . . . Then the Cardinal called all his officers before him and took accompt of them for all such stuff whereof they had charge. And in his gallery were set divers tables whereupon lay a great number of goodly rich stuff. . . .

There was laid, on every table, books reporting the contents of the same, and so was there inventories of all things in order against the King's coming. . . . Then had he two chambers adjoining to the gallery, . . . wherein were set up two broad and long tables upon trestles, whereupon was set such a number of plate of all sorts as was almost incredible. . . .

After this, in the King's Bench his matter for the præmunire being called upon, two attorneys, which he had authorized by his warrant . . . , confessed the action, and so had judgment to forfeit all his lands, tenements, goods, and chattels, and to be out of the King's protection. . . .

During this Parliament was brought down to the Commons the book of articles, which the Lords had put to the King against the Cardinal, the chief whereof were these:

1. First, that he without the King's assent had procured to be a legate, by reason whereof he took away the right of all bishops and spiritual persons.

2. Item, in all writings which he wrote to Rome or any other foreign prince, he wrote *Ego et rex meus,* I and my King; as who would say that the King were his servant.

3. Item, that he hath slandered the Church of England in the court of Rome. . . .

4. Item, he without the King's assent carried the King's Great Seal with him into Flanders, when he was sent ambassador to the Emperor.

5. Item, he without the King's assent sent a commission to Sir Gregory de Cassado, Kt., to conclude a league between the King and the Duke of Ferrar, without the King's knowledge.

6. Item, that he, having the French pox, presumed to come and breathe on the King.

7. Item, that he caused the Cardinal's hat to be put on the King's coin.

8. Item, that he would not suffer the King's clerk of the market to sit at St. Albans.

9. Item, that he had sent innumerable substance to Rome, for the obtaining of his dignities, to the great impoverishment of the realm. . . .

[2.4.108–17; 3.2.455–57; 5.2.5–68] [After being permitted to journey to York, the Cardinal was arrested for high treason at Cawood by the Earl of Northumberland. On the way south the Cardinal "waxed very sick."] The next day he rode to Nottingham and there lodged that night more sick; and the next day he rode to Leicester Abbey, and by the way waxed so sick that he was almost fallen from his mule; so that it was night before he came to the abbey of Leicester, where at his coming in at the gates, the abbot with all his convent met him with divers torches' light, whom they honorably received and welcomed.

To whom the Cardinal said: "Father abbot, I am come hither to lay my bones among you," . . . and as soon as he was in his chamber he went to bed. This was on the Saturday at night, and then increased he sicker and sicker, until Monday, that all men thought he would have died. So on Tuesday . . . Master Kingston came to him and bade him good morrow. . . .

"Well, well, Master Kingston" (quoth the Cardinal), "I see the matter how it is framed; but if I had served God as diligently as I have done the King, he would not have given me over in my gray hairs. . . ."

Then they did put him in remembrance of Christ His passion, . . . and incontinent the clock struck eight, and then he gave up the ghost and departed this present life; which caused some to call to remembrance how he said the day before that at eight of the clock they should lose their master.

Here is the end and fall of pride and arrogancy of men exalted by fortune to dignity: for in his time he was the haughtiest man in all his proceedings alive, having more respect to the honor of his person than he had to his spiritual profession, wherein should be showed all meekness, humility, and charity. . . .

This Cardinal (as Edmund Campian in his history of Ireland describeth him) was a man undoubtedly born to honor: "I think" (saith he), "some prince's bastard, no butcher's son; exceeding wise, fair spoken, high minded; full of revenge; vicious of his body; lofty to his enemies, were they never so big; to those that accepted and sought his friendship, wonderful courteous; a ripe schoolman; thrall to affections; brought abed with flattery; insatiable to get, and more princely in bestowing, as appeareth by his two colleges at Ipswich and Oxenford, the one overthrown with his fall, the other unfinished, and yet as it lieth for an house of students, considering all the appurtenances, incomparable through Christendom. . . . [He was] never happy till this his overthrow; wherein he showed such moderation and ended so perfectly that the hour of his death did him more honor than all the pomp of his life past." . . .

This Thomas Wolsey was a poor man's son of Ipswich, . . . and being but a child, very apt to be learned. . . .

[2.4.Entry] [The Cardinal's pomp and ceremony are described.] Before him was borne first the Broad Seal of England and his cardinal's hat by a lord or some gentleman of worship, right solemnly, and as soon as he was once entered into his chamber of presence his two great crosses were there attending to be borne before him. Then cried the gentlemen ushers, going before him bareheaded, and said: "On before, my lords and masters, on before; make way for my lord's Grace." Thus went he down through the hall with a Sergeant of Arms before him, bearing a great mace of silver, and two gentlemen carrying two great pillars of silver. . . .

[1.4] Thus in great honor, triumph, and glory, he reigned a long season. . . . And when it pleased the King for his recreation to repair to the Cardinal's house . . . there wanted no preparations or furniture. . . .

On a time the King came suddenly thither in a masque with a dozen masquers all in garments like shepherds. . . . And before his entering into the hall, he came by water to the water gate without any noise, where were laid divers chambers and guns charged with shot, and at his landing they were shot off. . . . It made all the noblemen, gentlemen, ladies, and gentlewomen to muse what it should mean, coming so suddenly, they sitting quiet at a solemn banquet. . . .

First ye shall understand that the tables were set in the chamber of presence . . . and the Lord Cardinal sitting under the cloth of estate, there having all his service alone; and then was there set a lady with a nobleman, or a gentleman and a gentlewoman, throughout all the tables in the chamber on the one side, which were made and joined as it were but one table, all which order and device was done by the Lord

Sands, then Lord Chamberlain to the King, and by Sir Henry
Guildford, comptroller of the King's Majesty's house. Then
immediately after, the Great Chamberlain and the said
comptroller, sent to look what it should mean (as though
they knew nothing of the matter), who looking out of the
windows into the Thames, returned again and showed him,
that it seemed they were noblemen and strangers that arrived
at his bridge, coming as ambassadors from some foreign
prince.

With that (quoth the Cardinal), "I desire you, because you
can speak French, to take the pains to go into the hall, there
to receive them according to their estates, and to conduct
them into this chamber, where they shall see us and all these
noble personages being merry at our banquet, desiring them
to sit down with us and to take part of our fare." Then . . .
they received them . . . and conveyed them up into the
chamber. . . . At their entering into the chamber two and two
together, they went directly before the Cardinal, where he
sate, and saluted him reverently.

To whom the Lord Chamberlain, for them, said: "Sir,
forasmuch as they be strangers and cannot speak English,
they have desired me to declare unto you that they having
understanding of this your triumphant banquet, where was
assembled such a number of excellent dames, they could do
no less under support of your Grace but to repair hither to
view as well their incomparable beauty, . . . and . . . to dance
with them; and sir, they require of your Grace license to
accomplish the said cause of their coming." To whom the
Cardinal said he was very well content they should so do.
Then went the masquers and first saluted all the dames. . . .

Then spake the Lord Chamberlain to them in French, and
they rounding [whispering to] him in the ear, the Lord
Chamberlain said to my Lord Cardinal: "Sir, . . . they confess that among them there is such a noble personage,
whom, if your Grace can appoint him out from the rest, he is
content to disclose himself and to accept your place." With
that, the Cardinal taking good advisement among them, at
the last quoth he, "Meseemeth the gentleman with the black
beard should be even he"; and with that he arose out of his
chair, and offered the same to the gentleman in the black

beard with his cap in his hand. The person to whom he offered the chair was Sir Edward Nevill. . . .

The King, perceiving the Cardinal so deceived, could not forbear laughing, but pulled down his visor and Master Nevill's also. . . . The Cardinal eftsoons desired his Highness to take the place of estate; to whom the King answered that he would go first and shift his apparel, and so departed into my Lord Cardinal's chamber and there new appareled him. . . .

Then the King took his seat under the cloth of estate. . . . Thus passed they forth the night with banqueting, dancing, and other triumphs, to the great comfort of the King and pleasant regard of the nobility there assembled. . . .

[4.2.33–44] This Cardinal . . . was of a great stomach, for he compted himself equal with princes and by crafty suggestion got into his hands innumerable treasure. He forced little on simony, and was not pitiful, and stood affectionate in his own opinion. In open presence he would lie and say untruth, and was double both in speech and meaning; he would promise much and perform little. He was vicious of his body and gave the clergy evil example. . . .

[2.3.60–65] On the first of September [1532] . . . the King, being come to Windsor, created the Lady Anne Boleyn Marchioness of Pembroke, and gave to her one thousand pounds land by the year. . . .

[3.2.41–42, 67–71, 400–6; 4.1.22–33, 108–12] [The King journeyed to France, 1532.] And herewith upon his return, he married privily the Lady Anne Boleyn the same day, being the fourteenth day of November . . .; which marriage was kept so secret that very few knew it till Easter next ensuing, when it was perceived that she was with child. . . .

It was also enacted the same time [1533] that Queen Katherine should no more be called Queen, but Princess Dowager, as the widow of Prince Arthur. In the season of the last summer died William Warham, Archbishop of Canterbury, and then was named to that see Thomas Cranmer, the King's chaplain, a man of good learning and of a virtuous life, which lately before had been ambassador from the King to the Pope.

After that the King perceived his new wife to be with child, he caused all officers necessary to be appointed to her,

and so on Easter Even she went to her closet openly as
Queen; and then the King appointed the day of her coronation
to be kept on Whitsunday next following. . . . The assessment
of the fine was appointed to Thomas Cromwell, Master of
the King's Jewel House and councillor to the King, a man
newly received into high favor. . . .

. . . the Lady Katherine Dowager (for so was she then
called) . . . persisted still in her former opinion and would
revoke by no means her appeal to the court of Rome; whereupon the Archbishop of Canterbury, accompanied with the
bishops of London, Winchester, Bath, Lincoln, and divers
other learned men in great number, rode to Dunstable, which
is six miles from Ampthill, where the Princess Dowager lay,
and there . . . she was cited to appear before the said Archbishop in cause of matrimony . . . and . . . she appeared not
but made default, and so she was called peremptory every
day fifteen days together, and at the last, for lack of appearance, by the assent of all the learned men there present, she
was divorced from the King, and the marriage declared to be
void and of none effect. . . .

[4.1.36–94] [The coronation is described.] First went gentlemen, then esquires, then knights, then the aldermen . . . , after
them the judges in their mantles of scarlet and coifs. Then
followed the Knights of the Bath. . . . After them came the
Lord Chancellor in a robe of scarlet open before. . . . After
him came the King's chapel and the monks solemnly singing
with procession. Then came abbots and bishops mitered. . . .
Then after them went the Mayor of London, with his mace
and garter, in his coat of arms. Then went the Marquess
Dorset in a robe of estate which bare the scepter of gold, and
the Earl of Arundell, which bare the rod of ivory with the
dove both together.

Then went alone the Earl of Oxford . . . which bare the
crown. After him went the Duke of Suffolk in his robe of
estate, also for that day being High Steward of England,
having a long white rod in his hand, and the Lord William
Howard [Norfolk] with the rod of the marshalship, and every
Knight of the Garter had on his collar of the order. Then proceeded forth the Queen in a surcoat and robe of purple velvet
furred with ermine, in her hair, coif, and circlet . . . , and
over her was borne the canopy by four of the five ports, all

crimson with points of blue and red hanging on their sleeves; and the bishops of London and Winchester bare up the laps of the Queen's robe. The Queen's train, which was very long, was borne by the old Duchess of Norfolk. After her followed ladies, being lords' wives, which had surcoats of scarlet. . . .

When she was thus brought to the high place made in the midst of the church, between the choir and the high altar, she was set in a rich chair. And after that she had rested a while, she descended down to the high altar and there prostrate herself while the Archbishop of Canterbury said certain collects. Then she rose, and the Bishop anointed her on the head and on the breast, and then she was led up again, where, after divers orisons said, the Archbishop set the crown of St. Edward on her head and then delivered her the scepter of gold in her right hand and the rod of ivory with the dove in the left hand, and then all the choir sung "Te Deum," etc. . . .

Now, in the mean season, every duchess had put on their bonnets a coronal of gold wrought with flowers, and every marquess put on a demicoronal of gold, every countess a plain circlet of gold without flowers, and every King of Arms put on a crown of copper and gilt, all which were worn till night. When the Queen had a little reposed her, the company returned in the same order that they set forth. . . .

[5.1.158–70; 5.5.Entry] The seventh of September . . . the Queen was delivered of a fair young lady, on which day the Duke of Norfolk came home to the christening, which was appointed on the Wednesday next following. . . . The godfather at the font was the Lord Archbishop of Canterbury; the godmothers, the old Duchess of Norfolk and the old Marchioness Dorset, widow. . . . The child was named Elizabeth. . . . [A description of the christening follows.]

When the ceremonies and christening were ended, Garter chief King of Arms cried aloud, "God of His infinite goodness send prosperous life and long to the high and mighty Princess of England, Elizabeth," and then the trumpets blew. Then the Archbishop of Canterbury gave to the Princess a standing cup of gold. The Duchess of Norfolk gave to her a standing cup of gold, fretted with pearl. The Marchioness of Dorset gave three gilt bowls, pounced with a cover. . . . Then they set forwards, the trumpets going before. . . .

[4.2.105–54] The Princess Dowager, lying at Kimbolton, fell into her last sickness, whereof the King, being advertised, appointed the Emperor's ambassador, . . . Eustachius Caputius, to go to visit her and to do his commendations to her and will her to be of good comfort. The ambassador with all diligence did his duty therein, comforting her the best he might; but she within six days after, perceiving herself to wax very weak and feeble and to feel death approaching at hand, caused one of her gentlewomen to write a letter to the King, commending to him her daughter and his, beseeching him to stand good father unto her; and further desired him to have some consideration of her gentlewomen that had served her, and to see them bestowed in marriage; further, that it would please him to appoint that her servants might have their due wages and a year's wages beside. This, in effect, was all that she requested, and so immediately hereupon she departed this life. . . .

JOHN FOXE

From Acts and Monuments of Martyrs
(1597 edition)

[5.3.175–77] . . . it came into a common proverb: Do unto
my lord of Canterbury displeasure or a shrewd turn, and then
you may be sure to have him your friend whiles he
liveth. . . .

[5.1; 5.2] . . . certain of the council . . . by the enticement
and provocation of his ancient enemy the Bishop of Winchester, and other of the same sect, attempted the King
against him, declaring plainly that the realm was so infected
with heresies and heretics that it was dangerous to his Highness farther to permit it unreformed, lest . . . such contention
should arise . . . among his subjects that thereby might
spring horrible commotions and uproars, like as in some
parts of Germany it did, not long ago; the enormity whereof
they could not impute to any so much as to the Archbishop
of Canterbury, who, by his own preaching and his chaplains', had filled the whole realm full of divers pernicious
heresies. The King would needs know his accusers. They
answered that forasmuch as he was a councillor no man
durst take upon him to accuse him, but if it would please his
Highness to commit him to the Tower for a time, there
would be accusations and proofs enough against him.

The King, perceiving their importunate suit against the
Archbishop (but yet not meaning to have him wronged . . .),
granted unto them that they should the next day commit him
to the Tower for his trial. When night came, the King sent Sir
Anthony Denny, about midnight, to Lambeth to the Archbishop, willing him forthwith to resort unto him at the
court. . . . The Archbishop . . . coming into the gallery where

the King walked, and tarried for him, his Highness said: "Ah, my lord of Canterbury, I can tell you news. For divers weighty considerations it is determined by me, and the council, that you tomorrow at nine of the clock shall be committed to the Tower, for that you and your chaplains . . . have taught and preached and thereby sown within the realm such a number of execrable heresies, that it is feared, the whole realm being infected with them, no small contention and commotions will rise thereby amongst my subjects, as of late days the like was in divers parts of Germany, and therefore the council have requested me, for the trial of the matter, to suffer them to commit you to the Tower, or else no man dare come forth as witness in these matters, you being a councillor."

When the King had said his mind, the Archbishop kneeled down and said: "I am content if it please your Grace, with all my heart, to go thither at your Highness' commandment, and I most humbly thank your Majesty that I may come to my trial, for there be that have many ways slandered me, and now this way I hope to try myself not worthy of such report."

The King perceiving the man's uprightness, joined with such simplicity, said: "Oh, lord, what manner a man be you? What simplicity is in you? I had thought that you would rather have sued to us to have taken the pains to have heard you and your accusers together for your trial, without any such indurance. Do not you know what state you be in with the whole world, and how many great enemies you have? Do you not consider what an easy thing it is to procure three or four false knaves to witness against you? Think you to have better luck that way than your master Christ had? I see by it, you will run headlong to your undoing if I would suffer you. Your enemies shall not so prevail against you, for I have otherwise devised with myself to keep you out of their hands. Yet notwithstanding, tomorrow when the council shall sit and send for you, resort unto them, and if in charging you with this matter they do commit you to the Tower, require of them . . . that you may have your accusers brought before them without any further indurance, and use for yourself as good persuasions that way as you may devise, and if no entreaty or reasonable request will serve, then deliver unto them this my ring . . . and say unto them, 'If there be no remedy, my lords, but that I must needs go to the Tower, then I revoke my cause from you, and appeal to the King's own person by this token unto you all,' for … so soon as they shall see this my ring, they know it so well that they shall understand that I have resumed the whole cause into mine own hands. …"

The Archbishop, perceiving the King's benignity so much to him wards, had much ado to forbear tears. "Well," said the King, "go your ways, my lord, and do as I have bidden you." My lord, humbling himself with thanks, took his leave of the King's Highness for that night.

On the morrow about nine of the clock before noon, the council sent a gentleman usher for the Archbishop, who, when he came to the council-chamber door, could not be let in, but of purpose (as it seemed) was compelled there to wait among the pages, lackies, and servingmen all alone. Dr. Butts, the King's physician, resorting that way and espying how my lord of Canterbury was handled, went to the King's Highness and said: "My lord of Canterbury, if it please your Grace, is well promoted; for now he is become a lackey or a servingman, for yonder he standeth this half hour at the council-chamber door amongst them." "It is not so" (quoth the King), "I trow, nor the council hath not so little discretion as to use the metropolitan of the realm in that sort, specially being one of their own number. But let them alone, … and we shall hear more soon."

Anon the Archbishop was called into the council-chamber, to whom was alleged as before is rehearsed. The Archbishop answered in like sort as the King had advised him; and in the end when he perceived that no manner of persuasion or entreaty could serve, he delivered them the King's ring, revoking his cause into the King's hands. The whole council being thereat somewhat amazed, the Earl of Bedford with a loud voice, confirming his words with a solemn oath, said: "When you first began the matter, my lords, I told you what would come of it. Do you think that the King will suffer this man's finger to ache? Much more, I warrant you, will he defend his life against brabling varlets. You do but cumber yourselves to hear tales and fables against him." And so incontinently upon the receipt of the King's token, they all rose and carried to the King his ring, surrendering that matter, as the order and use was, into his own hands.

When they were all come to the King's presence, his Highness, with a severe countenance, said unto them: "Ah, my lords, I thought I had had wiser men of my council than now I find you. What discretion was this in you, thus to make the Primate of the realm, and one of you in office, to wait at the council-chamber door amongst servingmen? You might have considered that he was a councillor as well as you, and you had no such commission of me so to handle him. I was content that you should try him as a councillor and not as a mean subject. But now I well perceive that things be done against him maliciously, and if some of you might have had your minds, you would have tried him to the uttermost. But I do you all to wit, and protest, that if a prince may be beholding unto his subject" (and so, solemnly laying his hand upon his breast, said), "by the faith I owe to God, I take this man here, my lord of Canterbury, to be of all other a most faithful subject unto us, and one to whom we are much beholding." . . . And, with that, one or two of the chiefest of the council, making their excuse, declared that in requesting his indurance, it was rather meant for his trial, and his purgation against the common fame and slander of the world, than for any malice conceived against him. "Well, well, my lords" (quoth the King), "take him and well use him, as he is worthy to be, and make no more ado." And with that every man caught him by the hand, and made fair weather of altogethers, which might easily be done with that man.

Commentaries

WILLIAM HAZLITT

From Characters of Shakespear's Plays*

This play contains little action or violence of passion, yet it has considerable interest of a more mild and thoughtful cast, and some of the most striking passages in the author's works. The character of Queen Katherine is the most perfect delineation of matronly dignity, sweetness, and resignation, that can be conceived. Her appeals to the protection of the king, her remonstrances to the cardinals, her conversations with her women, show a noble and generous spirit accompanied with the utmost gentleness of nature. What can be more affecting than her answer to Campeius and Wolsey, who come to visit her as pretended friends.

> ——"Nay, forsooth, my friends,
> They that must weigh out my afflictions,
> They that my trust must grow to, live not here;
> They are, as all my comforts are, far hence,
> In mine own country, lords."

Dr. Johnson observes of this play, that "the meek sorrows and virtuous distress of Katherine have furnished some scenes, which may be justly numbered among the greatest

* From *Characters of Shakespear's Plays* by William Hazlitt. 2nd ed. (London: Taylor & Hessey, 1818).

efforts of tragedy. But the genius of Shakespear comes in and goes out with Katherine. Every other part may be easily conceived and easily written." This is easily said; but with all due deference to so great a reputed authority as that of Johnson, it is not true. For instance, the scene of Buckingham led to execution is one of the most affecting and natural in Shakespear, and one to which there is hardly an approach in any other author. Again, the character of Wolsey, the description of his pride and of his fall, are inimitable, and have, besides their gorgeousness of effect, a pathos, which only the genius of Shakespear could lend to the distresses of a proud, bad man, like Wolsey. There is a sort of child-like simplicity in the very helplessness of his situation, arising from the recollection of his past overbearing ambition. After the cutting sarcasms of his enemies on his disgrace, against which he bears up with a spirit conscious of his own superiority, he breaks out into that fine apostrophe—

> "Farewell, a long farewell, to all my greatness!
> This is the state of man; today he puts forth
> The tender leaves of hope, tomorrow blossoms,
> And bears his blushing honors thick upon him;
> The third day comes a frost, a killing frost;
> And—when he thinks, good easy man, full surely
> His greatness is a ripening—nips his root,
> And then he falls, as I do. I have ventur'd,
> Like little wanton boys that swim on bladders,
> These many summers in a sea of glory;
> But far beyond my depth: my high-blown pride
> At length broke under me; and now has left me,
> Weary and old with service, to the mercy
> Of a rude stream, that must for ever hide me.
> Vain pomp and glory of the world, I hate ye!
> I feel my heart new open'd: O how wretched
> Is that poor man, that hangs on princes' favors!
> There is betwixt that smile we would aspire to,
> That sweet aspect of princes, and our ruin,
> More pangs and fears than war and women have;
> And when he falls, he falls like Lucifer,
> Never to hope again!"—

There is in this passage, as well as in the well-known dialogue with Cromwell which follows, something which stretches beyond commonplace; nor is the account which Griffiths gives of Wolsey's death less Shakespearian; and the candor with which Queen Katherine listens to the praise of "him whom of all men living she hated most" adds the last graceful finishing to her character.

Among other images of great individual beauty might be mentioned the description of the effect of Ann Boleyn's presenting herself to the crowd at her coronation.

> ——"While her grace sat down
> To rest awhile, some half an hour or so,
> In a rich chair of state, opposing freely
> The beauty of her person to the people.
> Believe me, sir, she is the goodliest woman
> That ever lay by man. Which when the people
> Had the full view of, *such a noise arose*
> *As the shrouds make at sea in a stiff tempest,*
> *As loud and to as many tunes.*"

The character of Henry VIII is drawn with great truth and spirit. It is like a very disagreeable portrait, sketched by the hand of a master. His gross appearance, his blustering demeanor, his vulgarity, his arrogance, his sensuality, his cruelty, his hypocrisy, his want of common decency and common humanity, are marked in strong lines. His traditional peculiarities of expression complete the reality of the picture. The authoritative expletive, "Ha!" with which he intimates his indignation or surprise, has an effect like the first startling sound that breaks from a thundercloud. He is of all the monarchs in our history the most disgusting: for he unites in himself all the vices of barbarism and refinement, without their virtues. Other kings before him (such as Richard III) were tyrants and murderers out of ambition or necessity: they gained or established unjust power by violent means: they destroyed their enemies, or those who barred their access to the throne or made its tenure insecure. But Henry VIII's power is most fatal to those whom he loves: he is cruel and remorseless to pamper his luxurious appetites: bloody and voluptuous; an amorous murderer; an uxorious debauchee. His hardened insensibility to the feelings of others is strengthened by the most profligate self-indulgence. The religious hypocrisy, under which he masks his cruelty and his lust, is admirably displayed in the speech in which he describes the first misgivings of his conscience and its increasing throes and terrors, which have induced him to divorce his queen. The only thing in his favor in this play is his treatment of Cranmer: there is also another circumstance in his favor, which is his patronage of Hans Holbein.—It has been said of Shakespear—"No maid could live near such a man." It might with as good reason be said—"No king could live near such a man." His eye would have penetrated through the pomp of circumstance and the veil of opinion. As it is, he has represented such persons to the life—his plays are in this respect the glass of history—he has done them the same justice as if he had been a privy counsellor all his life, and in each successive reign. Kings ought never to be seen upon the stage. In the abstract, they are very disagreeable characters: it is only while living that they are "the best of kings." It is their power, their splendor, it is the apprehension of the personal consequences of their favor or their hatred that dazzles the imagination and suspends the judgment of their favorites or their vassals; but death cancels the bond of allegiance and of interest; and seen *as they were*, their power and their pretensions look monstrous and ridiculous. The charge brought against modern philosophy as inimical to loyalty is unjust, because it might as well be brought against other things. No reader of history can be a lover of kings. We have often wondered that Henry VIII as he is drawn by Shakespear, and as we have seen him represented in all the bloated deformity of mind and person, is not hooted from the English stage.

CAROLINE F. E. SPURGEON

From Shakespeare's Imagery*

In *Henry VIII,* so far removed in treatment and spirit from
King John, the dominating image, curiously enough, is
again the body and bodily action . . . , but used in an entirely
different way and at a different angle from that in the earlier
play. The continuous picture or symbol in the poet's mind is
not so much a person displaying certain emotions and characteristics, as a mere physical body in endlessly varied
action. Thus I find only four "personifications" in the play,
whereas in *King John* I count no less than forty.

In a play like *Henry VIII,* a large part of which it has been
generally decided on good critical grounds is not written by
Shakespeare, the question which immediately presents itself
is whether there is any evidence or not in the imagery that
one mind has functioned throughout. For our present purpose, however, I suggest we leave this question aside, and
look at the way the running symbol works out as a whole.

There are three aspects of the picture of a body in the mind
of the writer of the play: the whole body and its limbs; the
various parts, tongue, mouth and so on; and—much the most
constant—bodily action of almost every kind: walking, stepping, marching, running and leaping; crawling, hobbling,
falling, carrying, climbing and perspiring; swimming, diving,
flinging and peeping; crushing, strangling, shaking, trembling, sleeping, stirring, and—especially and repeatedly—
the picture of the body or back bent and weighed down under
a heavy burden. Except for this last, I see no special symbolic reason for the lavish use of this image, other than the
fact that it is a favorite one with Shakespeare, especially the

* From *Shakespeare's Imagery and What It Tells Us* by Caroline F. E.
Spurgeon (London: Cambridge University Press, 1935). Reprinted by permission of the publisher.

aspect of bodily movement, and we find it in the imagery from various points of view in *King Lear, Hamlet, Coriolanus, King John,* and in a lesser degree, in *Henry V* and *Troilus and Cressida.*

The opening scene—a vivid description of the tourney on the Field of the Cloth of Gold when Henry and Francis met—with its picture of bodily pomp and action, may possibly have started the image in the poet's mind, as it did in Buckingham's, when after listening to Norfolk's glowing words he asks,

> Who did guide,
> I mean, who set the body and the limbs
> Of this great sport together . . . ?   (1.1.45)

Norfolk, trying to restrain Buckingham's anger with the cardinal, says,

> Stay, my lord,
> . . . to climb steep hills
> Requires slow pace at first . . .   (129)
> . . . . .
> Be advised;
> . . . . . . we may outrun,
> By violent swiftness, that which we run at,
> And lose by over-running;

and the utter uselessness of the treaty which was the avowed object of the costly Cloth of Gold meeting is brought home by the amazingly vivid picture of a support or means of walking offered to the human body when no longer capable of any movement at all: the articles were ratified, says Buckingham, "to as much end as give a crutch to the dead" (171). At the end of the scene the original image returns, and the plot against the king is thought of as a body, so that when the nobles are arrested Buckingham exclaims,

> These are the limbs o' the plot: no more, I hope.
>   (220)

We note as we read that many of the most vivid images in the play are those of movements of the body, such as Norfolk's description (2.2.26) of Wolsey diving into the king's soul, and there scattering dangers and doubts, Cranmer, crawling into the king's favor and strangling his language in tears (5.1.156), Anne's ejaculation about Katharine's deposition, and her divorce from the majesty and pomp of sovereignty, and Katharine's

> sufferance panging
> As soul and body's severing. (2.3.15)

Wolsey thinks constantly in terms of body movement: among his images are those of a soldier marching in step with a "file" (1.2.42), a man scratched and torn by pressing through a thorny wood (75), or set on by thieves, bound, robbed and unloosed (2.4.146); and in his last great speeches, which, in spite of falling rhythm, I incline to believe are Shakespeare's, he speaks of having *trod* the ways of glory (3.2.435), sees Cromwell *carrying* peace in his right hand (445), urges him to *fling away* ambition (440), and pictures himself successively as a rash *swimmer* venturing far beyond his depth with the meretricious aid of a bladder (358–61), a man *falling* headlong from a great height like a meteor (226) or like Lucifer (371), and finally, standing bare and *naked* at the mercy of his enemies (457).

The image of the back bent under the load recurs five times, and is obviously and suitably symbolic of Wolsey's state, as well as of the heavy taxation. Wolsey complains that the question of the divorce was "the weight that pulled him down" (407), and after his dismissal, sees himself as a man with an unbearable burden suddenly lifted off him, assuring Cromwell that he thanks the king, who has cured him, "and from these shoulders" taken "a load would sink a navy,"

> a burden
> Too heavy for a man that hopes for heaven!
> (384)

The idea of a man falling from a great height is constant in the case of both Wolsey and Cranmer; and the remonstrances made with their accusers are in each case exactly alike:

> Press not a falling man too far;. . .
>
> (333)
>
> . . . .
>
>   'tis a cruelty
> To load a falling man.   (5.3.76)

The queen draws on the same range of bodily similes. She speaks of unmannerly language "which breaks the sides of loyalty," "bold mouths" and "tongues" spitting their duties out, and her description (2.4.111–15) of the great cardinal, with the king's aid going swiftly and easily over the shallow steps until mounted at the top of the staircase of fame, is extraordinarily vivid.

The king also uses it with great force when relating his mental and emotional suffering and the self questioning that followed on hearing the French ambassador demand a "respite" [an adjournment] in order to determine whether the Princess Mary were legitimate, thus raising the whole question of the divorce.

He draws a picture of the word "respite" and its effect on him as of a rough and hasty intruder rushing noisily into a quiet and guarded place, shaking and splitting it, forcing a way in so ruthlessly that with him throng in also from outside many other unbidden beings, pressing and pushing, dazed and puzzled with the commotion and the place wherein they find themselves. "This respite," he declares,

>   shook
> The bosom of my conscience, enter'd me,
> Yea, with a splitting power, and made to tremble
> The region of my breast; which forced such way
> That many mazed considerings did throng
> And press'd in with this caution.   (181)

A little later, as he tells the court how he sought counsel from his prelates, he, like Wolsey, pictures himself as a man almost unbearably burdened, groaning and sweating under his load, when he turns to the bishop with the query,

> my lord of Lincoln; you remember
> How under my oppression I did reek,
> When I first moved you.   (207)

When we trace out in detail this series of images, we recognize that it is a good example of Shakespeare's peculiar habit of seeing emotional or mental situations throughout a play in a repeatedly recurring physical picture, in what might more correctly indeed be called a "moving picture"; because having once, as here, visualized the human body in action, he sees it continuously, like Wolsey's "strange postures" in every form of physical activity.

I must not, however, here be led into the question of authorship, beyond stating that the imagery of *Henry VIII* distinctly goes to prove that in addition to the generally accepted Shakespearian scenes (1.1 and 2.2, 3, and 4, the early part of 3.2 and 5.1), the whole of 3.2 and 5.3 are also his, and that he at least gave some touches to 2.2.*

---

* For a fuller discussion of the authorship of *Henry VIII,* see my British Academy Shakespeare lecture for 1931, *Shakespeare's Iterative Imagery* (Oxford University Press, 1931), pp. 22, 23.

G. WILSON KNIGHT

A Note on *Henry VIII**

I

Perhaps no other Shakespearian play presents so queer a case of academic disintegration and uncritical popularity. Scholars have for long written off the most important scenes as the work of Fletcher, while asserting that the whole lacks unity and design. This position has hitherto been left unchallenged. Actors have, however, generally recognized the greatness at least of individual scenes and persons in the play. Irving played Wolsey with Forbes-Robertson as a famous Buckingham.** *Henry VIII* was one of Tree's most successful productions, and Wolsey one of his best parts. Since the war Dame Sybil Thorndike has played Queen Katharine, and Charles Laughton, more recently still, Henry himself. The play appeals to the profession. The general public have mainly followed the actor's rather than the professorial lead. They have not been unduly disquieted about "feminine" endings; and, I think, rightly. Here I wish to plot out a short interpretation maturing from acceptance of the play's artistic and organic validity. Afterwards, I return to the question of authorship.

* From *Shakespeare and Religion* by G. Wilson Knight (New York: Barnes & Noble, Inc.; London: Routledge & Kegan Paul Ltd., 1967). Reprinted by permission of the publishers.

** There is a gramophone record easily obtainable of Forbes-Robertson's speaking of Buckingham's great speech, which Mr. Granville-Barker, in his lecture *From Henry V to Hamlet* (*Aspects of Shakespeare,* Oxford University Press) has called "the most beautiful piece of speaking I ever heard." I understand Mr. Granville-Barker's aspersion on "such creaking methods"; but I nevertheless suggest that anyone who thinks the speech is by Fletcher should buy the record and play it from time to time.

II

The King here is not the middle-aged, sensual, robustious, goodhearted but expeditious wife-killer whose successful promiscuity has endeared him to the hearts of the British public. He can be best placed by considering the response we make to such a stage-direction as: "Flourish: Enter King and Attendants." He is not primarily a character study and should certainly not be performed as a "character" part. Primarily he is King of England; dignified, still young, honorable, and every inch a King. We must not let our sympathy for Katharine and our knowledge of a certain self-deception within Henry's supposedly conscience-stricken desire to divorce her—both have undoubted support in the play—prevent our recognition of his central position and sacred office. For this is recognized, and stressed, by all the persons. The others do not blame him; nor should we. Certainly, during the early acts he is a little insecure, deceiving himself once, deceived by others often, and distraught by troublesome rivalries and ambitions. But at the end he is a king of power and a peace-maker, overruling all turbulent and envious discontents. Which brings us to another important thought.

The play is epic rather than dramatic in structure; or, perhaps, an epic which includes a succession of single dramatic movements. Three of these show an important similarity. Buckingham opposes Wolsey's ambitious scheming and quickly falls under an apparently false charge of treason. He was formerly haughty, aristocratic, intolerant. But he goes to his death already "half in heaven," forgiving all his enemies, praying for the King, a martyr of Christ-like strength. A sudden reversal, but more than paralleled by the fall of Wolsey. Wolsey is a crafty, unprincipled, and ambitious schemer and statesman. His indirect methods are exposed, the King's displeasure falls on him, and he next embraces a religious humility and poverty with only his robe and his "integrity to heaven" in place of his former glories. He preaches what is almost a sermon at his fall, urging Cromwell to serve the King without ambition, thus forgiving and honoring to the last the master who he nevertheless feels has been unjust and ungrateful to himself. He dies, as Griffeth tells us, in religious peace. Third, we have the tragedy of Katharine. She is shown first as a strong, almost domineering

woman who hampers Wolsey's policy. At her trial she excels
in innocent and wronged dignity, and shows scathing scorn
of what she considers Wolsey's injustice and hypocrisy, a
theme developed further in her subsequent scene with the
two Cardinals. But her story closes too in religious light. She
hears of Wolsey's death, prays for his rest, showing, however, that she is not yet free from bitterness towards him;
next listens to Griffeth's noble eulogy—which is, perhaps,
necessary to stimulate our forgiveness too—and at last
attains to perfect charity towards her wronger. Whereupon
follows her Vision, in which angelic figures, to solemn
music, offer her the garland of immortality from the land of
that "celestial harmony" that awaits her. She dies blessing
the King, like the rest, without resentment.

Notice how with all these we are never quite clear as to
faults and virtues, the exact rights and wrongs of it all, but
the rhythm from personal pride and sense of injustice and
unkindness—each endures the typical Shakespearian sense
of betrayal by friend or lover—to Christian humility, absolute
forgiveness, and religious peace is found in each. It must be
observed, too, how service to the King is uppermost in the
thoughts of all at their end and is inextricably twined with
the thought of duty toward God. Thus is unrolled the sequence
of individual tragic movements. The play is rich with both a
grand royalism and a thrilling but solemn Christianity;
orthodox religious coloring being present and powerful
throughout far in excess of any previous play.

But there is more, of less tragic impact. Countering and
interwoven with these we have the rise of Anne Bullen. The
King meets her in a scene of revelry and dance, and she has a
gorgeous coronation, staged for us by direction and description. She is presented as a lovable and beautiful woman, and
we are pointed by choric passages to rejoice in the King's
good fortune. The play culminates in the christening of her
child and the striking prophecy of Cranmer. These happier
elements are mostly associated with the future Protestantism
of England—hence the importance of Cranmer—whereas the
tragic elements are entwined rather with the Cardinals, the
Pope, and Roman Catholicism generally. The movement
from Queen Katharine to Anne Bullen is thus, partly at least,
a religious movement. Nor can the play be properly under-

stood without a clear sight of its amazing conclusion, to which the whole surge of the epic advances. Cranmer's prophecy is the justification and explanation of all that precedes it.

All these themes radiate from the central figure of the King. He is like a rock, the others are waves breaking round him. And he grows in dignity and power. Towards the end he dismisses the third trial in our story, that of Cranmer, enforcing peace and goodwill, and silencing the fiery Gardiner: all which is, of course, to be contrasted with the earlier unhappy trials of Buckingham and Katharine. So we have a most involved story-pattern in terms of a few years of one King's reign which nevertheless suggests a vast history and universal movement: the rise and fall of noble men and women, whose individual sufferings and deaths are in some way necessary to the structure of a greater than themselves, here the religious independence and national glory of England; and whose troubled stories, and the King's too, including his lapse from strict honesty with himself, are shown as necessary, or at all events preliminary, to their final flowering, justification and perfection in the child Elizabeth. Thus in producing the play it is perhaps best to mark it into three act-divisions: two mainly tragic, the third optimistic. The first ends with the execution of Buckingham and the second with the fall of Wolsey; the third presenting a rising action with the coronation of Anne Bullen, Katharine's Vision—which may be allowed to suggest the peace in eternity that has also received Buckingham and Wolsey—Cranmer's trial and reinstatement, the final christening, and the prophetic conclusion forecasting the happy reigns of Elizabeth and James I.

So the mystic riches of that eternity which bounds human tragedy here alternate with the more temporal glories of successful kingship, and both contribute to the inspired words of Cranmer over the new-christened Elizabeth, foretelling a divinely ordered prosperity, worship, and peace. That such blending of national and religious prophecy should be centered on a child is nothing strange: Isaiah and Virgil offer interesting correspondences.* And, indeed, the final scene

* See T. F. Royds, *Vergil & Isaiah* (Blackwell): an admirable short study of that very entwining of spiritual prophecy with national affairs which I find in *Henry VIII*. This book has helped my general understanding.

of *Henry VIII* is in essence close to a medieval, or modern, nativity play: and as such should it be rendered in the theater.

III

I shall now briefly notice *Henry VIII* in relation to Shakespeare's other work. I need not recapitulate in any detail what I have elsewhere written on Shakespeare's final plays. But it may be as well to repeat that they are saturated in religious transcendentalism and present plots mainly concerned with loss in tempest, jealousy, misfortune, and all evils, balanced against divine appearances, and the resurrection of lost loves to music, with a general stress on oracles, dreams, prophecies and chapels. These plays, following the somber plays, seem to represent a certain inward progress of the poet's informing genius from tragedy to religious light. They and the tragedies may all be called "personal" in comparison with the earlier histories. *The Tempest* presents a final and comprehensive synthesis of the poet's main intuitions, Prospero's farewell to his art thus resembling, inevitably and with no necessary trick of conscious allegory, something of what Shakespeare the man might be supposed to feel on looking back over his completed work. Prospero leaves his island to embrace again the community of men; and Shakespeare the artist writes another play with a theme national rather than personal and philosophic, an impregnating mythology Christian rather than pseudo-Hellenic or elsewise pagan, and a prophetic finale referring primarily to the two sovereigns under whose reign he has lived.

It is a logical conclusion enough. There is something almost inevitable about this play coming at this time. It is crammed, too, with reminders of the other final plays. Queen Katharine on trial before her own husband is almost a reincarnation of Hermione; as later, listening to music to solace her marital distress, she reminds us of Desdemona. Her Vision repeats, in Christian terms, the theophanies to which the others have accustomed us—the oracle of Delphi and the appearance of Apollo described in *The Winter's Tale,* Diana in *Pericles,* Jupiter in *Cymbeline;* and, of course, much of the same sort in *The Tempest.* In close connection with each of these—except only the examples from *The Tempest*—

occurs the rare word "celestial," used too by Katharine just before her visionary sleep. The recurrent forgiveness-motif in *Henry VIII* presents exactly the quality and depth of Prospero's forgiveness. Most important of all, the birth and child themes of the other final plays are reflected here in the glorification of the baptized child Elizabeth. I have elsewhere claimed that the restoration of Hermione and Thaisa to their husbands may be said to correspond to an intuition of a paradisal eternity such as that which lies behind, or may be said to lie behind, the restoration of Beatrice to Dante or Gretchen to Faust; whereas the finding of the lost child, Perdita or Marina, and, I might add, the importance given to the various children's happiness and success at the last moments of all the final plays, suggests rather the onward progress of creation within time; the words "time" and "eternity" being here deliberately used as metaphysical concepts arbitrarily applied to a poetic creation to bridge the gap between art and thought. Now in *Henry VIII* we find a similar contrast. Queen Katharine's vision of eternal bliss is set directly beside the more humanly joyous coronation of Anne Bullen, and not long after we have the baptismal ceremony of the infant Elizabeth. Notice how much happier this contrast is than the more cruel juxtaposition earlier of the King's revelling in Wolsey's Palace immediately before Buckingham's execution. It is as though time and eternity were seen converging as the play unfurls, to meet in exquisite union at Cranmer's prophecy: which again may remind us of the soothsayer and the prophetic conclusion of *Cymbeline*.

If in *The Tempest* Shakespeare gives us a comprehensive and inclusive statement of his furthest spiritual adventures, in *Henry VIII* he has gone yet further, directly relating those adventures to the religion of his day and the nation of his birth. In the prophecy of Cranmer I see the culmination not only of the epic movement of *Henry VIII* as a whole but the point where the vast tributary of Shakespeare's work from *Hamlet* to *The Tempest* enters the wider waters of a nation's historic and religious advance, to swell "the main of floods" to England's glory and, through her, the establishment of the peace of Christ on earth.

IV

All this, I shall be told, would be well enough, if there were ten syllables in each line of the great speeches here and not eleven. Frankly, I do not know how satisfactorily to answer this objection: because I do not understand it. I believe such pseudo-scientific theorizing is again here, as elsewhere, merely an unconscious projection of our sense of organic incoherence within the play due to failure in focus and understanding. *Henry VIII* is generally divided into scenes of what is usually considered "ordinary" Shakespearian verse, and those where there is a high percentage of eleven-syllable lines. Now, if these latter are by Fletcher,* we certainly have not an instance of Fletcher spoiling the Shakespearian art-form by weak collaboration, but rather, if we cannot, because of variation in style, see the play as an organic whole, we must observe Shakespeare trying (in vain) to spoil a Fletcherian masterpiece—since it is the best scenes that are considered un-Shakespearian; a masterpiece in some ways—in a certain selfless and Christian nobility and finality of restrained power—greater than anything Shakespeare had done himself outside *The Tempest*. But there is surely no necessity for all this. Shakespeare had long—in the latter acts of *Timon* for example—been finding the extra syllable a means, when he wanted it, to verbal mastery of an especially grand but reserved strength of statement. In *The Tempest* it is continual: Act 5 alone provides all the examples any one should want. In *Henry VIII* this style is finely used to mark the solemn cadences of the grandest scenes: Buckingham's Farewell, Katharine's Trial, her interview with Wolsey and Campeius, Wolsey's Fall, Katharine's Vision, Cranmer's Prophecy. And I find, on re-inspection, that the admittedly Shakespearian scenes have a goodly sprinkling of it too. Indeed, Shakespeare has only here carried a certain technical effect, which he had for some time been progressively and increasingly developing and had brought to a climax in *The Tempest*, just a little further

---

* The late Edgar I. Fripp once strongly opposed the Fletcherian theory in a letter written to me about my first Shakespearian publication, *Myth and Miracle*, suggesting, if I remember right, that I should incorporate *Henry VIII* in my general thesis. His letter redirected my attention to a play I had not then read for some years.

than before, emphasizing it especially in the most important scenes according to the quality of the occasion.

Moreover, these noble speeches are rich in the cadences of typical Shakespearian emotion and Shakespearian thought; though the expression is restrained, as in *The Tempest,* the metaphors are likewise Shakespearian;* and the general power is, indeed, such that, if Fletcher wrote them, he was clearly one of the two greatest poets in our literature, sharing that honor alone with the author of *Timon* and *The Tempest,* to whom he bears so striking and uncanny a resemblance.

---

* Miss Spurgeon certainly notes that a single typical strand of Shakespirian imagery is not found in the suspected scenes, while it is found elsewhere. But imagery and rhythm both naturally vary with scenic tone. And it is pleasant to find Miss Spurgeon writing that the evidence of imagery "by no means all points one way," and expressing her belief that Shakespeare "wrote the greater part of the play." (*Shakespeare's Iterative Imagery* in *Aspects of Shakespeare,* Oxford University Press.)

MARK VAN DOREN

Henry VIII*

Shakespeare's rest could not have been interrupted long by *Henry VIII,* even if he wrote every word of it. It has become a tradition to say that only five or six scenes are his, and that Fletcher, or possibly Massinger, is responsible for the remainder; although one extreme theory gives him the entire work, and another takes it all away. The question has interest, not because *Henry VIII* is important in itself but because in any view it is an imitation of Shakespeare; it is at the same time like him and unlike him. And the question will not be answered because in such cases we cannot know whether the poet has imitated himself or been imitated by another.

A certain resemblance to Shakespeare's later plays is all too obvious. Tempests, shores, flowers, music, and peace are incidental themes. Henry knows how to praise Katherine in the idiom of Pericles and Florizel: she is "the queen of earthly queens" (2.4.141), and her saintlike meekness is most rare. And reconciliation is rampant—several dramas, rather than one, busily develop it into a kind of orthodoxy.

Just there the resemblance ceases; or overleaps its limits and lands in imitation. For the successive dramas in which Buckingham, Katherine, Wolsey, and Cranmer submit their wills to Henry's are not dramas of reconciliation. The theme has been watered down; resignation is now the word, and its repetition through a series of unmotivated surrenders suggests machinery. Either Shakespeare has lost the impulse which gave his final stories their mellow power, or some other poet has never felt it. Three proud persons break sud-

* From *Shakespeare* by Mark Van Doren. Copyright 1939, © 1967 by Mark Van Doren. Reprinted by permission of Holt, Rinehart and Winston, Inc.

denly and bow before a dummy king who represents England, and a fourth who has never been "unsound," Archbishop Cranmer, basks weeping in the sun of his accepted monarch. It is like nine-pins going down, nor can we miss a tone of smugness in the proud ones as they pray. This is Buckingham:

> Go with me, like good angels, to my end;
> And, as the long divorce of steel falls on me,
> Make of your prayers one sweet sacrifice,
> And lift my soul to heaven.   (2.1.75–78)

This is Katherine:

> Remember me
> In all humility unto his Highness.
> Say his long trouble now is passing
> Out of this world; tell him, in death I bless'd him,
> For so I will.   (4.2.160–64)

And this is Wolsey:

> Nay then, farewell!
> I have touch'd the highest point of all my greatness;
> And, from that full meridian of my glory,
> I haste now to my setting. I shall fall
> Like a bright exhalation in the evening,
> And no man see me more. . . .
>   I have ventur'd,
> Like little wanton boys that swim on bladders,
> This many summers in a sea of glory,
> But far beyond my depth. My high-blown pride
> At length broke under me, and now has left me,
> Weary and old with service, to the mercy
> Of a rude stream, that must for ever hide me. . . .
>   O Cromwell, Cromwell!
> Had I but serv'd my God with half the zeal
> I serv'd my king, He would not in mine age
> Have left me naked to mine enemies.   (3.2.222–457)

The smugness of their tone goes with a smoothness in their verse such as Shakespeare had long ago outgrown. Not for years had he let his lines roll like this, or ripened his metaphors to rottenness. "Highest point," "meridian," "setting," "bright exhalation in the evening"—there is too much of it by Shakespeare's final standard, and although it is excellent in its way it bears no resemblance to the unique elliptical poetry he had recently been writing. "Swim on bladders," "sea of glory," "high-blown pride," "rude stream"—any competent poet could have developed the image thus, just as any workman of 1612 or 1613 could have worked out the vegetable autobiography of Wolsey in terms of his tender leaves, his blossoms, his blushing honors, his greatness ripening, and his root nipped on the third day by a killing frost (3.2.352–58).

The style of any good poet moves from simplicity to congestion, and once this end is reached return is difficult if not impossible. If Shakespeare returned in *Henry VIII* he was performing an extraordinary feat. He had performed many feats in his history, but not this one, of which nevertheless he was perhaps capable. At the same time, however, and in the same play, he imitated—or someone did—his last nervous style. It crops out everywhere, not only in the scenes assigned to him but in some that are assigned to his collaborator.

> The tract of everything
> Would by a good discourser lose some life,
> Which action's self was tongue to.　　　(1.1.40–42)

> Of her that loves him with that excellence
> That angels love good men with.　　　(2.2.34–35)

> And which gifts,
> Saving your mincing, the capacity
> Of your soft cheveril conscience would receive,
> If you might please to stretch it.　　　(2.3.30–33)

> For it is you
> Have blown this coal betwixt my lord and me,
> Which God's dew quench!　　　(2.4.78–80)

> If your business
> Seek me out, and that way I am wife in,
> Out with it boldly.　　　(3.1.37–39)

> Such a noise arose
> As the shrouds make at sea in a stiff tempest,
> As loud, and to as many tunes. . . . No man living
> Could say "This is my wife" there; all were woven
> So strangely in one piece.   (4.1.71–81)

These are imitations in the sense that their virtue has no bulk, their involutions no excuse. They may or may not have been written by Shakespeare, but it does not matter. They do not save the play for distinction any more than its gorgeous pageants make up for an absence of drama, or than its external compliments to Oxford and Cambridge, Elizabeth and James, have continued after three centuries to be interesting. The two styles in *Henry VIII* are two currents of water, one tepid and the other icy. The difference is to be noted, but it is also to be noted that the water is never wine.

   The style of certain passages in *The Two Noble Kinsmen* which criticism persists in suspecting to be Shakespeare's gives us a headier imitation of his brew.

> Draw thy fear'd sword
> That does good turns to th' world.   (1.1.48–49)

> O queen Emilia,
> Fresher than May, sweeter
> Than her gold buttons on the boughs or all
> Th' enamell'd knacks o' the mead or garden! Yea,
> We challenge too the bank of any nymph,
> That makes the stream seem flowers! Thou, O jewel
> O' th' wood, o' th' world, hast likewise bless'd a place
> With thy sole presence.   (3.1.4–11)

> Each stroke laments
> The place whereon it falls, and sounds more like
> A bell than blade.   (5.3.4–6)

But it is imitation, and once again the identity of its contriver does not matter. The lines are charming in their oddity rather than beautiful in their strength; the syntax is wrenched, the syllables are curled, for no discoverable reason. The quaint series of little triumphs grows tiresomely long, together with a story which cannot be believed and whose two fine heroes talk like one gold-plated man. The shortness of breath in Shakespeare's later verse was a sign of seriousness and power; here after a while it is weakness, for this verse lives only within the phrase, dying at each fall to gasp again. Such cleverness is senseless, as Shakespeare in his right mind never was. It drones, as he never did. None of his styles was an end in itself as this one is. He wrote to further ends: to say things, to tell stories, to mingle lives with lives. His one great end he could never have wished to put into a few words. Nor did he need to, since his many words would last.

JANE LAPOTAIRE

Playing Katherine in the Vision
Scene (4.2) of *Henry VIII**

The vision that she sees [in Gregory Doran's production
1996–97] caused us much debate. Finally, to my great relief,
the idea of the younger members of the cast tripping round
me in white dresses and cherub wings was scrapped for the
simpler (and to my mind more effective for an audience
familiar with the cinematic skills of Spielberg) pillar of golden
light. In this, surely as a reward for her forgiveness of Wolsey,
she sees "a blessed troop," "spirits of peace," who invite her
to "a banquet, whose bright faces/Cast thousand beams"
upon her "like the sun" (4.2.83–89)—what a potent reminder
of Spain, even at this late stage in her life and the play. Their
departure leaves her saddened to rediscover the wretchedness of her earthly state. But they have promised her eternal
happiness, the greatest accolade (if that's the right word for
the humbling she has achieved through suffering and Christian endurance): but, as ever, with her truthful mind, she
knows that she is not ready for this greatest of tributes yet.

With the same skill that led Shakespeare to introduce
the clown with the basket of figs and his jokes just prior
to Cleopatra's death scene, Katherine's second reverie is
abruptly shattered by a messenger (surely a Kimbolton
local) who in the excitement of his errand addresses her
with no formality at all: "An't like your grace" (100). In a
flash we see the old Katherine, but one whose years of
diminution in status have made her all the more status-
conscious. (She would never acknowledge the title that they

* From Jane Lapotaire, "Queen Katherine in *Henry VIII*," in *Players of
Shakespeare* 4, ed. Robert Smallwood (Cambridge University Press, 1998),
pp. 149–51. Reprinted with the permission of Cambridge University Press.

tried to force on her after the divorce—"Princess Dowager.") "You are a saucy fellow! / Deserve we no more reverence?" (100–1). The saucy fellow has come to tell of a messenger from the King, a messenger that even with the failing of her eyes that grows progressively worse through the scene, is one that she recognizes from Spain—another valuable echo of her homeland, now that she is so near the end of her earthly journey, and the messenger can be a useful tool to carry, at long last, an earlier message she had written to Henry.

Greg asked a very potent question at one point in the rehearsing of this scene, when it seemed to be stuck, not growing or going anywhere: "What would we lose if the scene ended after the vision?" Quick as a flash we saw what the end of Katherine's role was about. We have to see that she has no grudges against Henry; that she is still concerned for his welfare; that she must remind Henry of his duties towards the child of their "chaste loves" (especially as another from Anne Boleyn is on the way), and that she must make provision for her faithful servants, albeit that her estimation of how many she has is slightly awry: to the last she is the champion of the poor, although her manservants have grown poor because of their cleaving to her despite her change in fortune. The passion with which I colour "That they may have their wages duly paid 'em" (150) was based on Katherine having to send messengers home to Spain asking her father to send her money for food when she was pushed out into the paucity of Ludlow Castle in the years between Arthur's death and her eventual marriage to Henry, not dissimilar to the relative poverty in which she must have lived at Kimbolton.

The energy with which she has finally put her earthly house in order so that she may depart in peace costs her dear. She knows that she is near death. With her recently learned humility she tells the messenger to inform the King that "his long trouble now is passing / Out of this world" (162–63)— what a heartbreaking but nevertheless accurate description of herself!—and adds: "Tell him in death I blessed him, / For so I will" (163–64). What utter Christian forgiveness and love. This is all the more poignant now, of course, since we have seen her, as frail as she is, claw herself back from the jaws of bitterness and hatred. Again the word "chaste" appears. How strongly she must have held on to this, through all her years of exile and rejection: "I was a chaste wife to my grave" (170). And she leaves us, having detailed her burial instructions, with a last reminder of who she really is: "A queen and daughter to a king" (172). Spanish, noble, and dignified to the end, till she "can no more." Her actual last words, after she had heard mass at daybreak said by her Spanish chaplain, were in a moving letter to Henry, in which she declared: "For my part I pardon you everything . . . I commend unto you our daughter Mary, beseeching you to be a good father unto her . . . Lastly I make this vow, that mine eyes desire you above all things." "Humble et Loyale" to the very end. The Imperial ambassador Chapuys wrote of her "that she was the most virtuous woman I have ever known, and the highest hearted." Me too. It is a privilege and a joy to play her. May she rest in peace.

S. SCHOENBAUM

Henry VIII on Stage and Screen

Few first runs of Elizabethan plays created a stir on the same order as that of *Henry VIII* in the early summer of 1613, when chambers were discharged, i.e., cannons fired, heralding the arrival of the monarch for Cardinal Wolsey's festivities at York Place (1.4). The wadding with which one of the cannons was stopped smoldered and caught fire in the thatched roofing of the Globe playhouse, and the theater quickly burned to the ground. The event was plentifully documented, being commented upon in contemporary letters, ballads, and annals. A recently recovered letter of July 4, 1613, by one Henry Bluett, speaks of the full house at the Globe for "a play called *All Is True,* which had been acted not passing two or three times before," and the fire which left no one injured "except one man who was scalded with the fire by adventuring in to save a child which had otherwise been burned." (There is no doubt that *All Is True* and *Henry VIII* are the same play.) The theater was quickly rebuilt—this time with tiled rather than thatched roofing.

When the playhouses reopened after the restoration of Charles II in 1660, *Henry VIII* early became a favorite among Shakespeare's plays for revival, and remained so until the present century. The big parts—Henry, Wolsey, and Katherine—recommended the play to actors, and producers were attracted by the opportunities afforded for sumptuous decor and costumes. These became ever more elaborate. Inevitably the text, severely curtailed, took a back seat to spectacle; of the last act—when it was done at all—only the christening remained. The antiquarian impulse of the nineteenth century found expression in the quest for historical fidelity with respect to the domestic detail of Tudor court life: Henry became the King of Hans Holbein's celebrated portraiture, as other performers have since. So frequently has *Henry VIII* been acted that only selective notice of revival is possible here.

In his *Diary* Samuel Pepys (1633–1703) twice recorded seeing the play, the second time professing himself "mightily pleased with the history and shows of it." Thomas Betterton, the foremost actor of the day, played Henry, and a stage tradition traces his instruction in the part back—via the playwright-manager Sir William Davenant and John Lowen, a player with the King's men in the old days—to Shakespeare himself. However that may be, Betterton pleased audiences in the part, *Henry VIII* being performed consecutively for fifteen days, a long run in this period. Of his performance an early commentator remarked: "No one can or will come near him."

In the eighteenth century the play was acted most years. The Drury Lane revival of 1727 featured a resplendent coronation scene, with the added embellishment of the Queen's champion issuing a general challenge on behalf of the new sovereign. The scene made a great impression and was imitated in subsequent productions until outdone by the 1762 Drury Lane revival, which featured a cast of 130 for the coronation, including the Dukes of Aquitaine and Normandy, six Beef-Eaters, and "the Queen's herbwoman strewing flowers"—all, needless to say, unspecified in Shakespeare's text. Katherine became one of Sarah Siddons's favorite parts, and at least one knowledgeable spectator thought it the equal, in effort and perfection, of her celebrated Lady Macbeth. Mrs. Siddons's brother John Philip Kemble, a distinguished actor in his own right, played Wolsey, increasingly regarded as the leading male role. The great William Charles Macready made Wolsey one of his star parts. Curtailed productions, ending with Wolsey's fall, became the rule. One such was acted, by royal command, before Queen Victoria and Prince Albert at Drury Lane in 1847.

Charles Kean in 1855 restored some of the fifth act, of late years "entirely omitted," but it consisted almost entirely of the christening of Princess Elizabeth. He enhanced his staging with a moving panorama of London and a real barge for Buckingham's final exit. Pageantry triumphed in this production. The settings, of unprecedented splendor, with numerous tableaux and processions, required the curtain to be lowered for the scene changes. An actual coronation was featured. It was a long evening at the Princess's Theatre. Kean himself took the part of Wolsey; his wife, Ellen Tree (1805–1880), played Katherine. The production had a record-breaking run of almost one hundred nights, and was revived four years later. A young Oxford mathematician, C. L. Dodgson, not yet known by the pseudonym (Lewis Carroll) which would make him famous as the author of *Alice's Adventures in Wonderland,* saw the production, and was entranced by the spectacle: "the greatest theatrical treat I ever had or ever expect to have." Entranced also were two young American visitors, the brothers William and Henry James. "Our enjoyment of Charles Kean's presentation of *Henry the Eighth* figures to me as a momentous date in our lives," the novelist recalled a half century later; "we did nothing for weeks afterwards but try to reproduce in water-colours Queen Katherine's dream-vision of the beckoning, consoling angels, a radiant group let down from the skies by machinery then thought marvellous"—although retrospectively James found the spectacle "comparatively garish and violent." The production, revived at the same West End house in 1859, marked the high point of Kean's career. At the last performance he bade farewell to the stage. In 1868 he died, and his wife retired.

Henry Irving's revival in 1892, with himself as Wolsey and Ellen Terry as Katherine, doubled Kean's run. Well that it did; the revival had—for its time—been mounted at great expense (£16,500), overwhelmed by the grandeur of sets which aspired at once to sumptuous display and antiquarian fidelity. Years afterward Irving would declare, "For the abuse of scenic decoration, the overloading of the stage with ornament, the subordination of the play to a pageant, I have nothing to say. That is all foreign to the artistic purpose which should dominate dramatic work." In fact Irving's productions—not least his *Henry VIII*—admitted such foreign matter aplenty.

In the present century the Tyrone Guthrie revival at Sadler's Wells in 1933 featured Charles Laughton as the King and Flora Robson as Katherine. *Henry VIII* three years later inaugurated the open-air theater in London's Regents' Park. In Oxford in 1946 the play was chosen to honor the quatercentenary of the foundation by Henry VIII of Christ Church as a college and cathedral; undergraduates personated Wolsey and the Tudor courtiers in Wolsey's hall, while the cathedral choir sang Tudor music for Elizabeth's christening. Guthrie's nothing if not energetic revival at Stratford in 1949 featured Anthony Quayle as Henry, Diana Wyngard as Katherine, Harry Andrews as Wolsey, and a plenitude of bustling, talkative extras. With King George VI and the Queen (now the Queen Mother) in attendance, Quayle acted every inch a king.

"Peace, plenty, love, truth, terror"—this line from Cranmer's incantatory prophecy at the christening of the infant Elizabeth that brings *Henry VIII* to its triumphant close—was featured in posters and programs of the Royal Shakespeare Company's production in 1982. Richard Griffith made a stately sovereign in his prime, not diffident about embarking upon the exercise of Tudor absolutism, which came naturally to him. Gemma Jones, like so many who had preceded her in the part, was movingly eloquent as the jewel that had hung round the King's neck; she yet retained a slight trace of a Spanish accent in her voice: a nice touch. The music for this revival had a deliberately anachronistic Kurt Weill *Threepenny Opera* flavor, and the Tudor dances at Cardinal Wolsey's gala banquet at York Place (1.4) became stately tangos. Tailors' dummies rather than extras were called upon for the coronation procession, with the elaborate stage directions declaimed. It was not unnoticed at the time that a revival coinciding with another royal arrival— the birth, to Princess Diana and Prince Charles, of a future heir to the throne—furnished a suitable occasion for another celebratory revival of this celebratory play.

In the United States *Henry VIII* has been less frequently produced. The first American staging took place in New York in 1789, with Lewis Hallam and his wife as the King and Anne Bullen. A notably vital American actress in the romantic style, Charlotte Cushman (1816–1876)—the second American actress to perform on the British stage—played Queen Katherine in seven different seasons, last in 1874, when she was sixty. Physically awkward and extremely tall, Cushman now and then played Wolsey: but she was accustomed to taking male parts, including Romeo to her sister

Susan's Juliet. Cushman interpolated additional spectacle into *Henry VIII,* introducing, as an addition to the procession in 4.1, the coronation of Anne. In the nineteenth century E. L. Davenport (1858) and Edwin Booth (1863, 1878) were notable Wolseys. The Polish actress Helena Modjeska's fine acting techniques won applause for her Katherine despite her accented and unfluent English. In 1946 Margaret Webster's Broadway production with Walter Hampden as Wolsey, Victor Jory as Henry, and Eva Le Gallienne as Katherine conspicuously initiated the American Repertory Theatre. Buckingham (Richard Waring) descended a long staircase, evocatively furnished with battlements, to encounter "the long divorce of steel" which would fall upon him (2.1). Ms. Webster herself took the minor part of the Old Lady (2.3; 5.1).

A television version of the play was directed by Kevin Billington (best known for his work for British television, most notably *Upstairs, Downstairs*) and released as part of the BBC Shakespeare Plays series in 1979. For this production the camera zeroed in not on studio sets but on Leeds Castle, Hever Castle, and Penhurst Place. John Stride was a well-intentioned if temperamental Henry. Timothy West, "massive and scarlet" (in one critic's words) in his cardinal's habit, moralized his descent from power with this actor's customary authority. Claire Bloom—the star presence of this version—played an eloquently regal, middle-aged Katherine. Her vision (4.2) became a troubled dream.

POSTSCRIPT

The late Sam Schoenbaum's stage history could not, unfortunately, discuss what probably was the most important production of the play in the twentieth century, the one directed in 1996 by Gregory Doran, for the Royal Shakespeare Company at Stratford, with Paul Jesson as Henry and Jane Lapotaire as Katherine. (In 1998 the production moved to London, and then to the United States.) The words *All Is True* (an alternate title for the play in Shakespeare's day) were written in huge letters across double doors at the rear of the stage, thereby constantly reminding the reader of the deceptions or at least distortions of the truth that many of the characters—not least the king—engage in. It happens that one performance was attended by Charles, prince of Wales, who met with the cast after the performance. Paul Jesson, in *Players of Shakespeare,* 4th ed. (Robert Smallwood: 1998), reports that according to Charles, the world of the play was not much different from the world of the prince. Jesson reported:

> During a wide-ranging conversation the prince said, referring to the play, "It makes you realize how little things have changed. When one is born into a certain position you have people advising you all the time, whispering into your ear. It's only when you get to my age that you begin to work out who's telling you the truth."

Doran's political figures were for the most part drably costumed, but the production did not lack for visual and aural appeal. For instance, Norfolk's description of the Field of the Cloth of Gold in the first scene—a site in France where, in a tourney in 1520 Henry and Francis I met and lavishly competed—introduced us to a splendid Henry, crowned and dressed in gold, on a golden horse, with the entire company singing "Deo Gratias," and the christening at the end of the play again gave us both Henry and "Deo Gratias," but, to repeat, such scenes were undercut by the words and actions of the characters; "All is true" emphasized the falseness of much of what we witnessed, and made Katherine's uncompromising honesty the more effective. Katherine's slight Spanish accent, too, separated her from the figures around her, isolated her, so to speak. That a gulf existed between her and Henry was evident when Capucius, after she left the stage, tore up the letter (4.2) that she entrusted him to deliver to Henry; the implication was that Henry would not have bothered to read it. (We reprint, in this book, part of Jane Lapotaire's discussion of her interpretation of Katherine.)

Bibliographic Note: Many of the titles already listed in Section 4, "Shakespeare on Stage and Screen," have brief discussions of productions of *Henry VIII*. Some editions of the play, such as those mentioned in Section 12 of the Suggested References in this book, devote eight or ten or so pages to the stage history. For productions in the second half of the nineteenth century, see Michael R. Booth, *Victorian Spectacular Theatre* (1981). Hugh M. Richmond's small book, *King Henry VIII* (1994) in a series called "Shakespeare in Performance," is devoted to the stage history of the play: Richmond surveys productions up through the nineteenth century, and then concentrates on six productions of the twentieth century. Unfortunately his book was published before Doran directed the play for the Royal Shakespeare Company.

Shakespeare Quarterly is a good source for reviews of productions—not only in the English-speaking world but also elsewhere—since the middle of the twentieth century. *Shakespeare Survey,* an annual, includes reviews of British productions of the same period. For extracts from reviews of the BBC television production (1984), see J. C. Bulman and H. R. Coursen, *Shakespeare on Television* (1988), pp. 255–56. Paul Jesson and Jane Lapotaire discuss their performances as Henry and Katherine in Gregory Doran's acclaimed 1996 production in *Players of Shakespeare,* ed. Russell Jackson and Robert Smallwood (1998), pp. 114–31.

Suggested References

The number of possible references is vast and grows alarmingly. (The *Shakespeare Quarterly* devotes one issue each year to a list of the previous year's work, and *Shakespeare Survey*—an annual publication—includes a substantial review of biographical, critical, and textual studies, as well as a survey of performances.) The vast bibliography is best approached through James Harner, *The World Shakespeare Bibliography on CD-Rom: 1900–Present.* The first release, in 1996, included more than 12,000 annotated items from 1990–93, plus references to several thousand book reviews, productions, films, and audio recordings. The plan is to update the publication annually, moving forward one year and backward three years. Thus, the second issue (1997), with 24,700 entries, and another 35,000 or so references to reviews, newspaper pieces, and so on, covered 1987–94.

For guidance to the immense amount that has been written, consult Larry S. Champion, *The Essential Shakespeare: An Annotated Bibliography of Major Modern Studies,* 2nd ed. (1993), which comments briefly on 1,800 publications.

Though no works are indispensable, those listed below have been found especially helpful. The arrangement is as follows:

1. Shakespeare's Times
2. Shakespeare's Life
3. Shakespeare's Theater
4. Shakespeare on Stage and Screen
5. Miscellaneous Reference Works
6. Shakespeare's Plays: General Studies
7. The Comedies
8. The Romances
9. The Tragedies
10. The Histories
11. *King John*
12. *Henry VIII* (*All Is True*)

The titles in the first five sections are accompanied by brief explanatory annotations.

1. Shakespeare's Times

Andrews, John F., ed. *William Shakespeare: His World, His Work, His Influence,* 3 vols. (1985). Sixty articles, dealing not only with such subjects as "The State," "The Church," "Law," "Science, Magic, and Folklore," but also with the plays and poems themselves and Shakespeare's influence (e.g., translations, films, reputation).

Byrne, Muriel St. Clare. *Elizabethan Life in Town and Country* (8th ed., 1970). Chapters on manners, beliefs, education, etc., with illustrations.

Dollimore, John, and Alan Sinfield, eds. *Political Shakespeare: New Essays in Cultural Materialism* (1985). Essays on such topics as the subordination of women and colonialism, presented in connection with some of Shakespeare's plays.

Greenblatt, Stephen. *Representing the English Renaissance* (1988). New Historicist essays, especially on connections between political and aesthetic matters, statecraft and stagecraft.

Joseph, B. L. *Shakespeare's Eden: the Commonwealth of England 1558–1629* (1971). An account of the social, political, economic, and cultural life of England.

Kernan, Alvin. *Shakespeare, the King's Playwright: Theater in the Stuart Court 1603–1613* (1995). The social setting and the politics of the court of James I, in relation to *Hamlet, Measure for Measure, Macbeth, King Lear, Antony and Cleopatra, Coriolanus,* and *The Tempest.*

Montrose, Louis. *The Purpose of Playing: Shakespeare and the Cultural Politics of the Elizabethan Theatre* (1996). A poststructuralist view, discussing the professional theater "within the ideological and material frameworks of Elizabethan culture and society," with an extended analysis of *A Midsummer Night's Dream.*

Mullaney, Steven. *The Place of the Stage: License, Play, and Power in Renaissance England* (1988). New Historicist analysis, arguing that popular drama became a cultural institution "only by . . . taking up a place on the margins of society."

Schoenbaum, S. *Shakespeare: The Globe and the World*

(1979). A readable, abundantly illustrated introductory book on the world of the Elizabethans.

Shakespeare's England, 2 vols. (1916). A large collection of scholarly essays on a wide variety of topics, e.g., astrology, costume, gardening, horsemanship, with special attention to Shakespeare's references to these topics.

2. Shakespeare's Life

Andrews, John F., ed. *William Shakespeare: His World, His Work, His Influence,* 3 vols. (1985). See the description above.

Bentley, Gerald E. *Shakespeare: A Biographical Handbook* (1961). The facts about Shakespeare, with virtually no conjecture intermingled.

Chambers, E. K. *William Shakespeare: A Study of Facts and Problems,* 2 vols. (1930). The fullest collection of data.

Fraser, Russell. *Young Shakespeare* (1988). A highly readable account that simultaneously considers Shakespeare's life and Shakespeare's art.

———. *Shakespeare: The Later Years* (1992).

Schoenbaum, S. *Shakespeare's Lives* (1970). A review of the evidence and an examination of many biographies, including those of Baconians and other heretics.

———. *William Shakespeare: A Compact Documentary Life* (1977). An abbreviated version, in a smaller format, of the next title. The compact version reproduces some fifty documents in reduced form. A readable presentation of all that the documents tell us about Shakespeare.

———. *William Shakespeare: A Documentary Life* (1975). A large-format book setting forth the biography with facsimiles of more than two hundred documents, and with transcriptions and commentaries.

3. Shakespeare's Theater

Astington, John H., ed. *The Development of Shakespeare's Theater* (1992). Eight specialized essays on theatrical companies, playing spaces, and performance.

Beckerman, Bernard. *Shakespeare at the Globe, 1599–1609* (1962). On the playhouse and on Elizabethan dramaturgy, acting, and staging.

Bentley, Gerald E. *The Profession of Dramatist in Shakespeare's Time* (1971). An account of the dramatist's status in the Elizabethan period.

———. *The Profession of Player in Shakespeare's Time, 1590–1642* (1984). An account of the status of members of London companies (sharers, hired men, apprentices, managers) and a discussion of conditions when they toured.

Berry, Herbert. *Shakespeare's Playhouses* (1987). Usefully emphasizes how little we know about the construction of Elizabethan theaters.

Brown, John Russell. *Shakespeare's Plays in Performance* (1966). A speculative and practical analysis relevant to all of the plays, but with emphasis on *The Merchant of Venice*, *Richard II*, *Hamlet*, *Romeo and Juliet*, and *Twelfth Night*.

———. *William Shakespeare: Writing for Performance* (1996). A discussion aimed at helping readers to develop theatrically conscious habits of reading.

Chambers, E. K. *The Elizabethan Stage*, 4 vols. (1945). A major reference work on theaters, theatrical companies, and staging at court.

Cook, Ann Jennalie. *The Privileged Playgoers of Shakespeare's London, 1576–1642* (1981). Sees Shakespeare's audience as wealthier, more middle-class, and more intellectual than Harbage (below) does.

Dessen, Alan C. *Elizabethan Drama and the Viewer's Eye* (1977). On how certain scenes may have looked to spectators in an Elizabethan theater.

Gurr, Andrew. *Playgoing in Shakespeare's London* (1987). Something of a middle ground between Cook (above) and Harbage (below).

———. *The Shakespearean Stage, 1579–1642* (3rd ed., 1992). On the acting companies, the actors, the playhouses, the stages, and the audiences.

———, and Mariko Ichikawa. *Staging in Shakespeare's Theatres* (2000). Like Alan C. Dessen's book, cited above, a careful analysis of what the Elizabethans saw on the stage.

Harbage, Alfred. *Shakespeare's Audience* (1941). A study of the size and nature of the theatrical public, emphasizing the representativeness of its working class and middle-class audience.

Hodges, C. Walter. *The Globe Restored* (1968). A conjectural restoration, with lucid drawings.

Hosley, Richard. "The Playhouses," in *The Revels History of Drama in English*, vol. 3, general editors Clifford Leech and T. W. Craik (1975). An essay of a hundred pages on the physical aspects of the playhouses.

Howard, Jane E. "Crossdressing, the Theatre, and Gender Struggle in Early Modern England," *Shakespeare Quarterly* 39 (1988): 418–40. Judicious comments on the effects of boys playing female roles.

Orrell, John. *The Human Stage: English Theatre Design, 1567–1640* (1988). Argues that the public, private, and court playhouses are less indebted to popular structures (e.g., innyards and bear-baiting pits) than to banqueting halls and to Renaissance conceptions of Roman amphitheaters.

Slater, Ann Pasternak. *Shakespeare the Director* (1982). An analysis of theatrical effects (e.g., kissing, kneeling) in stage directions and dialogue.

Styan, J. L. *Shakespeare's Stagecraft* (1967). An introduction to Shakespeare's visual and aural stagecraft, with chapters on such topics as acting conventions, stage groupings, and speech.

Thompson, Peter. *Shakespeare's Professional Career* (1992). An examination of patronage and related theatrical conditions.

———. *Shakespeare's Theatre* (1983). A discussion of how plays were staged in Shakespeare's time.

4. Shakespeare on Stage and Screen

Bate, Jonathan, and Russell Jackson, eds. *Shakespeare: An Illustrated Stage History* (1996). Highly readable essays on stage productions from the Renaissance to the present.

Berry, Ralph. *Changing Styles in Shakespeare* (1981). Discusses productions of six plays (*Coriolanus*, *Hamlet*, *Henry V*, *Measure for Measure*, *The Tempest*, and *Twelfth Night*) on the English stage, chiefly 1950–1980.

————. *On Directing Shakespeare: Interviews with Contemporary Directors* (1989). An enlarged edition of a book first published in 1977, this version includes the seven interviews from the early 1970s and adds five interviews conducted in 1988.

Brockbank, Philip, ed. *Players of Shakespeare: Essays in Shakespearean Performance* (1985). Comments by twelve actors, reporting their experiences with roles. See also the entry for Russell Jackson (below).

Bulman, J. C., and H. R. Coursen, eds. *Shakespeare on Television* (1988). An anthology of general and theoretical essays, essays on individual productions, and shorter reviews, with a bibliography and a videography listing cassettes that may be rented.

Coursen, H. P. *Watching Shakespeare on Television* (1993). Analyses not only of TV versions but also of films and videotapes of stage presentations that are shown on television.

Davies, Anthony, and Stanley Wells, eds. *Shakespeare and the Moving Image: The Plays on Film and Television* (1994). General essays (e.g., on the comedies) as well as essays devoted entirely to *Hamlet, King Lear*, and *Macbeth*.

Dawson, Anthony B. *Watching Shakespeare: A Playgoer's Guide* (1988). About half of the plays are discussed, chiefly in terms of decisions that actors and directors make in putting the works onto the stage.

Dessen, Alan. *Elizabethan Stage Conventions and Modern Interpretations* (1984). On interpreting conventions such as the representation of light and darkness and stage violence (duels, battles).

Donaldson, Peter. *Shakespearean Films/Shakespearean Directors* (1990). Postmodernist analyses, drawing on Freudianism, Feminism, Deconstruction, and Queer Theory.

Jackson, Russell, and Robert Smallwood, eds. *Players of Shakespeare 2: Further Essays in Shakespearean Performance by Players with the Royal Shakespeare Company* (1988). Fourteen actors discuss their roles in productions between 1982 and 1987.

————. *Players of Shakespeare 3: Further Essays in Shakespearean Performance by Players with the Royal Shakespeare Company* (1993). Comments by thirteen performers.

Jorgens, Jack. *Shakespeare on Film* (1977). Fairly detailed studies of eighteen films, preceded by an introductory chapter addressing such issues as music, and whether to "open" the play by including scenes of landscape.

Kennedy, Dennis. *Looking at Shakespeare: A Visual History of Twentieth-Century Performance* (1993). Lucid descriptions (with 170 photographs) of European, British, and American performances.

Leiter, Samuel L. *Shakespeare Around the Globe: A Guide to Notable Postwar Revivals* (1986). For each play there are about two pages of introductory comments, then discussions (about five hundred words per production) of ten or so productions, and finally bibliographic references.

McMurty, Jo. *Shakespeare Films in the Classroom* (1994). Useful evaluations of the chief films most likely to be shown in undergraduate courses.

Rothwell, Kenneth, and Annabelle Henkin Melzer. *Shakespeare on Screen: An International Filmography and Videography* (1990). A reference guide to several hundred films and videos produced between 1899 and 1989, including spinoffs such as musicals and dance versions.

Smallwood, Robert, ed. *Players of Shakespeare 4* (1998). Like the volumes by Brockbank and Jackson, listed above, contains remarks by contemporary performers.

Sprague, Arthur Colby. *Shakespeare and the Actors* (1944). Detailed discussions of stage business (gestures, etc.) over the years.

Willis, Susan. *The BBC Shakespeare Plays: Making the Televised Canon* (1991). A history of the series, with interviews and production diaries for some plays.

5. Miscellaneous Reference Works

Abbott, E. A. *A Shakespearean Grammar* (new edition, 1877). An examination of differences between Elizabethan and modern grammar.

Allen, Michael J. B., and Kenneth Muir, eds. *Shakespeare's Plays in Quarto* (1981). One volume containing facsimiles of the plays issued in small format before they were collected in the First Folio of 1623.

Blake, Norman. *Shakespeare's Language: An Introduction* (1983). On vocabulary, parts of speech, and word order.

Bullough, Geoffrey. *Narrative and Dramatic Sources of Shakespeare*, 8 vols. (1957–75). A collection of many of the books Shakespeare drew on, with judicious comments.

Campbell, Oscar James, and Edward G. Quinn, eds. *The Reader's Encyclopedia of Shakespeare* (1966). Old, and in some ways superseded by Michael Dobson's *Oxford Companion* (see below), but still highly valuable.

Cercignani, Fausto. *Shakespeare's Works and Elizabethan Pronunciation* (1981). Considered the best work on the topic, but remains controversial.

Champion, Larry S. *The Essential Shakespeare: An Annotated Bibliography of Major Modern Studies*, 2nd ed. (1993). An invaluable guide to 1,800 writings about Shakespeare.

Dent, R. W. *Shakespeare's Proverbial Language: An Index* (1981). An index of proverbs, with an introduction concerning a form Shakespeare frequently drew on.

Dobson, Michael, ed. *The Oxford Companion to Shakespeare* (2001). Probably the single most useful reference work for information (arranged alphabetically) about Shakespeare and his works.

Greg, W. W. *The Shakespeare First Folio* (1955). A detailed yet readable history of the first collection (1623) of Shakespeare's plays.

Harner, James. *The World Shakespeare Bibliography*. See headnote to Suggested References.

Hosley, Richard. *Shakespeare's Holinshed* (1968). Valuable presentation of one of Shakespeare's major sources.

Kökeritz, Helge. *Shakespeare's Names* (1959). A guide to pronouncing some 1,800 names appearing in Shakespeare.

———. *Shakespeare's Pronunciation* (1953). Contains much information about puns and rhymes, but see Cercignani (above).

Muir, Kenneth. *The Sources of Shakespeare's Plays* (1978). An account of Shakespeare's use of his reading. It covers all the plays, in chronological order.

Miriam Joseph, Sister. *Shakespeare's Use of the Arts of Language* (1947). A study of Shakespeare's use of rhetorical devices, reprinted in part as *Rhetoric in Shakespeare's Time* (1962).

The Norton Facsimile: The First Folio of Shakespeare's Plays (1968). A handsome and accurate facsimile of the first collection (1623) of Shakespeare's plays, with a valuable introduction by Charlton Hinman.

Onions, C. T. *A Shakespeare Glossary*, rev. and enlarged by R. D. Eagleson (1986). Definitions of words (or senses of words) now obsolete.

Partridge, Eric. *Shakespeare's Bawdy*, rev. ed. (1955). Relatively brief dictionary of bawdy words; useful, but see Williams, below.

Shakespeare Quarterly. See headnote to Suggested References.

Shakespeare Survey. See headnote to Suggested References.

Spevack, Marvin. *The Harvard Concordance to Shakespeare* (1973). An index to Shakespeare's words.

Vickers, Brian. *Appropriating Shakespeare: Contemporary Critical Quarrels* (1993). A survey—chiefly hostile—of recent schools of criticism.

Wells, Stanley, ed. *Shakespeare: A Bibliographical Guide* (new edition, 1990). Nineteen chapters (some devoted to single plays, others devoted to groups of related plays) on recent scholarship on the life and all of the works.

Williams, Gordon. *A Dictionary of Sexual Language and Imagery in Shakespearean and Stuart Literature*, 3 vols. (1994). Extended discussions of words and passages; much fuller than Partridge, cited above.

6. Shakespeare's Plays: General Studies

Bamber, Linda. *Comic Women, Tragic Men: A Study of Gender and Genre in Shakespeare* (1982).

Barnet, Sylvan. *A Short Guide to Shakespeare* (1974).

Callaghan, Dympna, Lorraine Helms, and Jyotsna Singh. *The Weyward Sisters: Shakespeare and Feminist Politics* (1994).

Clemen, Wolfgang H. *The Development of Shakespeare's Imagery* (1951).

Cook, Ann Jennalie. *Making a Match: Courtship in Shakespeare and His Society* (1991).

Dollimore, Jonathan, and Alan Sinfield. *Political Shakespeare: New Essays in Cultural Materialism* (1985).

Dusinberre, Juliet. *Shakespeare and the Nature of Women* (1975).

Granville-Barker, Harley. *Prefaces to Shakespeare*, 2 vols. (1946–47; volume 1 contains essays on *Hamlet, King Lear, Merchant of Venice, Antony and Cleopatra,* and *Cymbeline*; volume 2 contains essays on *Othello, Coriolanus, Julius Caesar, Romeo and Juliet, Love's Labor's Lost*).

———. *More Prefaces to Shakespeare* (1974; essays on *Twelfth Night, A Midsummer Night's Dream, The Winter's Tale, Macbeth*).

Harbage, Alfred. *William Shakespeare: A Reader's Guide* (1963).

Howard, Jean E. *Shakespeare's Art of Orchestration: Stage Technique and Audience Response* (1984).

Jones, Emrys. *Scenic Form in Shakespeare* (1971).

Lenz, Carolyn Ruth Swift, Gayle Greene, and Carol Thomas Neely, eds. *The Woman's Part: Feminist Criticism of Shakespeare* (1980).

Novy, Marianne. *Love's Argument: Gender Relations in Shakespeare* (1984).

Rose, Mark. *Shakespearean Design* (1972).

Scragg, Leah. *Discovering Shakespeare's Meaning* (1994).

———. *Shakespeare's "Mouldy Tales": Recurrent Plot Motifs in Shakespearean Drama* (1992).

Traub, Valerie. *Desire and Anxiety: Circulations of Sexuality in Shakespearean Drama* (1992).

Traversi, D. A. *An Approach to Shakespeare,* 2 vols. (3rd rev. ed, 1968–69).

Vickers, Brian. *The Artistry of Shakespeare's Prose* (1968).

Wells, Stanley. *Shakespeare: A Dramatic Life* (1994).

Wright, George T. *Shakespeare's Metrical Art* (1988).

7. The Comedies

Barber, C. L. *Shakespeare's Festive Comedy* (1959; discusses *Love's Labor's Lost, A Midsummer Night's Dream, The Merchant of Venice, As You Like It, Twelfth Night*).

Barton, Anne. *The Names of Comedy* (1990).

Berry, Ralph. *Shakespeare's Comedy: Explorations in Form* (1972).

Bradbury, Malcolm, and David Palmer, eds. *Shakespearean Comedy* (1972).

Bryant, J. A., Jr. *Shakespeare and the Uses of Comedy* (1986).

Carroll, William. *The Metamorphoses of Shakespearean Comedy* (1985).

Champion, Larry S. *The Evolution of Shakespeare's Comedy* (1970).

Evans, Bertrand. *Shakespeare's Comedies* (1960).

Frye, Northrop. *Shakespearean Comedy and Romance* (1965).

Leggatt, Alexander. *Shakespeare's Comedy of Love* (1974).

Miola, Robert S. *Shakespeare and Classical Comedy: The Influence of Plautus and Terence* (1994).

Nevo, Ruth. *Comic Transformations in Shakespeare* (1980).

Ornstein, Robert. *Shakespeare's Comedies: From Roman Farce to Romantic Mystery* (1986).

Richman, David. *Laughter, Pain, and Wonder: Shakespeare's Comedies and the Audience in the Theater* (1990).

Salingar, Leo. *Shakespeare and the Traditions of Comedy* (1974).

Slights, Camille Wells. *Shakespeare's Comic Commonwealths* (1993).

Waller, Gary, ed. *Shakespeare's Comedies* (1991).

Westlund, Joseph. *Shakespeare's Reparative Comedies: A Psychoanalytic View of the Middle Plays* (1984).

Williamson, Marilyn. *The Patriarchy of Shakespeare's Comedies* (1986).

8. The Romances (*Pericles, Cymbeline, The Winter's Tale, The Tempest, The Two Noble Kinsmen*)

Adams, Robert M. *Shakespeare: The Four Romances* (1989).

Felperin, Howard. *Shakespearean Romance* (1972).

Frye, Northrop. *A Natural Perspective: The Development of Shakespearean Comedy and Romance* (1965).

Mowat, Barbara. *The Dramaturgy of Shakespeare's Romances* (1976).

Warren, Roger. *Staging Shakespeare's Late Plays* (1990).

Young, David. *The Heart's Forest: A Study of Shakespeare's Pastoral Plays* (1972).

9. The Tragedies

Bradley, A. C. *Shakespearean Tragedy* (1904).

Brooke, Nicholas. *Shakespeare's Early Tragedies* (1968).

Champion, Larry. *Shakespeare's Tragic Perspective* (1976).

Drakakis, John, ed. *Shakespearean Tragedy* (1992).

Evans, Bertrand. *Shakespeare's Tragic Practice* (1979).

Everett, Barbara. *Young Hamlet: Essays on Shakespeare's Tragedies* (1989).

Foakes, R. A. *Hamlet versus Lear: Cultural Politics and Shakespeare's Art* (1993).

Frye, Northrop. *Fools of Time: Studies in Shakespearean Tragedy* (1967).

Harbage, Alfred, ed. *Shakespeare: The Tragedies* (1964).

Mack, Maynard. *Everybody's Shakespeare: Reflections Chiefly on the Tragedies* (1993).

McAlindon, T. *Shakespeare's Tragic Cosmos* (1991).

Miola, Robert S. *Shakespeare and Classical Tragedy: The Influence of Seneca* (1992).

———. *Shakespeare's Rome* (1983).

Nevo, Ruth. *Tragic Form in Shakespeare* (1972).

Rackin, Phyllis. *Shakespeare's Tragedies* (1978).

Rose, Mark, ed. *Shakespeare's Early Tragedies: A Collection of Critical Essays* (1995).

Rosen, William. *Shakespeare and the Craft of Tragedy* (1960).

Snyder, Susan. *The Comic Matrix of Shakespeare's Tragedies* (1979).

Wofford, Susanne. *Shakespeare's Late Tragedies: A Collection of Critical Essays* (1996).

Young, David. *The Action to the Word: Structure and Style in Shakespearean Tragedy* (1990).

———. *Shakespeare's Middle Tragedies: A Collection of Critical Essays* (1993).

10. The Histories

Blanpied, John W. *Time and the Artist in Shakespeare's English Histories* (1983).

Campbell, Lily B. *Shakespeare's "Histories": Mirrors of Elizabethan Policy* (1947).

Champion, Larry S. *Perspective in Shakespeare's English Histories* (1980).

Hodgdon, Barbara. *The End Crowns All: Closure and Contradiction in Shakespeare's History* (1991).

Holderness, Graham. *Shakespeare Recycled: The Making of Historical Drama* (1992).

———, ed. *Shakespeare's History Plays: "Richard II" to "Henry V"* (1992).

Leggatt, Alexander. *Shakespeare's Political Drama: The History Plays and the Roman Plays* (1988).

Levine, Nina S. *Women's Matters: Politics, Gender, and Nation in Shakespeare's Early History Plays* (1998).

Ornstein, Robert. *A Kingdom for a Stage: The Achievement of Shakespeare's History Plays* (1972).

Rackin, Phyllis. *Stages of History: Shakespeare's English Chronicles* (1990).

Saccio, Peter. *Shakespeare's English Kings*, 2nd ed. (1999).

Spiekerman, Tim. *Shakespeare's Political Realism* (2001).

Tillyard, E. M. W. *Shakespeare's History Plays* (1944).

Velz, John W., ed. *Shakespeare's English Histories: A Quest for Form and Genre* (1996).

11. *King John*

Useful editions of *King John* have been prepared by E.A.J. Honigmann (1954), A. R. Braunmuller (1989), and L. A. Beaurline (1990).

There are two collections of essays on the play: Francis Shirley, ed., *"King John" and "Henry VIII": Critical Essays* (1988), and Deborah T. Curren-Aquino, ed., *"King John": New Perspectives* (1989). For a collection limited to earlier criticism (1790–1919), see Joseph Candido, ed., *Shakespeare: The Critical Tradition: King John* (1996). For readings concerning stage and television productions, see above, Section 4.

For the play in the contexts of other history plays, see above, Section 10.

Bonjour, Adrien. "The Road to Swinstead Abbey: A Study of the Sense and Structure of *King John.*" *ELH* 18 (1951): 253–74.

Burden, Dennis H. "Shakespeare's History Plays: 1952–1983." *Shakespeare Survey* (1985): 1–18.

Calderwood, James L. "Commodity and Honour in *King John.*" *University of Toronto Quarterly* 29 (1960): 341–56.

Campbell, Lily B. *Shakespeare's "Histories": Mirrors of Elizabethan Policy* (1947).

Dusinberre, Juliet. "*King John* and Embarrassing Women." *Shakespeare Survey* 42 (1989): 37–52.

Elliott, John R. "Shakespeare and the Double Image of King John." *Shakespeare Studies* I (1965): 64–84.

Honigmann, E.A.J. "Shakespeare's Self-Repetitions and *King John.*" *Shakespeare Survey* 53 (2000): 175–83.

Jones, Emrys. *The Origins of Shakespeare* (1977).

Ornstein, Robert. *A Kingdom for a Stage* (1972).

Pettet, E. C. "Hot Irons and Fever: A Note on Some Imagery of *King John.*" *Essays in Criticism* 4 (1954): 128–44.

Rackin, Phyllis. "Anti-Historians: Women's Roles in Shakespeare's Histories." *Theatre Journal* 37 (1985): 329–44.

Rossiter, A. P. "Ambivalence: The Dialectic of the Histories." In *Angel with Horns* (1961).

Shattuck, Charles. *William Charles Macready's King John* (1962).

Sprague, Arthur Colby. *Shakespeare's Histories: Plays for the Stage* (1964).

Tillyard, E.M.W. *Shakespeare's History Plays* (1944).

Vaughan, Virginia Mason. "Between Tetralogies: *King John* as Transition." *Shakespeare Quarterly* 35 (1984): 407–20.

Waith, Eugene M. "*King John* and the Drama of History." *Shakespeare Quarterly* 29 (1978): 192–211.

Womersley, David. "The Politics of *King John*." *Review of English Studies,* new series, 40 (1989): 497–515.

12. *Henry VIII*

Especially useful editions are those by John Margeson (1990), Jay L. Halio (1999), and Gordon McMullan (2000).

For discussions of the stage history of the play, see the bibliographic note at the end of the discussion of "*Henry VIII* on Stage and Screen" in this volume. For discussions of the play in a context of the other English histories, see Section 10 above. Some useful essays on the play are collected in *"King John" and "Henry VIII": Critical Essays,* ed. Francis Shirley (1988). Linda McJ. Micheli has provided an invaluable research tool, *"Henry VIII": An Annotated Bibliography* (1998).

Burden, Dennis H. "Shakespeare's History Plays: 1952–1983." *Shakespeare Survey* 38 (1985): 1–18.

Byrne, Muriel St. Clare. "A Stratford Production: *Henry VIII*." *Shakespeare Survey* 3 (1950): 120–29. [A review of the 1949 Guthrie performance.]

Felperin, Howard. "Shakespeare's *Henry VIII*: History as Myth." *Studies in English Literature: 1500–1900* 6 (1966): 225–46.

Foakes, R. A., ed. *The Arden Edition of the Works of William Shakespeare: King Henry VIII* (1957).

Kermode, Frank. "What Is Shakespeare's *Henry VIII* About?" *Durham University Journal,* N.S., 9 (1947–48): 48–55.

Leggatt, Alexander. "*Henry VIII* and the Ideal England." *Shakespeare Survey* 38 (1985): 131–43.

Magnusson, A. Lynne. "The Rhetoric of Politeness and *Henry VIII*." *Shakespeare Quarterly* 43 (1992): 391–409.

Micheli, Linda McJ. " 'Sit By Us': Visual Imagery and the Two Queens in *Henry VIII*." *Shakespeare Quarterly* 38 (1987): 452–66.

Noling, Kim H. "Grubbing Up the Stock: Dramatizing Queens in *Henry VIII*." *Shakespeare Quarterly* 39 (1988): 292–306.

Reese, Max Meredith. *The Cease of Majesty: A Study of Shakespeare's History Plays* (1962).

Ribner, Irving. *The English History Play in the Age of Shakespeare.* 2nd ed., revised (1965).

Slights, Camille Wells. "The Politics of Conscience in *All Is True* (or *Henry VIII*)." *Shakespeare Survey* 43 (1991): 59–68.

READ THE TOP 20
SIGNET CLASSICS

1984 by George Orwell

Animal Farm by George Orwell

Frankenstein by Mary Shelley

The Inferno by Dante

Beowulf (Burton Raffel, translator)

Hamlet by William Shakespeare

Heart of Darkness & The Secret Sharer
by Joseph Conrad

Narrative of the Life of Frederick Douglass
by Frederick Douglass

The Scarlet Letter by Nathaniel Hawthorne

Nectar in a Sieve by Kamala Markandaya

A Tale of Two Cities by Charles Dickens

Alice's Adventures in Wonderland &
Through the Looking Glass by Lewis Carroll

Romeo and Juliet by William Shakespeare

Ethan Frome by Edith Wharton

A Midsummer Night's Dream by William Shakespeare

Macbeth by William Shakespeare

Othello by William Shakespeare

The Adventures of Huckleberry Finn by Mark Twain

One Day in the Life of Ivan Denisovich
by Alexander Solzhenitsyn

Jane Eyre by Charlotte Brontë